Rymer
Rymer, Russ
Paris twilight

$25.00
ocn828723954
07/09/2013

Paris Twilight

Books by Russ Rymer

Paris Twilight

RUSS RYMER

Houghton Mifflin Harcourt
BOSTON   NEW YORK
2013

www.hmhbooks.com

Library of Congress Cataloging-in-Publication Data
Rymer, Russ.
Paris twilight / Russ Rymer.
pages cm
ISBN 978-0-618-11373-6
I. Title.
PS3568.Y58P37 2013
813'.54 — dc23   2013000616

Book design by Brian Moore

Printed in the United States of America
DOC 10 9 8 7 6 5 4 3 2 1

For Susan, at last

Before the old wound dries, it bleeds again.

— AESCHYLUS, *AGAMEMNON*

PART ONE

I

I'M NOT SURE HOW to explain this, why I am writing to you,
you of all people, and writing to you now, except for the simple circumstance that the rain has chased me into this place
and does not appear to want to let me go, and here in my confinement all I can find in my purse to occupy me are a pen, a nail file, a
piece of paper: prisoner's tools. I'm ignoring the file. Daniel, I need
a witness, and there's no one else to turn to. Can you imagine how
many witnesses we have lost by now, you and I, how little sense it all
makes, those ancient awful dramas, with no one around to remember how splendid they were? Oh, how I have hated you! And now you
are back on my mind because of the Brahms. And before that, I suppose, the train ride in from the airport. It was snowing. The winter
this year was *précoce,* as they call it here, and that afternoon was too.
With the flurries and the overcast, the day seemed hours ahead of itself, and reminded me of that other train ride, so long ago, when we
had decided to go back into New York despite the blizzard, the fields
and the Connecticut estuaries slipping by us, the snowflakes curling
bright against the windows, your head in my lap. I see now, sitting in
this dreary-day café, how unmoored I was becoming even so early on,
just off the plane, with the onrush of dark and the RER hurtling me
toward this city where I have none of the things I know to grab on
to to keep my mind from wandering. So, of course, the Brahms and
the train. And also, I confess, I'm emboldened by the knowledge that
whatever I set down here you will never read, that I will never know
your thoughts. Such comfort! You see, Daniel, that after all, you have
left me safe at last.

· · ·

It was a Thursday, that afternoon when I got in. I deserted the train at Gare du Nord, and, pushing out with the crowd onto rue de Dunkerque, I was tempted to try to walk it, even with the weather, but I had the bags, and I didn't want to arrive all soggy and sad and middle-aged in some terrible cold, grand lobby. They were putting me up at the Clairière. Anyway, my day was hardly over; they'd scheduled me for an evening meeting, which I dreaded, if only because Willem would be there, and I was nervous about seeing Willem. So I caught a cab, shards of war news on the radio as we swerved our way through town. In the deserts of Arabia, Western armies were gathering to drive Iraqi legions from Kuwait. From the news accounts emitting from the dashboard, the first pitched skirmishes were being fought right here.

L'Hôtel la Clairière de l'Armistice, when we reached it, was as monstrous as I'd imagined it would be, one of those push-pull places full of servile staff and imposing décor, all this uncomfortable comfort, walnut and crystal and that grotesque white furniture trimmed in gilt that always reminds me of dental work, or naval uniforms. My room wasn't ready, of course. I dumped my bags on the concierge, and the martinet at the check-in desk (his humility had been honed to a murderous edge) scrutinized my passport and refused my credit card — *"Déjà reglé,"* he sniffed. Already settled. It was almost as an afterthought (though with a world of forethought devoted to his gesture) that he handed me the message, just as a voice behind me boomed, "Mademoiselle." I stuffed the envelope into my purse with the luggage receipt.

The accent was clearly Anglo, and I responded with all the mademoisellian coquettishness my fifty years could muster. "Why, sir," I said, "you flatter me." I meant it as a quip, but really I was bracing myself. It's a reflex. Whatever was approaching, I wanted a stance to handle it. Of course, at the same time, I knew exactly who to expect, whose familiar Anglo accent I was hearing, and I turned and we embraced. My first thought was *My, he's prospered!* — do you remember what a skinny guy Willem used to be? — and then immediately I was reminded of my own prosperity and grew self-conscious. After a few seconds of squeezing the life out of me, he held me out at arm's length with locked elbows and a hand on each shoulder — why do men of a certain stature think women enjoy being grasped like a lectern? — and gave me *the expression*: you know, this tight-lipped side glance full of rue and fondness that's supposed to add up to the gaze of enduring love. "My God, you haven't changed a bit," he said, intoning, and I shot him my expression of enduring dismissal, and he said that, well, we could head out whenever I was ready.

I checked myself over in my mind — was my travel attire really presentable? My travel face? — and I heard myself babbling that he really hadn't needed to pick me up at the hotel, I could easily have caught a cab, that we could leave right away, why not, since I couldn't check in yet. We stepped out under the porte-cochère and he helped me into the back of a long, dark Mercedes that slid up to the curb and gave the driver a destination. I thought: *His first honest sentence.* On the way down the boulevard, he ventured another, more quietly. "Thank you for doing this, Matilde."

"You're very welcome," I said, and, after a while, "I don't call a paid month in Paris much of a sacrifice."

"It's an exorbitant amount of time," he said. "Maybe five weeks, we still don't know."

"Well, I told you when you called, you're not exactly dragging me away from anything."

He looked at me slightly mystified, as though I had answered a question about something else.

I had thought the ride would be a short one; that's generally how things work in such arrangements, proximity being at a premium. But we headed down the boulevard to the highway and out of the city center into the neighborhoods of some inner *banlieue*. The traffic, at first, was more clotted even than I remembered it, even for late on a weekday afternoon. Willem leaned over the seatback to inquire. *"Les manifestations,"* the chauffeur answered — he was an Algerian, Willem would later inform me, whose name was Drôlet — the protests *"contre la guerre."*

The snow flurries had abated, and as soon as we escaped the city, the roads cleared of other cars. A small village flashed by, and another and smaller one, and then we were on a winding country avenue passing the walls of enclosed estates, until finally the Mercedes turned up a pea-gravel driveway that led through the lawns of a large old chateau. Former chateau. It was a hospital now. There were no indicators of such, no glaring emergency bay, no QUIET signs lining the road or speed bumps on the drive, and no name on the art-nouveau beveled-glass door, but it was irrefutably a hospital. With a little practice, you can smell them a mile away.

There was a small lobby inside the beveled glass, but no public waiting room and no records window staffed by admitting nurses, only a stocky, efficient, daunting woman in a silk dress and sensible heels sitting behind a table who half stood when the door opened and then relaxed when she saw Willem and nodded us wordlessly toward some double doors. The doors gave a click when she reached beneath the table, and we went through into a hallway.

Inside, things were brighter and more antiseptic, but hardly less sumptuous. Willem felt my gaze on his cheek, or sensed my raised eyebrow, and said — did I imagine he was chuckling a little? — "Come along, you'll see," and we caught an elevator up to the top floor, the floor you needed to use a key for the elevator to reach, which Willem produced from his key ring, and then he ushered me down another hallway into a small, book-lined conference study where a dozen or so men were milling about, eating little sandwiches and sipping coffee. As we entered, a quiet fell, and all of them simultaneously moved to put down their plates.

"Hello, gentlemen," Willem said as we bustled in, and he steered me past the crowd to a man standing out of the light and modestly apart, and introduced us.

"Professor Anselm," the man said to me, softly. "I'm honored."

"Mr. Sahran," I said back, hoping I'd caught the pronunciation right. He was a trim man in a quiet suit, shorter than me and maybe younger, late forties or so, aristocratic in his bearing and with an extraordinary limpid gentleness in his gaze, though it was the sort of gentleness you would never want to cross. I took him to be a consul or envoy — he was one of those men tightly coiled within their composure whom you rarely run into anymore outside the foreign service, but what on earth (I reminded myself) did I know about the foreign service? I couldn't help feeling that if he was honored, I was obscurely in peril.

"We are very grateful that you are able to take this on," he said, and his eyes probed mine for an exploratory second. "I trust you had a nice trip? Your accommodations are acceptable?" he asked, and when I answered the rhetorical pleasantry with a rhetorical nod, he answered my answer with a little smile. "Good," he said, and it was understood that some contract had been efficiently negotiated and signed.

"Well, Dr. Madsen, I leave all this to you." Sahran shook Willem's hand, and then mine again, with a slight, quick bow of the head, and left the room, and two other men in cheaper suits left with him.

The subsequent hour was a ritual, more or less standard, of putting together a surgical team — the wrinkle being that this team was so very disparate and each of us so very new to the others, except for a couple of the Pakistanis, I guess, who knew each other, and Willem and myself, of course. And of course there were the other anomalies, which were glaring, but I thought I would hold off asking about those until the ride home, when I would have Willem to myself again. Papers were handed out, and introductions were made, names and degrees, but without, I noticed, current affiliations. Willem asked some pathology and peri-care questions and addressed a few hematology concerns to the perfusionist, the man who would run the heart-lung bypass machine, and turned to me when we got to my role in things. Matilde Anselm, I told the group, and trotted out the insta-CV. No one had warned me to edit my history, so I let them have it, or the bones of it, at least, skipping over the unpleasant stuff, the Singleton business, starting with Bryn Mawr undergrad and continuing through post-D at Sloan-Kettering "with post–Doctor Madsen" (no smiles from the group), all the way to head of cardiothoracic anesthesiology at St. Anne's in New York until a few years ago. Teaching since (I didn't say *since the unpleasant Singleton stuff*). Currently on sabbatical.

Willem thanked me and cued up a couple final members and then gave us what amounted to marching orders. "As you see, you are among an exceptional group of professionals," he said, "but what we're here to do is nothing more than a routine procedure, albeit in exemplary fashion. We have ten days minimum before the operation, and probably several weeks. But you should be as entirely prepared as if it were happening tomorrow. Whatever you need to do to familiarize yourself with this facility, do it immediately. Dr. Mahlev here is your coordinator. He has schedules for each of you to come in to checklist your equipment and go through your protocols. Whatever you need, ask him. Be thorough. Remember, there is no backup; it's all on you. This is the last time we will see one another *ensemble* until we meet over the patient. You've each been given a telephone number. You must call that number twice a day, wherever you are, so that you'll know when you're needed —"

"No beepers?" I interrupted. "We're not to be on call?"

"Not yet," Willem said. "Just be sure to phone. Every morning early, every evening late, without fail. Any other questions, direct them to Dr. Mahlev."

"But Willem . . ."

"Thank you," Willem said to the group, and then to me, "Drôlet will take you back to the hotel."

So I didn't get to clarify anything with dear Willem on the ride home after all, and out of weariness, I didn't talk with Drôlet either, though I suspected somehow, as I watched his silhouette against the passing lights, that my driver knew a lot more than I did about what I had gotten myself into.

La Clairière was aglitter when we got there, and the pageant of early diners traipsing through the lobby in evening dress and formal wear confirmed my determination to hole up humble and eat in. Some poor lackey tricked out like an organ grinder's monkey in crimson tunic and braided pillbox hat and dragging a gilded luggage cart led me to my room. It was enormous. At any rate, I couldn't see a bed from the door when it opened, and that was always enormous enough for me. Then behind the first room came another, and then another, a whole grand suite, which I already felt at sea in long before I bumped into a bedroom.

As I fished in my purse for some change to tip the bellhop, my hand brushed against a soft, sharp-cornered object that my tactile memory recalled from only the briefest acquaintance. How long it seemed since the concierge had handed me the envelope! It gave me a jolt. I dug up some coins, but a voice in my head whispered, *Suite!* and even as another voice grumbled, *What does the room size have to do with the tip?* I dropped the coins and pulled out a twenty-franc note instead and pushed it into the waiting white glove, which folded it into instant invisibility with the practiced skill of an illusionist. We walked the long walk back to the door, and I locked it behind the departing train of minion and cart. Then, before doing what I knew I must do next, I put down my purse on the dining table and found the phone and ordered up a lovely-sounding *filet de poisson grillé*, not really because it would be so lovely, along with its lovely *tarte aux légumes*, but because it was the first thing on the menu. Along with the cheapest glass monsieur might recommend. Then I went into the kitchen and boiled some water and returned with a monogrammed napkin and some green tea steeping in a Spode cup.

What was I thinking while I did this? I wasn't very hungry, nor the least bit thirsty. As I look back, I imagine that I was setting the scene, commencing an order of service, adorning the altar with chalice and cloth, and I wonder: What did I sense? A portent? Of a sacrifice? Or was I merely heeding the conviction that any messenger who has waited so patiently deserves to be met with ceremony? I settled myself in a dining chair and settled my glasses on my nose and set out my napkin and my saucer and my cup and took a little breath of resolve or resignation, I'm not sure which, before reaching back into the purse.

The envelope was of expensive linen, one of those subtle sizes easy to the hand that you never find in American stationery, and to the touch as crisp and lush as taffeta, embossed with a company name that ended *et Associés.* So: A law firm? The flap was sealed with a dime-sized daub of bright red wax. Inside was a single sheet, folded once, its message in longhand, the same cursive hand that had penned my name and the words *par courrier* on the envelope's face and *novembre 1990* at the top of the page.

Ma très distinguée Madame, the note began. *I wish to alert you to certain unhappy recent events, and to confer with you about subsequent matters which you may find of importance.* Without further elaboration, it requested me to contact, "with due regard for urgency," a Monsieur E. Delacroix Rouchard, provided a telephone number and an address on rue Delembert in the seventeenth arrondissement, and closed with *Avec mes plus respecteux hommages, je vous prie, Madame, d'agréer l'expression de ma très haute considération,* one of those ornate cordialities (translation: "I'm in no rush, are you?") that only the French, among the nations, remain silly enough to come up with and pompous enough to pull off. I called the number, but the phone kept ringing with that dreadful flat buzz that is the most awful sound in the daily life of any place on earth, and no one picked up, not even to yell *Ne quittez pas!* and put me on hold.

I wasn't surprised. An office where an attorney addressed his own envelopes (Did he melt the wax too? I wondered. Was he himself the courier?) was not likely to be one where staff would still be working at this hour. So I finished my tea and dabbled at my dinner, and took a bath, and retired with a book whose secrets were guarded by my exhaustion, for almost immediately it lay open beside me on the duvet, and I woke after a while to turn off the light, and succumbed back into a dream that must have lasted most of the rest of the night, of swirling snow past a speeding train, a sensation of being unable to understand anything close by, of everything immediate flying past in a frenzy too fleet for me to grasp, while the trees and houses guarding the horizon stayed sharp and clear and precise to the eye, so that there were in the world only two things I was certain of: the feel of your hair beneath my palm, and the horizon, as patient and gradual and slow to pass as a thing remembered, even as it melted into distance and stillness and white.

II

T HE WOMAN MANNING the reception desk of Rouchard
et Associés, Avocats, struck me instantly as a sort I'd met a
thousand of and never once been inclined to like, maybe in
small part because none of them has ever been the least inclined to
like me either. *"Oui?"* she said by way of welcome, without looking up
from a ledger, her tone tinged slightly with some odd extra quality —
was it incredulity? Was she aghast at the sheer effrontery of my stepping through the door? I gave my name and she warmed up enough
to chide me, or at least to chide (the implication was blatant) "those
people who don't think to make an appointment."

"Just happened to be in the neighborhood," I rejoined, but to myself, for she'd already sped from the room to fetch her boss.

In the abrupt abeyance of hostilities, an oddly domestic commotion arrived at my ear — a buzzy little incantation, like the creak of
a porch swing or a deck of cards being shuffled and reshuffled, that
I identified, after a moment, as the quiet musings of a bird in a birdcage, though where the cage was, I couldn't tell. Looking down at the
receptionist's abandoned desk, the too-many-times-polished veneer
not worth polishing beneath the vase of fading Jour des Morts chrysanthemums, I saw that she hadn't been reading a ledger but making one, in the old French banker's style, scribing a grid of columns
and rows onto the blank pages of a leather-and-clothbound accounts
book, using a ruler and a ballpoint pen. Her desk held no computer
monitor, no Minitel. The telephone — the very beast I'd been pestering from afar, for I had rung Rouchard's number again in the morning, fruitlessly, several times, before heading over to happen to be in
the neighborhood — was an ancient black lump of Bakelite with a ro-

tary dial. The newest object that I could spot that might have cost a penny was a twenty-year-old correctable Selectric set on a gray metal typewriter stand. The little bird chirped, and its voice was like the dry, careful setting down of cards in a convalescent wing that once was part of my rounds. The obsolescent wing, the other interns called it, a room where patients who'd worked so hard and paid so much to secure a few extra minutes of life ran out the clock with hearts and gin rummy, and time filtered in through the yellowed drapes and settled like dust on anything that stopped. I felt my certainties plummeting.

Daniel, when did my first impressions turn so traitorous? You remember how I relied on them, how whatever I sensed at the outset would always turn out to be true. By now my old clairvoyance has become a game of bait and switch, and the shine of bright promise turns out to be gilt in the long run, and my monsters do something human as often as not. Indeed, when the receptionist returned, I no longer saw a gorgon but a long-faithful lover fiercely defending her companion's final dignities, knowing her battle was lost.

The man who emerged with her had a hint of a shuffle in what was left of his stride, and an air that said he accepted his own fate genially. Monsieur Rouchard was stooped and impeccably mannered, his coat impeccably tailored to the bulge of a dromedary back, his yellow bow tie deliriously askew beneath an iodine goiter, his gray eyes clear amid the moles and liver spots of a face that was no longer handsome, though it had been. The tinge I'd heard in his secretary's voice was outrage.

"*Docteur!*" he exclaimed, and his speech still had a deep, young timbre. "*Enchanté.* May I get you a *café*? A tea? Nothing? Please excuse our mysterious note. For someone so prominent, you are not so easy to track down, *non*? Not with what we had to start with, which was not even a name. Finally, we reached your university and learned our good fortune, that you are already on your way to us!"

He took my arm and steered me toward an alcove off the lobby, a space just big enough to accommodate a half-couch, a couple of chairs, and a diminutive coffee table, and also the phantom birdcage, inside of which a trio of orange-faced finches busied themselves flitting from peg to perch. "Now, tell me," Rouchard was saying, "do you have a late aunt from Ohio who then moved to Fort Worth?" I did indeed, though I had to give this a moment's thought, for I couldn't possibly picture her. She was storied in our family, but the only time she and I had met, I'd been too young to remember.

"She was not actually my —"

"Blood relation, just so," he said. "But do you recall her name? . . . Yes, Bettina, of course. And her sister, Alice, is your mother, *legal* mother, deceased also, can you remind me when? . . . A decade ago. Well, you see, we are like the surgeon, we must be sure we have the right patient." He glinted with the pleasure of it. "Now, my last question. What do you know of a gentleman named Byron Manifort Saxe? Nothing? Nothing at all. I see. Sit down, please, and let me tell you why we are searching for you so eagerly."

Byron Saxe, he explained, was a Parisian pensioner who had recently suffered a medical catastrophe that put him first in a hospital and soon thereafter in a cemetery, prior to which transition he had composed a will leaving an estate that Rouchard's firm was still engaged in assessing, not having checked all possible channels, but that seemed to consist primarily of a single item of property, an apartment his parents had purchased for him fee simple in the spring of 1933 and in which he had resided without interruption, except for one notable sojourn, ever since, and that he had bequeathed, along with its contents and whatever else in the way of assets the lawyers might be able to find, to me.

"To whom?" I asked.

"To you, madame," he repeated.

"Then there's clearly been a mistake."

"*Non,* madame."

"But I told you, I don't know this man."

Among the finches, a scuffle broke out, with a flurry of wings and a spatter of scattered seed, but no sooner had it commenced than it resolved itself, and the satisfied chiding took up where it left off.

"Unimportant," Rouchard said, "since evidently he knew you."

The first reaction to bubble up through my disbelief was anger. I'm not sure where my hostility rose from (though I can say that in this one instance, my shopworn clairvoyance was still spot on). Partly, it annoyed me that the attorney addressed this final sentence not to me, but to my left hand, a common indiscretion. You remember my disfigurement, my compass-rose scar with its talent for fascinating children. All children and some few adults, though the adults were generally of a ruder sort than this one. At any rate, my answer retrieved his gaze. "I'm sorry," I said to him. "I must decline to accept this, this..."

"Gift," Rouchard said, finishing my protest, and the light in his clear eyes steeled into something less amenable. "But let me assure you, Doctor, this is no gift. You have been appointed sole executor of the estate of one Byron Saxe, who may not have had much in the way of possessions or, let us conjecture, family, but who was nevertheless a legal person and who has conferred on you a legal obligation, which we will help you adjudicate. We have gone ahead with a necessary step and publicized his death in the proper journals so that any other claimants may have their chance to come forward. Due diligence will require some interlude, and then we will have documents for you to sign — there is quite an amount of paperwork involved, his instructions being elaborate, if I may say. I am glad, in the meantime, that coincidence has placed you here in Paris, so you can begin to put affairs in order. The first thing you need to do is visit the apartment, which I understand may be in less than commendable shape, owing to the nature of his disaster, but which has a number of his things in it, such as they are."

And with that he placed, in my left hand, a key.

Getting from rue Delembert across the river to the address Rouchard supplied me with was not so difficult a task, except for the condition I imposed on myself of giving the slip to the man who could most easily get me there. Drôlet was waiting outside. I hadn't intended to employ him that morning; hadn't even imagined, as I ate my room-service egg and toast and made my call to the hospital and my calls (in vain) to the Bakelite lump on the secretary's desk, that the driver would be around. But hardly had I exited the Clairière's elevator and begun my trek across the lobby than he materialized in front of me. "You wish us to go, madame?" he inquired.

Well, no, not *us*. But there he was, so we went. The car was a godsend, I confess. It was drizzling out. How blessed I was, headed for my rendezvous, not to have to rely on the fabled patience of a Parisian cabby as I slowly scanned the façades of buildings for the door bearing Rouchard's number. And how relieved I was, coming back out of Rouchard's office, not to face the daunting implausibility of hailing a return cab in the rain, vacant public Peugeots being as magically water-soluble in Paris as empty yellow Checkers in Manhattan. So I was feeling kindly toward Drôlet and his conveyance as I hopped back in and he asked me where to go next.

Kindly — but I still wished to give him the slip. As I looked down at the memo paper covered with Rouchard's scribblings, caution whispered that this location wasn't one I wanted the world, or at least my chauffeur, to know about just yet.

"Hotel, please," I answered.

"As you wish," Drôlet said, and something about the tone of his consent, the hint of ironic distance, the temperature-less control, affirmed my decision. I would think better of him, with time. Now, I had a momentary urge to throw acid on all his virtues: the absurd professionalism, the compliant pliability that so thinly veiled a resolute contempt, his confident familiarity with a world that seemed out to confound me at every turn. I upbraided myself that my tempest had more to do with jet lag than Drôlet. Or maybe I wasn't accustomed to servants, only students and patients, and the specter of obedience deranged me. Or maybe it was just that, after Rouchard and Saxe, I had no tolerance left for even one more mysterious stranger in my life.

Whatever its source, my annoyance had the happy effect of sealing me away from everything. I was securely, familiarly alone. The Mercedes accelerated, turned, turned again, and as we twisted our way out of the quiet neighborhood and into the havoc of the bigger streets, I snuggled into the leather as into a nest. The greater the chaos outside, the calmer and more sequestered I was in my rolling cloister, defended by Drôlet's guardhouse silence and the sentinel raindrops coursing down the tinted glass. My mind cleared. I let all that had just happened sink in.

Or, let us conjecture, the lawyer had said, *family.* Could he know how fraught the word was? Did he understand my impoverishment? Of course he did — at the very least, he knew that I was a foundling. Whatever he had been able to ascertain about the deceased apartment owner — which didn't appear to be much — he'd vetted the heir quite thoroughly. He'd even resurrected old Bettina, my gadabout, globetrotting black sheep of a Quaker elder aunt. He must have known how absolute my solitude was.

There was something, though, Rouchard had no way to comprehend: the security I'd established within that solitude. I grieved — still grieve — the loss of Alice. She and Roy, my "legal" father, were far more than legal in their parenting, were parents complete and entire, and their collegial home and the whole collegiate world of two esteemed professors (he the classicist, she the mathematician) exceeded every need and want a child growing up could have. You knew them, Daniel. Did I ever begrudge them their due? I still can feel the tug at my waist as Alice cinches, from behind, the ribbon of my communion dress, the rough grasp of intensely interlocking gratitudes. I'd arrived in her life when she'd reached an age when she'd given up wishing for children.

When Alice died — two years after Roy did, Daniel, and sixteen years after you — I found a consolation to assist me through my grief, a stance: I exulted in my invulnerability. I offered fate no more hostages. No parent of mine was going to get sick and need care; no child of mine would lose her way and need rescue. Where could hazard attempt to invade such a life? There was no one around me to leave the door ajar, to forget to latch the latch.

Though now it seems I'd left more than a door unattended. A whole side of my life, of which I'd had no inkling, was gaping to the elements, and through that gap had walked a man as parentless, spouseless, childless (as Rouchard took pains to stress), sisterless, brotherless, cousinless, loverless — as solitary — as myself.

Was that how he had recognized me, this Saxe person, whoever he was, through the kinship of our kinlessness? *Let us conjecture.* The question was more than a perplexity. The experience of being recognized by a stranger unsettled me. Not because I didn't know who *he* was — quite otherwise. I had a panicked intimation that I didn't know myself, had been oblivious to my own existence, for here I'd been given notice that there was something essential about me an unknown man had known but I had not. Still did not! The stranger who could explain it all was dead.

Did I really desire the explanation? Obviously, anyone else would. Offered the key to her life, with an apartment thrown in for good measure, she'd not be so quick with the "I must decline!" Never mind avarice: Where was my curiosity?

Anyone else wasn't me, though—hadn't that always been true! The futures of these *anyones* had surely grown seamlessly out of uninterrupted pasts. The progress of their young, budding lives hadn't been determined by a decision at some crucial point, a decision made, a decision carried out, the juncture of the carrying-out still evident in the invisible scar of psychic sutures, like the line in the bark of a grafted tree. For me, as not for them, the offer to unseal the past, to expose the full inheritance, was not a blessing I could blithely accept. What horror might lie beyond the curtain? I traced, with a fingertip, the edges of the other—the not-so-invisible—scar, the cicatrix clasped like a round pink barnacle to the back of my left hand, the surface of which always felt beneath my touch like the face on an antique cameo. It was a villainous face on a cameo of abuse. No. Only the bravest adoptee could welcome such an offer without a hesitation in the heart.

I deliberated over this as the Mercedes angled deftly through the snarl until, as we approached a great wide circle, our advance was cut off by a rapid flash of moving color and a thump so loud it wasn't drowned out by Drôlet's *"Merde!"* The car lurched, and I grabbed the back of the front seat to keep from landing on the floor. *"Conard!"* Drôlet yelled as a crowd of runners dodged around us across the road, noisily, for many of them were blowing whistles, flowing through the traffic as heedlessly as loose leaves driven before a great wind, and a couple of them ended up bouncing over Drôlet's hood. They bounced well, fortunately; fortunately, we hadn't been going very fast. One of the two never lost stride and evaporated into the confusion; the other one did a somersault and tumbled out of sight beside us. I leaped for the door—this drew a further ejaculation from Drôlet—and then nearly fell myself, for we hadn't quite stopped when my heel hit the pavement.

A delivery van screeched to a halt behind us; its driver laid on the horn. I squeezed between bumpers and knelt beside the person we'd collided with just as he pushed himself up onto his knees. He wore

jeans and boots and a wool cap and was pillowed in layers of shirts
and jackets; a brown bandanna masked his face. I grabbed an elbow
to help him to his feet, and the bandanna slipped its knot, and it was
then I saw that it wasn't a man at all. She was russet-haired, young
like the others. The expression in her copper eyes was caught crazily — seized — between two extremes, opposite realities, like those
frames in a film where one scene dissolves into the next and for a moment the overlap forms a single image. Her eyes and her cheeks were
flushed with elation and fear and exertion, the excitement of danger,
a residue of anger. Intruding on that was a grave still gaze of watchfulness. Could I call her gaze recognition? It was exactly such for me,
one of those moments when amid the haste of everything else, everything comes to a stop. The two of us knelt on the wet pavement in
the canyon between two automobiles, she in her boots and her road-
soiled jeans and me in my dress and my overcoat, bathed — amid the
blaring horns and receding keening of whistles and pounding of footsteps — in silence, and for some expanse of time briefer than a second, that was all there was, that silence, and then elation won, and
haste reclaimed her and she pushed me away and was gone.

I stood and looked out over the sea of cars frozen in their odd array, bobbing at rest like boats in a harbor, and then they all moved
forward a few yards and halted again, as though the tide had turned.
The Mercedes remained where it was. Drôlet's door was open and I
couldn't see him — had he run for help? Was he coming around to
find if I was okay? — but then I spied his coattails. He was doubled
over, popping up and down, searching between and under cars, until
at last he stood, triumphantly gripping a chrome hood ornament. He
held it aloft like a scepter and smiled, and I smiled back.

I could hardly hate him at the moment. I'd gained my own souve-
nir, a brown rumpled square of cloth, and when I bent to pick it up,
my eye settled on something else for which I felt a sudden and overwhelming and unexpected fondness: the oil-marbled cobblestones of
a rainy Parisian street. *I'm here!* I thought to myself. *Here! Standing
where American professors of anesthesiology so rarely get to stand, in
the middle of lanes on l'avenue de la Grande Armée!,* and when Drôlet
ushered me back into the sedan with a ceremonial flourish of the
Mercedes logo, I waved him off with my bandanna and told him, no,

I'd walk. From the distance, I could hear the sirens of the police vans racing in reinforcements and caught on a gust of the vaguest breeze the faintest ghost of tear gas. I extracted my bag and my umbrella from the car and slammed the door and zigzagged toward the curb through the idling maze like a last straggler hoping to catch up.

III

B EFORE I COULD TURN the key, but after I'd inserted it in
the lock, I was swept by a strange compulsion to check my
hair and smooth my dress, as though someone might actually greet me, might be at home to usher me graciously into the life of
Byron Manifort Saxe. Perhaps a welcome feast had been prepared! I'd
already dutifully wiped my shoes on the doormat, the entrance's only
amenity, and knocked, timidly, and then again, less so. There was no
bell. My shoes were soggy. The outfit I had chosen for consulting with
a lawyer had turned out to be not so smart for a foul-weather crosstown hike. I had pictured this as my leisure day, one in which I would
recover from travel and act the tourist, take a saunter, sit in a café, get
reacquainted with the city: an uncomplicated day *à Paris, avec moi-
même,* since I had myself to myself for the moment, before my official
duties closed around me and I had to start thinking professionally.
Already, I was scheduled to be at the hospital on Saturday, and for a
Sunday brunch with Willem. Well, at least I'd achieved the *moi-même*
part by getting rid of Drôlet, but I was hardly alone with Paris. My
adopted mission clung to me like an overzealous chaperone. It was a
condition unbefitting a *flâneur.*

I did attempt a bit of a wander, strolling down avenue d'Iléna
and then veering off through quieter side streets toward the river.
The Seine, I saw as I reached the *quai,* was at full flow, not flooding
(not close), but straining its granite channel — the weather must be
dreadful in the Vosges! The current that usually makes such a deco-
rous curtsy as it courses through the city had a rumbling rudeness in
it: France's river acting boorishly un-French. Thinking it might be fun

to traverse the rampage over the most delicate of the city's bridges, I headed toward the Pont des Arts.

I'd spent a lot of time in this city over the years, beginning (encouraged by Roy and Alice) with a college semester abroad (in Lyon, but near enough) and continuing through a convention here, a consultation there, the last of them, come to think of it, years ago. As a result, I have the sort of elementary familiarity with Paris that means I can usually get where I'm going though I never really know where I am. As people tend to, I've loved the city since the moment I set foot in it, though not as so many Americans (and, I suppose, so many Frenchmen) do, in a quaint Maurice Chevalier way, and not in a Hemingway or Scott Fitzgerald way. My favorite Paris has never been one of mustaches and gastronomies, wartime intrigues over pot-au-feu and slow indiscretions involving Gitanes and calvados, of madness by absinthe and death from dissolution or cheese mold or *l'amour*. We don't die of *l'amour*, anyway, Daniel, as I told you, as you know, as we both know, love dies of us.

At any rate, I don't have the attention span required for proper dissolution, or even for proper indulgence, can never remember the name of the dish that was so divine last night, or the vintage of an excellent wine. If, as the master said, Parisian life is dominated by two passions, for ideas and for fornication, my Paris was dominated by only the first. My affection was not for the voluptuary's city, but for a harder and lighter one — of music on the one hand and science on the other, Gabriel Fauré to Marie Curie, *Tannhäuser* (second version) to the Observatoire, a city of cosmic order strung together by endless miles of cold stone streets that could be walked as beautifully on an inclement day as any. Which is good, since I love to walk, though on this day I gave up, finally, and took a coward's refuge in the Métro. I changed trains at Concorde and rode four stops, slipping beneath the angry river, and exited at Sèvres-Babylone.

The escalator carried me to a place where I'd never been. A vast intersection, a busy bend around a park lined with Beaux Arts façades — it struck me at once as not only un-Parisian but oddly un-itself. Its grand expanses lacked grandeur, and its grandeurs — those façades — lacked the conspiratorial confidentiality that makes impressive

Paris enticing as well. I'd been in the *quartiers* that lay to either side of here, rue du Bac and Saint-Sulpice, tourist places, retail places, sure, but nevertheless as intricate in texture as this strange place was bald. Its baldness wasn't ugly so much as deadpan, undistinguished, interchangeable. Unlike any Paris I'd ever seen, this spot could be anywhere, or at least in any of many elsewheres: Buenos Aires or Beirut, Dupont Circle, Astor Place. There was one exception to the elevated drab: the nouveau-deco face of the (according to its neon tiara) Hôtel Lutetia. Rouchard's instructions directed me quickly down boulevard Raspail away from the square and into a warren of narrow and narrower streets, where I walked until I found myself at the dead end of an impasse, facing a giant gray door.

Press in the code, leap the transom; I spun in the center of a cobblestoned courtyard for a moment, an umbrella ballet — Pas de Deux with Bumbershoot — searching for a resident, a concierge, a stray deliveryman, anyone who could direct me. No one was about. The atelier windows lining the ground floor were dark, and most of them shuttered, and so I headed through the only door that seemed a likely bet, in the corner farthest from the street. It admitted me into a little oval alcove at the foot of a narrow spiral staircase. The stairs curved up steeply for five or six stories, hugging the silo wall. All this felt like a rear exit to some establishment, not a main entrance, but it was what I had, so I went up. Top floor, Rouchard had said, and I climbed until I couldn't anymore and the ascent leveled out into a short, brutish stub of a hallway. The hallway had three doors. One door sported a ceramic tile decorated with a blue amphora and a Greek surname, another emitted the hollow plink of a slow drip into a water tank — the WC, I surmised — and the third was distinguished only by a coir mat reading (was it the exclamation point that made it seem sarcastic?) *Bienvenue, Mes Amis!* I smoothed my dress and turned the key in the lock.

The door cracked open, and I staggered back a step. A breath of air had splurged out, and what an evil breath it was, corrosive, mephitic. My eyes smarted, and I turned my head as I stepped inside as though to evade the brunt of something. "Anyone here?" I called. No answer, no echo; the place was neither occupied nor empty. "Hello?" I felt the wall for a light switch, found none. Clasping the bandanna against my mouth, I stepped urgently through the darkness to where a scrim of light announced a window obstructed by a shade. The shade was like any window shade except that it was made of an infernal heavy flesh, the grasping black fabric of a mourning dress. I gave its hem a quick yank and the curtain reeled to the top of the window and slapped a couple times against the molding for good measure. I twisted the window lock and flung the sashes open as wide as they could go. The air and light of a rainy November midday flooded the room.

What there was of it to flood. The apartment before me was hardly larger than a parking space, so tiny that I didn't feel *inside* it so much as perched upon it. A narrow bed covered with an embroidered, tasseled counterpane and a bolster to serve as a daytime divan took up half of one wall; a small yellow writing table and hard-bottomed chair were set against another, next to a vertical dresser with a dozen drawers. In addition to the front door, there were two others, behind which I would discover, later, a bath with a half-length clawfoot tub and a sink in one case, and a cluttered walk-in closet in the other. That was all. My European real estate portfolio apparently comprised a single smelly room. And within these walls a man had lived for more than half a century! Most of his life! With that knowledge burdening my appraisal, the room didn't strike me as a room at all, more a coffin. Tidy as one too, I thought. The counterpane's tassels were lined up evenly an inch off the floor; its surface was still dented with ... what? ... the shape of Saxe lying there?

The notable piece of disorder was an old camp stove tipped on its side on the floor halfway under the dresser. A plume of spilled kerosene, evaporated now, had spread from it across the wooden planks — I could see where the wax had lifted into an eczema of scales and chips and blisters — to a shabby hook rug. That explained the odor. That and a lead-lined wooden icebox containing no ice but half a quart of milk gone to cheese and two rinds of cheese gone furry and some other perishables that had perished long ago. I emptied the little crypt's contents into a plastic bag I found beneath the sink, and then righted the stove — only for ceremony; its reservoir had long since gone dry as bone.

Why hadn't the place exploded! The spooky silhouette etched into the floor wax, a flattened phantom with its arm flung out, gave me a shudder. Raindrops spattered in off the windowsill; they seemed restorative. I bundled up the corrupted rug and lugged it clumsily down the stairs, trying not to grasp it close against me, trying not to trip, trying not to breathe any more than I had to. I ejected it through the door into a puddle.

No sooner had I turned to head back inside than a voice yelled, *"Non! C'est interdit!"* I peered around — no one at all in the courtyard, but, once again, the screech of the raptor, and in a few seconds the door of one of the ateliers burst open to emit a short, round woman in a brown housedress, herself emitting great effusions of protest. The sheer volume of her invective protected me; had she spoken more slowly, I might have caught every word. The point was certainly clear. I was not to dump my crap in the *cour* for her to have to pick up, what did I take her for, a mule, a slave? I fully intended to move it, I promised her (dodging the question of what I took her for), as soon as I figured out the *lieu* of the *poubelle*. My journeyman's French slowed her for a critical second, just as she drew near.

"Qui êtes-vous?" she asked wonderingly, her voice suddenly bell-like, a wind chime of innocence, and then she figured it out for herself and the rasp resumed. "You're here about that Saxe!" She crossed herself, without piety, and without pity plowed ahead: the garbage area was over in a room behind the mail drop, and, concerning the mail, I needed to attend to it. His box was becoming a problem for everyone, and everyone's problem always turned into hers, she was a human mop for all their messes, a scandal it was, and here came another fine one to burden her more, as though that were possible, as though it mattered. She raged her way back whence she'd come. I managed a shouted *"Merci, madame,"* before the door slammed, then picked up one end of the miscreant rug and dragged it like a corpse across the cobbles in the direction her finger had indicated.

I found the mail drop there also and saw what the scourge had meant — the box marked SAXE was so packed that letters stuck from the slot like leaves of an old corsage. It was locked, but when I went back upstairs for the freezer-chest refuse, I found, in the blue bowl on the dresser top, just where you'd expect it to be, a mailish-looking flimsy silver key that opened the postbox nicely to unpin the avalanche. The envelopes I extracted were mainly of two types, neither (let us conjecture) personal: junk, which I trundled around the corner to join the stinking carpet in the trash, and bills, which I carried upstairs, along with the one item I couldn't categorize, a manila envelope with *M. Saxe* scrawled on it but no postage stamp and no address. I placed the little bundle on the yellow table and then, on the Métro heading back to the hotel, I wondered why I'd done that. Who was I so carefully leaving all that for, if not myself? I was probably now responsible for M. Saxe's accounts — I would be, wouldn't I? — and what kind of spendthrift might he have been, though his lodgings implied otherwise. But, oh my God, how long had he lingered in that hospital? And if his debts were now properly mine, what propriety guided me in opening his personal mail, as I assumed the manila envelope to be (the envelope was marked *confidentiel*)?

The more I thought about my unwanted inheritance, this insane imposition, the more agitated I became. I even smelled volatile heading home, my good clothes, already damp, now perfumed with a soupçon of stove oil, and as soon as I reached my suite in the Clairière, I dialed Rouchard's number to make an end of the travesty. I was fueled with resolve and dudgeon, flushed with anger at the presumptuous lawyer and even more at my own compliance, for letting myself be dragooned into spending my leisure day in glamorous Paris performing maid service for a dead man. Perhaps it was the case that the esteemed firm of Rouchard et Associés closed early before the weekends, or maybe there was another explanation involving the brusque secretary I'd made the mistake of deciding to like after all. At any rate, no one answered the phone. That was all right; I would deal with it on Monday.

IV

DANIEL, YOU KNOW HOW I hate it when the rain clears away in the middle of the afternoon, have always hated it. Surely you remember that about me, how I could handle almost any event, weather-wise, could face down a tornado, outlive a drought, except for that one exact, particular thing: the day that starts out stormy, only to abandon its conviction by three or four thirty and dwindle into cerulean. I look up at the empty sky and emptiness explodes inside me! As though love had fled, or a child were lost, as though all intensity—the morning's moodiness, the day's drama, a cloistered inwardness—had come to nothing, had forgotten what it was about. A dreary day that improves by lunch is a parable of youth and optimism. Let it happen at teatime, and it reminds me, creepily, of early-onset Alzheimer's, a blank sky scrubbed, at the edge of evening, of every clue of all that had transpired.

So it was odd for me, as I left the hospital Saturday afternoon, to see that the rains had lifted and be glad. I was even gladder the next morning as I headed to meet Willem through a tinsel-glitter day that verged, almost, on warm. Pristine sidewalks, not a spot of Parisian dust in the spotless Parisian air, all before me appearing so perfect in every minute detail that it was as though a smudge had been snatched from my eye, as though the crystal air itself had been chiseled into a magnifying lens. The morning was all the more precious for being stolen, not from the rainy week just past, but from the season about to descend. There wouldn't be many more like this, not for a while. We sat outside on slat-bottomed chairs, at a trendy little place on a square near the Place de la République, the customers around us hushed and heliotropic, faces arrayed chins up toward the low, sharp sun, like identical daisies in a window box. The place was named Le Faux Henry.

"Tell me all you've been up to," Willem said. He was. enthusiastic to such a cheerful extreme I was afraid he might rub his hands together. He had on a thick, cabled alpaca sweater, jeans, and soft calfskin loafers with the soles still pink, the sort of casual dress that made a point of not dressing down, posh enough to put you in mind of the fineness of the suit left hanging at home, and the fineness of the home the suit is hung in, though his home of the moment was as provisional as mine (albeit, I suspected, even more luxurious). His jeans were creased. His air of ease was plump as a peach. Hadn't it ever been thus with Willem? Even when we were students together in med school: plump as a peach, even then.

We'd met in our first year, when we were both still downy with ideals and indecision, still dabbling in undergrad lit and music and philosophy (and also, for a while, in each other), still awhirl with the meaning of it all, and from there we survived the whole long course of it, from the oak and slate, chalk and bromide of Professor Maasterlich's unpassable Introduction to Surgical Practices lectures on through our graduations and residencies and the commencement of our specialties.

And later we'd worked together, sporadically over the years, but often, and I'd watched him put on the assertive adult plumage of the Lifelong Purpose and grow into his identity. He became Dr. Madsen, for better or worse, with all his devotions and pomposities. Not a bad person, as far as I knew; just a surgeon, society's most ambitious and useful, and so most amply rewarded, sadist. And I was the anesthesiologist, his Tonto, his Panza, his abettor and antagonist, letting him work even deeper mischief by quelling the sting of it, never quite sure whose side I was on, his or the patient's, or mine. I still remembered him as I'd first seen him, the clumsy shy novice blustering his way toward confidence.

And then came the Singleton affair, that horror, Willem and I both accused of gross malpractice — negligent homicide, in effect, not to put too fine a point on it — in the case of a woman who had died during a routine valve replacement when it seemed she should have lived, according to the very fine medical expertise of the very fine lawyer her very wealthy family retained. We prevailed, though at some cost to our friendship, each of our lawyers preferring a strategy of every man for himself and to heck with solidarity. Willem and I were never sure if we were in it together or if one of us was about to be thrown beneath the other's bus, which I'm sure would have happened the instant one of our lawyers found it the least convenient to shift blame entirely to either *the cutting into* or *the putting under* — to Willem or to myself. Our long affiliation did not survive the victory.

It had been eleven years since the suit. My news of Willem during the interim had come through the journals and the OR gossip, how he'd branched out from surgery to charity, from heart to whole patient, and from there to the whole of society; was flying around the globe setting up public-health initiatives, keynoting conferences, and humbly accepting high honors; had established his own international foundation; was the fresh face of enlightened medicine; and in all those years I didn't see my old colleague at all. Nor hear from him, until the invitation arrived to collaborate again, in an unusual but exciting case. I'd been so glad to get the call. More than I'd missed Willem, I'd minded the breach between us, and the operation he described sounded like a healing within a healing, a mending of a rift.

And maybe I should have thought about it more before jumping to agree. And maybe that's why I didn't, my fondness for a long-missing friend whose faults and frailties I thought I knew to a T. Sitting at the Faux Henry, I sensed something new about my friend. Or at least, something I'd never noticed before — at the core of his sweetness, a hard, unyielding pit of privilege. That bumbling, boyish smile of his gleamed with new warning: Take a bite out of this bonhomie, and you could break a tooth.

Eleven years. I'm sure I'd changed too.

For the moment, he was eager to gab, as long as we gabbed about nothing: museums, plays, concerts, food. Where had I been amusing myself? Where indeed! At any rate, I had something else on my mind.

"You don't like the facilities?" he responded, baffled. "Have you let Mahlev know?"

"Of course I like them, Will, they're top-notch. If anything —"

"Because, well, look, why don't we go over there together this week? I told him your needs, that you must be kept completely happy."

"Willem, it's not that. What about the patient? When do I meet our mystery man?"

"You have the profile," he said. "It's sufficient, and I can tell you whatever else you need to know."

"Don't be a putz, Will, c'mon." He'd dumbfounded me thoroughly. I protested that I didn't care if I was administering Novocain for a root canal, I wanted to see the patient, even if that wasn't how everybody else worked; it was just how I did things, as he well knew. The patient's anxiety level, for example, was for me alone to judge, in person, and that was just for starters. I'd want to get a good peek at his jaw too, judge if his chin was prominent or weak. The length of the line from lip to larynx (or, more technically, from chin tip to the edge of the thyroid cartilage) can make a life-and-death difference when you go to stick a tube down someone's throat, which is why we anesthesiologists walk through the world compulsively judging everyone's thyromental distance. Introduced to a stranger at a party, we don't think, *Soulful eyes,* or *Lovely hair,* we think, *Get a load of that thyromental distance!* And still it was never included on the chart. Hadn't Willem got me here so things would be done right? Ergo, we needed to meet, this man and I. "It is a him, isn't it?" I said. I'd studied the sufficient profile and noticed that its sufficiency lacked a basic thing or two, like gender. Like a name.

"Perhaps."

"Willem, for Chrissakes."

"Look, Tilde —"

"Please don't 'look' me!"

"Look, okay, sorry, I know this may not sound orthodox to a disciple of the great god Maasterlich, but if this weren't an exceptional situation, then you — *we* — wouldn't be here. The whole thing demands flexibility. No, you can't interview our client, because our client's not around —"

"Meaning he's still in Lahore."

" — right now. What makes you think —"

"Oh, gee, I don't know. Maybe it's just not possible to visit France these days without bumping into the crème de la crème of the Pakistani med corps, never mind a Pakistani potentate. Don't screw with me, Willem. I know how to use my feet."

"I recall," he spat back. "Why not run toward something, for once?"

He paused a moment for this to sink in, then said, "He's not from Pakistan."

"Who?"

"Your potentate. Sahran's from Paris."

"Right," I said. "Why don't you tell me a little about Mr. Sahran."

Which he did, precisely: a little. How Emil Sahran was that rare distillation, a man from a haute Paris family of North African descent, a family established and wealthy enough to have amassed considerable influence, which Sahran had expended (in part) advancing third-world health. His efforts were long-standing but had escalated dramatically in the past year, after he had a run-in with cancer. Lymphoma. An early diagnosis, a successful lymphectomy, and a deft application of radiation had cured him, but the experience had confirmed his conviction that the practices that had saved his lucky life should be available to those on earth least lucky. He redoubled his efforts, in part through an exceedingly handsome endowment to Willem's foundation, currently being finalized, and also by escalating his own work.

Sahran handled the delicate political side of trauma relief: getting care to refugees and field surgeries to civilians caught in civil war, and sparing the survivors of natural disasters the subsequent disaster of cholera. He ran interference behind the scenes, flattering the vanities of dictators and calming the suspicions of local chieftains so the medical teams could safely get into the villages. That's how Willem and Sahran had met, one monsoon-season night between the Niles, in the guest bar of a rattletrap, previously grand colonial hotel in Khartoum, a city made of sand and no higher than a sand dune, where they'd begun a conversation whose eventual fruits included the Frenchman's fiscal support for Willem's foundation. And also, eventually, Willem's involvement in this surgery, for which Sahran was the major-domo.

"Calming suspicions?" I ventured. "Or flattering vanities?"

Willem snorted. "Look," he said. "I owe him, and I'm delighted that I do. He does things his own way, but he does them right, which for you means you'll have everything you need. You'll have more essential information than any physician in any operation that's ever been performed. Your patient's been tested and retested and re-retested, and you'll get the full dossier. And if there's some iota of mystery that you can unearth that you think needs addressing, ask me. I'll tell you."

"All right, then," I said, not to be shrugged off with boys' adventures in colonial Khartoum. "Who's the patient?"

"Who's the patient," Willem echoed, with dismay. His head rolled in frustration. "Who is the patient. Well, that's easy: Someone interested in privacy and able to afford it. And in dire need of a new heart. That's it. That's already more than you need to know."

I pursed my lips, aware that I'd hit a dead end. I looked around at the basking crowd and caught an image from on high of the two of us, statuary gnomes squabbling amid the hollyhocks.

"What beautiful weather," Willem said, clinching his victory with largess, turning his face to be a flower too. He peeked at me sidelong and placed a conspiratorial hand on my arm. "It's okay," he said, and then, in the voice of another, "Only a house divided against itself can stand." He laughed, and I couldn't help it and laughed with him.

"Are we finally entering our golden age?" he asked.

Joined at the hip, I thought, not happily.

The day was too lovely to defile with a direct route home, and once our curdled brunch had ended — none too thankfully soon — I kissed Willem's cheek and headed out, intending to get lost. I succeeded, but only geographically. The farther I got from Willem, the clearer it was that I wasn't going to leave him behind. The man was like the human corpus we delight in describing to schoolchildren: mostly water. Only a quarter of Willem was solid; I'd give him maybe 30 percent, at the most. The rest, for me, was a shifting, murky gel of memory and apprehension. Our brunch together had punched big holes in the great cosmic membrane, that essential diaphragm that seals the present safely away from the past. Now the barrier was breached and the phantoms released, and as I walked I struggled to get my mingled lives re-sorted out.

Toward something, for once . . . was that really what I was, a runaway from love? That's what he'd meant, in all his snottiness — and a runaway not just from love, but from him. He'd paused to let his arrow land, and when it did, I had the reaction I'd always had when his arrows landed, back in those days when I knew him a little better. Poor Willem, he'd always been the type who couldn't fire back without revealing his position, who couldn't land a punch without setting himself up for the kill. Which was why being the target of his zingers had often given me a bit of guilty pleasure, as it did now. *Why, Willem!* I'd thought to myself with amazement, and some fondness, after his outburst in Le Faux Henry. *After all this time!*

But as my guilty pleasure faded, offense blossomed within me: even to consider the question was to collude in his presumptions. Yes, we'd had a fling, a student affair or whatever you wanted to call it — a mistake, an entanglement — and yes, it was I who'd ended it, who'd done the spurning, and it had been decades since I was able to remember it with any precision beyond some dim scenes of resentful sulking in places where we couldn't avoid each other, Maasterlich's classroom prominent among them. But I remembered it well enough to know I hadn't ditched Willem because I loved him too much, as agreeable as that formula might sound to him in retrospect; to the contrary, there hadn't been any love worth ditching, not on my part, anyway. And now, these many years later, to be diagnosed with a fatal character flaw by the light of a carried torch! (And to have poor great-god Maasterlich obscurely singed in the indictment.)

Maasterlich! Once the heartless old bastard had been invoked, he refused to be evicted from my thoughts. Heartless old softhearted bastard. Concerning surgery, he was more than merely a teacher: he was a paradigm, a pure example of the form in action. In his lectures, he'd carved into our young, unblemished minds with consummate skill and with an absence of mercy, to our eventual good, of course. *Eventual* was the key: you had to do some healing first before you could admit to the benefit. We cringed, we railed at his cruelties, his excessive incisiveness, his trite formulations: "Failure to prepare is preparation for failure"; "Anything worth suturing is worth suturing twice." We searched his character for any imperfection that would diminish his dominion, give us a fighting chance.

We found what we sought in the doubleness of his nature, his (as we insisted on seeing it) Janus face on a bipolar soul. For he'd hammer us on procedure, hammer and hammer and hammer, and when he had us as hardened as tool steel, he'd soften us up with philosophy — if that's what you could call his wandering, melancholic free associations — the combination driving us crazy with its inconsistency. Every time we encountered this ruminative side, this pudding within the granite, it seemed to us as weirdly misplaced as a swamp on a mountaintop. That's how we felt; we felt it was something freaky, and suspected we'd been badly used — had he led us up the face of the Matterhorn just to plant our flag in a bog? Yet dutifully we climbed, and dutifully we bogged, not realizing until later that the two sides of his pedagogy weren't hard and soft, but hard and harder yet. He taught like a surgeon, but it would mean something to me, much later on, that Professor Maasterlich was an anesthesiologist by specialty. He knew how to dwell in the middle realms.

My walk had led from the square up Quai de Jemmapes, where I paused by the old canal to watch some boys bombard with windfall chestnuts a boat they'd fashioned out of alley flotsam. When the enemy craft had been decisively sunk and they'd run off to make and launch another, an impulse drew me away and up the hill through an indecisive *quartier* where vendors sold Arab goods from sidewalk stalls beneath the tolling of cathedral bells and from there eventually to the perimeter of the Parc des Buttes-Chaumont.

In front of the *guignol* stage at the entrance to the park, children were gathered in a noisy flock under a translucent harlequin awning to await the puppet show. The sun through the awning chalked the pavement with a flowing pastel rainbow, and the children too. They chased one another in circles in the kaleidoscope light. I turned into the park along a path lined with benches, where men and women sat talking or (mostly) silent, taking in the sun in their church clothes, rocking prams, or hidden behind newspapers whose headlines feted me with impending war, with mounting protests and sham diplomacies, along with the winnings and losings of the *fútbol* teams.

"What marvelous fortune," Maasterlich had congratulated us one important afternoon — important for me, anyway, as I could still recall every word of that lecture, and evidently Willem could too (he'd been slumped in the chair right beside me) — "that we might by chance assemble here at the advent of surgery's golden age." Then he had itemized: how, with superstition and ignorance banished at last from the operating theater (so recently!), surgeons and anesthesiologists now worked as one, saw as one, our diverse disciplines marching united in the cause of human improvement.

"As you go forth from here to pursue your chosen specialty, you will keep that in mind, won't you? Many methods, one goal," he said, hectoring, pacing the pit at the front of the amphitheater lecture hall, a lumbering scold. "Herein lies our profession's strength! Correct?"

"Can't wait to find out where this one's going," Willem muttered.

"Then tell me this, please, regarding our precious unity," our professor demanded. "Why is it that the definition of the anesthesiologist's success is precisely the definition of the surgeon's failure?"

Silence dwelt among us.

The path brought me to the lake in the middle of the park and lured me on around its shore, a lake so dominated by the precipitous island in its center that the placid pool seemed parenthetical, a moat for a citadel. Only in relation to the lake was the island big at all, but it loomed far larger than its size, with its histrionic crags and battlements, a bonsai mountain, enormousness in miniature. Crowning this basalt pillar was a little belvedere surrounded by columns, a sibyl's temple in a summit glade of trees. A high, single-arch bridge connected the island to the shore. The chasm it leaped was as narrow and deep as though cut with a cleaver, so deep that the span, though short, had proved uncrossable for many; its nickname (I learned later) was le Pont des Suicidés. I didn't venture to traverse it, preferring my privileged prospect of the island to the experience of the island itself. I located an empty lakeside bench and collapsed to absorb the view.

"You in this room are — are about to become — the two necessaries of modern surgery, surgeon and anesthesiologist," Maasterlich had said. "In major procedures you will neither of you work without the other at your side. You will be equals in your precision, the rigors of your task," but that didn't mean we should mistake each other for friends, he said, "for you must understand that you subscribe to opposing creeds. The surgeon's one job is to change someone," Maasterlich said. "Your success will be judged by how deftly you effect that change; your fame will depend on how dramatic and daring and unnatural are the changes you effect." For those entering anesthesiology, he said, "Your core job, your one imperative, is to leave someone unchanged. Never underestimate the force of this distinction," he instructed, "for it doesn't live in the operating room — it lives in the world. In truth, you are enemies joined at the hip. It's a miracle of human comity that you will get along at all!"

As Maasterlich launched into "the world," his flights of significance and ramification grew even loopier — how we should relish our essential incompatibility, how that was the mark of any golden age worth crowing about, for "only a house divided against itself is strong enough to stand," take Spain, for example, in those halcyon centuries before the Catholics chased away the Moors, or Germany before it incinerated its Jews. What had befallen these societies when they'd achieved the purity they'd so desperately sought by driving out the best they had?

The snickers had begun, along with a quiet groan or two. "Things to do," Willem explained, slipping past my knees with his books under his arm just as Maasterlich got to "the Soviet before the purges," but I hardly noticed his departure, was riveted by the scene before me, which remains bolted into memory intact, the folding wooden seats in their descending rows, the lecturer's rostrum as heavy as a catafalque, the blackboards on which figures and terms had been dispelled by erasure and overwriting and erasure again into swirling calcite cumuli, a billowing fog of chalk, as the hulking madman in the fog-smeared suit stalked the pit, raving at whoever was left.

"You surgeons, your belief is in improvability, perhaps ultimately in human perfectibility. Your journey is linear; its compass always points toward progress. Good! It must! How else are you to take knife and bone saw and commit the irrevocable? You don't turn away. You are epic. You step through. Your violence has the name of optimism; it is the violence to push the moment to its crisis."

And then he addressed the opposing side, or rather, as I heard it, me, for in the next few minutes, the rest of my life was determined, its banes and blessings defined and named. "You anesthesiologists, your journeys are lyric and, if they are to be successful, circular," Maasterlich said. "While the surgeon's every sun ascends to noon, to the zenith, you, by contrast — you will traffic in twilight." In those hours when the surgeon opened to the examining lamp recesses that were never meant to see the sun or feel the air, in those same bright hours I would lead the conscious mind into proscribed darknesses. But with caution: I would never push the moment, would shy from the brink. That would be my talent, in a nutshell, knowing where the brink was and when to shy, when to release my patient to retrace his path back upward toward the light, to surface in the very ripple where his dive had commenced, with no more than a dime of a bruise or a Band-Aid over a needle prick to remind him of his hour in oblivion.

Except for those — and this was something Maasterlich failed to mention, a phenomenon not easily discussed that some of us would notice over the years and learn to be on the lookout for — except for those patients who remembered, not the surgery, but the oblivion. It didn't occur with every operation — heart procedures seemed to be the worst — or in every patient. Only in a very, very few patients, actually, and maybe only those very few who were fated to such perceptions anyway, who already knew how death inhabits life. We could spot the signs when the patients came around — a hollowness in the eye, a metallic blankness haunting the gaze in the aftermath of surgery — and then, usually a couple days later, the delirium set in. For these few, the awareness lingered of how, in the course of outrunning pain, they'd traveled to the border of mortality.

Rarely did the sensation become permanent, though there were those occasional witnesses for whom the stupor and the haunted eye never fully lifted, and we had a name for those people, gleaned from a paper in a German academic journal that was the only piece I ever read that addressed the syndrome, likening it to the mindset of survivors of historic trauma and referring to its exemplars as *die Wiedergänger*: the revenants, returners from places that could not be described. Generally, though, the condition persisted some several hours, a day or two at most, and finally was gone, and the hollowness and the blankness abated into ordinary cheer.

Then, for some reason, as I was sitting on the bench, looking out at the templed island and the Suicide Bridge and the promenade along the lakeshore, and thinking about all these things and Maasterlich, a horrible realization sprang into my mind, as motivating as a bee sting, that I'd left the window open.

V

I DON'T REALLY KNOW where my frenzy came from — was I alarmed that too much light might leak in and stain the gloom of that dank box? — but I got myself to Sèvres-Babylone as quickly as I could. I was irritated, predictably. As I drew nearer I became aware of another and insurgent emotion. My irritation felt like a cover for something more perverse, less admissible, and as I walked down the impasse, pushed through the entry into the *cour,* climbed the precipitous stairs, and turned the key in the lock, I put a name to it: anticipation. My destination had been transfigured by its status in my mind: what had been, on my first visit, an enigma, something unknown that the world had withheld from me, had become my secret knowledge, something private I was withholding from the world. Could anything be more precious?

The apartment itself was exactly as small and shabby as before. It was brighter, at least, and the odor had fled through the neglected window — had the poison cloud done a pirouette around the yard, I wondered, before winging off over the city? I found a sponge and mopped up the puddle of rainwater under the sill, and then I retrieved ammonia and a bucket from beneath the bathroom sink and a broom from behind the bathroom door and kept on going. The cleaning ritual mollified me, dispersed the remnants of my disturbing brunch. But if it was Willem I fled, I was drawn by something — by someone — else, and as I knelt on his floor and encountered his world inch by inch, I felt I was getting my first vague glimpse of the face of Byron Saxe.

The thing I saw there initially was desperation, a derangement that culminated in the grim silhouette, that ghastly snow angel carved in the floor wax by the excoriating kerosene. Its implication was confirmed to me some days later by the excoriating housekeeper, Céleste, who described with undisguised delectation how Saxe had passed out in the fumes from the overturned stove and then spent two days unconscious (due to either a concussion from his fall or *sa marinage* in gas fumes before he was found). His brain never really recovered.

Smaller signs gave me greater pause. Maybe the weather stripping that sealed the door tight against the hallway light could, along with the blackout curtains over the window, be explained by the bottles of film-developing chemicals stashed near the sink beside a Japanese camera — had this chamber also served Saxe as a darkroom? But how was one to explain the peephole hidden by a sliding cover positioned a meter off the floor in the corner of the room, which would afford anyone cringing there an excellent surveillance of the stairs? How, except with a diagnosis of extreme paranoia? And I began to suspect that the weather stripping was engineered not to keep the hall light out of the apartment, but to keep the apartment's light and all signs of internal life invisible from the hall. What on earth had the poor man been afraid of?

Along with all this, though, I encountered a paupered dignity, a grace in the proportions of the room as he'd laid it out, in the bolster propped against the wall to make the divan comfortable, in the careful conceits of his day — that so spare an individual would bother to wax his floors at all. Can you read a man by Braille? My sweeping palm tried. The distressed floor wax smoothed away easily; the phantom all but vanished. In this way, even as I encountered Saxe, I erased him. I tossed out his toothbrush and his shaving kit, mapped with a moist sponge my own private kingdom cleansed of the dust of his life, directly in the center of his world, a beachhead of safety whose borders I dared extend only so far.

What on earth was I afraid of? The closet, for one thing — I couldn't imagine invading so personal a precinct. It felt as though his shirts and shoes might rise up to defend their owner's privacy. Even less could I bring myself to open the drawers of his dresser. So I mopped out my little ammonial empire, which enlarged satisfyingly with every pass of my arm and every backward shuffle down the floor, until I bumped into something and felt behind my denimed fanny the leg of the writing table.

Of the two varieties of fate — the one that seeks and the one that lurks — I've always feared the latter most, and the table leg gave me a start. Of course it had been there all along, and of course I had known where it was — how often in life are we surprised by the inevitable, the crease beside the eye, the spot on the skin, the lump in the breast that wasn't there yesterday but must have been? So here's where my search for safety had brought me: directly to the thing I feared. For the table was the prelude to the dresser that was prelude to the closet — atop the table was his mail.

The evening was waning by now, and it was getting too dark to read, but the gloaming also emboldened me, afforded me some cover, cast a welcome shadow over my surreptitious mission. The first envelope I opened was a bill from a neighborhood tailor, the second was another bill, and the third, forwarded from some establishment named Café Portbou, was an itemization, apparently, of toll calls racked up on its phone. The fourth was a statement of account from a hospital, which I scrupulously avoided inspecting, alarmed at what I might see, and the last two were utility bills I greeted with the same reflexive outrage that I lavish on all bills as a matter of policy before even reading the damage. The damage in this case was spelled out in print so faint that I had to carry the invoices over to the divan, in order to determine in the light through the window if the totals sounded reasonable. Two hundred and thirty francs, one said. Was that a lot?

My brain was still calculating when it struck me — *quelle idiote!* — exactly what I was doing: straining to read a utility bill in the dark. Hadn't I just completed a microscopic survey of the premises? I had found, excluding the one radiator and the water out of the tap, not the least indication of any public infrastructure whatsoever. Could the gas charge be an assessment for a percentage of the heat, a hot-water tithe? Implausible, even in implausible France, and anyway, what of the electric? There was in the entire benighted joint no wall switch, no outlet, no place to plug in a TV or hair dryer or toaster oven or table lamp, no ceiling light or wall sconce, nothing in the category of artificial illumination beyond two old glass-flued hurricane lamps parked on a shelf, which is precisely why I was sitting by the window holding out a page to catch the last drops of daylight like a child catching snowflakes on her tongue. Considering that the apartment boasted the amenities of a cave dwelling, the bill, which was clearly someone's error, seemed to have been mailed mistakenly not just to the wrong address, but to the wrong century.

I leaned back into the bolster as I mulled over this mystery, my eye idly straying from the paper in my hand to take in the evening sky, the stalagmite landscape of chimney pipes and rooftops. The evening was of the sort in which night doesn't fall so much as day ascends, lifting from the ground mist-like through a palette of finely hued heavens, from frost to orange to indigo, and above it all a single bright planet chased a newish moon across a china-bright dome that had become, when I awoke from sleep sometime later, richly black and densely peppered with stars.

It had gotten quite cold in the room. I stood up to close the window sashes before I'd really surfaced into consciousness, before I realized that I didn't know where I was. Haven't you done this, woken up in a strange room in a foreign locale and felt yourself adrift without handholds in the silence of the place that is not the silence of any place you know? At the window, in the darkness, sight mingled with slumber, and it was as though I were floating above a city, moored by the least substantial coordinates, sounds, glimpses, impressions as precise as the individual stars: a lit window across the *cour,* a puddle of lamplight on cobblestones, someone talking in a room somewhere, and from somewhere else, the thump and clink of a table being set, and each of these things spilling into the air out of different lives (the lives being lived in this building) reached my perception from far and farther places, from different times in my own life, so that the scene below me became this intricate collage, a heritage quilt of misplaced moments. I surveyed the yard with great satisfaction. Could it be? Could they really all be here, all these prodigal memories finally summoned home again, as though my past had gathered to greet me beneath my tower, under the glistening sky?

These benign bewilderings collided with wakefulness as I pulled the sashes to before at last collapsing into ordinary addlement. Then something happened that riveted my attention and drew all my reminiscences into one. Somewhere, in some unseen room, someone began playing a piano. I didn't recognize the piece right away. The player stopped and started, practicing a passage over and over. What struck me first was the persistence of the music: alone among the night sounds, it didn't dim when I closed the sashes and latched them. It still magically saturated the room and the darkness as though broadcast out of my own spinning mind. I think, in fact, that I located the melody in memory before I identified it musically, pinpointed it on a particular night before a particular doorway in Lower Manhattan where you and I stood listening on another cold hour full of comfort and wonder. Do you remember? Would you? Though the piece we overheard through the window that night was the whole thing, the full adagio, two pianos, four hands, an overwhelming culmination of sound and thought, and the playing infusing the darkness of Saxe's apartment was only one side of the duet. Hearing it was like straining to recognize in profile someone I'd met only face to face, and it took me a while to comprehend the thing I was confronting, that this was our Brahms, or half of it anyway.

You would remember, don't you? Daniel, who could have thought we would make of that sidewalk, that marble stoop so sweetly hummocked with snow, our embarkation point? We were trussed up like Eskimo and alone in that bubble of brittle stillness that cold and snow imposes. We'd only just paused to say goodbye when someone pulled the drapes aside to crack open a window of the recital salon — that they inside could be enjoying such heat that they had to let some of it go! — and a keystone of light spilled toward us. A slab of amber dropped across the blue-white snow.

We looked up into the chamber — isn't it one of those delicious things, to glimpse the crimson beating heart of *within* from the icy exclusion of *without*, to view our intimate life, usually so fuzzy and indistinct, from a clear and frozen remove? It's like floating in the cold of the cosmos and knowing all of Earth, its every hearth and campfire, furnace and candle. I can count the times I've experienced that duality, can count them on two hands, no fingers raised: once on a starry, motionless night in the December of my seventh year, or was it my eighth? It was near Christmas. I'd paused in the yard with the sled reins clutched in my mitten, home later than I'd promised, my urgency to arrive arrested by the stolen vision through the kitchen window of Roy and Alice walking out of and into the light, busily being my parents, busy getting our dinners ready, and knowing without regret that these belonged to me, these alive, these busy people, but that somehow I wasn't theirs, that their faces, framed in the window side by side, were impossibly far away.

So: that moment and this one, on the sidewalk in front of the conservatory, you, your violin case slung on its strap across your shoulder, eager to get to your teaching and to get inside and out of the chill before it wrecked your fiddle's tuning, and then the curtain parted and the window opened, and out slipped the adagio on a carpet of light. Who could separate sound and warmth? The two arrived entangled. We stood bundled in each other's breath, listening to the music as though the music were a way — as though it were intended as a way — of listening to each other's listening. We were engrossed in a deep, keen unison when the last chord hit. Do you remember the last note of that movement? A brief suspended silence as deep as a cleaver's chop, and then four hands find their tone exactly as one, landing so gently on a chord that fades to nothing. Systole, diastole: sound, silence, sound . . . silence.

Come in, you encouraged, *and we'll hear the rest.* But I shook my head, preferring my prospect of the golden room to the experience of the room itself, and then you climbed the steps and went inside and I watched until the door closed before I walked off, and I suppose as I think of it that our idiot Willem, in all his snottiness, may not have been so wrong after all.

VI

A T FIRST GLANCE, after I stepped inside, I found it hard
to differentiate Café Portbou from any of its pestiferous
brethren: an array of Cinzano ashtrays on a battered zinc,
a bottle of pickled eggs and a basket of croissants, racks of cigarettes
and phone cards and Métro tickets over the cash register, linoleum
floor and mirrored columns and a handful of little round tables surrounded by pressboard-bottomed chairs, the whole smelling strongly
of espresso and tobacco and mildly of disinfectant. Black-and-white
photos from another era lined one wall, inevitably of celebrities long
since forgotten who had stumbled in, the frames jostled slightly out
of alignment and never set back straight. Near them, in the nether regions by the restrooms, a short bank of video games blinked through
the shadows, erupting at intervals into blaring come-ons, in English,
lamentably, desperate for some bored customer to pay attention and
drop a coin. One console featured a lurid image of a fighter jet zoom-
ing straight toward me, wing guns ablaze, pilot grimacing hatefully
through the cockpit glass. Air War, it was called, which seemed appropriate, or at least ironic. You could say the war had led me there.

I'd spent the week — the week that followed my chez Saxe cleaning frenzy — like any good salaryman, commuting crosstown twice
a day. A very un-good salaryman, actually, I confess, for although
my starting point and destination were unvarying, my journey was
lackadaisical, and I wandered and lingered at will, gawking through
the precipitation, coveting through shop windows (most obses-
sively admired: in a window on rue du Four, amid a bristle of stiletto
heels and sexy flats, a pair of fleece-lined gum boots), stopping in at

Shakespeare and Company to peruse the books, making sure to be in Saxe's room at the time each night when the music started. I bought a pretty, down-filled quilt to spread over Saxe's counterpane, and also three bottles of lamp oil — enough to last me several years, I realized later — to fill his glass lanterns, which emitted, after I'd wiped the soot from the chimneys and knocked the ash off the cotton wicks, a glow that was sufficient to read by yet still vague enough that the music was not outshone, and what could be seen never obstructed that which could be heard, and the softness of the room, its lack of edge and corners, complemented the strange indeterminate source-lessness of the playing. Debussy joined Brahms on the program, and Mendelssohn and bits of Fauré and bits of other things I didn't recognize, all of it bits, fragments lingered over, repeated and repeated, around and around and around, yet the whole of it strangely beautiful, the playing accomplished, searching. At some point, I would lock up and wander home to my hotel, and make my call to the hospital.

One day early I rang Rouchard. His secretary explained that he was out of town on business and would be in touch upon his return. Was there something I needed? Not a thing, I said, and I headed out to begin my commute, descending in the elevator, striding through the lobby to the street, where no Drôlet awaited me. We'd struck a bargain: on the occasion that I needed a lift to the hospital, I'd contact him the night before. Otherwise, sayonara. His absence as I stepped through la Clairière's doors always gave me a little burst of happiness. I'd overthrown my jailer! I was practically a modern-day Marianne, wasn't I, bearing high the Revolution's standard! So, okay, it was a demitasse revolution; nevertheless, my first morning gulp of Paris sidewalk air always gave me a caffeine jolt, and each day started victorious.

The snow of my arrival didn't repeat, but the cold resumed and deepened, and the gray of the season set in with evident obstinacy, another reliable certainty. Half of the days, it rained, but never hard, and the scene I surveyed from under the hem of the hotel umbrella entranced me. The daylight hours grew more and more wan and sordid, but they diminished in number. The gay shop lights, illumined earlier and earlier, the slow glow through drizzle and music from somewhere else gave the impression of a world in night flower, a neon reveille to announce a nocturnal dawn. I stopped in, finally, and bought myself the boots.

On one of my longer and wilder excursions I ended up on a path through an emerald park, not realizing, until a soldier made the long march down the lawn to tell me so, snapping to attention directly in front of me with a click of polished heels and a spring-loaded salute, that I had managed to breach the grounds of the Élysée Palace. He was as inorganic as a lamppost and as splendid as a cockatiel, done up as Napoleon might have done him up, buttons bright in a tricolor swallow-tailed coat, a dress cap with a patent leather visor, but his barked *"Bonjour, madame!"* was clearly a request not a nicety, and an order not a request, and meant that I should go, now, and quickly. I was entertained by this, really— *"Bonjour!"* I trilled back, silly old thing—thrilled that my dowdy American cluelessness would elicit the same formality this centurion accorded his emperor.

But it wasn't entertaining, not really. Out in the larger world, a war was on the way, and the carbine slung across his ceremonious chest was straightforward, ugly business, and every day the protests chewed another grim bite out of the city. I could feel tension's grip tightening, even in the apostasy of my distraction, even in my luxurious isolation, even in my sumptuous hotel suite or in pretty neighborhood bistros, when the news came over the television. The news was of arrests and injuries as the street *manifestations* multiplied, and I never heard bulletins of these encounters without thinking of a spinning, tumbling body and red hair lank with rain. The brown bandanna was still in my purse.

On another day my favored route to Sèvres-Babylone was obstructed by barricades and sentries, and I detoured around to an alternate route and was scanning the corner for street signs when I encountered a familiar name scrawled across a window in chipped black and gilt. It hadn't been on my mind to seek Café Portbou out, but here it was, and I thought, *Why not*, and went in.

The only people in evidence inside were two customers standing at the zinc. I set my purse on a table by the window and eased into a chair. A waiter materialized in good time, a gaunt, middle-aged man who struck me as being almost as rigid, but not nearly as polite, as my Élysée soldier. His tunic was a black apron.

"Madame," he said with disapproval, staring off somewhere else as though I were an impediment to his destiny soon to be circumvented, and I felt more an interloper than I had on the palace lawn. I asked him for a black tea, and managed to get in *"et aussi"* before he fled, for he'd sprung from my side as though jettisoned by a shock, and when he turned around, I asked if anyone here might know a man — at this the waiter backed up a dismissive step and his head began to shake — named Byron Manifort Saxe. That stopped the headshaking, all right, but I got no response; instead, he sped off as he'd tried to do before, and the hand that brought my tea, and with it a piece of cake, was very sweet and generous and slow, but it wasn't the hand of the waiter. It belonged to another man, young enough that his face was fresh and still unlined, though his sandy hair was thinning, who sat down across from me and introduced himself with a handshake as Passim.

He wore a tan suit without a coat, the vest buttoned across a starched white shirt. The jacket would be hanging behind a door in a back office somewhere; that would make him the manager. He pushed the plate with the cake in front of me. "This is our grande torte Portbou," he said. "We are famous for it. In truth we order it from a bakery in the *banlieue* like everyone else, but the truck arrives early, and our wonderful customers are kind enough not to notice." He pushed a napkin next to the plate and set a fork on the napkin. "You are searching for someone."

I allowed that I was.

"Tell me, who might you be to this individual?"

Good question, I thought to myself, and responded, "I understand he may have owed you some money, and I would like to settle the debt." This had not been, in fact, remotely my mission in entering, for the reason that I'd had no mission at all, only a chance opportunity. On the spur of the moment, though, the phone charges seemed a plausible bandage to cover my raw curiosity.

"Ahh," Passim said with relief. "I was worried I would have to inform you of the news." He placed his hands flat on the table. "Byron was a regular here, yes. He was also a friend of ours. Cafés have friends, just as people do, and he and this room enjoyed quite a history. In truth, he doesn't owe us anything. He could have used the phone for free, of course; it was not a problem. He paid for his meals, which is more than some people do; he came every day, and paid by the week. But he insisted on reimbursing us whenever he made a call." He shrugged. "That's okay; it's how he wished it. Then for a while he didn't come in, and I sent him that phone bill. Mostly, I was kidding him, trying to find out what was going on. Now I'm sorry. I will ask that you please ignore what you've received. Byron owes me nothing, and I am sure he owed nothing to anyone else."

"Is there anything," I asked, "anything you can tell me about him?"

I could feel Passim appraise me — who was this woman who knew too little to care so much? A wisp of suspicion crossed his eyes, then fled. "You must come visit us, madame," he said. "As it turns out, you have chosen monsieur's favorite table, though he would have been here promptly at five, and I would have served him a beer."

Passim left me alone to finish my cake, which indeed tasted famous and which the waiter, though still not seeing me, nevertheless refused to let me pay for, and when the fighter-jet game screamed "Air war!" I bolted back the dregs of my tea and left, but not so quickly that Passim couldn't meet me by the door, his hand outstretched, and if the thing he held in his hand had been a grenade, it could not have caused a greater explosion in my life.

"This may be yours, then," he said. "I wasn't sure what to do with it."

To tell you about that, I must explain about the letter — the first letter, signed *A.*, from the woman whose name was Alba — and I am mystified that I haven't already done so. Perhaps it is because the letter, or rather the *event* of the letter (the letter itself being so obstinately unremarkable), occupies a space in my mind that is so nonplussed, so dumbfounded, that it exists as a kind of abeyance, a reality I still can't quite let myself admit to, though, God knows, it's a reality I'll never escape.

The large manila envelope I'd pulled from Saxe's mailbox had stayed safely sealed until one night in the apartment when I got the lamps glowing and settled down to wait for the music (with some anxiety! I was never sure on any given night if the serenade would commence again or not), and I decided the time had come. I say this like it was an occasion, but it wasn't, not at first. After all my avoid-ance of it, the envelope's content proved to be as ordinary as a shop-ping list, which, in fact, it was, in a way: the single page, carefully penned, was primarily about some shoes. It began with no date. That is, the first thing it said, at the top of the page, was *No date. No place.* This was in English, as was the rest of the text, which continued with *Beloved.*

> Have I thanked you for your beautiful shoes? Oh, not enough! I know how you are, you won't even remember buying them. Or perhaps you will remember the abuse I heaped on you for your kindness. So I must also thank you for forcing them on me. Who ever could sus-pect that the item she sees for sale through a pretty vitrine on rue de Rivoli will save her life in some other and unimaginable world, & that's where I am now, for what I have seen these last recent days is nightmare. I write quickly because Valentín and Rosa will be depart-ing with the mail. There were moments I didn't have the will to get to here, it was so very far. Even my faithful *alpargatas* would have given up, I'm sure, & it was only your lovely Rivoli boots that sol-diered on, took one step and another and dragged me to safety. Oh, that they might abduct me home (is that what you instructed them, or did you just say to take me away? I wish I knew!). How I love you, my dearest & only & I will write more soon.

I suppose my reaction to this missive could have been embarrass-ment—professions of love and commercial satisfaction mushed together in a sort of purple-prose product endorsement. Had I just read a bodice ripper, I asked myself, or a brochure for bodices? But whatever questions I had for the letter, and I had some—*Byron, you salty dog, you were a bit more spry, weren't you, than the doddering im-age I had of you!*—the letter posed a greater one to me: Is this what I wished to be doing, is this who I *was,* an eavesdropper, a peeping Tom?

The effect was saddening, and I could feel its immediate under-tow. The intimate glimpse of Saxe's life estranged me from Saxe's sur-roundings, just when I was feeling so . . . residential. *You trespass,* the letter admonished me, and the scolding was sufficient that I locked up and left before the piano could begin to play and spent my concert hour stalking the back streets of Saint-Germain-des-Prés, seeking out bookshops and art galleries, anywhere I could pretend to stare at a wall of bindings or a wall of paint while my mind beat me bloody. Who was I fooling, inhabiting this man's vile little corner as though it were my private pied-à-terre? Though, okay, it *was* mine, veritably, by the fluke of his bizarre intent, but still, what could I be thinking, lurking around in the evenings, kicking off my shoes and getting all comfy in my fancy quilt with a cup of tepid tap-water tea (I had even considered buying a kettle and was stopped only by the thought of rehabilitating that murderous stove) and settling in to read a book — or, for that matter, a stranger's mail?

This wasn't why I was here. I'd been put in charge of disposing of an estate, a simple bit of business, especially since the estate was on the order of minuscule and of the character of dingy. Except for providing me with the amusing diversion offered by the Mystery of Mr. Saxe, my duty hardly rose above the onerous and needed to be dispatched with, not indulged in.

With that self-caning, I set to work over the next few days, arriving at the premises early and diving into my chore with admirable purpose. Out went all the miscellaneous bric-a-brac of Saxe's life, the ordinary items that may have been as meaningful as prayer beads when strung along the habit of his days but that were now utterly valueless. The developing chemicals I emptied down the drain, and the camp stove hit the trash with a little more vengeance than perhaps it deserved. I dispensed with my superstitions and flew into the dresser drawers. The top ones held socks and T-shirts (into the trash) and boxer shorts (trash!) and the bottom ones a horrible collection of paperwork, a bureaucratic midden of twentieth-century domestic life — more bills, tax documents, correspondence of complaint and request, all consigned to neat stacks of neatly labeled file folders. I gave the drawers a cursory rifling — I found a folder marked *Electricité* but nothing particularly enlightening; nothing, for instance, labeled *Anselm* — and shut them again, leaving them as I'd found them. It would all require more sober dissection on another day. But the closet!

I flung open the door as though my assault required the advantage of surprise. Perhaps it did — I was certainly outnumbered. The space was crammed with an impressive wardrobe hanging from two rows of rods lining all three walls. Cotton shirts, woolen pants, short coats and long for varying degrees of cold and inclemency, shoes, boots, two bathrobes (one silk jacquard, one flannel), and five suits, two with vests. I caught myself finding all of this interesting, musing on what it meant that his suits had Spanish labels and his shoes were a forty-three, that his raiment cost more than his apartment. Were his dress clothes meant for church (or for synagogue, actually, since the only thing I'd not discarded from the sock drawer was his yarmulke), or for promenading through Père-Lachaise on Sunday afternoons, or for gift shopping on rue de Rivoli? But I snapped out of my musings and turned myself back forcibly to my task, my more literal deconstructing of his closet. All of this — all of it — would have to go. I pulled much of the wardrobe out onto the divan, with a double satisfaction — there, try reposing on that! — and drew up a quick inventory, and when I got home to the Clairière that night, I called Goodwill and arranged a pickup for the next day, which was the day I encountered the armed roadblock and discovered my detour and met the proprietor of Café Portbou, who'd handed me the second letter and said, "This may be yours."

A second letter!

I knew what it was right away, of course — in all outward aspects, it was identical to the one I'd pulled from the mailbox (Passim had left that one there when he delivered the phone bill): a large flat envelope with *Saxe* and *confidentiel* scrawled across its face. Its effect was utterly different, though. Its detonation was retroactive. The first letter had seemed to me a plain enough relic, a memento mori, some laggard piece of Saxe's corpus slow to get the word, that had, like hair and fingernails, gone on growing an hour or two after his decease and would by now be as dead as the man was, dead and over. The second letter told me that the first had been no such thing. What I received from Passim and now held in my hand was a live, ongoing correspondence, and what did that mean for me? I'd been put in charge of tidying up for a dead man; was I now supposed to drive a stake through affections still alive?

"Under the door, just yesterday," Passim said. "Some of them arrive like that."

"Some," I said.

"The others she drops off in person. He liked to read them over his dinner."

"How many . . . ?"

"Once a week, twice," he said. "Other weeks nothing." The news so obliterated the obvious question that it didn't occur to me until I'd turned away and almost left, and I had to lean back through the door to inquire.

"Not the least idea," Passim answered. "Couldn't tell you her name."

I had no time then to look at the envelope's contents; I had to race. The Goodwill truck was idling in the impasse when I got there. My consternation was running a little high, but in emotion, at least, the driver had me bested. He seemed furious to be there, furious at having to wait. I couldn't tell if this was a provisional condition or simply how he was, his personal expression of what he thought it meant to be Parisian. At any rate, his irritation rose with every stair he climbed (*"Pas d'ascenseur?"*) and soared when he got a good look at the state of my gift (*"Pas de cartons?"*). No boxes and no elevator and I had to plead (*"S'il vous plaît! Désolée!"*) and ply him with a tip, but at last he did the job.

Actually, his underling, a gangly and beleaguered teenager, did the job, the part of it that I could see, mounting the stairs over and over to grapple with armloads of loose garments while the driver handled the truck end of things, which evidently took a lot of handling. The transfer consumed most of an hour. On the teen's last climb, I tipped him also, gave him more than I'd given his boss just for the satisfaction of it, and he handed me an ornately itemized receipt (so that's what Pas de Cartons had been doing down there!) on which the monetary value of my generosity was left blank for me to fill in, I'm sure because the job boss didn't want to climb five flights to haggle.

The receipt listed seventy-three items of clothing, seven pairs of shoes and boots, and three hats (two felt fedoras and a Panama), and how I wish I had it all back to look at again, knowing what I now know of Saxe and wishing as I do for any piece of evidence of which I might ask questions. I would check every sweater for Spanish moth holes, every pocket for Algerian sand, peruse his trousers for waist size and inseam length and every coat's collar for a tailor's label, its shoulder for the shadow of a nonexistent star. But they were all gone, and in their place a dark, vacant chamber that showed all the traditional signs of residential rout: shards of shirt cardboard anchoring skittish caravans of dust, a coin or two, a regiment of decommissioned hangers, a paper clip. The closet, stripped, presented only three surprises: a door in the far wall obstructed by clothes rods and anyway locked and sealed (I tried it), a shiny right shoe — should I adjust the receipt to read six and a half pairs? — and a square metal security safe, also locked. The music that night was more spectacular than ever before, and Liszt rolled like a tide into my chamber, along with the Brahms again — rumbled amplified through the ransacked closet as though through the horn of an enormous gramophone.

VII

BELOVED,
    I fear we are to lose our refuge. Nothing has happened, but it won't be long. I haven't told Lotte or Maria Xavier. I don't wish to worry them. I heard the propeller overhead yesterday, its drone peeking through whenever the racket of the wind & the children died down. Again this morning. It's maddening, like having a mosquito in your skull. I can't spot him, but I know he's there & what he's doing. If death is a seamstress, as they say, she's a conscientious one, & she's come to take our measure. Oh, it makes me weary! Not even afraid, just tired again, in advance. I'm looking back on what is to come and bearing the weight in my bones. I hope they come in loud this time. When the Heinkels cut their engines out at sea and coast in silent, there can be no rest at all, it's the worst of waiting. How are you, dearest? You see, I don't even ask. Poor you! I load you up with my sorrows & never inquire of your news. Received letter of 17th, thank you. So Byron's sticking with his plans? I think it is good, please tell him. Yes, you are right, Ganivert 40 is a distant mirage, our *glycinage* [?] so impossibly long ago, but you are real, and I carry you next to me always. Bless you for tuning the piano. If it awaits, I know I won't be long. There, I hear him. When did their everywhere god become so tiny? They've reduced omnipresence to a mean little speck in the sky. Do you know what makes me mad? That this little speck understands my fate & I do not. Is that what war is? A migration of the senses such that one's life is visible only from afar & to a stranger? But oh, well, we are always at war, if that's the definition.
    Save me (and you, *pobrecito!*) from all my loose thoughts. I love you.   —A.

· · ·

"Madame."

I looked up from rereading the letter, rereading it for the twentieth time and re-mulling its implications, and saw that we had reached the hospital. Had reached it, evidently, a while ago, since we were parked on the pea gravel with the wipers off, the windshield dappled with rain. I offered, "Oh, I'm sorry," and hastened my things together, and instructed Drôlet to come inside. "It's cold. I'll be at least an hour." He said he'd stick with the car.

Upstairs — I'd been bequeathed a precious key to the elevator — I went to find a coordinator. I wanted to check over the setup. Not for any practical purpose, mostly for reassurance. Whatever had been gnawing at me since my arrival in this place had been gnawing harder and harder in recent days and with every conversation with Willem. The nurses' station was vacant, so I wandered down the hall to Mahlev's door and stepped inside. Stepped with trepidation; he was such a big guy, Mahlev, but whatever majesty his bulk conferred was stolen away by enthusiasm — he was recklessly kinetic and always, for some reason, on the three or four times we'd now met, so glad to see me that he'd smash into others or, as today, the corner of his desk on his way to say hello. I could never greet him without fearing I'd bring on a zeppelin disaster.

When it was clear we'd both survived, I said, "You thought by now you'd have the room assigned."

"Yes, yes!" he said. "Let's see, where are we putting you? Three, I think." But he seemed determined to double-check and tapped away endlessly on a keyboard on his desk, his face all pallid in the green glow of the computer monitor. Was the issue really so complicated? In my several visits, the hospital, or at least its surgical ward, had never seemed anything but idle, an impression emphasized by the whiteboard calendar on the wall over Mahlev's desk, on which the end of November and beginning of December were snow-blind white, except for a name in brackets. The name was Sahran. Mahlev peered darkly at the monitor, muttering dates ("The twenty-ninth? No, no, the thirtieth") and hours and room numbers and looked up at the ghostly whiteboard again, and finally he said, "Yep," and led me down the hall and through the recovery room and deposited me at the door to OR 3.

The wall switch inside the door didn't ignite the room lights, only the big surgery lamp over the table, but that was okay; the lamp was more than ample. The operating room was among the finest I'd ever had a chance to use: table, anesthesiology machine, scrub table, displays, x-ray light box, bypass machine, even the IV poles as gleaming and unblemished as if they'd just come out of the box, which they well may have. I spent some time making sure I knew where my essentials would be, going through my mnemonic, the helpful phrase all of us have tucked away in our brain tissue whose acronym spells out a checklist of must-have items. "Us" being me, of course, the anesthesiologist, the person you find in the minutes before any surgery mumbling the mantra that isn't a prayer. There are some standard, garden-variety mnemonics — Maasterlich had offered up a few of his favorites, mostly ribald — but I'd adopted a ditty from a Greek tragedy, since I'd already been made to memorize it for some classics seminar. Or maybe Cassandra just suited the scene. Where others go funny, I tend to go tragic, anyhow.

"Still There Drips In Sleep Against the Heart," I chanted to myself and began mentally ticking things off: syringes, tape, drips, intubation tray, suction, airway, heparin. It was just a nervous exercise — there weren't any drugs or bags or anything yet. No endotracheal tube, no line-in catheter. I pulled the overhead operating lamp — it was a very fancy model, one I'd never seen — around on its articulated arm until its shadowless glare was centered over the table. The table, without its protective veil of blue shroud and red wound, reflected back blameless as a saint's face.

There is always something eerie about an operating theater not in use: hushed, lambent, shiny with soundlessness. In no other venue on earth does so much transpire leaving so little trace. Ritual gore is swept aside and tidied up so efficiently that fifteen minutes after the most invasive and drastic procedure, when a new team convenes over all-new gore, it is as though nothing had ever happened there before. You would think, wouldn't you, that this space, of all spaces, would confess its history. Shouldn't a taint of such a past persist? Yet coming into a room like this one, expectant before an operation, I'd wonder that a place of intensest concentration and ultimate consequence, of deepest mortal struggle, could be washed so spic-and-span. Washed by Lethe (same seminar). Harm sank into oblivion, and the waters closed above it.

"'Still there drips in sleep against the heart grief of memory,'" I repeated, oratorically this time, taking the lamp as my stage light and assuming (in error) that I was alone. But there was no memory, *should be* none, not in any OR of mine, not if I could help it, for memory and forgetting were my province, just as Willem's province was restoration through carnage. The ancient chorus had words for that too. "'From the gods who sit in grandeur,'" I continued, readying to give Willem his tragic due, but it was someone else who finished.

"'. . . grace comes somehow violent.'" The torso that emerged into the halo of light wasn't Mahlev's, and neither was the voice, though I recognized it.

"Oh, hello," I said, embarrassed, and in a flustered attempt at recovery, I reached my hand across the table.

"I've startled you," Sahran said. "Forgive me." He took my hand in both of his and held it, held it a moment too long for cordiality, as though he were appraising or adoring it, as though I wore a fisherman's ring and he were about to go down on his knees.

"They've given us a beautiful room," I said nervously, retrieving my extremity. "Good of you to come and check it out."

"Have they," Sahran said.

"Not every patient is so conscientious," I said.

"Nor every doctor, Dr. Anselm."

"Matilde," I offered.

"Emil," he countered, and invited me — *S'il vous plaît, tutoyez-moi* — to address him informally. "But would you mind, terribly, Doctor, if I stuck with your title? I know you may think it absurd — many doctors do, all that MD mystique — but there's some consolation to be found in mystique backed by merit, and since our relationship will be ultimately a formal one, I admit the formality comforts me."

I could feel my cheeks burning; I'd never been accosted with such brash propriety.

"So, yes, Dr. Anselm, it must look odd," Sahran said, "me, here. Today I'm not here as a patient, though, thankfully. You see, I enjoy a complicated relationship with this hospital."

"I'm sure I don't need to —"

"Need," he interrupted. "What's need? You are curious, so I am telling you. You were informed you'd be in a private hospital. But even among private hospitals, as you see, this is a special place." Sahran called it a "diplomatic facility," though not belonging to a particular nation. It had been founded, he said, during the Algerian conflict, "when some of my brethren felt the need for a medical . . . alternative, shall we say," where Muslim extra-nationals could be assured of proper treatment. Sahran declared it "an encouraging sign" that the place was currently little used, except when, say, a visiting Saudi prince was in town and in need of medical care. In service of such clientele, it was kept in tiptop condition.

"One thing to understand is that, technically speaking, we are not standing in France. You and I, we are here by invitation, diplomatically secured," Sahran said. "And as it turns out, I am a diplomat of sorts. I stress the 'of sorts.'" He smiled softly, and assured me of the simplicity of what he called "the situation. An operation is necessary, and for convenience it is best done in France. But not in the French jurisdiction. Why? Because of you, quite frankly, and the other doctors we have enlisted who are not all licensed to practice here. And so I have made arrangements and resolved the problem. As matters go, it wasn't difficult. Am I clarifying things?"

He was, in part. Willem had assured me before I left New York that all relevant credentials issues would be handled on his end, and now I knew what he'd meant. Sahran and I headed out from the table toward the recovery room. At the swinging doors, I reached for the lamp switch, and he paused to look back, as though he were afraid he'd left something behind. "It's beautiful, you're right," he said. He scanned the air, slowly; whatever he sought, it didn't lie on the floor; it was floating in the ether. "Ever seen a battlefield?" he asked, by which he meant a historic one, "like your Gettysburg?"

I said I didn't favor them, preferring more pacific parks; for instance, just the other day I'd walked through Buttes-Chaumont, and I would have prattled on longer in this prattling manner if he hadn't said, "In its own way, a battleground too," and returned me to his point. He'd visited Gettysburg once, when he was in the States, just as he'd visited other, similar spots. "Verdun, same thing," he said. "Very odd experience. You go there looking for an answer, some evidence.

And here's this trench and that bridge, exactly where you'd read they'd be, and aside from that: nothing, nothing that can enlighten you. Whole armies bled into the dirt, and it's all disappeared. After all that violence, not even a ghost." His eyes finished their circuit of the room and came back around to mine. "Not even a ghost," he said.

I went to thank Mahlev ("Please, don't get up!") and retrieve my things, and found the big man in a dither. "Oh, here you are!" he exclaimed and said with flustered apologies that he was just coming around to find me, that he'd directed me to the wrong OR. "You'll be in number five." He wanted to take me back in, but I said, No, no, another time, no big deal, I'm sure the room is similar. My ritual had fulfilled its symbolic purpose regardless of practical accuracy. I still felt anxious, but not concerning the facilities.

When I got to the elevator, Sahran was there too, with his overcoat on and a newspaper folded beneath his arm. He'd already pressed the down button. He carried a leather briefcase and was wearing a rain hat with a wide flat brim and a string under his chin, an item whose floppishness had the strange effect of emphasizing his dignity. The bell dinged; the doors opened. We talked small on the ride down, on our way through the lobby — did I have friends here? Was I missing New York? — and my impatience grew with each exchange. As we paused on the pea gravel in front of his car, I mustered my resolve.

"Mr. Sahran . . . Emil . . . I appreciate your explanation," I said. "You're right, it helps. But based on what you've told me, I have no idea what legal authority we're under here, if any, and I would hate to find out that that was really the point."

He took this without flinching, and his face managed to appear contemplative and even a little sad under the silly rain hat. Then he said, "I'm hosting a dinner before the surgery period starts, at my place, and I would enjoy it very much if you could join us. Some evening soon. I will let you know. May I count on you?"

I heard myself respond that I'd be delighted.

"Good, then," he said. "Goodbye, Matilde."

And I told him goodbye and was almost to the Mercedes before it occurred to me that I hadn't gotten my answer and before I registered the name.

· · ·

The phone was ringing on the table by the couch even as I unlocked the door to the suite, and the voice spilled out of it before I could even say hi.

"What the hell, Matilde."

"Willem, hello. I thought I might hear from you."

In fact, I'd resolved, during the ride back into the city, to give him a call. My afternoon at the hospital had sunk in on me slowly, but during the ride my thoughts had avalanched, and with them my composure, and I knew nothing would settle matters except a long-delayed mano-a-mano heart-to-heart with Willem, though I certainly didn't need the tirade that now greeted me. Willem had heard from Sahran, and Willem wasn't pleased. I was sabotaging the effort, he shouted, was making him look bad, was paranoid, was a troublemaker, was —

"Replaceable."

"What?" Willem said.

"Replaceable. Willem, I'm an anesthesiologist. There are scads of us. You could probably even find a few in France. If my questions make you uncomfortable, get rid of me. Get someone you like."

"I've considered it," he said.

"But."

"It isn't up to me. He wants you."

"Who?"

"Sahran, naturally. Who else?" For some reason, Willem said, that was beyond his ability to fathom, Sahran was insisting I be on the team. And anyway, he, Willem, didn't want me to go either, it was far too late for such changes, we had an operation coming up and soon.

"November thirtieth at seven A.M.," I ventured.

"Soon, like I said."

"Seven A.M., Willem! November thirtieth! A specific time on a specific day. It's on Mahlev's computer."

"Yes?"

"Willem! We aren't taking out tonsils!" Why was he feigning ignorance of fundamentals? With me! "You can't schedule a heart transplant, because a heart transplant requires a heart, and, geez, you just never know when a heart might become available," I said. "Or do you?"

"Implying what?" he said.

"I'm not implying anything, I'm asking you. Do you know? Have you arranged for someone to donate his heart at a time convenient for all? Unless you can convince me that this is not what it looks like, then I am out of here; it doesn't matter what you think. I may be a lot of things, but I will not be an accessory to murder."

"Of course not, Tilde. You must calm down!"

I was giving myself the same instruction but could feel myself not cooperating. Everyone had heard of such horrors — a surgery where an organ was secured through lavish payment or lavish threat, by abduction or attack, or by means of a contract made with a healthy but impoverished donor to provide for his family forever, educate his kids. All it took was money and power and will: diplomacy. My hand was shaking and the phone receiver drummed against my ear. "At the very least," I said, "you're jumping the queue." For however sick Sahran might be, he was clearly not at death's door, was still gadding about with a long way to go before he could be considered urgent. "At the worst —" I said.

"Stop it!" Willem barked. "You're being hysterical." He understood my alarm, but I was wrong. "It isn't what's going on." He hadn't seen Mahlev's calendar, he said . . . didn't care what was on it . . . no time was set . . . probably just something penciled in . . . dibs on a room . . . their bureaucratic way. Yes, the setup was unusual, Willem said, but not fundamentally. "Fundamentally, we're waiting for a heart, and when we get a heart, we'll go. Just like in any transplant. Tilde? Do you hear what I'm saying? You're blowing things way out of proportion."

"Out of proportion," I said.

"Wildly," he said. "How many years have we known each other? I did not bring you over here to do anything illegal. Okay? I promise you. Will you accept that, and quit this crazy talk? If this were scheduled, why are we sitting around waiting a whole month? If I knew the time, why would I make you call in twice a day?"

Well, that was true. "Oh, Willem, I don't know," I said. "I guess so. Why do I feel so unsure about this?"

We agreed to argue again soon, and I hung up. Then I picked the phone back up and dialed room service and ordered a glass of white wine. Before it arrived, I called again and changed the white to red and ordered some dinner to go with it. I watched the television until the food arrived and at the same time kept an eye on (as though it might jump, or flee) the telephone. *Soon,* I thought, *he'll call back, won't he? Once he's calmed down a little? Call and tell me something to assuage my despair. How many years? Surely he knows how I feel.*

When I finished eating, I took a long shower, then got out my suitcases and threw my clothes and toiletries in them along with a bar (or three) of l'Hôtel la Clairière de l'Armistice almond-scented bath soap. And then I picked up the phone again.

The front desk confirmed no messages. "Could you send up a bellhop, please?" I said. "With a luggage cart, thank you. No, that's okay. I'll be checking out."

May I tell you a story? Did you ever experience an occasion when you learned some lesson that wasn't in the syllabus, that wasn't the moral the fable was supposed to impart? For instance: It's a late-fall weekend and I am in the Girl Scouts — or is it still the Brownies? — at any rate, one of those children's paramilitaries with caps and sashes and pledges and badges for this and that, and the leaders have got us out on what they've advertised as Nite Hike, which basically means we are tromping through the woods in the dark, our sneakers in the mulch and our camping gear on our backs. The exercise is meant to teach us fortitude in confronting our girlish fears, I suppose, and certainly the path is lurid with terrors. It's epically, interminably, endlessly long, and every branch is a bony claw and the tiniest peep from off in the forest is the baying of predator death, and the waves kiss the lakeshore with a lugubrious little suck that means the depths are rising to snatch us under so that later we'll be dredged up covered with pond slime and white as pickled onions with our skin sloughing off and our eyes eaten out by arthropods, and eventually we get to a campground where we pitch our tents and roll out our sleeping bags by the light of a bonfire that is itself an errant piece of reddish hell, throwing shadows deeper than the night. Several bumptious hours later we emerge from our sleeping bags to find our orderly covey of tents smiling beneath a diamond sun and we boil our oatmeal over a pale agreeable domestic flame that cauterizes all our fears and banishes our demons forever.

That's my story, though I now know the trek could not have been longer than a mile or maybe two, and I see that at the end of it I didn't feel I'd faced down an enemy so much as met a lifelong friend and discovered something crucial: that you can build in darkness the village you'll inhabit in the light; that superstition may blaze the trail for reason; that the thinking mind will find its way in blindfolds, by blunder and grope, through the dimmest corridors to brilliant places it otherwise would never have known.

The morning after my flight from la Clairière, I woke in Saxe's bed, or rather on top of it, rolled up in my quilt and attired in a terry-cloth hotel bathrobe I'd pilfered along with the soap. The sun streamed through the windowpanes onto the evidence of my nocturnal bivouac. After the taxi ride and the repeated bumping ascents trying to get up the precipitous stairs before the *minuterie* went out, I'd entered and dropped my suitcases inside the door and hung my better dresses in the closet, where I visited them now to see that they weren't rumpled, as though they were tucked-away children and I needed to be sure they weren't forlorn or scared. Then I walked out to Portbou, had a café au lait and a famous croissant at Saxe's favorite table, and begged Passim for recommendations on neighborhood emporiums, and I returned to my apartment after a circuit of the *quartier* lugging new towels, a set of sheets, a tablecloth, votive candles, instant oatmeal, a bottle of red *vin de table,* a pint of skim milk, tea, a teakettle, and, my pièce de résistance, a small chafing dish with extra Sterno refills. A subsequent trip brought a bag of ice and a bouquet of Gerber daisies.

With the bag and the pint in the icebox and all my purchases in place, I emptied my suitcases into dresser drawers and onto bathroom shelves and closet rods; this, though, after first giving the closet a serious dusting out. My timing was lucky, as I'd stumbled upon an important element to life at Saxe's: for a few minutes midmorning, the sun through the window caromed off the bureau mirror and ricocheted into the closet, lighting its depths like a magnesium flare. At least, that's what it did this morning; perhaps for the one time in the year, the way, on the solstice, the sun's rays line up through the columns of Stone Age temples, requiring a sacrifice. The glare lit every hanger scratch and drifting dust mote, every ding in the old horsehair plaster. I dragged a suitcase in, and as I anointed the renovated closet with fresh clothes, the sun shifted farther and glinted off a shiny object, a nugget of Nibelung gold embedded in the side of the cave. It was a key, hanging from a nail in the wall beside the sealed-up door. Its correlate sprang immediately to my mind.

The safe. I had avoided thinking about that armored presence crouching in its corner, simply because it was obdurate, and I don't mean by that only that it was heavy for its size and refused to budge when I kicked it. The strongbox struck me right away as a stubborn problem hard to solve, and I had no use for another of those, I already had Willem. Now, with the solution glittering directly before me, the problem went from impossible to irresistible. I pulled the key off the nail, knelt down, and tried it in the key slot.

Nix. Right away I could see it was a no-go, male and female absurdly mismatched. But with the hunt initiated, I went to do something I'd been meaning to do for a while: search through the blue bowl of odds and ends wherein I'd found the mail key that first afternoon. I retrieved the bowl from the sock drawer — I'd stashed it next to Saxe's yarmulke — and dumped its contents onto the divan's counterpane. Here was all the predictable boy detritus: cuff links; a gold-filled wristwatch with a broken band; coins; an odd large medallion stamped with a spread eagle; more coins; a menthol inhaler; an old transit pass; a borrowing card for Bibliothèque St. Geneviève, expired; and amid it all, a leather pouch shaped like a teardrop and sealed with a zipper that gave a dull grating clink when I shook it and that released, when I opened it — bingo! — a gaggle of keys. They displayed the variety you'd expect of any worthy lifetime collection of mystery-keys-to-forgotten-doors. Two were skeletons, two others small enough they might have opened jewel boxes. One resembled the key I'd found in the closet, cast brass, unplated, its bow ornamented with a vine motif forming the letter *W.* Among them were several that looked like plausible candidates, and I swept up the entire menagerie and dove back into the closet to see what I could do. Surely one of these would work. It must!

Except that none of them did. Some fit the slot and wouldn't turn, others not even that, and after I'd tried several a second time — out of disbelief, or to give luck a chance, or maybe just to wallow in my despond — I sat on the floor in a puddle of disappointment surrounded by an audience of cheerfully useless keys and facing a smug, impervious, and seemingly inviolable box, and that's when it occurred to me. I can thank Maasterlich for the revelation, or any of those other teachers who drummed it into our heads. For that matter, I could thank myself, for don't I drum it into the heads of my own students? One day you will make a misdiagnosis, I tell them, and it will be for the predictable reason: you were looking so hard for what you expected that you missed what was right in front of you.

Right in front of me, eye to keyhole, as it were, was the lock of the door in the back of the closet. I'd given the knob an inquisitive twist on first meeting, but I had never really inspected it, at least not sufficiently to appreciate its ornamentation, the tendrils covering the knob and the escutcheon with a rampant brass garden of vine. I felt around on the floor as my eye took this in, and the awareness struck, and my fingers came up with the original key, the one I'd removed from the nail, and I set it into the slot, and gave it a turn, and that's how I came to be admitted into the palace, and so into Corie's life.

PART TWO

VIII

COWARD, YOU LEFT before we could settle up. I'm thinking about our oldest and most idiotic argument, the thing I always told you I would hear no more about, about whether we would ever have children. Which meant: whether I should want them. I never wanted them, Daniel, as it turns out, and now I can tell you happily that I never will have them, so one of us is finally an authority on the thing we both used to rant about. You were correct on one point, and there was a price to pay, though it wasn't the one you predicted, that everyone prattles on about. I haven't mourned for that rejuvenating force of the future, the pitter-patter of little feet, the sky-blue gaze of tomorrow from the depths of the perambulator. You see, I haven't betrayed the future with my lack of children. This is what you learn when you cross the mysterious bar and childlessness becomes part of your identity, this is what I want to tell you that you could never have known: I didn't betray the future, but the past.

To whom will I pass on the stories I was given? Whom will I tell about you? I am the last carrier, a testifier without an audience. My family's endless heritage ends with me; its meanings are my responsibility, mine alone, now. Sometimes the accumulation of decades — perhaps, sometimes, centuries — crashes against me like a storm surge hitting a seawall, but there is no release; beyond me there is nothing, no one to relieve the burden, assume my duty, hear my tale. More to the point: my parents' tales. That is what children are, in the long run. You could make it definitional: your child is the person who carries your parents' tale. It's the job of your future to make sense of your past.

I hear your quibble: *But Tilde, what centuries? You never had actual parents to give you a tale to pass on. Okay, Alice and Roy, adoptive ones — that's love, but it's hardly a lineage.* Point taken. But point not taken, all the same, for Roy and Alice were parents to me, ample and sufficient, and their family and its sagas all I knew. Which is all the more reason why I think, today, as I sit here in Portbou, that I was never really orphaned until I was orphaned by my childlessness. I never produced an heir who could relate my history back to me.

That's correct: Portbou. I got the heave-ho at the old place, Daniel, that dreary-day café where I began this saga, the place I wrote you from yesterday. It wasn't a place I'd have entered if the rain wasn't hounding me. Dingy, in a word. The lack of affection turned out to be mutual. You'd have been amused by it: bum's rush, don't *oubliez* your *chapeau.* Swept out of my rain refuge by the swish of a dishrag. I guess my residence in the banquette was threatening damage to the bottom line (not to mention the damage to my bottom) and so at any rate, now I must begin you a new letter from a friendlier clime. Passim will defend my squatter's rights against all comers, at least today. It's Saturday. The offices that supply his lunch clientele are closed, and, poor Passim, there just aren't that many comers to defend against. Even the impervious waiter, whose name is Jeko and who extends his neglect more benignly these days (we share a bond. It turns out he visited Perth Amboy once, and he brings up New Jersey at the oddest times), won't complain if I dawdle the hours away penning you a letter about forgotten disputes, all this childish childlessness stuff.

I guess what I'm trying to get at is this: The whole parade of generations is driven by the need to solve a mystery, a mystery we can never solve, and so we pass it on. The mystery is the meaning of individual moments in our lives, the lost step, the leaf's twirl, the close of an eye, the sound the chair made when the chair was pushed back. Example: You and I standing on a sidewalk in the snow on an evening that we don't yet realize is irreversible. Now, there's a mystery I would ask to have answered. I would like to say: What does it mean that I was given a life, and that the life I was given turned around such an instant? May I submit the question? To whom do I address the envelope? *Recipient Unborn?*

For a while, I addressed it *Recipient, Corie Bingham*. Not because of her beauty and her youth — splendid decrepit beauty, tattered youth. I blame it on her eyes. They had a color, sometimes, when they looked into mine, that shone as dim as verdigris, like light in deep forest, but that usually were copper, a cheap trinket gold blushing through the brown, just as I'd seen them in the seconds of our first meeting, as I would see them on our second meeting, and upon our third, right here in Portbou. And they were empty, so terribly empty. But I am getting ahead of myself. I haven't even told you about the palace I discovered at Saxe's place when I turned the key and opened the closet door.

In truth, it wasn't that easy.

I couldn't even locate the keyhole until I'd chipped away an ancient piece of electrician's tape that someone had pasted over it that had long ago hardened into shell. When I did finally get the key into the lock, it worked smoothly — the tumblers clicked, the bolt scraped open. That's all. The key worked, but the door didn't budge. Its edges were sealed with caulk and plaster and tape and paint, every sort of thing, and I went to work gouging all this out, stabbing away viciously with a table knife and a spatula. I also had to dismantle two clothing rods from their brackets. The visiting sunbeam abandoned the closet and left me swearing in the dark, but finally I could feel a little give in the door when I pulled on the knob and so I gave it a mighty tug, using all my weight, and then another, and with a third, the thing flew open so fast, with a great shower of dust and a racket of falling plaster, that I thought the whole wall had come away in my hand.

In my passion to get the door open (which I suspect was fueled by my pique at the stupid safe), I don't think I even considered what might lie on its other side, had probably expected to find a bricked-up entry or a crawlspace or a utility corridor. I especially hadn't stopped to imagine the consequence of an alarmed neighbor greeting my thundering demolitions and home invasion with the wobbly barrel of *grand-père's* old bird gun hastily loaded with *grand-père's* buckshot. But there was no wall and no neighbor, none of that. At first there was just silence and a blinding barrage of light, which landed on the floating cloud of plaster dust like judgment on Lot's wife and re-calci-fied it into a solid, impenetrable curtain, a brilliance so tangible that I moved my hand to push it aside as I stepped through.

The room I stepped into past this curtain of dust was the antith-esis of crawlspace. It was one of the most extraordinary I'd ever been in. In shape, first of all, for it was oval, and in size, though wall to wall, it was only maybe five times as big as my residence next door. Its true immensity was vertical. Above me, way, way above, was a violet sky, a tempera stratosphere dotted with puffy clouds and a few darting swifts and trimmed at the horizon in gold leaf. A crystal chandelier hung from a central mandala over an empty expanse of parquet.

My eye lingered on the spectacle of the chandelier — it must have held a hundred bulbs; it dangled from the sky like the gondola of a fabulous balloon — before taking in the room's peripheries. There was no furniture. The back wall was painted, above the head-high wainscoting, with a bucolic landscape of trees and fields. On the op-posite long wall, this pastoral was interrupted by tall windows, cata-racts of glass, and the wall at the oval's far end was pierced by French doors that opened into a second room.

I moved toward it, disregarding the fact that each step I took made me less and less the handywoman whose work on a door had acci-dentally breached a wall and who could explain away everything, re-ally, to whoever showed up, and more and more the willful and egre-gious intruder. My hesitancy, my native good sense, was overpowered by a magnetic apparition. In the middle of the adjacent room, vis-ible through the double doors, stood a piano. I approached it in a trance: a Bösendorfer prewar (that is, pre–Great War) Imperial, its mirror-lacquered top propped open, its gold frame glowing like a banked fire, a leather-upholstered bench shoved under it. Some mu-sical scores were stacked loosely beside it on the floor; a Mozart so-nata was open on its stand. I circumnavigated it in a marveling orbit, taking it in from all sides. So this was the mysterious conservatory whence were broadcast my nightly serenades! The room that housed the instrument was no less fine than the one before it, though the mural was supplanted by wine-hued satin wallpaper, the chandelier by several sconces with alabaster shades, and the copious ornamental filigree along the edges of the ceiling and descending the chamfered corners of the walls was silver leaf, not gold.

I would like to say that I paused at this point to yell hello or otherwise announce my presence, would like to claim that propriety, or at least timidity, constrained me from going farther, but I don't remember any of that to be true. Somehow, the piano that had for so many nights so boldly invaded my space, irrespective of walls and borders, invited me now to return the favor. I padded softly — I had kicked off my shoes during my labors on the door and was barefoot — but without a qualm into the next room and the next and the next, surveying each of them slowly, each of them seeming to my astonished eye larger and more sumptuous than the last. They were successively easier to breach, too, as though their escalating grandeur allowed me to pretend I was touring some lavish public museum, not somebody's home. In one room the parquet gave way to polished marble, icy under my feet, and another had a skylight and was entered through a colonnade of smooth, fluted columns. There was a hunt room that looked like it had been carved — floor, walls, ceiling, molding, and mantel — from a solid block of walnut (racked over the fireplace: several of *grand-père*'s long guns), and a library whose upper shelves were arrayed around a mezzanine balcony reached via a cast-iron corkscrew stair. All the rooms beyond the piano's conservatory were darkened by heavy drapes drawn across tall windows, and all beyond the conservatory were furnished and appointed opulently: dense rugs rapturous underfoot, the tables topped with flower vases, in which, however, there were not any flowers.

There was nothing anywhere remotely alive, askew, or out of place, no open novel or tossed cap or gray ash in an ashtray that betrayed a human presence, except those musical scores. The scores, and a couple smaller indications, like a copper pot — alone, out of dozens hanging from hooks above a bank of ovens — set with a spoon, and an upturned porcelain bowl in a drying rack on a kitchen counter next to one of the sinks, and, in the pantry (a storeroom larger than Saxe's quarters), which was otherwise barren of food, five cans of minestrone and half a jar of instant coffee. Then I reached the study.

The study — I call it such; it was dominated by a monumental mahogany partners' desk—wasn't what you'd call cozy, but it was at least more modest than the grand halls leading up to it. Within it was concentrated all the clutter and aroma of life that had been petrified out of its compatriots. What happy chaos! Clothes and books lay scattered about on nearly every horizontal surface, on chairs and couch and floor. Idly, I opened a couple of the volumes. They were textbooks. Like schoolbooks everywhere, they were each personally branded with a signature inside the front cover. The signature said *Bingham.* The desktop, oddly, was pristine, but a smaller writing table, set in front of an uncurtained window, was burdened with notepads and dictionaries. A straight-back chair was set before it; a lavender sweater was draped over the chair back. A small end table off to the side held an electric teapot, a crystal drinking glass bristling with pencils and ballpoint pens, a ceramic coffee cup, and an open box of tea bags, which explained the nice smell: orange pekoe, wafting into the air from the half-empty cup.

I froze. All the fear and trepidation I should have let gather with each successive room—nine rooms' worth of fear (not counting the pantry)—took hold of me. I leaned to lay my fingers against the cup. A thin wraith of rising steam coiled around my head and I thought: *Warm.* The ceramic was smooth as glass and flushed as fever. I straightened with a start. Was that a sound? A step? I scurried on tiptoe around the desk and paused at the door, plastering my back against the wall like the spy I was or the burglar I'd be mistaken for.

Nothing.

I steeled my resolve for a dash back to my own place, praying that nobody had settled down in the rooms between me and my refuge, but something stopped me before I could bolt as surely as if a hand had grabbed my ankle. Beside me was a low book cabinet, a mess of envelopes splayed across its top: manila envelopes, some creased and dog-eared, some crisp and new, their flaps unsealed, all of them apparently empty and each hand-labeled *M. Saxe — confidentiel.*

The discovery disoriented me, a confusion that would settle into distress later when I had a chance to consider the implications but that now just hit like a slap. Whatever generous invitation the piano had extended was rescinded by those envelopes, by my collision with that name in this place. What could it mean? I sensed an ensnaring malevolence. I was in the presence of something more knowing than I was. I felt run to ground, surrounded by what I did not understand, a conspiracy of coincidence, and just as my extreme vulnerability and the emergency of needing to escape struck home, another noise came, and this time it was definite, a loud, mechanical *ka-chunk*.

I burst from the room. Without caution, without any restraint or plan or control, I shot through the shadow realm, crazily dodging furniture, mewing with terror, spinning through the whole long array of chambers until I reached the sunny conservatory—if the piano had not had its lid raised, I honestly think I might have tried to leap it—and the oval salon, and I jumped through my portal as though one step ahead of the hounds and slammed the door behind me and leaned against it.

I leaned against it for a long time, until my panting died down and my heartbeat settled and my reasoning self, my half century of hard-won composure, could begin to reassert sanity. *No one heard you,* my composed self said. *You pounded away on that door for an hour and nobody came because nobody heard, and now you're back where you started from, and safe. But you must erase your tracks.*

I opened the door a crack: silence. I got the broom and dustpan and stepped back under that lovely, placid summer sky long enough to sweep up the worst of the evidence. The door, I observed, had no knob on the far side, and no escutcheon. It had been, from the palace point of view, just one more panel in the wainscoting until I'd erupted through it. Now it was not so invisible. My intrusion had pulled some paint away and splintered a piece of molding, which I tried to push back into place, without luck. I swept up plaster shards and paint chips and dust, and made it as good as I could get it. Then I retreated with my dustpan and broom and turned the vined key in the viney lock, except the lock wouldn't work—I seemed to have sprung that too—but anyway the door stayed shut and I jammed Saxe's shoe against it just to be sure and retired to the divan in exhaustion.

IX

[No place]

November 24

Carlos, my only,

    I am so terribly afraid to write to you. My whole existence pines to hear your voice tell me you've received this. But I know I'll have no word & no assurance — as soon as this letter leaves my hand my aloneness will be back & unbearable. But I must trust in luck, it is all that's left for me. Valentín gone. Communication getting more dangerous (for you, dear!), & I know it will get worse. I'll get you news as I can. Unhurt, a little sick recently, I guess to be expected. We've been warned to use an *adresse intermédiaire*, please note & watch for postmark Genève, and forgive if I sound not quite myself, it's how it will have to be for a while. Are you safe, my love? I'm sure you heard how the Ebro fell. A horror, unnecessary. Retreat a despair — how exultant we were those first weeks! Internationals decamped, do we even exist anymore, for the world? Trying to reach Barcelona. Things may settle, though I fear [illegible — three lines] poor little one, [illegible] less lonely with him coming, but it isn't so, only more aware of you. How could all this be happening in this way? Will write from B., maybe things stable there, we will see.

    The letter — in an envelope addressed to Saxe and awaiting me in Portbou, and that I opened at Saxe's Portbou table — came bundled with two other documents: a flyer for an upcoming antiwar rally and another old letter, penned, for once, by someone other than A.

    This second missive was nearly as confounding as A.'s letters, except that it contained an important key. A couple of them, actually (well, three, if you include the revelation that A.'s full name was

Alba): a date, 1939, and a place, Le Vernet, that rang a dull bell in my mind. Here was a thing I'd heard of, courtesy of old Aunt Bettina, who had haunted my childhood like some incorporeal goad—never there physically, yet the source and locus and inspiration for a hundred breakfast lectures on the dangers and depravities of history, especially in the era of the Spanish Civil War. It seems my aunt had considered herself a great friend of Spain, and, traveling with her husband in Europe in the 1930s as part of a Quaker relief effort, was close enough to events to respectably claim an opinion. Roy and Alice, stay-at-homes that they were (unique among their conference-trotting faculty set, they'd never gone abroad), had treasured her adventures and regaled me with accounts, when I was far too young to care, of how the elected Spanish Republican government fought the revolt of the Fascist "nationalists" and of the horrors that had ensued and of the many defeated Republican loyalists who had ended up in French internment camps like the one named Le Vernet.

I recalled few of the details beyond the sulfur taste of unwanted extracurricular history lessons. But I did remember that the era was not one to enter unprepared, this war being more replete with atrocities on all sides even than your everyday, average war, and endless in its convolutions. Why can't Europeans ever learn to conduct their internal spats along simple, straightforward, blue-and-gray, Redcoat-and-Minuteman, easy-to-comprehend lines? Though, to be serious, I would later confound the stories, the cautionary family tales of the ancient bloodbath in Spain with the television newscasts of the American quagmire that overshadowed my youth, and robbed you of yours, and I would come to wonder if the sulfur taste wasn't the flavor of premonition.

The history book I would purchase on a subsequent outing to serve as a concordance to the letters and a guide through the thicket (and to repair my regret that I hadn't paid better attention as an eleven-year-old) had the effect of restoring Roy and Alice's depictions to full luster: how the Republicans, cut off from the world but supported by Russia and the volunteers of the International Brigades, fell to Generalissimo Franco's Fascists, who were supported by the Spanish Catholics and the ruthless Falange, Mussolini, Hitler, and Henry Ford. How when the war was over, Franco didn't relax in the afterglow of victory but continued with a brutal cleansing campaign of reprisal, murder, torture, terror, imprisonment, and exile, the exiles being the lucky ones among the leftists, the refugees who made it across the border to France.

Vernet d'Ariège
February 17, 1939
Dear Monsieur Landers,
    You may remember your wife introducing us at Hospital Obrero on your visit. I'm also a nurse with Red Aid. I write concerning her and asking if you have news on her whereabouts. I must hope she is already with you, but I have recently heard she was captured. Here is what I can relate. She and I made it away after Ebro and it was our intention to head to Barcelona, but with some worry I would be hunted there by Communists, as last time. (I am with POUM. On the front such things never mattered.)

And that was just more of the mess, how the Republicans were riven by fratricide, much of it instigated by their Moscow allies, pitting leftist against leftist, anarchist against anarcho-syndicalist against Communist against Workers' Party of Marxist Unification (or Partido Obrero de Unificación Marxista, this woman's POUM), an anti-Stalinist organization Stalin tried to exterminate, and so I continued reading.

We did not take the train straight to the city, as I would be recognized, but were able to ride most of the way on convoys and stayed a couple of days in a village where Alba knew a family. They'd hardly enough for themselves. They thought we'd be stupid to go into the city, and so we walked instead towards the mountains. Open country where the roads were blocked. Alba well, and excited to be walking towards you, this meant everything. She decided she should make a last detour. Not to Barcelona but Madrid, to be sure friends were safe. Also she was feeling her condition and wary of the climb, I think. So we said goodbye. I write from a French camp. We are prisoners, so the dangers are different. The guards allow women to bicycle into the village to market and the post. I am so miserable with myself that Alba would be here with me now if I had only insisted. Please write with anything you have heard. Brigaders brought in last week recount they heard she was seized and taken to Jorge Juan police station. Maybe by Falangists, I'm not sure, but anyway she was seen to be detained. Can something be done? I will write you with any news.

Saludos,

Salina Contrerras

PS: Arrival today confirms Falange. Saw Alba loaded on truck to Ventas. I do not know this man. POUM, though.
— S.C.

• • •

Mobilisation
CONTRE LA GUERRE!!!
LA VIOLENCE CONTRE LA VIOLENCE
quand c'est nécessaire!!
ARRÊTEZ L'IMPERIALISME AMÉRICAIN
Le moment, c'est maintenant!!!
OÙ ÊTES-VOUS???

Where are you??? The protest rally advertised by the mimeographed flyer was to take place this very night — *The moment's now!!!* — in some establishment (this alone made it sound possibly amusing) called the Winter Church.

Faites partie de la solution —
— Venez! —
à un meeting pour décider d'un plan d'action
Le comité pour la Justice et la Paix
à 21 heures
Église d'Hiver

"Air War!"

The announcement and ensuing rat-a-tat-tat interrupted my perusal of the flyer. I slid the handwritten pages and the mimeographed one back into the envelope and gave Passim an ungenerous stare. "Have you told her?" I demanded.

He blinked at me. "I've told her nothing," he said. "We haven't spoken. It came under the door, like the others."

"So she has no idea what's happened to Saxe." I tried hard to make the sentence sound grim.

"I suppose not, no," he said, his voice contrite. Then, cheerfully: "If I see her, of course I'll explain to her."

"Don't," I said.

"Non?"

I considered the options for a second. "No. Best not. Just tell her I do need to meet her."

"First time I run into her!" Passim exclaimed.

"Well, maybe you could *make a point* of running into her," I said, my frustration breaking through, and I immediately felt unreasonable. Passim's head bobbed in deferential objection.

"Actually, Passim, never mind," I said. "I should handle this."

His nodding continued, though now in agreement, and he was still annoyingly agreeable as I left the café and headed home. In truth, I left excited. Out of the blue, a name — Dilthy — had sprung to mind, and with it, a method and a plan.

Cutting away from my route before I entered my impasse, I began a topologist's circumnavigation of the block, which basically meant: I put my left shoulder by the wall and walked. *Block* is too simple a description to apply realistically to many street squares in Paris, and this jagged acre was a worthy demonstration of why. It was riddled with alleys and cutoffs and setbacks and turnabouts, curlicues and cross streets. I'd perused my Michelin map of the district but could not begin to guess what *rue* or avenue or boulevard the palace's windows might overlook, what vista they commanded. I tried to reconstruct in my mind the inner contours of the grand flat that I had, just a few hours ago, toured: two rooms and then a corner, four rooms more and a corner again. It was hopeless. I couldn't fit the internal trip to any aerial overview. That's where Dilthy came in.

Dilthy was a blind surgeon I once knew, or, rather, a surgeon who had in the middle of an accomplished career lost his sight. He was sometimes called in on difficult cases where every attempt at diagnosis had failed. He'd attended one of my own operations, a parathyroidectomy gone cryptic. The patient showed every symptom of overactive parathyroids, the little neck glands whose hormones regulate calcium levels. Her bones had been chewed to brittleness, and her

heart was at risk of a dangerous arrhythmia, but there was a catch
in the diagnosis: two of her four parathyroids, makers of the culprit
hormone, had already been removed. A hyperparathyroidism patient
deprived of parathyroids was, in essence, no longer a patient — she
had crossed into the category of medical oddity and would be placed
on constant dialysis that would keep her connected to tubes for the
rest of her bedridden and most likely not-so-lengthy life, and that's
where Dilthy came in. The man couldn't read an x-ray or a patient's
chart, but his hands were exquisite and his diagnostics sensual, and
he traced every structure and organ of our patient's excavated neck
until he was fondling — with an almost erotic slowness and attentive-
ness — her clavicle, where he came upon the evildoer hiding under
the fascia. Evildoers: two rogue parathyroid glands that had sponta-
neously developed far from their home in the middle neck and set up
shop in the woman's shoulder, there to pump out their poisonous su-
perfluity. They were removed within the quarter-hour, and the woman's life resumed.

I wanted Dilthy with me now. My tactile exploration of the block
brought me down garbage alleys and onto loading docks, through an
underpass where I couldn't be sure that the property I sought wasn't
crossing directly overhead, and past locked courtyards, where, without a key or code, I had to abandon my method altogether. After I
had jogged around a jigsaw's worth of curves and juts, thwartings
and discouragings, I bumped at last into a telltale sign. A sign, literally. Set into the wall a foot below the blue ceramic plaque announcing rue Nin was an older sign, its metal signature rusting through the
paint, that read (as best as I could make it out) R E G N VER.

I smiled at this pentimento as though greeting an intervening angel, a memory rusting through my consciousness. Wasn't Ganivert —
rue Ganivert 40 — the address of the mysterious *glycinage* in one of
A.'s (aka Alba's) letters? I turned and idled down the avenue's length.
The building numbers were in the 100s, but the numbers, I told myself, like the name of the street, could easily have been altered, and
when I got to the building I was looking for, I did find a FORTY carved
in the red stone of the entry that directly repudiated the *136* by the
curb. The number wasn't the giveaway, only the confirmation, for I'd
spotted my quarry from half a block away. It would have been hard

to miss, frankly. The façade of 136 (née 40) receded squarely from the street to accommodate a jewel-like park or yard fenced off from the sidewalk by tall iron pickets topped with gold spear points. The gate in the fence was framed by a columned entry gazebo (of classical pretension; it reminded me of the belvedere atop the island in the Parc des Buttes-Chaumont) whose lintel bore, along with the obsolete number, a name, The Wisteria, spelled out in its English entirety, definite article and proper noun, both capitals and both tittles, in sculpted red-stone vinery. I walked under the lintel and into the gazebo. Beside the locked gate was an aluminum-and-plastic-faced intercom directory on which the Wisteria's residents were itemized alphabetically. I ran my finger down the list. None of the names was familiar.

Qu'est-ce qu'on fait? There are times — rare enough, I assure you — when there's a benefit to being a middle-aged, middle-class woman of middling complexion and middlebrow appearance whose capacity for, say, breaking and entering, no one would ever suspect. I waited, and in not so very great a while, a man arrived and unlocked the gate and let himself into the yard, and I followed along behind him with a smile and a nod and looking benignly flustered. He paid no mind, even held the gate for me. We sashayed down the short walk together and when he'd gone into the building and the door had closed, I turned to the mailboxes, a row of old, varnished oak fasciae set into the marble wall. I didn't have to look far to find what I sought. I started at the right end of the row, which I thought might represent upper floors, and the name I coveted was the very first one I encountered: LANDERS, C., undoubtedly the very Monsieur Landers to whom had been addressed the letter from Le Vernet announcing the capture of Alba, "your wife."

On my way out, I turned to stare up — yes, those could be the windows. The Wisteria's crowning floor was obviously an outsize penthouse, its mansard palisade tall as a top hat. Which pair of windows belonged to the study? I wondered (might someone be looking out?). How many more lay beyond it, opening into rooms I had not even reached? Beyond ogling, I wasn't sure what to do next. There was no buzzer for Landers, C., and even if I could buzz him, what would I say? *Hi, I stole into your flat this morning?* And *Oh yes, I've also been reading your mail?* I was out of my depth. I headed back to Portbou. If nothing else, I could find the gentleman's number in the café's phone book and make my confessions at a somewhat safer remove.

I also had a question for poor, beleaguered Passim; a few of them, actually. I was suddenly of a mind to present the whole problem to him, draft him fully into my mission of locating the individual who seemed to hold the key, this phantom letter courier. I turned the corner and saw the café door, and all such plans sped out of my head, replaced by an urge to flee, or to clench my fists and bellow. Standing in his uniform at parade rest next to his limousine was Drôlet. I didn't run, and didn't scream, not yet. I marched right past him and into Portbou. Passim was standing there by the zinc, twirling a rag in his hand, nervous. He shrugged at me as I entered. I could hear Drôlet behind me, pushing through the door. "Salaam," he said.

"Salaam. *Keefak?*" Passim returned politely, with a bow of the head. How are you?

Before the driver could answer, I wheeled to face him. "How dare you!" I said. "Why have you come here!"

I had not realized until precisely that moment what solace I'd taken in my hideaway, how much my secret had meant to me. And to have my idyll's walls breached by, of all people, my Clairière capo — and, by the way, when had he breached them? Had he tailed my hotel umbrella on an early visit, known where I was all the while? My indignation mounted, but my invective devolved into a stutter that I must concede was uninspired, repetitions varying only in volume.

"How dare you follow me!" I shouted as I edged around the immobilized chauffeur and backed toward the exit, and then, to clinch the deal (and did I actually clench my fists? I think I did), "How dare you!" and I turned to storm out and barged full force into the embrace of the man coming through the door. Which is to say, right into Sahran's embrace.

The car whispered smoothly through the traffic, headed down Saint-Germain toward the Invalides. Sahran leaned near to me in the back seat, his knee drawn up beside him and his thoughts knotted up in some big ardent tangle of life and law and art. Even absent art and law, my life was feeling tangled—witness the fact that I was here, wherever here was, listening to Sahran's soliloquy, whatever it meant.

Does a person's portrait become universal only when the person himself is forgotten? Since, according to the Islamic traditions—hadith—saints are generally not depicted in art, does that make oblivion sacred? "Forgive me," he said, with a laugh, "I'm off on a toot!" He allowed me a moment to admire his Americanism. "But you will see. This is exactly what Ralu will demand of me when we get there." Wherever *there* was, whoever *she*. "But it's an interesting question, after all: Must one be personally obliterated to assume one's true importance?" It was clear, at least, that we'd traveled far from the phrases that had launched our journey, the pleas and exhortings, the supplicating without supplication that had won my agreement to come along.

Sahran's wooing in Portbou had convinced me of his diplomatic bona fides. He'd released me right away from our collisionary hug, a good thing, since I consider being hugged while angry a lackluster combination. It smacks of the straitjacket. You would remember, Daniel, I should hope you'd remember, never to try to constrain me when I'm riled, or, even worse, placate me, or especially touch my neck, I lose all irony. I lose control and I'm liable to throw an unironic punch (and have done so once or twice) if not something sharper.

Sahran happily eluded that fate, for the moment, and my emancipation from his clutches drained away my panic. Also, it calmed me that his hands, as he released me, quickly smoothed the length of my arms and found my hands and squeezed them, and I was also soothed by his voice. "I would never have come if I weren't worried. May we sit for a moment?" He assured me the imposition was his, not Drôlet's, that he was concerned that my abandonment of the Clairière was the result of burdens he'd placed on me, and could I perhaps accompany him on a mission, nonmedical but possibly of interest, in essence a simple parcel delivery, and we could talk on the way.

It may have occurred to me that I wanted answers from Sahran and this would be a good way to get them. Or maybe I am getting too fancy about all of this, and the thing that really reached me was the thing that happened first: the fact of being held, if just for an instant and especially while upset — of being constrained by calm. That and the sensation, after so many flights on so many days through strange streets and empty rooms, of being brought up short and hard by something alive and by someone with warm hands. The car whispered smoothly toward the Invalides.

We cruised around the monument and on through *rues* and further *rues* until after half an hour we entered a shabbier outlying neighborhood of industrial apartment blocks and vacant lots patched with grass and pestered by windblown trash — the trash with its commercial colors at least not as sad as the sad, depleted grass — and surrounded with tumbledown fencing. One large lot was markedly more kempt and hopeful than the others, its chainlink intact, and, inside the fence, a concrete basketball half-court with a well-used net and a circle of concrete tables with concrete benches. The concrete wall behind this scene was painted with a colorful mural of happy butterflies and dancing glow worms and fantasy critters cavorting in a forest of giant flowers. We'd reached our destination, the second stop on our itinerary and the next stage of our separate missions: Sahran's to deliver his parcel and mine to learn something new about Sahran. *And we could talk,* he'd said — and hadn't we! I had, at least, compelled by Sahran's interest, but his interest, while it warmed me, had the noticeable side effect of fending off my inquiries.

I got some basic developmental history out of him: he was thoroughly Parisian, third generation, tried-and-true and born-and-raised, though the way he spelled his name, without the *e* the French would append to make Emil Emile, betrayed his heritage. His great-grandfather, a Tripoli newspaper editor, had arrived in town in the 1890s to cover the Alfred Dreyfus trials for his paper. He was a charter Dreyfusard, and not just between the lines — the Arab and Muslim press of the time had weighed in strongly on the side of the beleaguered Jewish lieutenant and against French anti-Semitism, how things change! — but whatever his critiques and condemnations, he loved France the way Dreyfus did: enough to stay there, despite it all.

Down the decades, the family had suffered all the standard immigrant dislocations, but the cultural duality they experienced as crippling ambivalence was passed on to the great-grandson as ambidexterity: he could think as well in one worldview as another, as well with the *e* as without, and that's what recommended him to his trade, about which I'd learned a little from Willem. Now I got the bulk of it. Sahran was a roving freelance troubleshooter, called in to mediate particularly intense (and therefore often particularly secret) flash conflicts between Muslim governments (and Muslim groups and individuals) and the pervading, impending West, efforts that whisked him off on sudden, and sometimes protracted, sojourns to desperate locales, from the Horn of Africa to the Balkans, from Morocco to Astrakhan Oblast, though he saw his interventions in less geographic terms. "It's really quite simple," he told me. "Basically, I'm a letter carrier between the abstract and the tangible," those properties belonging to the Western and Islamic factions, respectively, especially in times of war. Americans preferred to fight at as great a remove as possible ("Someday, when they figure out how, they'll fly their planes from a desk in DC") and the Arabs at close quarters, even if *close* meant dying by the bomb that killed their enemy, there was nothing more tactile than that. Though the equation could work the other way, he stressed — witness the Muslim preference for abstract geometric patterns and calligraphy over representational (concrete) painting or sculpture — with the effect that after you'd been at this awhile and had spent enough time as a letter carrier between the two irreconcilable poles, you no longer really knew which was which.

Along with such elaborations, I received some helpful household hints on personal comportment, to wit: If you don't want to be located, don't place traceable calls from your local café to a hospital owned by an embassy. For the most part, whatever I learned about Sahran, I picked up indirectly. Maybe that was his method, I thought, to answer my doubts by showing me something of his life.

Just past the playground, we glided to the curb and stopped before the scowling entry of what appeared to be an old manufacturing mill, and Drôlet jumped out to open my door. I stepped from the car and waited by a wooden sign with a glow worm painted on it that was set on the sidewalk by the building's steps. It was a lonely neighborhood. Some urchins rolled up on rusty bicycles, mute with curiosity. I was feeling inconsolable. Sahran and Drôlet walked back to open the trunk. The sign read ÉCOLE ISLAMIQUE DE JEUNES FILLES.

My disconsolation had its source. Our spiral through Paris, from one unfamiliar site to another, had exacerbated a more general vertigo induced by my flight through the grand apartment. Whenever I lost track of my whereabouts, my thoughts converged on a name: Bingham, the name that had leaped at me like a spider out of a book. And then my thoughts went to the person who owned the book, who drank tea and went to class and wore a lavender sweater, who penned letters in one apartment that were intended for a reader in the apartment next door, though none of the letters ever traveled directly, only via a subterfuge, through the *adresse intermédiaire* of a café a quarter mile away.

As I contemplated this infernal circuit, around and around and around, a spider's image came to me. I felt I was being wrapped in silk, spun about like some hapless piece of prey. Throughout the afternoon motoring around with Sahran, my mind whirled in this vortex, stuck in the groove of a mantra: I must find this person; she was the knower whom I must find. It was a perilous quest, for the woman I hunted was a woman I couldn't escape. Being with Sahran didn't help matters. The seediness of the *quartier* around the Islamic school had revived my suspicions of him. I'd let them go dormant on the early part of the journey *malgré moi,* but with every mile out from the center of Paris, as the discord grew between the luxury of our ride and the deprivations surrounding it, my discontent resumed. Then Drôlet opened the passenger door, and instantly the hush of leather upholstery and the rustle of silk on cashmere as Sahran pulled his overcoat collar closed around his neck were swamped by an inswarm of gutter cold and brick dank, and I thought, *Why wouldn't he? Why on earth wouldn't he?* How could a man with such outsize means, such exorbitant power in such a poor community, *not* be tempted to save his own life by buying someone else's?

Our previous stop had offered up no such class disparity. We'd gone to an art museum. We'd arrived before its grandeurs as humble supplicants, if anything, going in via the servants' entrance. We deserted the car (and Drôlet) in an unmarked, subterranean, brightly lit, and immaculately clean garage and then trudged through an immaculate warehouse with polished concrete floors and a bustling wilderness of office cubicles and then past an immaculate secretary and into the corner domain of a young woman whom Sahran introduced as Mademoiselle Curator Someone-or-Other, though, observing her empire, foolish me, I took her for an empress. He and she had some business to transact involving discussions of money and provenance and drying rates and the validity of certain receipts and appraisals and documents of authenticity, the results of which conversation left Sahran clearly cheered.

I occupied myself gawking at her office, which was baubled out with *objets de prétention* that even I could tell were extraordinary, and when the business was concluded, Sahran shook the empress's hand and asked a final favor. Those were his words: "final favor." Might he show Dr. Anselm the companion piece? Though he understood this might be far too much trouble, the building being closed today, et cetera, and maybe he should just come back later in the week.

But it's no problem at all, Mademoiselle said, standing and smiling, and she begged his forgiveness that she couldn't accompany us, as she was awaiting a call.

"D'accord! À bientôt!"

"Emil!"

"Yes," he said.

"When can we deliver . . . ?"

"But why?" he said. "I've brought the limo."

"Ah!" she exclaimed, and launched off toward the warehouse, calling into the wilderness for assistance. We set off too, in a different direction. A guard took us through a back hallway and, with pauses to unlock doors and disarm motion detectors, into a room as vast as an airport terminal. Then he disappeared. The ceiling was all skylight, the floor a gloaming through which contorted figures romped, some pygmy-sized, others enormous, set about in a scramble that dizzied my perspective; we'd stumbled on a contest of terrible inequality, a tiff between giants and elves. The guard, wherever he was, must have reached the light controls, wherever they were, and the sculpture gallery sprang circuit by circuit into life.

"You're doing me a great favor," Sahran confided as we entered the collection. He stopped before a large nude, which he studied with full concentration and equal leisure before moving on to a big stone bear. He clearly had a destination and clearly was in no rush to reach it. "I have more old friends in this room than in any place in Paris," he said. "Which means, any place in the world. My life has been saved by some of them, I would say." I describe him as leisured, but I wouldn't dare call it relaxation: Sahran wore a brown suit and a sedate tie, and he kept his jacket buttoned and his shoulders back and the silk knot tight to his collar. I found myself wishing I'd worn my better pants.

"Over the years," he added. "Today, I wished for a private last moment among my friends, away from the crowds."

I raised an eyebrow and touched my hand to my chest, an offer.

"Oh, n-no, no, no," he stuttered, and clutched my wrist a second. "Not away from you. Please, I wouldn't be here without you. You have sprung me in!" He would have been far too embarrassed, he said, to request this tour for only himself. "So now you see how you've been used!"

When we'd wandered through the galleries for more than an hour (the guard scurrying invisibly ahead to intercede with alarms and lights), we rounded a corner and stopped before a Gauguin, and then a painting by Pierre Bonnard, and another by Bonnard, and then, a few steps down the row, we came to a large oil portrait of a woman dressed entirely in black and wielding a furled black umbrella emerging from an exuberant, primitive forest, approaching us down a sandy path. We and she seemed headed for a direct confrontation, which I suspected she would win. There was a hedge of pansies by her dainty foot, and a mottled, deranged-looking cat, whose ball of yarn had rolled out onto the path. Emil stood before it awhile, then said, "I adore her. What do you think of it, Matilde?"

I said I liked the woman but wasn't so sure about the artist.

"Then you'll never be alone," he said, for apparently a lot of people, generations of them, had found the crudeness of the painter's representations . . . crude. "But we agree about Madame. I love her because of what she's been through," he said. "We don't really know, because we don't know who she was. But regard" — and he itemized the clues: the path that had brought her out of the wood and into the garden, out of the tangled thicket to a place where her thoughts, "her *pensées*" (her pansies) could be arranged so prettily, the clouds at her back, the umbrella she could now safely lower — "they speak of a tragedy survived." He noted the woman's left ring finger, with its large wedding band heavy as a halo. The finger was bent back so that, alone among the fingers of her hand, it disappeared from view beyond the knuckle, "as though it's been amputated. Has a marriage been cut short? Is this her sorrow?"

He continued looking at her as though something were about to occur or be revealed. "They say the man painted only two full-length portraits," Sahran said. The other was across town in the Musée Picasso, and he encouraged me to see it. It was of another woman in a black dress, "but she's very, very different and quite honestly I can't stand her. The painting's nice, I just don't like the girl." And there was this one, whose career Sahran spelled out for me in meticulous detail, how it had been given to the Jeu de Paume gallery by one Madame Gourgaud, "née Gebhard," he said, "widow of Napoléon Gourgaud, a baron who bought it during the Great Depression from the previous owners, who may have needed the cash on account of the times, though I can only guess."

I commented that he certainly knew an impressive amount about the painting. Sahran nodded, insensitive to my sarcasm. "You know," he said, "when he did a portrait, he didn't start with a person and then fill in the landscape around her. He'd paint the landscape first. Yes! Incredible! Then he'd impose the person." This despite the fact that the landscape was entirely fanciful, since the artist had never once gone to a jungle or seen such trees (let alone all the vipers and lions and desert Bedouins he most enjoyed depicting). The sitter was right there directly in front of the artist, Sahran said, yet he had to bring her forth out of an imagined setting. "She's literally emerging. He's *deriving* her from the scene."

Derived from . . . imposed onto. I thought: *Now, there's a fine line, and I've been both.* Sahran said, slyly, "How could you not like him?"

It struck me as a complicated question.

"Les pauvres!" Sahran said as we descended the stairs to exit. He paused at a landing to take in the view over the sculpture gallery, and I realized he was sympathizing with the artworks. "They must be freezing, poor things!" It was a very grand space, he said, as he supposed people preferred. "But so cold! Were you ever in the Jeu de Paume, in the Tuileries? Only four years ago, you could have seen these things there."

I said that I hadn't gone.

"A shame," he said. "It was magnificent. I mean, it was not magnificent. Magnificent is exactly what it wasn't. Everything was in the small old building that used to be the royal tennis courts, and the whole place was intimate and cramped, unglamorous; there was no distinction between the art and the people, they were all of them creatures of Paris. The light was yellow, like at a street fair, and the people would huddle, they would argue. They disputed with the paintings! Everything was ordinary. When you came up the stair and saw the van Gogh, you cried.

"At least," he said, "I did. Every time. Now, when I come, I admire. *Hélas!*"

The drizzle ceased for a blessed minute as we parked in front of the school, and seeing the opportunity, Drôlet flung open the trunk and, with the aid of a man who had quickstepped out of the building, began extracting a large rectangular swaddle of white cloth. Its emergence seemed improbable, like a scarf pulled from a magician's ear; the thing looked as big as a Ping-Pong table, and when they had it free of the car trunk, they whisked it inside and we followed. We must have appeared like pilgrims in a saint's-day procession, following the mysterious, held-aloft icon as it led us down hallways to another office, one not at all like the office we'd just left. It had, for starters, another sort of empress. Madame Ralanou had an institutional matron's imperial disposition, all black and white with a little bit of somber in between. But she was done up in Easter-egg pastels, pale blue headscarf, floor-length skirt, a blouse of eyeleted pink. Black, white, and pale, but her eyes were bold with primary mischief, and it was clearly her mischievous side that was pleased to greet her visitor. With an offhand gesture, standing behind her desk, she dismissed the package to the fringes of the room. "You always bring such trouble," she said to Sahran. "When will you leave me alone?"

"Ralu, this you can't shove in the corner. No, no, unwrap it. We must welcome it to its home. Is Odile in?"

"In? Of course she's in. You cannot see her!"

"Come," Sahran said to me, and, cheerfully violating the headmistress's injunction, he beckoned me out of the office and down a dim hallway whose length was an experiment in sound: sounds gathered and sounds lost. The doors were ajar, and each classroom we passed spilled its hubbub into the common mix, and then there was a decrescendo until we approached the next door and the volume picked up again. Sahran seemed to navigate by the voices like a ship by the rhythm of foghorns until we turned a corner and came to a room that emitted hardly any sound at all, one in which a woman was speaking into silence, speaking so softly we couldn't hear what she said. Sahran touched a finger to his lips, and we stood peering in through the door.

There were twelve or fifteen students, teenage girls, sitting on blue benches, attentive. The woman glided among them as she talked, glided up and down the aisles with her arms swaying as she stroked the rims of her wheelchair's wheels. She moved toward us, and then away, to the blackboard, and then again toward the back of the room, and at her closest I could see a round pleasant face with cratered eyes, their sockets apparently empty beneath eyelids sealed shut. Mid-aisle and midsentence, the woman stopped abruptly, paused for a scant moment, and then, as though she'd caught a scent on the still air, pivoted the chair to face the door.

"Emil?" she said, in a whisper. We had made not a sound; even now he seemed not to breathe. Regardless, she answered her question with an exclamation of certainty. "Emil! You've come!" and she slipped to us across the room in a single glide as simple as a stone's flight and raised her face to his kiss, the round face under the hijab, the eyes closed permanently.

"I've brought someone for you to meet," Sahran said, bending to her ear. "Are you able?"

"Wait for me," she said. Maybe it was the expression that then crossed his face that I had been brought to see.

A nervous excitement filled Ralanou's office. A celebration was set to commence. Or maybe *celebratory* overstates it. It wasn't quite a jubilee. Some staff had gathered, and wax-paper cups had been set around and filled with fruit juice, and a tin of sugar wafers had been opened and the little stacks of cookies set out on a tabletop in their pleated cupcake papers. The source of the nervousness had been balanced on a mantel and leaned against the wall, a painting so recognizable in all its details — black dress, sandy path, pansies, umbrella — that my first reaction upon seeing it was that I had just been party to a heist. "They say he painted only two," Sahran said. "But as you see, they were wrong." It turned out, "as the appraisers have now been obliged to concur," that the artist had done another full-length commission, one that might have been a sketch or study for the one we'd seen on exhibit. *If it's a study,* I thought, *it's certainly a fully realized one.*

Though it turned out that what I was looking at, the picture perched on Ralanou's mantel, was not even the fully realized study. It was a fully realized imitation of the fully realized study. Sahran (on a later occasion, over a full dinner on Île Saint-Louis, not here amid the sugar wafers) explained the setup. It seemed the painting's previous owners had had a twinship of portraits, two paintings by the same artist largely identical, and before selling off the one that eventually made its way to the museum, they'd given the other, in service of a debt, or perhaps in extravagant friendship, to Sahran's parents, in whose home it had hung throughout his childhood, on a living-room wall.

Recently, no longer wishing to carry the insurance and worried about the security required by such a treasure, Sahran had sold it to the museum for an "amusing" sum of money, on the museum's obvious condition that the work survive appraisal, and on his condition that the museum commission a faithful copy from a reputable portraitist to replace the original that had lived two generations on the Sahran family's wall, though Emil did not intend it for his living room or for any other room in the old house, which he was in the process of selling as well, part of a general and drastic divestment. His commission from the museum he'd donated to the Islamic girls' school, and he was giving its headmistress the copy of the painting as an eternal reminder of whence the school's endowment had derived: from a piece of blasphemous human representation.

And, there, I did finally learn something about Emil Sahran, that he preferred for even his profoundest generosities to contain a touch of devilment.

"Tamathil!" Ralanou declared, squinting at the painting and then, again, harder, at her benefactor. "The angels will not enter."

"But Ralu, Ralu, this isn't such an image, look at it, she is entirely symbolic. Have you ever seen a tree like that, or such a woman? She's a pattern, an allegory. We were just talking about this, weren't we, Dr. Anselm?" He gave me an actual wink. "At any rate, she now belongs to you, so you'll have to learn to live with her." Ralanou's look was skeptical and glad, glad, I imagined, that someone cared to so insistently overrule her skepticism. Somebody handed me a cup of red juice, which I immediately set down, because I saw that Odile had entered the room and that Sahran had scurried over to steer her through the assembly. As the chair came to a stop before me, the woman lifted her face in my direction with a happy, vague expectancy and lifted a hand an inch off the chair arm, inviting. I was aware of the crowd swiveling its attentions to encircle us, and over the cordon of shoulders, at just that moment, I noticed something about the portrait of the woman in black. Otherwise so faithful to the sibling we'd viewed in the museum, it lacked a central detail. No deranged cat lurked in the garden; no ball of yarn had been dangled across the path.

"Odile, this is Matilde Anselm," Sahran said. "She's a physician, from America." I took the offered hand, which gathered to my touch and curled itself softly around my fingers. "Tilde," Sahran said, "allow me to introduce you to my sister."

"Enchantée," I told her. Gently I squeezed the hand.

X

D O YOU REMEMBER . . . actually, let me rephrase that. I know that you cannot possibly have forgotten the night we were brave enough to rescue that woman by Washington Square. It may even have happened on that same trip, I think, of course it did, on our way from Penn Station in the snow. Dark so early — winter, after all — but still, it was late enough that there wasn't anyone out in the cold, no one about on Fourth Street except the two of us. The parked car, when we passed it, looked like it had been there for days — snow on the door handles and on the windshield, a little cap of snow on the parking meter — and if the car hadn't moved or made a noise (I can't remember what it was exactly that drew our attention), we might not even have noticed. We were talking, our heads down, picking our way through the icy patches, and I remember we got a few yards beyond the car and stopped. You looked at me and I looked at you, and we both said, "Did you see that?" And then, the unexpressed *What are we going to do about it?*

For what we'd just glimpsed was one of those things you hope you never see. Through the misty side window, in the dark, their not being under a streetlight: a man beating a woman into the floorboards, holding her hair with one hand and punching her as hard as he was able. We crept back to the side of the car — it was rocking with the struggle — and even as we approached, the fist lifted and landed and landed again, the woman fallen out of her seat onto the floor, her foot in the air. You handed me your violin solemnly with both hands, like it was a Torah or an infant, and looked around and took a breath — I was so proud of you; I knew what that deep breath held — and then you banged on the window. Are you recalling this yet? How you banged so hard on the car window, and the commotion froze, and then a face came boiling up close and pink behind the glass and the window cranked down. "What's going on?" you said, funny you, your voice a baritone I'd never heard. But the face in the window was the woman's face; the man had crumpled.

"What!" she demanded. "What do you want?"

"Are you okay?"

"What do you *want!*" Shrieking.

"Is everything..."

"Mind your own business!" She furious; the man contorting into a tighter and tighter ball, hands covering his eyes. She shoved him aside, irritated — he's in the way — and half crawled over him to get her head out of the window.

"Mind your own fucking business!"

"Okay, okay!"

"Fucker!"

"Sorry! Just checking."

"Fuck off!"

Didn't we have a laugh about that, walking on down Fourth Street! Laughing with relief that the assault had been only shadowboxing, an S & M play date, relief we hadn't had to do any fighting ourselves. Laughing with pent-up agitation at the fear we still couldn't shake, our emotions kicked loose by adrenaline. Laughing at the absurdness of absurdity. Permit me, sir, to carry your violin; Madam, may I help you off the curb? Fuck off, fucker. New York! You just never knew, not in New York City. Couldn't we have laughed for years about it, about New York, and how you never knew in New York City if you were saving a life or breaking up the party. Laughed for years, if we'd had them. But instead, for years, the story has turned more worrisome, because as it turns out I have become a helper, Daniel. I've trained myself to be alert to signs, but it's still not always clear to me, judging from the signs, who needs help and who doesn't. Why couldn't I just have told him, when I was so warmed by his interest, that I was glad to help out but not to love, told him on the long ride to l'École Islamique de Jeunes Filles of my strongest fear — not fear, conviction, persisting after all these years — that whatever I love I will cause to be slaughtered? I thought she needed saving, the girl in the car, and

you thought so too until we heard her screeching that she didn't. But
I didn't hear your silence . . . Was it actually the same night, Daniel?
The very same? It was, and I didn't know the signs. That's all. You
were silent, and I didn't hear your call.

I left the Islamic girls' school soon after my introduction to Odile.
She was weary and wished to retire, and Sahran wheeled her back to
her quarters, a neat, dorm-ish room at the far end of the first floor,
ascetically furnished with a narrow bed and a dresser, a table and a
lamp and a large mirror in a heavy wooden frame. ("My guests complained that I had no window," Odile explained to me of the last item.
"So now I do!") Sahran stayed at the school to discuss necessary
things with Ralu. He assigned Drôlet to drop me off, *a simple parcel
delivery,* wherever I desired, and since I desired to not lead him back
to my already violated neighborhood, I named a restaurant I liked in
the Marais.

I dismissed Drôlet with honest gratitude. I was embarrassed that
I'd ranted at him in Portbou; he'd been doing only what he'd been told
to do, drive there, wait here. Bistro l'Urquidi was open. The maître d'
recognized me and seated me at a quiet corner table in deference to
(I'm surmising here) my evident weariness — he was, after all, the experienced pit boss of an established Parisian bistro and could tell a
rattled woman when he saw one — and I threw myself on the mercy
of the kitchen and left, two hours, a steak frites and cognac later, con-
solidated if not entirely restored.

At least my foolhardiness had been fortified. At some point after
the oysters, I pulled out the envelope that Passim had handed me that
morning and reread its contents, and the arrival of the *plat du soir*
found me staring at the words *Église d'Hiver* and the announcement
of the evening anti-war protest at the Winter Church. I felt a mounting resolve: *I must find her.* It was late and I was tired, and I wasn't
sure what I might discover or even quite what I was looking for, what
possible trait might differentiate this person from among the crowd
of demonstrators. But it was a chance, at least, and I couldn't think of
another.

D'Hiver was something foreign to my experience, even including my
limited quota of society weddings and political funerals — an over-

flowing church. I found it by the overflow. The crooked, one-lane street was blocked by an angry moil, faces blanched white by the glare of the pole lights set up next to the television vans. The building at the center of it all was one of those medieval pocket cathedrals that infest French back alleys, its statuary eroded away by car exhaust, its Gothic portico opening not onto a magnificent square but directly onto the street via a stubby flight of stairs. The demonstrators chanted and handed out leaflets, pumped out protest through amplified megaphones. Giant stilt puppets danced above the crowd, titans above the mortals. I pushed through resolutely, eyeballing the multitude for a glimpse of lavender sweater and wishing I'd pressed Passim harder for a better description of my quarry. Meaning: any description at all. At last, I squeezed in through the Moorish doors and succeeded — by dint of a tactical elbow and sheer boneless fluidity of form — in getting myself into the nave, all the while cursing my handbag, whose size and square corners made it surely the only item of its fashionable description anywhere in the hall and which presented a logistical nightmare.

My entrance was more glacial than grand, and by the time I found a workable vantage on the proceedings — pressed against the ancient stones at the rear of the church — the services were well under way. I have no idea what I was standing on or whom, but it was enough to loft me barely above the crowd, and I could see, when the hands and placards lowered, a distant raised presbytery as overrun as the pews, people reposing on the altar and lounging against the organ. Among them, cordoned off, was a cluster of individuals who were clearly official. They exuded the entitlement of visiting clergy. Several, the protest organizers, I supposed, were middle-aged and smartly groomed and decked out in purposeful suits, and the others were more rableaisian, in the official rent garment and unshorn cheek of street revolt.

One of the latter group fulminated into an intermittently working microphone to intermittent cheers — he seemed alarmingly more roused than the people he was rousing — until, with some hideous shrieks and crackles, the microphone gave up the ghost entirely. A priest raced up — of unsure denomination; he wore a western leather fringe jacket over his vestments — and there ensued a lot of fidgeting and consulting under and behind the pulpit and many incantations of *Un, deux, trois,* and finally the priest gave a raised-fist victory salute that was greeted with a loud and general cheer. Right had triumphed, if only over the PA system. He introduced the next speaker, and another young revolutionary stepped forward to commence his reiteration. His chosen nom de anti-guerre was Che.

I don't know what contributed so to my reverie at this point. I can say there's no lullaby on earth more lulling than a good antiwar rally; the form is even more comfortingly formatted than the liturgies this chapel was built for, and the breviary more orthodox. I'd attended more than my share — they became quite the rage, you know, in the years after you left to go to war — and they'd done no good, for if they'd done any good, why were we here yet again? Oh, the rallies achieved what we'd wanted them to, and stopped an evil war, I suppose, eventually, in good time. But not in time to do any good for me, or especially you, and maybe that's where my thoughts went. They also went insistently to the opposite of all this shouting, to an intimate moment amid another (if smaller) gathering: Emil bending over the wheelchair handles to confide to his sister (as though offering her something delicious), "Another classics major."

I'd smiled and nodded affirmingly, there among the cookies and the punch, though how my nod could possibly affirm anything to a blind woman, I didn't know, and I was left wondering two things simultaneously: *Why am I acting like an idiot?* and *How did he know that?*

"Emil tells me you like the Parc des Buttes-Chaumont," Odile had said, with a quick in-catch of breath that revealed how shy she was about making the opening conversational gambit.

"I've been," I conceded. Evidently, she had also.

"To the island?" she asked, to which her brother conjectured, in all silliness, "Yes, to the sibyl's temple, to receive her oracle from the virgin."

"Emil! Don't interrupt!" Odile reproved him. "Anyway," she said, "sibyls aren't virgins." As she delivered this corrective, she reached down and caught his knee in a painful pinch, and I could see where she'd make an effective educator.

"No?" he said.

"No! Emil, that would be a Pythian temple. A Pythia is a virgin. You always want to pretend to know everything, so you need to get that right." Then, to me, with energy: "Right?"

I can tell you with precision the state of my knowledge of Pythias, which was absolute zero, goose egg. But I know all about girl bonding and understood what was required. "Right!" I declared, with energy. And then Odile expounded, for her brother's edification (and to flirt with me), on the essential difference between a Pythia and a sibyl. The Pythia, it seems, was the oracle of Delphi. She was always young (at least in Delphi's early years) and never spoke for herself during her trances but channeled the voice of the god she served. A sibyl was an older prophetesses subserving no deity. Her divinations flowed straight from the well of her bitter experience and out of her own pain and madness.

"Sounds like an important distinction," Emil admitted, but his humility was dubious and Odile laughed and would have pinched his leg again if he hadn't yanked it away. I noticed that his jacket was open, and his tie gone altogether. I told Odile that unfortunately I hadn't made it to the temple yet.

"Oh, you must go!" she said. "I always leave a coin when we visit. Not because it's a tradition or anything. I just like to."

Che wrapped up and relinquished the mike to Karl, and by the time Karl approached his peroration, I'd had my fill and couldn't bear much more and couldn't remember what profit I'd imagined from attending this enterprise in the first place. A myriad of humans mashed together, marinated in murk and packed in stone — what had I been thinking? I was grasping at straws in a haystack. As I began calculating the slim odds of an easy exit, the fringe priest's voice returned to thank Karl and introduce the next speaker, an American, he said, here from "*le* Middle West" to express the outrage of the American people at American capitalist aggression, and he turned the hall over to "Alba."

The placards were in full flurry so I couldn't see the pulpit, but the name rang like a steeple bell and as soon as I heard it, I began to strategize in a different and opposite direction. Alba! With difficulty, I descended to the floor and headed east. It was ten times farther to the front of the church than to the exit, and at some point during that distance, the crowd underwent a change of state, transmuting from flood to solid, a single massive ingot of infragrant flesh. Movement was impossible, breath barely. "This will not stand!" the loudspeakers blared. "No, it will not . . ." and the words drew me on in an almost effervescent excitement — could this be her? — undimmed by the slimness of the evidence. "We offer our lives to this struggle!" the voice said. I was going on only a name, after all.

". . . if a matter of *their* lives, *their* deaths, then no less for us!" The exhortations billowed like a sheet in the wind, but between the windy cheers (she had the crowd at full froth) and over my pushing and shoving (as though sound could be drowned out by exertion, but it can) I heard her harangue. "We're not afraid, if that's what is required of us. No, this shall not stand!"

The declarations poured direly forth, but as I powered my dreadnought purse through the impossible sea, my mind was consumed with nothing more radical than a delicate question of comportment. What would I say to her, if this was indeed her? I didn't know. I would know when we met, maybe. Even a good first look at her would give me some clue about how best to proceed. Sitting at l'Urquidi, I'd pondered the central question: If I found her, should I tell her about Saxe's demise? Despite all my guilt-tripping of Passim, I'd decided definitely not. Wouldn't that halt the letters, shut down our communication right from the start? Which was the opposite of what I desired. As I pushed my way toward her, I rehearsed my concocted alternative. I would tell her that Saxe had sent me, that I was his emissary, here to convey his greetings, that he wished us to meet and to confer.

By the time I made it close to the pulpit, the woman named Alba had long since departed the stage. The headliners were done and the dead horse had been turned over for flogging by second-stringers, and the rally had lost enough steam and spectators to permit a few atoms of oxygen back into the air. I stared at the frayed ranks in the presbytery and saw no women there at all, and I pressed up toward a carved wooden side door that looked as though it led backstage. A man sat on a stool by the door, reading a book as calmly and intently as though he were ensconced in a carrel in the Bibliothèque Nationale. I made for the door, and his arm shot out.

"Please, I need to meet someone," I said.

"Credentials," he stated. It wasn't a question, any more than he was swayable. He was tall and sallow and dressed in a ridiculous Sgt. Pepper jacket, with epaulets and brass buttons, and sucking on a bonbon in his cheek.

"I need to see Alba," I said, and he gave me a look that said *Doesn't everyone?*

When there's nothing left to do, I reminded myself, there's no risk in a chance. "Bingham," I said, with energy. "Her name is Bingham. Please tell her Dr. Anselm's here."

He mulled over this careful confection of specificity and title, sucked on it meditatively the way he did the bonbon, and then he stood and put the book on the stool and went through the door. Several minutes later, he was back.

"Sorry, lady," he said, and made to sit back down. But before the door closed I caught a view of the person he'd been speaking with, and it seemed to me I could place her somewhere — something about her hair, her hair seemed to shine like fire. And then it clicked, and as it did and before the shock of it enveloped me, I put the probabilities together. The probabilities were precise — goose egg, absolute zero — but I thought: *If it's so, I must try.* I opened my albatross, my ship's anchor of a society purse, and fished around in it until I found the tattered cloth.

"Please, could you just give her this," I said, my hand outstretched.

He sucked on the bonbon some more, this time with mild irritation, then disappeared, and after a much shorter interval the door flew open and Corie stood there, clutching the bandanna, her hair glinting red in the backlight and a look of confusion on her white face, verging on vague emergency. Her eyes went straight to mine. Could I call the look recognition? Hiding in her eyes was something I had seen only occasionally in my career and never outside the ward. I stood in her gaze for a length of time I couldn't and still can't measure because all the things I might have measured it by had ceased: the room's cacophony and the fidgeting of the bouncer had frozen into silence and a statuary stillness, and there was only the light off her shoulder and her hollow gaze, the tin gaze of a returner.

"Saxe is dead," I said.

XI

THE CAT WAS MOSTLY black, with a white chest and forehead and long hair, and it was coming down the street following the child on the scooter. It had a housecat's character, I guess naturally enough, a berserk alertness to everything real or imagined, distracting it in so many directions that when a car passed or a pigeon flew by, you could watch the synapses sizzle — it would halt and dawdle, jolt and wander, and then, just often enough to stay in the game, jog full tilt down the sidewalk with its tail straight up till it caught up with the child.

I watched through the windows of Portbou, thinking about it: how differently we get through the world. The child was four or five and was wearing Day-Glo sneakers, taking a walk with her father on a placid morning — for her it's an event — and he a slight gentleman in a drab corduroy coat and woolen cap, and she'd insisted (on threat of a tantrum: I can hear the ultimatums!) on bringing along her scooter, which was yellow and had blue wheels and a red handle, and which she pushed with her right foot down the sidewalk carefully, at a snail's pace, her head bowed in focused concentration on the wheels and on her Day-Glo foot and on the pavement, trying so hard to get it all correct, it was serious work, learning how to scooter, learning how to scooter as a next installment in learning all there was to be learned, and by her side her patient, drab father — it's not an event for him; for him, it's an hour out of events — ambling in place with his mind far away, present just sufficiently to pleasantly attend to his daughter's progress, a soft lumbering bass line to the child's tense melody, and then zoom, here comes the electrified cat, the personification of a nonlinear line, blasted off course by every ion, by every backfire and stray thought and sun mote and passerby, but getting there, nonetheless, nonetheless the quickest of them all. I sat and watched them through the café window and waited for Corie to arrive.

That was how we'd left it: We'd agreed to meet. It was all we'd been able to manage amid the chaos and with her handler standing guard — not the bonbon gendarme, but one of the suited impresarios I'd spotted earlier loitering behind the cordon in the apse, a compact, too-well-appointed hard-faced man with a heavy gold bracelet and thinning hair pulled back in a ponytail who stepped out from the back room to eye me with open suspicion. "Massue—" she started by way of introducing us, but he was having none of the friendly with me. He shook my hand brusquely and herded Corie back behind the carved wooden door before we could trade more than two dozen words, though not before she'd assented, with a nod, to my suggestion of a time to meet. Then she was gone, a beefy forearm around her shoulder, and that brought an end to the evening, though the evening wasn't over. It lingered like a headache. I went home and got to bed past midnight, knowing there'd be no music, not tonight, but wondering what she might have chosen had she played, what ceremonial Internationale she would have picked as the soundtrack for her triumph.

I was dreadfully on edge, and every drift toward dream deadended in a recollection that brought me wide awake again. What on earth was it? Something Sahran had said, I thought, but pound as I might on my memories of the day, I couldn't quite dislodge it. The border of sleep was guarded by confabulations. A woman raced toward me down a garden path littered with bears, counting the bodies, *Un, deux, trois, deux, trois,* as she tapped them each blindly with her parasol. A man wheeled past in an office chair chased by puppets through a thicket of tree-sized flowers. Sahran had said . . . Sahran had said . . . The music caught me slumbering.

At first, her playing was exceedingly pianissimo, in deference, I suppose, to its being two A.M. Whether on account of the hour or not, her anthem was a brief one, a short, whispered Chopin nocturne that frightened me with its sadness. It was a piece more bare than any I'd heard her perform. I rose from the sheets and went into the closet to attend to the notes more closely, and as I did I edited my impression: the nocturne itself was familiar — no, not a nocturne, one of his waltzes. I'd just never heard it played so desolately.

Then, before I could press my ear to the door, the crash came: a horrible pounded mis-chord, as though the pianist were out to destroy the piano, chopping off the elegy midphrase with the violence of two hammered fists. I stood in the closet as motionless as one more garment suspended on a hanger, alarmed, on alert — but there was no coda. The silence got long, and after a while I returned to bed. At least the commotion had dispersed the sentry of Chimeras, for I slipped past them successfully into sleep.

The woman who stepped through Portbou's door at ten thirty prompt the next morning seemed a thorough stranger until I realized what the strangeness was: it was the first time I'd seen her unattended by drama and emergency. I'd wondered how she would approach our little command performance, this summit with an older woman who had already, in two brief previous encounters, assaulted her with an automobile and stalked her through a church (and also, although I hoped she didn't know it, raided her domicile and rifled through her books). Had I been her, I might not have shown at all. But ten thirty came, and Corie stepped through the door.

"*Bonjour, madame*," she said, reserved, as I stood to greet her. The poise in her voice was businesslike, as was her hair, twirled into a chignon. It was a negligee pose; it emphasized the shape it pretended to obscure, the shape of confrontational unease. Her valise was a bicycle messenger's bag. Judging from the bag, I felt bad for the bicycle. But I liked the girl all the more. At least I had an answer to my question: How did she intend to play the morning? Demonstrably undemonstrative. She clasped the bag awkwardly under her elbow so that she could pull off a wool glove to shake my hand, and I confess the awkwardness gratified me: the maneuver entailed a little unintended curtsy.

"*En anglais, si vous voulez*," I said, gently. Gentle was the only stance I could come up with to undercut such poise. "*Je suis améri-caine aussi,* you know. Like you, mademoiselle."

"Yeah, sure," she said, her Midwest drawl asserting itself as soon as she reverted to her mother tongue. Her reversion invited my own. I'd been confounded myself, frankly, about how to approach this business. I wasn't sure that I wouldn't be the one in the hot seat, justifying my actions to my junior. But now the roles were suggested and set, and if she wished to hide behind a pugnacious propriety, I had my own safe refuge. Professor was something I knew how to do.

"Please," I said, and motioned her to sit as though this were my private office and the chair were the scholar's chair across my desk. She slipped out of her coat and hung it on the rack by the door, then came back and, instead of sitting, opened her bag and pulled out the brown bandanna. She held it toward me, exhibit A, and then let it drop onto the table, her head held a little to the side, her eyes transmitting suspicion.

"A coincidence," I said. "Purely."

"That was you," she rejoined.

"I know, it's strange. I'm very glad you weren't hurt. I'm as surprised as you are, believe me."

"But you kept it," she said.

I nodded. "Yes, I kept it."

She stood silent for a moment more, her thoughts seeping through some deep slow aquifer, and then, as though she'd reached a resolution, she pulled out the chair and sat down. She replaced the bandanna in the courier bag and dragged out one of the familiar envelopes. "I guess you want this," she said, all business again. "I usually deliver them to Mr. Saxe, but I guess it's okay . . ."

"It's okay," I assured her.

"They're —"

"Alba's letters," I said.

"Yes."

"But you are not Alba."

"No." Her face pinkened defensively. "I'm Corie Bingham."

"I see," I said. Corie. It was the first time I'd heard her Christian name. I let the silence hang in the air awhile, waiting for her to challenge me again — *how come you don't know who Alba is?* Was it a sign of surrender that she didn't ask? If so, it was the only one I was going to get.

"I liked her name," she blurted, recalcitrance resurgent. "I mean, I do like *her* too, especially. But I'm a Spanish translator. Spanish, Catalan, Basque. I translate these for Mr. Saxe."

"And Mr. Landers?" I said.

"I've never met Mr. Landers."

"Don't you work in his house?"

"Yes. I stay there. Mr. Saxe said it was okay. He gave me the key." She'd been there, she said, three months, almost. I was dying for a description of Saxe but didn't dare ask. She reached back into the messenger bag, extracted a cardboard box, and set it heavily on the table. "These are the ones I've already done," she said. "Mr. Saxe approves them, and then he gives them back for me to attach to the originals and file."

Her face looked stricken; she feared a faux pas. "Gave," she corrected, and grimaced. "What *happened* to him?"

And with that small thaw we began our exchange, which dispelled a few mysteries and opened so many more. She told me how she'd encountered Saxe: a colleague at the university where she studied comparative linguistics asked her if she knew anyone fluent in English, Spanish, Catalan, Basque, and the smaller languages of the Pyrenees, which she did, because she was. Fluent, that is. They happened to be her specialties. Saxe had interviewed her right here, at this very table, and retained her to translate a trove of old letters into English, for which he paid her in installments (the last of which she mysteriously had not received) and with the bonus that she would be allowed to camp out in a nice apartment not too far from campus, as long as she maintained a minimal footprint there, until the job was done.

"So, are you throwing me out?" she said, in a tone that invited me to do so.

"You mean you've finished?" I asked.

"No. But . . ."

"How many to go?"

"Twenty, maybe. Twenty-five? A couple more weeks, I guess. The semester's ending and . . ."

"Then I sincerely hope you'll continue," I said. I told her to let me know how much she was owed and said there was only one amendment I wished to make to the arrangement she'd struck with Saxe. "I prefer not to do this here. We'll meet at Landers's, and you can show me whatever you've finished. We'll start tomorrow."

In her impassive face I read relief and comprehended suddenly the fear that had haunted her morning, of imminent homelessness. That was the chip on her shoulder. Or at least the most recent and evident among her collection of shoulder chips. Did it also explain the violent chord? I had imagined (luridly, but without any evidence) that she was upset at being brutalized by her brutish handler, the pony-tailed thug she called Massue, but maybe her fear was of someone closer to hand: brutish me.

Jeko stepped over to take our orders, gingerly. The drama of my yelling match yesterday, followed by my abduction in a limousine, had produced a marked effect on Portbou's proprietors: I turned out not to be the woman they'd assumed, was more interesting, possibly, though possibly radioactive. I had their full attention, at least, and as Mademoiselle Bingham reverted to French to order, I gave my attention to her.

The girl before me was smaller than I'd realized. She was beautiful in whole, without, I saw, being beautiful in any particular part. Her fingers were tapered and slightly crooked, and her mouth was thin-lipped and straight, a quick, acerbic slash across her softly rounded face. Her compact solidity was redeemed by a striking grace. It wasn't a willowy grace, or delicate, or athletic. It was, withal, intelligent, for she was as smart as she was obstinate. Her intelligence was of the nitroglycerin variety, unstable, dangerous to carry, and the grace it occasioned was one of fluid moves and gentle settings down, the eternal care and extreme self-awareness of bearing an incendiary burden.

All this I figured out later, after I'd seen an explosion or two. Right then, she struck me simply as an example of a physical self overmatched by its aura, and I flashed on the game your nieces used to play during those Pennsylvania retreats, those family vacations. Remember those getaways? Remember Stamps and Buses? We'd spring ourselves from the homestead to go out prowling for ice cream. Your parents' old Impala, Delaware River glinting past the windows, Olive and Ruth amusing themselves in the back seat — how old those girls must be by now! — dividing the world up according to this system they'd devised.

As they explained it: There are things in the world that are marked with where they're from — postage stamps, for instance. And then there are things that are marked with their destinations, like interstate buses. But you never knew to look at it where the bus was coming from, or where the stamp might go. And how long did we sit there, careening through the Water Gap with those two girls, their hair blowing in the river breeze, dividing the universe into stamps (Candlelight! Seedlings! Cedars of Lebanon!) and buses (Raindrops! Immigrants!). You had to be a kid to truly comprehend it — I never could get why meteors were stamps and meteorites buses. (When I tried to explain the system to Sahran, he asked what it was called when something that was in one's past was in one's future too, and I answered, "I'm a doctor. I call it remission.") But I do remember there were things you couldn't know whence they came or whither they went (Shooting stars!), and the girl before me struck me as one of those. All I could know of her was that she was here, graceful and willful and momentary.

Her eyes had appraised me just as sharply. At least, that's how I explain the uncanny thing she did halfway through our breakfast, a simple action that subtly, by her grace, changed everything into its reverse, for afterward I was never again, with her, the professor in control of the defiant student, far from that: I was never again in control. She reached her arm slowly across the table, over the pot of tea and her *pain au chocolat,* and lay four narrow, crooked fingers on the back of my left hand, covering the scar. I was shocked at the feel of it, the feel of skin on my skin, the feel of her shock at the way the rough scar felt. I looked down at her fingers on my hand with the dumb, searing focus of the child on the scooter staring at her foot on the sidewalk, and then back at Corie's silent face. "A burn," I explained. "An accident, maybe, I don't know. I was a kid. I don't remember."

Did I imagine that her wide eyes were moist, staring at me so forcibly? Moist and smart and impassively calm, setting me down gently.

And then, of a sudden, all those things were dispelled by a second emotion that washed through like a shore wave over beach pebbles, and for a moment her expression reeled with panic and I thought: *Panic for me.* Then she was calm again, empty-eyed, and I watched the calmness harden into the same suspectful opacity she'd worn when she walked in the door.

When we were done talking, which is to say when we'd wrapped up the preliminaries and were too tired or timid to descend into the next deeper level of things, we left Portbou and said goodbye on the sidewalk. Of course we were headed in the same direction. For reasons I couldn't quite name, I did not want her to know that, or to know where I lived; there was a cold deceit hidden in my fond farewell. More dangerous, as it turns out, there was a fondness within my deceit. As we took our leave, I felt the heat on the back of my hand spread into general yearning. She headed off toward rue Nin, and I turned to wander — where? I didn't know — until it would be safe to follow, and no sooner had I wheeled about than I found myself face to face with my little gypsy-ish family clan — the father and his daughter and her housecat — straggling back on my side of the street.

Maybe they'd been to the park. Now, surely, they were headed home. In retreat they didn't display the neat tripartite experiment in perception that had been their distinction before, with one of them oblivious to where he was, one hyperaware of it but only in terms of her task, and the last oblivious to nothing whatsoever and keenly aware of all. Now they seemed unified in weariness. The father carried the scooter, and the daughter carried the cat.

She lugged it like a stuffed toy, her arm garroting its chest, its forelegs stuck out straight ahead like a sleepwalker in a horror flick, its little pink tongue stuck out a little too, its back legs bouncing loose against her leg — dangled this way, the cat was nearly as long as the child. It didn't seem to object to this rude transport, though as they passed me I discerned a wacko tolerance in its expression, and immediately I retrieved something I'd thought was lost for good, the recollection I had chased around my skull in the middle of the previous night. Sahran had said . . . Sahran had said . . .

Sahran had said "a tragedy survived." But then later, turning down the museum hallway away from the painting and away from his thoughts of storms and forests and missing ring fingers and folded umbrellas and the woman who had managed to get through the worst and had only good to look forward to, he'd said something else that I've neglected to report to you. Sahran had said, "Or maybe not."

XII

I T'S ALL ABOUT THE CAT, isn't it?"
"What's that mean?" Sahran said.
"The cat in the painting," I said.
He waited.
"Yours didn't have one."

We were strolling under the trees along the Quai d'Anjou, fresh from a lovely dim restaurant, looking out across the river from Île Saint-Louis, indulging in the rarity of a clear-skied twilight that looked more wintry than the standard rainy evening. With the overcast dispelled, winter had lost its veil, and an arctic iciness crazed the wide heavens like frost across a windowpane. I envied the sky. Involuntarily (or maybe not), I was shedding my cover, but with no gain of clarity. The meal had been sumptuous, from foie gras to *île flottant*, and the conversation as seductive as I would allow myself to allow. I rattled on about the Église d'Hiver without putting a name (Corie Bingham) to the quest that had brought me there, and I brought up my other new friends without giving any more than their names. "You have your diplomatic ways," I prodded Sahran, one diplomat to another. "How would I go about getting in touch with a guy named Carlos Landers? He isn't in the phone book." Sahran jotted the spelling down on a little notepad and then slipped it back in his pocket and didn't ask me why. "And also a guy named Byron Saxe," I added, why not. "Middle initial *M*."

Throughout the meal, and with each step down the quai, I could feel my Sahran surveillance mission slipping from its original intent. Was that the source of my irritation? Despite the evening's pleasures,

I was edgy as a horsefly. Later I would see how deep my tension ran, how angrily I resisted the thing I was drifting into. I was like a teenager, equal parts tantrum and temptation, unable to keep the heat of attraction from igniting my animosity. That was part of it. The rest was pure expectancy (and no less adolescent). I'd come up with this little insight about the cat and hoarded it till the moment I could present it to Sahran as a gift, a token. Which now, as we walked, I did.

"See, it's no wonder that you're such a conflicted optimist," I said, for I'd decided that that's what he was. "You grew up with a vision of life in which the future was unobstructed and the road was clear. But then one day you go to the museum and you see the *real* painting and discover that this strange little cat has rolled a ball of yarn across the path. Two steps ahead."

"And now I'm no longer so sure."

"Exactly: Is the string an amusement or a snare?" I said. "A plaything or a trap? A lure or a warning? Has the artist painted a history of survival? Or a forecast of a tragedy?"

"Huh," Sahran said, pausing to face me. Then he turned away and strolled on. Was that to be my reward? A pat on the head? Well, it hadn't been much of an insight, truth to tell, but he might at least have gone through the motions of admiring it. I felt my testiness spike. And, oh, how adolescent all my griping felt! But even as I instructed myself, *Get over it,* another voice yelled, *See?* And my suspicions added, *Such a kulak! Of course he'd take whatever heart he wanted.*

"About this rally," Sahran said, slipping past my subject and into one of his own, to my increased annoyance. Though here, even I had to admit, my pettiness was getting grandiose, since the subject he wanted to talk about was me. "What happened? You had a flyer; you went to the church."

"It was a mess, complete chaos," I said, but I'd said it already — I'd brought up the *mobilization* at table. Now, alfresco, I didn't want to discuss it.

"I'm sure it was extremely organized," he said.

"Oh, so you were there!" I exclaimed with mock surprise, intent on being intolerable. "I missed you!"

"No," he answered earnestly. (Hopeless!) "I was not." We reached a corner and turned away from the Seine and onto a narrow street of blank, high, garden walls and house façades sheer to the sidewalk. Sahran held my elbow as we crossed the cobblestones and kept it when we'd made it to the other curb. "But this is France," he said, "where we choreograph our chaos. Disaster's a ballet. Even our sex is stylish. Ask any Frenchman. Even our bad sex. Have you gone to a big *manifestation?*"

"Well, at the church," I said.

"Go to a big one sometime. You'll be interested. Much, much more tense than American demonstrations, it's a particularly French sort of violence. It's something you just can't find in the States, you don't have the streets for it. But always, like a hurricane — at the center of the fury there's a quiet core. In the middle of even the worst Paris protest is a huddle filled with calm negotiation. Really, I promise you, ten or a dozen strongmen from opposing sides, placing their bets, making their moves."

"I see you know all about this," I said, hearing in my head his sister's voice: *You always want to pretend to know everything.*

"I guess I ought to," he said, wise enough to ignore the provocation, and he said he'd lived in the city a long time. "If twelve Parisian strongmen are negotiating anything, I'm sure I know at least six of them."

Before I could even think, *La-di-da,* I heard him think, *Don't la-di-da me.* Fine, then. I was clearly in the mood for a fight.

"Let's say five," Sahran said. "To be on the safe side. Did you like what they said?"

"Who?"

"The speakers, the protesters."

"How could I not?" I declared, foursquare in defense of everything I'd derided at the time. How foolish I would have looked to myself (wasn't war his subject, after all? Wasn't the Middle East his region?) if I'd bothered to look at myself (but hadn't war been my subject too?). "Nothing good comes of bloodshed, that's all they're saying. Of course I agree. Don't you?"

"Hmm," Sahran said. "What happened to 'grace comes somehow violent'?"

With our turn into the side street we'd traded our oceanic vistas for a canyon horizon, and the arctic ice ran like a river overhead. We paused before a row house whose handsome eighteenth-century stone façade was hung with a sign announcing CENTURY 21 and SALE PENDING. "That's just Aeschylus," I said, preachy. "This is a war. An *actual* war, not some stage war, and it's about to happen. And it will be horrible. It's quite a serious matter." I couldn't quell the childish thought that Corie would be proud of me.

"You astonish me," Sahran said, and for a moment I could glow with the pleasure that somehow I'd caught him off-guard even though I was in his territory. It was to be a momentary moment.

Sahran said, "Because, you know, you do heart transplants. For your purposes, without bloodshed there can be no good at all. You're in the only legitimate line of work in the world where the correlation is one to one: someone can't live unless somebody else is killed."

It was my turn to stop and I did, but I didn't turn, just stopped dead in my tracks as though the sentence were a barrier dropped across the sidewalk and I wasn't sure how to step over it. I could feel my temperature plummeting. "I see," I said when I'd gathered the full force of his meaning. "Emil. So this isn't just a casual conversation we're having, is it?"

"Come in," he said.

We were standing in front of his home.

I'd spent the broad expanse of the day, between breakfast with Corie and my dinner date with Sahran, at Saxe's home — my home — romancing a file box full of letters. I'd skimmed the one just hot off Corie's press, then decided I'd come back to it and cracked open the archive to begin at the beginning, which, since the early letters weren't so reticent about their time and location, I learned was in Bilbao, in May of 1931, a year when spring came late but strong and the fuchsias in the Etxebarría had blooms as big as butterflies. Unlike the earlier letters I'd read, each of the translations in the box that Corie'd handed me was accompanied by its original, tidily paper-clipped together with the corresponding envelope if there was one, though the stationery of choice, especially early on, was a blue airmail onionskin that folded up to form its own envelope. The contents documented a woman in the delirium of young love and a new marriage, and then, after several years of adventurous and unceasing honeymoon — and before I had to lay the reading down to get gussied up for my evening — a desperate separation brought on by a war in which they both enlisted, he in Paris managing the underground railway funneling foreign volunteers and supplies through France and across the Pyrenees into Republican Spain, and she in the actual fighting, as a nurse in a blood wagon and in field hospitals, in battle and behind the front.

As I read, I resisted a gentle but unrelenting hallucination, fought it like an undertow. It was evident, of course, that the papers I held were translations, that behind each page were two pairs of hands, wielding separate pens. I'd understood that ever since I'd read the second letter and long before Corie's explanations. Still and all, I couldn't get the identity of the author separated from that of the interpreter, the woman living most of a century ago from the one living right now right next door. Onto every adventure and mishap and horror related by the Alba of 1937 and '38 and '39, I pasted the modern girl's face. This was Corie's doing! — so I grumbled. She was the one who'd conflated their identities, declared their equivalence from the pulpit of the Église d'Hiver (and how many other soapboxes?). Somehow her public affidavit had convinced me of their kinship, assured me their affinity was real. Only later would I grapple with the worse danger, that Corie might be convinced of this as well. For now, locked away in my solitude, an onionskin counterpane spread around me on the divan, sitting like a brown bird in a nest of blue petals, I tried to gather clues to one Alba's nature by reading the other one's letters. My hand burned; the letters were my salve.

Toward evening, I put them aside and went to get myself ready.

Sahran's apartments excited that emotion that he always produced in me, radical ambivalence. I desired to stay; I was desperate to flee. His rooms were gracious, beautifully decorated and arranged, of course, but also, at the same time — perceptibly, invisibly — frayed by long habitation, by generations tracing out their lives and days within this shell until they'd worn it into their own comfortable and abiding shape, like the contour of a river boulder carved by a patient current. I wanted to sink into the lap of a velour armchair, to bask in the yellow warmth pooled beneath a table lamp and lose this infernal chill (and here came the ambivalence) that Sahran's words had induced in me.

At least my adolescent quibbling was gone, purged by a tsunami of real anger over real things, anger and fear. But even here the tables had been turned, for the issue Sahran had raised — and he'd raised it like a cudgel — concerned the very surgery I wished to interrogate him about. The turnaround caught me off-guard, to say the least.

Once off the street, I went inert. I was cryogenically suspended. Sahran propped me upright in the living room like an umbrella in an umbrella stand while he closeted our coats. He came back and half invited, half pushed me into one of the armchairs, then went over to a cabinet, returned with two glasses of red liquor, and pressed one into my hand.

"Just guessing," he said. "There's ice if you want some."

"Christ, no," I told him. "But thanks." I wanted it to boil like a witch's brew. I took a swallow, noted with surprise that it was bourbon, and waited for the glow to blossom, and when I felt sufficiently thawed to give it a try, I said, "Not *killed*, Emil. For someone who needs a heart to live, someone else must donate a heart. The person dies, that's true. Of another cause. No one is killed."

He had walked over to stare out a window, his back to me. "When?" he said.

"When what?"

"Does he die?"

"Technically? When his heart stops."

"And what stops his heart?"

I saw where this was going, but could think of no reason to draw the drama out.

"Potassium chloride," I said. "If it doesn't stop on its own."

"And ice," Emil said. "Don't forget that you pack the heart in ice."

"Not me, Emil, please. But okay, I take your point, the surgeon. A surgeon packs the heart. But the donor is legally brain-dead before the operation. His heart is still going, but he's not."

"Why put him under, if he's so dead? For the hell of it? You want to be sure he isn't awake while he's dead?"

"Emil, what are you doing? Everything you're asking, you know already."

"But you do anesthetize him, right? This corpse. Before you remove his heart."

"That's the procedure. It's a way of keeping organs alive, regulating blood pressure, that sort of thing. Minimizing pain too, but his pain's all in his spine at that point."

"His pain," Emil said. "You know, it occurs to me that only two parties in history have been legally empowered to split open a human chest and cut out a beating heart. An Aztec priest. And you." He turned from the window. "But for some reason that I can't understand, you get to consider me a monster."

So that was it . . . so he hadn't been oblivious. And I saw of an instant that he felt the same push-pull, terrified attraction that I did. I stood from the chair. I wanted to go straight to him. Instead, I walked to the liquor cabinet. "It's an appropriate question," I said carefully. "Except I think that you have it turned around." Carefully, I picked up the decanter from the cabinet top. Should I go ahead and spew the whole history? Well, part of it, maybe. And if spewing required a little sustenance? I gave the decanter a tilt. "Do you know the name Luckner Cambronne?" I asked.

I allowed him time to say, and when he didn't, I went on. "You see, I've never cut anything out of anyone," I said. "But one thing I'm in charge of is a patient's blood supply. I've given a lot of patients a lot of blood over the years and because of that and because I practice in the United States of America, a lot of that blood has come from Port-au-Prince. Until recently, when AIDS came along, Haitian blood was widely used, for the simple reason that it was cheap and plentiful, owing to a reliable supplier: Cambronne."

Luckner Cambronne, I explained, "or, as he was known, the 'Caribbean Vampire,'" was a pillar of American medicine, though he wasn't a doctor. He was a bank teller who rose to be a lieutenant of Papa Doc Duvalier, heading up the dictator's Tontons Macoute terrorist militias and, not incidentally, a lucrative international blood concession. Lucrative for Cambronne because he could pay peasants almost nothing for their plasma. The problem was, many peasants he didn't pay at all. The successful merging of terrorism with medical supply brought marvelous efficiencies. There were never any problems with shortages. An ample flow was guaranteed. Cambronne also provided American medical schools with Haitian cadavers, hundreds of stiffs, the sources of which might never have been questioned if he hadn't also initiated a sideline supplying Haitian steaks to restaurants.

"Do you see what I'm getting at?" I asked. I'd never "killed" one of his precious heart donors, I said, had never anesthetized a donor, "never taken part in a harvest, but I can tell you with near certainty that I have had a role in the traffic of murdered men . . . So now it's your turn: answer me. Do you find me a monster?"

I had paced around the premises while I recited my history lesson, around couches and around chairs and around end tables and coffee tables, and my tour of Sahran's room brought me finally around to Sahran. We stood face to face, some paces apart, duelers at the end of the count. I said, quietly, "And then tell me why the hell not."

He was silent and I was. I had hoped that the combined effects of venting my emotions and dousing my sobriety would ease my agitation, but the more I'd talked, the angrier I'd become.

"Okay," I said finally, "then I'll tell you," and I said that the only reason I hadn't been a monster back then was that back then I hadn't known that such things went on. "But I don't have that excuse anymore. I am on cosmic parole. It's no longer adequate for me to say I didn't know where this came from. I have to be sure. And one day, maybe in a week or two, I will help switch out one human heart for another, and when I do, you have to tell me, Emil, will I be a monster?"

"No," Sahran said, softly but with a panicked urgency. He set his glass down in such a hurry the liquor sloshed onto the tabletop, and he stepped toward me.

"Because only you know the answer, so tell me: Will I be?"

"No," he said, and he had gotten close enough, and I punched him on the shoulder.

"Will I?"

"You are not, dear," he said. "No, you are not!"

Hitting him felt surprisingly therapeutic and so I hit him again, harder and in the middle of his chest. "Because I don't feel sure, Emil. I don't feel sure about anything. Because something's very wrong."

"Because . . ."

"Because, damn it, you aren't sick!"

"You mean because you're hitting me?"

"Yes!" I shouted. "Yes, because I'm hitting you! Because we walk all over town, and go to restaurants, and climb the steps to Sacré-Coeur! Because of marzipan, and profiteroles! And cordon bleu. And foie" — and I poked him in the sternum with my fingers — "fucking" — and I poked him again, and he reached out for me, and I guess unfortunately the way he reached, his touch found my neck beneath my ear and I felt the restraint, you know what that does, you could have told him, Daniel, you'd have explained what even that gentle restraint might cause to occur, considering the circumstances, me as upset as I was.

" — gras!" I yelled, and let him have it full in the face.

Then Sahran disappeared; he disappeared from view. What with the coffee table being right behind him, I guess, and I must have hit him pretty hard, he vanished. There was a terrible *ka-whump* sound with a frightening *croûton* crunch inside of it, and I looked down and saw him lying there on his back with one leg up on the table. He didn't move except to lie there blinking and I dropped down onto my hands and knees and for some reason, ever tidy, I first scurried over to grab my glass, which was spinning where I'd flung it, bourbon on the Aubusson, and then I crawled back over to Sahran with the glass in one hand, and with my other I stroked his chest.

"I'm sorry!" I said to him.

He raised one hand and gingerly checked his mouth. "Not at all!" he said — dazed, he made no sense, his voice kind of jaunty like it was teatime and he was getting set to offer me a crumpet and inquiring lemon or milk?, like the needle had skipped its groove and I'd knocked him into a completely different protocol. "Not at all! It's just, there's been a . . . some misinterpretations, you see. You have the wrong . . ." His speech was slowed to a stutter by his dabbing at his lip, and I had to wait for him to come up with the word. He dabbed and thought and dabbed some more, and then it seemed to occur to him. "Sahran!" he concluded.

"Sahran," I said.

"Yes, the wrong Sahran. Because, of course, as you can see, my heart's not sick." I leaned my ear closer; he was getting kind of wispy. "Odile's is," he said. "Mine's not, but Odile's is. She's your patient. She's very, very sick, Odile."

"Oh," I said, but it wasn't a word, it was just an exhalation, and when I kissed him I could taste his blood like rich living salt on his lip.

It was some time much later that I woke in the dark, startled out of a drifting, lost, gossamer happiness by some odd barb of anxiety and then relaxing as I recognized what it was. "I completely forgot to call," I marveled.

"Zut," the voice replied, sleepy.

"Is that bad?"

"Très! You must."

"But I'm here, I'm with you."

"I'm only the boss," he said. "I'm not your coordinator." He chuckled as I struggled out from the crisp sheets and, as payback for such cheerfulness, I pulled a blanket off him to drape around myself as I headed for the telephone, the phone I'd seen in the hall. There's one right here, he protested, right by the bed. "Just be sure they don't trace it." His grin audible.

When I hung up, I found the chair where I'd laid my things and I felt along its pillow for the hush of my dress, for my slip and un-dies and bra and the clingy hose, was that everything? (Surely there's a mnemonic.) Shoes downstairs. Purse downstairs. I leaned to kiss Emil lightly as I passed, his forehead smelled so sweet. His fingers reached for my arm, but I said, no, I should go, and when he made to rise I put a hand against his chest, he knew by now to pay attention to that. "Please, don't. I'll let myself out."

"Is that what you want?"

"It's what I want."

"Are you . . . it's all okay?" he asked.

The dear, I thought.

"Will I see you?"

"Yes."

Emil said, "Drôlet's by the curb."

· · ·

He was indeed, dozing with the bill of his cap pulled down onto the bridge of his nose, in the passenger seat of the slumbering limo, a shade within a shadow, but I didn't disturb him. I turned and walked the other way. I was doing him no favor, I knew — had I allowed him to drop me off, his duties would have been concluded for the night, and now he would rot by the curb till dawn, poor Drôlet, crumpled up like Jonah. It was not that I was still trying to protect my hideaway's whereabouts — somehow that privacy too had been shed when I shed my clothes, but I didn't care. There was a place I wanted to visit that had to be visited alone.

In a way, I'd already reached it: the city at night. Remember how we used to walk around Manhattan, you and I, in the wee hours, visiting the chestnut vendors' encampment, the night stalls of the carriage horses? Such secret places, and how glad I was that I had you to go with, Daniel. But resentful too. I knew we weren't there as equals; at 3:00 A.M. in a city like New York, you could go wherever you wished, but I could go only with you. How fiercely I sensed that my town had things to tell me, private murmurings so delirious and strange they could be heard by no one else, if I could only slip away from convention some night and meet it one to one. Which is why the Paris that I loved best was the one that insisted on being a place where the office girl could stop on her way home and drop her briefcase by the zinc and have a glass of Belgian by herself and watch the game, and set down her francs and pick up her briefcase and go, without attracting interest or incident, where the sound of heels on a deserted sidewalk at midnight might be just a woman lost in thought or compelled by the plain necessity of getting from somewhere to somewhere else and not the sound of some poor creature driven by fear for her life.

After leaving Emil's, I walked toward the river (it's the thing about Île Saint-Louis: *from* equals *to* there, and you can't possibly walk away from the Seine without walking toward the Seine) and then down the length of the Quai d'Orléans. I crossed the little frog's jump of the Pont Saint-Louis — *Let us cross over the river* — to the prow of the other island, and skirted the back gardens of Notre-Dame, and hopped another bridge to the sycamore shore of the mainland — *Let us cross over the river and rest under the shade of the trees* — and went up through the scatter of smaller streets that lay between the river and the boulevard. When I'd peered down from the span, the Seine had glinted back as scalloped as chipped obsidian, and now, blocks away, I could still smell its lush, heavy cold. A car passed; somewhere a clochard sang as he clanged his way through a garbage can. Then I was beyond them, and my own clicking heels were all that was left to be heard, though the tiny mechanical click my heels made was hardly much of a racket, was the dry precise ratchet of giant calipers sizing up the silence. My one heel clicked and then the other, and the duration between them was profound.

Then at some point, midblock on some blunt, straight street, the sky transformed. The river of arctic ice that had led up to Sahran's place now led me away from him, flowing overhead, idling around me, herding me gently along, pooling around the bridges and over the squares and quickening again as I entered narrower channels. I noticed it when I slowed or turned a corner; then I could feel the current brace against my back, but in all it was dim — dim, faint, and languorous — until, on the blunt street on the way to Saint-Séverin, the river jolted to vivid life, blared rudely into color as though a circus roustabout had pulled the big lever to set the grand carousel spinning in the sky and opened the curtain on spectacle.

The river above me wasn't at all like the one I'd crossed on the Pont Saint-Louis, my Old Man, my customary river, a tide of darkness lugged by its own rumbling weight to drown in a distant sea. This one was a crosscurrent and a contradiction, a rippling, twirling treadmill, all farce and carnival, a clanking mad contraption (*Confetti borealis?* I amused myself. I was daffy with delight) that stooped to engulf me then billowed aloft again, beckoning me through dun alleys, along blank *défense d'afficher* battlements, on an upended carpet of light, orange and turquoise, violet and blood. Is it any wonder I wished to fall up, to be swept away? You don't feel abandoned, Daniel, do you, that I would desert my dark, my slow, my gradual descent toward you to chase this shiny banner? Oh, silly, sagging, ridiculous me, wasn't I more than fifty? Oh, what had I done?

Nothing terrible, nothing wrong came the answer. Nothing at all bad. And hadn't it been lovely, with lovely Emil, whatever would we be now? He and me, Emil and I, what were we to do? *Nothing* came the answer, again. There's nothing to be done. He'd been such a prince, Emil had, understanding what a younger lover couldn't, how to bring me to the river's edge, knowing he wasn't the river. And hadn't he been gentle, Emil, and hadn't he known the gentlest thing of all, to let me glimpse his gratitude, how grateful he was to get to know this girl. This old girl could have kissed him, and didn't I! Kissed and kissed and kissed him, and felt his grateful heart pump hard beneath my palm in the plummeting dark, beneath the skin and breastbone where I'd hit him, how life breaks out afresh when you think you've long ago spent your allotted due.

A car roared into the square by Mabillon, managing the corner on two wheels and looking as close to capsize as a dinghy in a storm. It was a powder keg of rolling noise, flapping flags waved by screaming men perched on its windows and pounding the roof as they chanted the slogan of the *fútbol* team that had just won a match in some longitude where the sun still shone, a one-car victory parade lost in space. It orbited the block twice in search of an audience and finding no takers (except startled little me) roared away in the direction of Saint-Sulpice. I was afraid the commotion had dispelled my celestial overtow, but then the silence returned, and after an insecure second or two, the aurora emerged from hiding and winked back into place, and the conveyor clanked into motion again, tugging me onward, though its ribbons now were darker.

"Let us cross over the river and rest under the shade of the trees," the chaplain had said, the trees on this gun-gray day being a row of spreading tulip trees not far from the family homestead of our several summer vacations, though it wasn't summer now, but wintry, and though the lawns sloping down to the Delaware were marked by no shade at all from the trees that were bare beneath the drizzle and the sunless clouded sky, and I could hear beneath his plush, practiced sentences the threadbare warp of an oft-used eulogy. "Those words," the military chaplain said, "were pronounced by the general" — General Jackson, he meant, Thomas "Stonewall" — "and they were Stonewall's last," and he informed us that the wounded Jackson had delivered two final messages out of his delirium. The first was an order to his lieutenants to pass the infantry to the front. The second was an order superseding the first and all before it, "an invitation to peace, to rest.

"And so we must honor these two sides of the life of the young hero who will be with us now no longer. That he pushed to the front of life's battle, that he answered the call of his generation and gave full willing measure in defense of his country. Now he calls us to that harder mission, to let" — minuscule pause as he pasted in your name — "Maxwell Daniel Coddington rest, rest in the grace of God's mercy, under the shade of these trees."

And, oh, how I loathed him, the military chaplain with his chapbook eloquence, hate him still and have never hated anyone more faithfully, with the one exception. Hated him first for even thinking he could sum you up so tidily, you fucking hero, "full willing measure" indeed, and at such a moment, before such people as we were, and then, much later, and growing with each year, hated him for even thinking that we could conceivably let you rest, that you would ever conceivably let us let you rest, you hero. The unholy, lying, incompetent, duplicitous impostor of a pasteboard priest.

When the chaplain had done all the damage that words could do, the honor guard accomplished the rest, firing its volley into the air. The honor guard, Maxwell Daniel, being a day-labor cadet with a target-practice .22, and after the gun had been emptied, and the trumpet played by a high-schooler on loan from the halftime band, and the dirt shoveled onto the mahogany, and before everyone had made it back into the sorry cortege of a hearse and one sorry limousine, the sergeant sought me out to chat. He stood there in the drizzle, he having met you over there, he said, and having driven across the state when he learned the news, to be here at the graveside, done up in his dress greens, because he remembered you, and you'd struck him as a nice young man, someone to watch, that's what he said, someone to keep an eye on. In full dress greens, though I suspected he was no longer in the service, suspected the real reason for his extravagant long-distance courtesy call was not to bury the dead but to keep alive his own unresolved experience, to keep it unburied by time, and so he'd come here to me, wanting to reminisce, of all things, with me, of all people.

The torrent of light above me dimmed to a trickle, and then as suddenly as it had appeared, it dispersed in a last high scattering of sparks, leaving me with a standard-issue Paris night sky and with the realization that I was walking up rue Nin. My beautiful neon stream was sutured shut, and the street lay quiet and soft below the streetlights, the buildings dormant and mute. The only lit window on the block was on the top floor of 136, in the study of Carlos Landers's apartments.

I stopped across the street to peer up, wondering if she was busy at her translations, wondering why my happiness must ever be like this: not quite happiness, but a happiness now and then, systole, diastole, as the heartbeat goes — on again, off, a joy, an interminable contraction, another brief joy, the duration between my joys so deep that it would swallow you up if you let it, Daniel. And, oh, how I'd been swallowed. It was a terrible thing, always knowing ahead of time the end place of every runaway gladness — the smell of chestnuts in the night mists of Manhattan, the weight of Emil above me in the dark — to know how every gladness would end up: as a foil, a measure, a yardstick for grief, calipers sizing up sorrow.

Standing across the street from the Wisteria, I wished that I smoked cigarettes or that I had a broken heel or some other outward and evident excuse to linger like this, watching for a shape or shade to cross that square of light and provide me with a sign. Might I somehow glimpse the creature whose name, I now knew, was Corie? Might she somehow see me, if she looked out? If she did, what would I do? How would I explain standing here at such an hour, alone as I was? Or as I thought I was, until the shadow moved.

I feel that I saw it before I saw it move, but by then it was almost upon me, a vague apparition, some burlap pilgrim loosed from another time, the shawl that covered her bowed head clasped at the neck in cold fingers. When she passed under the streetlight I could see that it was the concierge, Céleste, in her tattersall coat, her feet shod in boots that looked as though she'd torn them off a Cossack, back when Cossacks existed. She reached the Wisteria's entry pergola and unlocked the gate and let herself into the yard but didn't proceed up the path. Instead, she crossed to a far back corner of the lawn, where she disappeared into blackness. I watched her through the pickets as she reemerged, and as she turned from closing the gate, she saw me too. She seemed shocked without being in the least surprised. "It's you," she said, in her customary milk-of-kindness rasp, and asked me had I gotten lost or had I quite stupidly locked myself out, and I said no, I was only headed home, and she said, "Now?"

We walked together toward the end of the block — she would escort me all the way around the maze and back to our courtyard, grousing, "Alone at this hour, *complètement folle,* the crazy thing, doesn't she know she's not in New York anymore?," as though my nighttime indiscretions didn't describe hers equally. My mind was still stuck in some other place, on the sergeant in his dress greens relating his story, the awful story I've never told you of the fated soldiers, and of lying on the grass beside the airfield, and I remembered how I'd listened, taking in his tale while I silently inscribed his name on the list of those whom I would ever after hate, the list that was now up to three and included the sergeant in his dress greens, and (in ascending order of importance) the duplicitous military chaplain, and you.

We weren't far down the sidewalk when the light snuffed out, and Céleste and I both noticed it, our heads jerking toward the darkened window, and noticed each other noticing, the window gone as dark as all the others.

XIII

PALMA, MAJORCA
Boo! It's a letter, my love, can you believe? They are letting us send mail! We're no longer categorized as *incomunicado*. Did you get that *carte postale* they permitted me, forever ago? "Señora Alba Solano Landers is pleased to announce, from her unending confinement, the end of her confinement . . ." I am well, generally. My current illness is worry and is chronic. They promise we can receive mail too, even packages. Please write today and say you are safe. May this long silence have been our last!

"Do you have this postcard from Alba?" I asked.

Corie shook her head. "Unless it's out of order," she said. We were sitting in Landers's study drinking the orange tea, she in an armchair, me on the neighboring couch, clutching a blue aerogram in one hand, its English twin in the other. "So many are," she said. "Anyway, it's the first one I've had like this . . ." Leaving "this" undefined, she stood and went over to her writing desk and began to rummage through her papers, and I turned back to the page.

I say "we" but that's not true. My privileges have been granted to only a few women deemed less criminal. And me! The matrons have got it in mind that I am some prize they've laid hands on, all because Carmen de Castro was a student in my father's school and she's now the director of prisons. So they exempt me from some of the favorite torments. I get more than sardines and biscuits & my mat isn't straw & I don't have to assemble for head count each morning and sing "Cara al Sol" & "Viva Cristo Rey," and they don't lock me in a cell at night.

I sleep with Alena in a room in the rectory. Of course it's locked, but it's clean, and on the top floor so it's bright & not damp & the window opens and I don't have to look through bars. I have a table!

"So grateful for a table," I said. The exclamation mark was doubled in the original, per Catalan. Or not Catalan, as Corie had explained to me with evident pride (this being her area of expertise), but a subdialect of Aranese that Alba and Carlos folded into their correspondence, along with a smattering of other regional vocabularies, as their private language.

"Oh, I know," Corie said, about the gratefulness.

Even flowers, when I rob the garden (Sister Serafina disapproves, but left me a vase to put them in). I pinch the stems with my fingernails. They would never trust a democrat with scissors! The price of my amnesty is only beginning to dawn on me.

"See?" Corie said, returning couch-side with a familiar white regulation-sized envelope familiarly tagged *C. Landers* and *40, rue Ganivert.*

"The first one to come like this," she said.

I looked at the envelope and then, quizzically, at her, and her exasperation was as instantaneous as an exasperated teacher's before a balky student. She snatched Alba's letter from my grasp and shook it in my face.

"*Regard!*" she commanded. "Aerogram!" and she turned the blue onionskin over to display the addressee, a name I didn't recognize, Corail Barayón, in Ginebra, Suiza, and then with her other hand she held out the regulation-sized envelope, her forefinger clamped so tightly above the postmark, Genève, Suisse, that the nail was white. "Envelope!" she declared. "She's using her intermediary, and he takes her letter . . . and puts it" — and she dipped the aerogram in the envelope with ostentatious helpfulness, twice for good measure, so the most abject of imbeciles could grasp the concept — "and relays it on."

"But she's already been captured," I said, abject. "They let her send mail." It wasn't one of my most functional mornings.

"It's for him," she said, her eyes bulging, "to keep from implicating Carlos."

"Oh, of course," I said. "Got it." I could hear from her voice that I clearly understood nothing about love. We returned to the letter.

. . . also a cigarette, every Tuesday. It's like permission to cut flowers without scissors: a cig but no match (you must ask Serafina for a light). The Mother Superior has a Blaupunkt, & on Friday eve the nuns gather in her rooms to hear the broadcast from Madrid, & they invite me. Alena gets to crawl on a real rug for a while (this is why I go) & teethe on Madre's spoons while the news fades in & out of atrocities we Republican loyalist traitors committed, all these garroted priests & ravaged nuns. They don't look at me. I feel them not looking. They take my pulse. Have I absorbed my error? They bring me to Mass. Will I repudiate my heresy and be accepted into the One Apostolic Faith? This is the price: they aim to baptize me! Whoever deemed me important enough to be treated humanely has deemed me human enough to be remade into a Catholic. It would be a nice demonstration for them, but, oh, well, their job is impossible. That I would consent to worship the pope who "lifted up his heart to God" on news of our torturers' victory! Dead clergy is no news to me. Dead anyone, for that matter. Could I forget the stadium at Badajoz? The Almería road?

And here I relied on Corie's explanations, of a town's population herded into a bullfighting arena and massacred, of a hundred thousand civilian refugees fleeing a battle along a coastal road being shelled by ships and strafed by Fascist planes and machine-gunned by Italian troops.

Or, as far as the radio goes, General de Llano's slobber on Radio Seville, urging the legions of his Column of Death to rape every woman they could. Anyway, if they would strip me of this one last shred of principle, the dignity of nonbelief, they should never have made it my last. With all else lost. A republic, and you, & the thing I have left is my stubbornness, which they will never get from me. And Alena, too, I have my Magdalena, she's my lovely and she's enough, she's all. She's so very much you! If you could only see her how she thrives, my little bliss! Right now her knees are red from crawling around the patio looking for grass to chew on, the stems sprout up through the concrete, it keeps me busy keeping the grass out of her hands & wiping the sand from her knees. She pulls up a stem and calls it a toy the way her mother plucks daisies and calls them *oreja de oso*, and she seems to have no idea she's growing up in a prison, & thank their god for that! And then the thought destroys me that you cannot know her, she who is all that I know.

"She's had a child," I said.

"Right!" Corie answered, and then paused so long, staring at me in a sort of spooky suspension, that I worried she was suffering a seizure. "Summer?" she resumed. "Late spring? Anyway, a while ago. It's been more than a year since she wrote."

This was the fourth of our morning huddles, and like the earlier three, it thrilled me. This was partly the relief of legitimacy reclaimed — I was entering through the front door, after all. Every time I rang from the street (Corie had labeled the apartment's doorbell *Alba Landers* to guide my initial visit) and was buzzed into the building, I felt honorable, felt I'd been given a dispensation for my crash through Landers's wall. *Where the crime's committed is where the crime's forgot*, as the master said. The remainder of my joy was proximity. I'd encouraged Corie to fly through her written translations (they were, as a consequence, notably inferior in word choice and penmanship to those she'd done for Saxe) so that we could go through the texts together. I wished to discuss each one, I said, to compare the versions sentence by sentence to be sure I was getting everything correct, but that explanation reversed effect and cause, means and ends, for the letters (for me) were mostly an excuse to talk. I'd felt since first meeting her that the girl had something to tell me, a confidential message to relate. Not knowing what the news might be, I hoped I might catch a clue in her voice and gave her voice every opportunity. And so the letters were both pretext and impediment. If I could, I would have tossed aside paper entirely and made her read to me aloud.

"And then there's this one," she said, and held up the next scribbled page for us to muddle through.

Emil and I had by then spent more than a week together of outdoor mornings and indoor afternoons, robed and stylishly otherwise, of long walks, and of leisurely dinners in restaurants where we rarely had to order to be served. I hadn't repeated either my fisticuffs or my *folle* flight home but let Drôlet drive me back early enough to indulge my other secret infatuation and catch some music through the closet door. My infatuation with the man I comprehended. Lust and luxury required no new vocabulary. But what was it about the child that so intrigued me? I discerned in the accident of our meeting—our multiple meetings; the chance collisions on a street, in a church, in a study—a chain of coincidences so extremely unlikely, I saw no alternative to fate, and that was part of it: Who can turn away from fate? And, too, I was riveted by her multiple natures—angry, haunted, protective, intolerant—a convergence of contradictions I couldn't have combined in a carboy were I the world's best chemist.

Superseding all these was another motive, rooted in my profession, for if I'm not the world's best chemist, I'm yet a pretty good anesthesiologist (and, I want to say, not such a shoddy chemist either, pharmacology being, along with physiology and procedure, among the three Ps that Maasterlich drummed into us). Given my particular trade, I'm drawn to anyone whose vital signs hint of peril. Ultimately, that's how I explain it. Corie's signs screamed trouble. I recognized the blankness in those eyes, and though I didn't know its root, I knew the realm wherein she traveled, and knew that at its far frontier the precipice awaited, where sleep trips into profundity as suddenly as despair trips into violence.

It's the anesthesiologist's creed: in calm lurks danger. We are ever (forgive me; they're Maasterlich's words, not mine) alert to the inert. In the operating room, that alertness would have been partly, blessedly technological. I would have had a bank of blinking CRTs and beeping alarms to monitor her every hidden state, EKGs and pulse oximeters to keep me apprised of her condition, and I would have watched those signs like a hawk does a sparrow, the way a lover peers into a lover's face, with just that sharp a hunger. Here on rue Nin, there was none of that to help me, only her eyes. So I watched her eyes, and listened to her voice, and tried fanatically to figure out where, within Corie's calm, Corie's disaster lay.

"More tea?" she said. We declared an entr'acte and headed to the kitchen to heat some water. She'd relocated the electric kettle and the tea bags from the study (Had she tidied up the joint for my inspection? I wondered, and I derived some self-importance out of that). Our kitchen jaunts and my occasional trips to the water closet (it was, may I assure you, no closet) had allowed me my only furtive glances into the interior of the mysterious *palais*, so I was glad that this time, after the kettle had boiled and we'd poured our libation, we didn't plod back to our posts, per usual — kitchen to dining room (furnished with a Biedermeier banquet table, its both ends bristling with a silver candelabra) to marble-floored colonnade to study — but diverted to the library. Corie felt at home in the room, obviously, though guiltily so. She'd taken as gospel Saxe's instruction to inhabit without a trace. She perched on her chair with a wren's timidity, poised for flight. Getting that deep into the premises was tantalizing for me, and I snatched at the chance to draw her further astray. My artifice was transparent (embarrassingly: I professed an interest in period wall coverings), but it brought the invite I'd hoped for. Corie's reservations — she was unsure if this was acceptable, though she accepted me as an authority — were in full blooming conflict with temptation. Temptation won by a nose.

I'd wondered if my memory had inflated the size and fineness of the rooms; now I found it hadn't. If anything, their grandeur had been emphasized by Corie's habitation here and the address on Alba's letters; they made the place more actual. This impossible hallucination, this architectural confection, had been and still was somebody's workaday residence, which rendered it all the more boggling. Cavernous room after cavernous room, I expressed my awe at everything we encountered. We came through the French doors into the conservatory, and, as Corie began effusing on the satin wallpaper, I reeled in sudden dread of the iceberg that lay just ahead. Damned idiot!

Oh, why hadn't I picked another pretext! Surely she would insist on showing me the hand-painted pastoral and the tempera summer sky that were the pièces de résistance, in wall-covering terms, of the entire flat. And of course we would then stumble on the evidence of recent forced entry. Would she alert the police? Would I then confess that I lived next door and end my infernal ruse? I had wanted so, so much to do exactly that, over recent days, had wanted to confirm our friendship with this central admission of who I actually was, but not right now, and certainly not like this. I hadn't figured out what context might best help me broach the matter. I was pretty sure trespass and vandalism weren't ideal ingredients.

We approached the piano, me trying, in defiance of all known optical principles, to cast an eye around the corner. How much devastation had I actually wrought in there? Visions of wholesale wrack and wreckage billowed like cumuli in my overbusy brain, and I made up my mind to stall.

"Oh, look," I said innocently, nodding to the music on the floor, "someone's been playing! Is that you?"

Corie stared at the piano as though surprised that it was there, then shook her head, pursed-lipped. "No," she said.

"You don't play?"

"Not really."

I took in her lie and set it beside my own, two candelabra on a table. They reflected each other, functional items of unexpected intricacy. Her denial disappointed me — I had fantasized adding a recital to our regular conversations, had anticipated listening to music unmuted by subterfuge. But her reluctance to play — to even admit that she could — placed in my path a denser obstacle than any closet door. Her insistence on secrecy reaffirmed my own, and on the spot I swore to myself that I wouldn't reveal my abode, absolutely not. The moment I confessed that I lived within earshot, I would lose Corie's music to Corie's shyness forever, the music that had sustained me through so much and that now I saw (I was recalling the pounding finale of the waltz) as another and necessary vital sign requiring my monitoring.

At least our encounter with the Bösendorfer succeeded brilliantly as diversion, for Corie, morosely focused on the instrument, didn't invite me farther, not at first. Not until I actually took a step back toward the study. Then she called out, "Oh, but you have to see this!"

"We should get back," I said, trying to sound indisputably foregone.

"One more room!" she replied. "It's the best." And she ran on without me, out of the chamber of her guilty secret and into the chamber of mine.

I waited for the horrified scream, the gasp of concern, and when at last I followed her, it was mostly to find out why nothing of the sort had come. She was standing directly under the chandelier, twirling like a dreidel, making the clouds spin. I approached her, my face turned up to feign observation of the handiwork while my lowered eyes scanned the floor and the wall panels for the incriminating mess.

"Isn't it lovely?" Corie asked, and, still peering skyward, she stepped to the wall and began tracing the room's circumference with her hand, her fingers ticking off the groins in the wainscoting like a playing card counting bicycle spokes.

"Lovely," I said, and she caught my vagueness and stopped, stopped precisely where my fear had feared she'd stop.

"What?"

"Nothing," I said, and meant it. There, where I knew full well my eruption into this chamber had left its garish evidence, sugar swirls of gypsum dust and jagged splinters yellow as lightning, there was nothing to see, no indication at all. The floor shone so spotless and the transom I had split was so flawlessly intact that I had to guess which of several panels I had burst through. The one before which Corie stood? Or perhaps the one beside it? I *had* burst through, hadn't I? Where, though? I was left with two prospects: that I had dreamed the entire adventure, or (far less plausible) someone had come along with glue and wax and carefully scoured away my signature.

I'm not sure which possibility was more alarming to contemplate, but my alarm, such as it was, took the form of giddiness. I was reprieved! Who cared how! "Nothing at all," I repeated in wonderment, and Corie, faced with such enigmatic gaiety, gave me a big silly smile. It was a smile completely outside her usual stormy nature, a shiny new facet of her character. Here: one more contradiction to mix into the carboy! On impulse, I grabbed her hand and bowed, formally, stretching one leg behind me. If I couldn't hear her music, I would imagine it for both of us.

"Mademoiselle?" I said, and straightened, and she picked up on my gambit and put a hand on my waist and took a step, and then another, and we waltzed a circle around the gleaming parquet, both of us laughing. We waltzed our way past fields and forests and picked up our pace past a flock of sheep and a flock of windows and began a second circuit of the room, and just as we reached again the entry into the conservatory our *cotillon à deux* collapsed as abruptly as if

the plaster heaven above had fallen in shards around us. My tune —
I'd begun humming our accompaniment — tailed off in tatters. She
doubled over, clutching at her waist. I debated, startled, between
comic and dire — a reciprocal curtsy? a burst appendix? — but my
thoughts were severed by a low solid growl, gagging out of her like a
tumor being born. With another spasm of contraction, she lurched
upright and bolted from the room.

I raced after, slowly enough to be sure not to catch her, unsure
what I'd done or ought to do. She halted, panting, inside the study
door, and I could tell that her flight from far precincts had only compounded her pain. She'd ricocheted out of her unaccustomed cheer
and into torment. Her aspect had darkened like a mire about her.
Instead of plunking down in her chair as usual (armchairs called
to Corie's inner skydiver), she stood with her back to me, erect and
motionless.

Did I see, or could I only sense, her trembling? I reached a hand
and gently pulled a distraught lock of hair from her shoulder. "It's
okay," I lied, quietly, stroking her hair and lying. "It's going to be okay."

Then she turned, and the face that greeted me was in no need of
consolation. With a forcible mobilization, she'd fought her way back
to composure. I watched her cross the last yard, her defiance crest-
ing in fear before settling back into the gaze. Her nostrils still flared
with the exertion, but her voice was steady and empty. "Resume next
time?" she asked me. It was not a question. In a flash her shape had
shifted from wounded to hostile to impervious, and it was the last,
the calm at the tail end of the storm, that chilled me. There was resolve in it, I just couldn't tell for what.

XIV

B Y THE TIME OF our resumption, two days later, her equi-
poise was immaculately repaired, its luster restored as miraculously as the woodwork in the oval room. All I could
know, as I searched for a relic of the crisis, was that harm had sunk
into oblivion, and the waters closed above it. We did our usual, amid
the ordinary, no mention made.

"She's in trouble," Corie informed me as soon as I stepped inside
the door, with such a hustling in her voice that I took it we might yet
effect a rescue, were we quick enough. She held a letter, which she
read aloud as we hastened back to the study, skipping the salutation
and whatever opening pleasantries and diving straight into the paragraph she'd been on when I rang the bell, translating it straight from
the page to my ear, so that this letter remains one of only two, among
Alba's many, of which I have no written English version.

> I've told you I draw the others' envy, but what would they wish me
> to do? My comfort is for Magdalena's sake, she's the only child on the
> grounds. I would give up all my privileges, except for the one of being
> allowed to accompany Alena in hers. I'm not ashamed. The life she
> enjoys is far from the least she deserves. But haven't I earned a better
> opinion? In Ventas —

"Another prison," Corie inserted.

> . . . with the women given *la pepa* —

"A seed, or, I think, a bullet: sentenced to die," she said.

> . . . as I was, didn't I use my status to save them from the firing squad?

And not just a few! My status has attracted cruelties too, though I don't pretend to be special. They hung a woman here last week for laying a wreath of flowers on her son's grave. There's a teenager here with burst eardrums from electric shocks to her ears, an eighty-year-old who cannot leave the latrine for they destroyed her gut with liters of castor oil and sawdust, for the sport of it. All in the name of the God they wish to convert me to. I'd rather die! Why am I made so alone? The brand I bear should balance any pain of theirs, the scars —

and here Corie broke off to say that she couldn't make out what was written, and she indicated the place where water or some other liquid had dissolved the ink into a Rorschach cloud of blue pastels and dark linings and eaten the text like a fog bank. Her finger shook. I was as disturbed as she was. Far from deriding Corie's connection with the poor, afflicted Alba, I increasingly shared in it, though on my own terms. Didn't I know how this luckless woman felt! What it was like to be kept from a loved one by war. I admired her nurse's sentiment, between the lines of all her early letters, insisting on procedure and professionalism amid the mayhem. We could have shared a slow drink over that, she and I! Yet in other ways, I couldn't begin to conjure this Alba who, beset by every ravage and hardship, still found a way to love, to bear a child and raise her. In prison! Who could fathom such fortitude? I'd tried to imagine her giving birth in a killing zone, and was shaken by the horror. Little by legible bit, the handwriting worked its way free again.

... breast & my back, especially, that demon's logo, that five-armed, five-footed devil. How will you delight in me? Only with anger. I don't feel the burns anymore, but I cannot get rid of the face, she was always so in love when she attacked me, luxurious with her time, attentive, lingering over her art, it will take me a lifetime to live down the disgust. I tell you this wrongly, I am being cruel, but really only weak, my dear & I say I don't want to upset you but I do. I need you to hate her too, your help in hating them all.

There was an incursion of more fog.

... or to apologize. Must I tear my dress & say look at this, this catastrophe of what remains of a woman — now tell me to my face you resent my baby's room!

Corie's voice was agonized, and hearing her read in real time, spitting out the words as Alba must have dashed them down in ink, as Alba might have spit them had she spoken her mind not written it, I felt that more was merging into a single seamless whole than a letter and its translation. Two women, author and translator, sang in unison before me. I had long conflated them, Alba and "Alba," the letters I read being penned by both. For these several minutes they were one. Then the buzzer sounded.

I jumped. I'd never before heard the doorbell's chime. (It chimed like a toad.) Corie, who'd heard it time and again, seemed startled too and sprang up to check the watch she'd set on the writing desk.

"Oh!" she said, a plea. She looked around frantically, as though she were about to stash me in a cupboard, then she grabbed up the pages of her other just-finished translations and shoved them into an envelope and shoved it into my hands as she herded me out. "Next time," she whispered. "Tomorrow." She shoved my coat into my arms and shoved me out the door.

The door closed with the cacophonous *ka-chunk* of good old-fashioned munitions-grade hardware. I deliberated, standing in the hall, whether or not I should knock on the door and demand to know what the hell was going on, but a moment convinced me to accede to Corie's panic — it was something else she could translate for me tomorrow — and I headed for the elevator. I must have been its most recent customer; the cage was still waiting on my floor, but just as I reached for the handle to open the gate there was another decisive, mechanical clunk and the cage began descending.

I'd missed my ride! And I thought, *So, no big deal, I'm a New Yorker, when you can't get a cab, you walk.* I headed down the stairs. They were narrow and spiraled squarely around the elevator shaft. The lift motor whirred to life again and the cage rose past me, and I caught a glimpse of its passengers, a man and a woman. Did I recognize his face? I'm not sure I saw it. But the play of shadow across his figure as the light worked its way through the moving lattice made something surface in my mind. Maybe, as the detective explained to the photographer, it's easier to identify people in the dark. Distractions of color and ornament fade away and you're left with the essentials, the way a person moves, his proportions and bulk, the ponytail pulled from the balding pate. Or maybe the shadows in the passing cage just echoed the shadows in the Église d'Hiver the brief single time we'd met.

The walk around the block should have allowed me sufficient opportunity to contemplate, but I arrived no wiser at Saxe's place. Somehow, in the scramble of my eviction, Corie'd left me in full possession of her fear, and her fear grew healthily as I fed it bits and pieces of my own. Was she in some sort of trouble? Danger? I stepped into the closet and then back out to pace my room in agitation, then stepped into the closet again to move some hangers around fitfully on their rods (thinking, *You know, Tilde, it's about time you locate a laundromat*), and stepped out again and then back in, and at the end of these convolutions and circumnavigations, I stood before the panel door with my hands on my hips. I reached to pull the knob.

It was an odd thing, sneaking by the back way into the same home I'd minutes ago departed as a guest. I felt like an actor with dual roles in a play, as though my impostor self were out to catch me in the act of being legitimate. But too late, too late — Legitimate Me was no longer there to be caught.

Initially, it seemed there was no one to catch at all — silence was all that emitted from the rooms ahead. For the first time ever, my course through these premises was not a voyage of wonder. Every marvelous, captivating thing was either to my purpose or in my way. I prowled from hassock to column to lamp resolutely aiming toward the study, listening for trouble as I went, but when I finally heard what I was listening for, I'd gone too far. The trouble was right behind me.

I was all the way past the door that led to the library when I heard the voices, or rather Massue's voice and Corie's protesting stammer, coming out of it. Three shadows sprawled into the room. It was the room I'd just passed through. If the place had been brighter or if he'd glanced my way, he would surely have seen me, but it wasn't and he didn't. He crossed the carpet and flopped himself onto a couch.

A woman followed but didn't sit, just stood beside him like an IV pole. I didn't know her. He still wore his knee-length leather coat. He propped his stocking feet on the coffee table as though in his den at home. I couldn't see Corie. I stood there trying to take in their conversation undistracted by my predicament — he was haranguing her awfully on some point. The rest of me was trying to figure a way out of my predicament, undistracted by their conversation.

"I suppose, but . . ." Corie said.

"Suppose? You chose this. Or am I missing something?" She tried to answer, but he insisted, "What am I missing? You say you're in the struggle. So *this* is what you mean, correct? This."

"It's an apartment, Massue. It comes with the job."

"I think what Massue is trying to say —" the woman started.

"Oh, the job!" Massue pushed on, not needing clarification. He rattled a sheaf of papers in the air, which I could see with dismay were a fistful of Alba's letters. Corie crossed into view, reaching, but he snatched them away.

"'My dear beloved C.,'" he read, his derision slathered in treacle. "My dear fucking Christ! You know, Corie, you already *have* a job."

"That's right," the woman said.

"A responsibility. It's an American war, you're an American voice."

"People respond to you," the woman said.

"No one else can say what you do. You're American, you're . . ."

"A woman," the woman offered.

"You're young, attractive, a woman. People are drawn to you. They feel your passion."

I could see the woman nodding. "They feel it," she said.

"But only if you're out there being passionate," Massue said, "not holed up here over your letterbox. Look, people miss you in committee."

"We do!" the woman declared.

"That's the whole reason we're here. We want you back with us. And I need you on the street. You should be leading things! Stopping this madness! You're the best I have, but you've gone halfhearted, and do you know how disappointing that is? How demoralizing for everyone? You have to decide. Read history or make it, it's up to you. But for me, I need an activist, not an archivist."

"They aren't just letters, Massue," Corie pleaded. "She's fighting Franco."

"Exactly! Not lounging around on her ass. You want to know why you admire this woman?" He shook the letters at her again. "Because *she wasn't here*, that's why! She *left* here and went *there*. She'd have laid down her life for you. For *you!* And this is how you repay her. Hiding away in her . . . *appartement*, sipping from her china" — he mimicked a sip, his pinkie held out mincingly — "while your comrades do the work. Such sacrifice!"

"Massue," the woman cautioned.

"Fuck it!" he said. He welled up from the couch in a violence of leather and bile and tossed the letters disdainfully onto the coffee table. They skittered across the glass and scattered to the floor. Corie scurried after them, and the woman stooped to help her. Massue said to the two bent backs, "At least change your name. I'm not sure Alba suits you. C'mon, Louise."

I recoiled from the indictment as though he'd spat it at me — I'd jumped too when he leaped up. And then I kept on going, mincing through the rooms as fast as I was able. I wanted to head back the way I'd come — for one thing, I'd left my door ajar — but how? Circle through the library? It might be just the path they'd choose to take. So I kept on toward the front rooms, propelled by Massue's invective. They were approaching rapidly behind me, and I sped, barely keeping out of sight, trying not to knock into anything, and in my haste, when I reached the front door I almost blew it with the chain lock — why did Corie insist on engaging the damned chain lock every time? I had the door in mid-yank before I saw that it was hooked, and I caught myself, and released it, and snuck out into the hall.

My relief was crushed by a cannon volley. It wasn't artillery, of course, though it sounded that loud to ears so sensitized by panic. The *ka-chunk* of the door latch thundered down the corridor. Had it roared as rudely inside? I raced for the stairs.

I was hardly even a full flight down when the door flew open. I froze. They stepped out into the landing, as furtive as I had been inside. They moved silently and didn't talk, their shadows looming down the wall as they peered over the banister into the elevator well.

"Flics," Massue growled: Cops. "Fuckin' *merde."* The shadows re-

ceded and the door closed and I ran without caution now because I knew precisely the amount of time I had—the time it takes a man to get his boots on in a hurry—and that turned out to be about right, because the next thunder I heard was his steps berating down the stairs behind me. There were interludes of quiet when he came to a carpeted landing, and then the banging resumed.

I reached the lobby in a near faint—if I hadn't already tripped the alarm, I'd have run outside and made my way coatless around the block. Now, surely, Corie would be watching from the window: I was caught. What would be the terms of my surrender? Then I noticed, as I hadn't before, that the stairs continued on from the lobby, and that's where I went, where they would take me, down into a basement.

Can you lose a pursuer by losing yourself? It was as much of a plan as I had. The stairs bottomed out into a concrete corridor that swerved like a sewer through a labyrinth of utility rooms and storage lockers. There was little light beyond the occasional glint through coal-grimed transom glass, and I passed a furnace room and a large iron-smelling fuel tank and had just miraculously navigated an alcove where a dozen phantomy bicycles were chained in the dark to a central phantomy bicycle rack—these precincts must get more traffic in the sunny months—and gone around a corner and was headed down another hall when out of the gloom the Minotaur appeared right before me, leaping out of the shadows into my path, a beefy arm cradling a laundry basket. I let out a yell.

Céleste made no answer. She was as impassive as I was panicked, taking me in almost casually, and it was just then I heard the terrible crash. The room behind me erupted in an apocalypse of rent metal and ripped flesh; my pursuer had discovered the bicycles. The collision seemed to go on and on for an unusual number of seconds, seemed to have first and second and third acts and encores and intermissions and to prolong itself through ornate cadenzas of bell and bone and spoke and tube, aluminum and obscenity, during all of which commotion Céleste's gaze never faltered from my face and never betrayed even curiosity, much less alarm, at the noise. When the symphony seemed to be petering out, she handed me the basket. "Washroom, first door to the right," she said, and stomped off toward the collision zone to set the world on its axis one more time.

Her nightingale voice wafted back around dark corners, demanding "What's the meaning of this!" and "Who let you into this building?" and then, in response to the obvious query, insisting no, the only thing she'd heard was the noise of a clumsy bicycle thief.

From my position, with my head in the maw of a front-loading washing machine, I sensed the malign shadow pause at the door, and I heard Céleste more loudly. "Then is it laundry you've come to help us with, monsieur, or shall I call the police?" Followed by "I thought as much" and her generous offer to escort him to the street. "Let's try it with the lights on, why not?"

She returned a few minutes later and said to me, crossly — she hadn't squandered all of her brimstone — "*Non, non,* not like that," and snatched away the basket and pointed me down the hall to the passage that would let me out directly into my courtyard.

Brushing past her as I escaped the room, I heard her say, low and in English, "You have not so nice friends."

"She's hardly the first," Emil complained. He *was* complaining; he sounded grumpy.

"Everyone's always the first when it comes to that, Emil," I said. "Everyone's first love is the first love in the world. Anyway, that's not the point." It definitely wasn't. Corie's meltdown had pried open, by a smidgen, my reluctance to talk about her. I felt the need for a confidant. I wasn't quite confident Emil was the confidant I needed, but he'd have to do. In the car, going down the highway, there were only the two of us. "The point is," I said, "what makes you so certain she's in love?"

"She's doubled over in agony!" he exclaimed. "What's that sound like to you?"

"You mean she's a girl, so what else could it be."

"Oh, poof," Emil said.

"It's so trite," I scolded him. "Can I suggest some other plausible possibilities?"

"Plausibilities!" he said. "Please, I bet you will. But could you, first," and he asked me to locate a map in the glove compartment. "They've changed all this around." The old grump; *all this* being the highway, a long straight stretch through field and forest named (propitiously for our purposes) Voie de la Liberté, though now the Way of Liberty had swerved into a tangle.

We'd given gray Paris the slip for the day, springing Emil's Citroën out of its garage for a spin through the Champagne region, stopping in Épernay to tour the caves of a famed vintner and lifetime friend of Emil's. (My lifetime had had no famed vintner friends, I castigated myself. That must be where everything went wrong.) Emil had said we absolutely must go, because I'd never been. As we wandered through the cool chalk, bottle-bottom burrows under the hillside, this bibulous catacomb, I suspected another motive, that we were here because he'd been so many times. Épernay was yet another way station in Sahran's sentimental tour.

It was also indisputably ideal for a picnic, conditions being right, and with some wishful denial concerning the chill but thankful for a dry day, we pulled a quilt from the trunk of the Citroën (I recognized it; it was the same quilt that had swaddled Headmistress Ralanou's blasphemous painting) and spread it on the lawn of the little church where, in another month, the blast of an antique cannon would initiate the Feast of St. Vincent and the procession would begin. There we broke bread in our overcoats and uncorked a hand-labeled bottle of local product, courtesy of the lifetime friend. It was beyond lovely, with the sun's rays diverging through the passing clouds converting the valley below us into a scene from a Bible frontispiece. The friend had asked Emil if he'd be returning to attend the feast, but Emil said no, not this year, he wouldn't be in France then, and that's why he wished to come early.

"Salaam," I said, hoisting my champagne flute and making an awful toast. (Peace. Was that so awful?)

He laughed. "*Haraam*," he responded.

"Harrumph yourself," I said after I'd had my gulp and balanced my glass on the blanket and set about slicing up *fromage* and *saucisson* and bread. "What's a *haraam*?"

"A prohibition," he answered. "According to the traditions of Islam. For example, prohibited fluids, like champagne. My sister would not approve."

I told him it wasn't a news flash that his personal Islamicness was of the secular variety.

"Are you informing me you're not a virgin?" he asked, and I swung at him (although playfully this time) with the baguette. *I have got to quit hitting Emil!* I scolded myself, but it was difficult. I found his ruptured lip so devastatingly cute I wasn't sure what I would have to do about it on the day that it finally healed up.

I said, "No. But you do have a liquor cabinet loaded with Jack Daniel's. For starters."

"Permitted," he protested. "Really! You have a common misconception. And I can eat mangoes. And garlic, as you've witnessed." And he could also drink beer and gin, according to some schools, not necessarily the most restrictive ones. "It's the fermented grape that's specifically off-limits," he said. "Cheers." He took another sip of prohibited fluid and I handed him a sandwich.

"Anyway, I'm not a secular Muslim," he said. "I'm a fallen one. There's a distinction." One, he made clear, that had nothing to do with the booze.

And so began a thread that would weave through our afternoon's chatter, alongside the one about Corie's predicament ("What if she's devastated by the war? She's an organizer, you know. That comes with a lot of pressure, and I'm sure she's got school pressures too"); alongside accounts of his upbringing in two cultures, the first one lapsing Catholic and the second ardently Muhammadan (as I called him only once; though fallen, he considered the term more blasphemous than wine), and mine in a more or less Unitarian clapboard New Jersey two-story house with a carriage lamp on a pole out front to light your way up the flagstones. We feasted until we could ignore the cold no longer and then packed up the picnic and drove on into Reims to take a look at the cathedral (either because I'd never seen it before or because he'd seen it so many times, one or the other), the heat in the Citroën cranked all the way up to broil. The temperature seemed to be plummeting out in the land in the graying afternoon, and it was good to be back in the car, even lost in the highway construction and lost in conversation, searching for a map.

"So," he said. "Those are your plausibilities? Homework and war."

Daniel, do you remember old Mr. Samson, your great-uncle, or maybe he wasn't really family, but he was certifiably great, at least;

he gave you a metal clarinet when you were a kid, remember? From Savannah? And remember how we always made him tell us why he moved all the way down there to Savannah, Georgia, when he was a young man, what a funny place to spend the rest of your life and raise a family, we thought, when he could have gone anywhere, to Trenton, or Newark, or Philadelphia. (How very long I've loved you, Daniel! Even when I first loved you, I thought: *I've loved you all of my life.*) And he'd look all muddled and mystified and he'd say, Why, Savannah's so lovely, anyone would want to live there; it has three short *a*'s and a *v*, a double *n* and a silent *h*. It begins with a secret and ends with a hush. What could be more irresistible? And we laughed, and he laughed because he'd made us laugh, but we knew there was a chance he was serious at heart — that he'd devoted his life to a city because he liked the way its name was spelled.

I'm not unsympathetic — I've always thought I'd be happy as a clam in Kyzyl or Samarqand or some other place I've only seen on a globe, on account of that self-same sonority. But it isn't place I'm thinking about, Daniel. It's vocation. Someone gave you a tin clarinet, and you became a musician, and sometimes I wonder about how these seeds are set, how they can be as infinitesimal as a grain of pollen yet grow to absorb your whole life, and I wonder about who I am and why, why I'm not just an anesthesiologist, but a cardiac anesthesiologist. And then I think of the thrill of it, the heart part.

It's not really my part, the part that belongs to me. After I put a patient to sleep and before the surgeon opens up his chest, we set up a drape, positioned like the blade of a guillotine across the patient's neck, except it's not a blade but a cloth, a low blue fence between our official purviews, the surgical team's and the anesthesiologist's. It's a part of procedure. To one side of it lies the patient's body; to the other side, my side, his head. His face is masked under another cloth, and all the tubes for probes and the airway cannula and IVs, the whole tangled basket of catheters and wires is there — all that belongs to me. And the name of this fence, this vocational barrier, this cubicle divider, is the ether screen, though some of us amuse ourselves by calling it the "blood-brain barrier," Willem says, in our case, because I have the brains and he doesn't mind the blood.

The thing is, I don't mind the blood either (you can't, really, and do this, but I promise you you've never seen anything like the color of blood in surgery; running through the tubes to the bypass machine, it's more solid and weighty than any inanimate red). Back when I was a resident, they encouraged us, as part of our training, to slip around the ether screen and get some feel for the other guy's job, and one day the surgery was a transplant — it was a fairly new procedure then — and the surgeons asked if I'd like to help out.

I scrubbed in and pulled on a fresh set of gloves and when the suturing was done and all that was left was the final settling in, I reached in through the chest spreader and cupped the scared little organ in my hands, clenched up hard like a kitten, and when toward the end it started to beat in my hand, I can't begin to tell you how that felt. It's mortality's orgasm! There's no sensation even remotely close. I still feel a twinge at the end of any chest surgery when they twist the stainless-steel sutures to clamp the sternum shut; a twinge of loss, saying farewell to that colorful inner kingdom with its bizarre dramas and vivid pageantry and mystery and heroism, seeing all that closed over with the pimply, hairy overcast of a standard-issue stretch of human skin. It's like pulling a tatty gray trench coat over your party dress when Mardi Gras is done.

I bet you didn't know this, Daniel, that the heart doesn't beat on command.

We drop a new one into someone's empty chest and its nerves aren't even hooked up to anything, and it will lie there dormant for a while, and then, of its own accord, it will start to beat. As soon as it feels blood (and if it doesn't get the hint, we give it a shock to nudge it, or a little massage of encouragement). But generally it doesn't need reminding and as soon as the clamps are released and the first cor- puscles spill from the sutured vein, it senses them, as though the heart can taste what the heart has swallowed, and of its own will, or the last life-will of the person whose heart it used to be, it picks up its duty right where its duty left off and goes to work pulsing this strang- er's blood through this stranger's body. It's voluntary, so to speak: au- tonomous. There's no cable of communication between the body and the organ beyond the message in this offering of blood, this blood- brother pact. I can't think of it without wonder, the sensation in my hands of the first faint spasm of acknowledgment and acceptance, and then collaboration — this willingness, this ultimate generosity.

But that's not what I'm trying to get at; I've wandered. I was telling you about how I picked my course, and I'd already picked it by then, you see. I suspect my direction depended on something as unsubstantial as the beauty of a word or a phrase, the sound of a name that gripped my imagination the first time I heard it, the way the name Savannah grabbed the life of Mr. Samson. I had no idea what the phrase meant or what it was, but I knew without hesitation that I could rest there the rest of my life, reside inside the splendor of the tetralogy of Fallot.

I have Kathy to thank, Kathy Brooks. She planted the seed, standing up there in front of the class, Mrs. Cummings's sixth grade, Verdant Avenue Elementary, and relating for show-and-tell how her infant brother was going to Baltimore to get an operation to save his life because he had a hole in his heart, and Mrs. Cummings jumping in to elaborate that it wasn't like a bullet hole. It was a hole between his heart's two halves — one that all newborns have, that's supposed to heal over as you grow but doesn't in some individuals — and that this was just one of several problems with Kathy's brother's heart, who had a syndrome known as a tetralogy. Mrs. Cummings wrote it on the blackboard, right under *Maryland* and *congenital: tetralogy of Fallot.*

And then she went on to tell us, being too excellent a sixth-grade teacher to let the opportunity pass, everything she could about the heart and its workings and its evolution. I sat there murmuring, "Fallot, Fallot, Fallot," as she said it was part of what made us humans, that the primitive heart was a single chamber, and then, like a frog's heart, three, but we higher mammals had a four-roomed heart, two ventricles and two atria, the rooms securely separated by valves and walls of muscle, and that's how the pump worked, and it didn't work well if any of the walls had holes in them. She was a very good explainer, Mrs. Cummings, Kathy nodding authoritatively in concurrence with everything she said, standing up there in front of us all, proud of her brother for being so complicated and evolutionary. And so, along with a profession, I acquired a conviction that day. The thing that makes our human heart human is its internal divisions; or, as Maasterlich might say, a heart undivided is one that cannot stand, and that's why, until today, I hadn't wished to tell Emil any-thing about Corie, anything at all, or even reveal her existence, just as I never told Corie about Emil, for the two belonged to different cham-bers, whose breach might somehow be fatal.

And, oh, that I had continued to abide by Mrs. Cummings's delin-eations, but I needed a friend in the matter, and I didn't have to tell Emil everything, only barely enough, and that's what I did. I never said she was the girl next door, or anything so precise, or anything about the letters. Only about the death that lurked in her eyes like winter on the horizon and that she was a friend, a friend of mine in trouble. He would in that, at least, prove helpful down the line.

"So . . . activist," Emil said. We were back amid the plausibilities.

"I said organizer."

I wasn't sure of the distinction, and Emil ignored it, surging on without pause to render his verdict on activists, a category that, dip-lomatically speaking, constituted a special case. Their passion on public issues masked a personal stake, he said, and if you were nego-tiating with them you had to remember to address the hidden per-sonal issue, not the declared public one. "They like to think they're saving the world, because saving themselves is far too hard in a world that has no values." They weren't wrong about the world, Emil said, "but they want its values to be more absolute, because only then will they be safe" from demons closer to home.

"Well, there's more than one kind of demon," I said. "It still doesn't mean she's in love," and I suggested Corie's studies again, or that maybe she was reliving some terrible childhood tragedy, like a deadly disease that felled a dear friend. Or an accident.

"The train wreck," Emil said.

"The freak train wreck," I said, accepting the invitation to impro-vise. "The favorite brother killed in the collision."

"The trestle washed out by the flash flood. And he ran back into the burning car to rescue the toddler from the mangled mom."

"Exactly!" I exclaimed; now we were getting somewhere. "Some-thing like that. Or how about her music? She's a musician, you know. A good one."

"What sort?" Emil asked.

"Piano. Classical."

"Hmmm," he said. "I don't know. Classical music, destroyer of young adults."

"Too improbable?"

"Not at all," he said. "In 1830."

"She cares about it," I offered, defensive. "Do you know what she practices?" I ran through some of the titles stacked beside the Bösendorfer. "Duets," I said. "Advanced stuff. Of course she only plays half of—"

"Et voilà!" Emil declared. He practically bounced off the bench seat.

"Oh, come on!" I said before he got the words out; I know when I've got myself good and cornered.

"But it's obvious!" he gloated.

I reminded myself I wasn't hitting Emil anymore. "So, go on," I said.

"Well, let's see. He's tall, blond, brooding. Concert pianist, international circuit, and he's run off with another."

"Why assume he's a he?"

"Good point. She's tall, blond, and brooding. And your Little One will never, ever replace her."

"And she cannot believe the pain," I said. "And she will spend her life playing over and over her half of all the duets they used to play together."

"Aïe!" Emil exclaimed, stricken.

"Ouch!" I agreed.

When we'd driven a while longer, he said, "She will, though."

"What?" I asked. We'd turned a corner, and the shadows had shifted inside the car.

"Find another. Everything that happens, happens over again."

I agreed with an "Uhn" and dusted off my Marx to suit the premise. "The first time as tragedy, the second time as farce. That's in history."

"Life, just the same," Emil said. I'd made him laugh. "Except that in life the first time's a tragedy and the second time is too."

A ways farther, and he said, "What if she's facing something worse?"

"Than?" I said.

"A broken heart." Even more awful than the pain that will never end, he said, was the moment Corie realized that it would end, "when she sees she'll get over it perfectly well."

"And that everything worth dying for turns out to be survivable, and life is larger than all the things she thought her life was about, and what did it all mean if the most important thing in the world didn't mean anything anyway? That sort of thing?"

"Precisely," he said. "What if she thinks she's figured it out, that the only way to make love last a lifetime is to cut the lifetime short."

And I thought, *What wishful nonsense — do we really so easily outlast love? —* but I thought it to myself.

We'd navigated the detour and were invading the inner city when Emil asked, "So, who is it I should be jealous of?"

"What do you mean?"

"Your tragedy," he said. "Who was your musician?" I didn't answer. I was flashing on you while trying to look like I was thinking of no one at all, but he persisted. "Tell me about Willem."

In general, I never minded our pokes and jabs, Emil's and mine. I knew that someday our relationship would decline into sweetness and pleasantry, and I was happy that we weren't there yet, that we maintained our disputation. Ardent is as ardent does. But this — this was beyond the pale, even or especially for us. I felt sucker-punched, after all our speculative Corie silliness, and I made to say so. "Tell me about Willem," he said, and I burst out, "Oh, now!"

But before I could get my breath in gear, he interjected, "I know, I know." He knew, he said, that Willem didn't mean anything to me, and said, "I just wonder what you might mean to Willem."

"That's not what's going on," I said.

"Ahh, so something *is,*" Emil said, all pleased and gotcha. "Going on." And I allowed that I'd been worried about it too, but you had to know Willem; just because he and I were squabbling didn't make it a romance.

"What would you call it, then?"

"Diplomacy," I answered. "Can you handle another plausibility?"

"Fire away," he offered. So I explained how I saw Willem, that he wanted assurance that he was okay in my eyes, because he couldn't stand the thought that someone out there might disagree with how he viewed himself. We used to be a team frequently but hadn't worked together in years. The last time we had, things hadn't ended so well. That's all. "He wants to be sure I still respect him," I said. "Wants it enough it resembles a passion. But it has nothing to do with affection." Except for himself, maybe. "Exoneration is more like it."

"Over the Singleton thing."

"Oh," I said. This was getting worse and worse. "You know about that."

Sahran shrugged: of course. "But Willem won."

"He did indeed."

"And you did too."

"In a way. Yes, we both won. The suit was dismissed."

"And then Willem kept on going without a blink and became this saint on the medical-mercy front, acclaimed for his humanity. And you quit your profession."

"I did nothing of the sort!" I protested. I'd left my staff job to teach more, was all. Okay, to teach much more — much, much more and to run a department. I still operated. "I'm here, aren't I?"

Sahran said, "It looks to me like you're the one who's needing exoneration."

"Look," I said, and now I was irritated. This wasn't ardent, this was tedious. There was, as he might say, a distinction. "I'm sorry, sorry to disappoint you. It was a terrible thing, a terrible case, and I actually don't feel good about it, win or lose." Win or lose, I wanted to say, someone had still died on the table, under the influence of nature or anesthesia or the shock of surgery, the jury deciding in favor of the first, fortunately, but my own internal jury being not so thoroughly convinced. I'd put the patient under and she'd stayed there, was how it looked to me, stayed there where I couldn't get to her and couldn't pull her back, no matter what I tried. Such things happen, but it isn't something you want to relive after a lovely picnic on a leisurely day off. "And if you are really interested, you should probably just get the court transcript and read it for yourself and decide if you want me working on Odile, or anywhere near her."

"I've read it," Sahran said.

That took me aback, I confess. I felt simultaneously surrounded and exposed, trapped in the moving car in the deepening dark and impending weather, maneuvering through the snarl of central Reims with a man who'd seemed to like me, or so I'd thought until I found out he'd vetted my dossier.

"So," I said, aiming for a little bitter irony, sidestepping injury, trying for a stance. "Yet he deigns to accept me anyway!"

"Because," Sahran said.

"I beg your pardon?"

"I wanted you *because*, not *anyway*. Because of the case. Because you quit your practice. It's why I wanted you."

Notre-Dame de Reims was a fortress of night when we arrived, its buttresses rising out of the low, yellow puddle of streetlight like the palisade of some terrible *île des morts*, its heights unseeable against a glowering sky. We dodged in through the transept doors, car to chapel across a moat of cold. A Mass was in progress. A smattering of congregants, or tourists more likely, speckled the pews before a droning sacerdote. A religion in remission is as mournful to behold as a religion ascendant is scary, and the opulent desolation of the scene unsettled me, obscurely. I felt I'd stumbled on a cluster of survivors of a plague.

"And they demolished a neighborhood to make this big enough to pack the whole crowd in," Sahran informed me; so now he knew everything about the thirteenth century too. I was still unnerved by our malpractice conversation. But I didn't speak. Neither of us spoke much at all, out of self-consciousness, not pique. Every step on stone echoed like the bang of a gavel, and I could hear my whispers slither up into the vaults to join a permanent sibilance, an incessant sly vesper of accumulated gossip that heckled our progress around the transept and back down the aisle of the nave. I've visited cathedrals in daylight, when the sun streaks in through the rose windows and the bus hordes gawk at the names chiseled on the floor tombs, tablets burnished by travel sandals to the brink of legibility — *We read their monuments; we sigh* — but here, tonight, as the votive candles glowed in their niches, ruby ranks of sins committed, sins confessed (they were the sole heat in the enormous room, a vast cold cavern of virtue warmed only by flickers of remorse), I felt the tables turned. How few our numbers, beset by these legions, these perished generations — *and while we sigh, we sink; and are what we deplor'd.* The sparse house was packed to overflowing.

In a while, outnumbered by the solitudes and jostled by emptiness and more chilled indoors than we would be out on the street, we cast our lot with the barometer and fled for a stroll around the block.

The barometer had betrayed us. A cold rain had started up. The cobbles were flashing with quicksilver gusts as though schools of minnows were pestering the surface from below. Sahran deposited me under a stone angel and dodged out to the car and returned with an umbrella, his arm outstretched to gather me beneath it. "Up for this?" he asked, and I assented. I didn't want to get back in the car with our conversation still so uncomfortably unresolved, and the church had offered no respite. A walkabout, even a drippy one, seemed advisable, though there was little use conversing even away from the church. The cloister's whisperings had crescendoed into the drumroll of rain on our umbrella, and when we rounded the corner behind the great church and spied the glowing marquee of an open pub, we made for it.

The interior of Le Chemin Vert smelled of yeast and old damp wool and sawdust and was predominantly dance floor, or what I took to be, though there was no band, and the jukebox and an old plywood upright piano were both blessedly silent; the piano didn't even have a bench. A necklace of unoccupied tables was strung one deep along the walls. The crowd, such as it was, was convened at the room's far end, plastered against the zinc in rough single file, standing (there were no barstools) like a police lineup run amok or a boozy reenactment of the Elgin Marbles.

Behind the zinc, a bartender patrolled like a priest behind a communion rail. He was doing a more prosperous business than his counterpart in the cathedral. He had a clientele and, from the looks of it, a faithful one. It was a local crowd. You could tell by the way the conversation paused as we entered, and the heads turned. But we weren't a friend requiring greeting, and we weren't the wind blowing the door open, requiring that someone traverse the expanse and slam it shut again, and so the heads turned back, and the hubbub recommenced. I made a note of it: we were less than the wind. But the place was warm and the warmth embraced me. Sahran shook out the *parapluie* and stashed it with our coats, and we fitted ourselves into the frieze and bellied up to the bar.

He was still brooding on the cathedral, and after we'd ordered some fermented and unprohibited hops ("Cistercians of the Strict Observance. Two, please," he instructed the barman), he resumed narrating how the church was shelled by the Kaiser's artillery in 1914 and everything in it set ablaze. You could still see the damage from the street if you stepped out and looked up, which was a nonstarter for me. I'd had my faceful of rain. To escape the long shadow of Big Bertha I drifted into an inspection of our companions at the bar. On the far side of Emil stood two men, similar in age (older) and disrepair (extensive), but of opposing physiques and demeanors, the one being carved of abiding stone and the other strung of wire. The first man was a monument of concentrated force and brooding solidity, his face rough as a quarry road and his voice like grit in a concrete mixer, qualities undoubtedly fostered by an infinitude of hand-rolled cigarettes like the smoldering stub now staining his fingers.

His companion was a flibbertigibbet scarecrow, a lanky imbecile who hopped in place in St. Vitus calisthenics whenever his friend spilled a gravelly word, grunting in response and keening wide-eyed from a mouth distended in a perpetual whistle. His hands jerked and glided in a spastic choreography whose exaggerations endowed them — and him — with an odd ceremonial stateliness, a psycho pomp and circumstance. Even at a bar none of whose patrons were much less shopworn, the two men made an exotic set, though I was the only one paying them any mind.

The drafts came, and Emil and I toasted each other for the second time that day. His prescription had elicited a brew called St. Hermes, which arrived in Trappist tulip glasses that had me feeling all the more serendipitous about our choice of location, as if we'd done much choosing. When I looked back over at Emil, I could see his complexion sombering, as though he'd held off crying until he had a beer to cry in.

"I have a favor to request of you, and it's much more than a favor," he said.

I waited — the inevitable needs no prompting — and he said, "Odile's going to need you."

"She has me, of course," I assured him, softly. I patted him on the arm. "But the person Odile needs is Willem. He's the best I've ever seen at what he does. He'll make her right."

"I know he will," he said, inspecting a spot on the bar, his lip gnawing tight against his teeth. "But she'll need you especially. Will you promise me something? Will you not let anything come between you and her?"

"Of course. What could possibly?"

"This kid."

"Corie?" I said. "Corie's okay."

"Uhn," he said, unconvinced. "She sounds like a brat, to tell the truth." To which I insisted no, just smart and young, and he asked what my attraction was. "Do you know?"

I couldn't consider the question without picturing the damage in her eyes and feeling her touch on the back of my hand. "I don't," I said. "Somehow I keep thinking there's something she could tell me if I just knew what to ask. Like she's a witness." And as I spoke, and as I asked myself, *A witness to what?*, another's eyes appeared to me, and the touch I felt was yours. "Or a messenger," I said. "She's like a fortuneteller turned backward."

"A survivor," he guessed.

I nodded. "I see her injury . . ." Then I tailed off, but he picked up the thought and completed it. "And you think she can say what happened . . . You know what, though?" he said. "Everyone's not built that way. Odile is. She was scarred at birth. She was a survivor from day one. But what if your Little One's the opposite? Maybe fate is pulling her, not pushing," he said, and said it was a known phenomenon with political radicals. They might be motivated by some personal or historical injustice, but more often their grievances grew out of no bad history at all. "The hard core, terrorists, you search their pasts and you know what you find? Happy childhoods in Pleasantville." If they were haunted by something, it was a something-in-waiting. Emil christened the syndrome pre-traumatic stress disorder. "What if this disaster in your Little One's eyes is one on the way? Do you really want to be around for that? I wish you weren't mixed up with her, is all, and for purely selfish reasons. I want you around for my sister."

I said I understood, and I held up my palm to take the oath forsaking all competing complications, but he wasn't going to treat the matter blithely. "Swear to me," he insisted.

I heard his earnestness, and without even thinking *But what of the letters we're translating, what of our talks on rue Nin?* I lowered my hand to his arm and squeezed it, a firm, steady grip, sincerity's talons. "I promise."

That relaxed him, and he cheered up a little. "You know that we're twins," he told me, and I said, "No!" — shocked. Close in age, I had guessed, but I hadn't guessed this, and I confessed that I'd thought Odile was somewhat younger. "Sorry," I said, and that got another laugh, this one rueful.

"By twenty minutes," he allowed. They were minutes separating good luck and bad, between making it to the curb and getting caught in traffic, safe or in harm's way. "She got the palsy, and so the blindness and the paralysis," and somehow, as if that weren't enough, the afflicted heart. Odile had had a whole life of health emergencies, he told me. She was handed all the curse in that way — such was her reward for letting him go first — while he received only blessing.

"Like your cancer, for instance," I ventured.

That paused him. "So you know about that." It was his turn to say it. I shrugged: of course. "Willem mentioned it."

"The lymphoma," Emil asserted, to be sure.

I said, "Right." And he said that if you were going to get cancer, "get that one," non-Hodgkin's, hundred percent recovery if you catch it in time, "and they did." He considered it a bullet dodged, and that was blessing enough. His good luck had deepened his debt.

Early in life, he told me, he'd made it one of his blessings to see Odile through her trials. And did so, until this one, when necessity was intervening, and it bothered him that, the way things stood, he couldn't be around to help her navigate this ultimate peril, and it wasn't a matter he would ever leave solely to Willem.

"You two are opposites, that's why," I offered. "Willem's a cutter and you're a diplomat, you prefer the talking cure."

His head shook. "We're not that different," he said. "In that regard. He stabs. I manipulate. We're both in the business of performing an evil to do the world some good. We're like the general: we have to believe that the ends will absolve the means."

"Then maybe you should have more faith in him," I offered.

"Oh, well!" Emil exclaimed. "Hasn't he enough in himself!" He enumerated: Willem's faith in medicine, in his practice, in progress, in his ability to do good, "and to be good, as a consequence." He had the secular man's full faith in reason: rationality was Willem's innocence. Which was exactly why Emil had hired him, he said, "because in the service of those delusions he's made himself into someone who can help me. You see, I can be sure that he'll help me, because you can get a rational man to do anything," there being an excellent and reasonable argument to justify any particular act. It was something else all good diplomats understood, "that there's no such thing as rational morality," and I wish I'd thought to ask him, right there, what all this philosophy had to do with Odile's surgery.

But I didn't, and it wouldn't have mattered anyway, for Emil's graveness had lifted and, with a quaff from the tulip glass, he launched into another of his "toots," about how morality defended on reasoned grounds always came down to self-interest — we should be good to others so they'll be good to us in turn — but that self-interest was at best amoral. "At best. And that's the catch." You can't base morality on amorality, he said. "The formula doesn't add up."

At any rate, for the surgery, he wanted someone who could slough off doubt, someone impervious to hesitation, and that was Willem. But when it came to putting his sister under and observing her journey and escorting her back and welcoming her home, he wanted someone else, an individual who knew the full consequence when something awful happened. Not abstractly and reasonably, but viscerally, and with a searing intimacy. "Someone fallen," he said. "I don't want anyone who has never faced the penalty. I want someone who has, and who's taken it to heart."

One time, after one of her girlhood surgeries, he told me, Odile had hit a snag coming back to consciousness. It wasn't even a big procedure, though major enough to require general anesthesia, and she'd come through all of it fine until the end, when she seemed to be headed for a fate like Mrs. Singleton's. For seven hours after she was wheeled into the recovery room, Odile had lain in a coma, on the bottom of the deep end of the pool, family and doctors huddled around her gurney like pallbearers, her vital signs steady but dire, and Emil only a kid himself, of course, but he thought he would go insane standing there small amid the helpless grownups, knowing his small sister was right beside him but that he couldn't get to her to pull her back out of the dark. And then, mysteriously, the lines on the displays had budged a bit, and the beep of the monitor quickened, and deep inside her, Odile began her ascent.

No wonder the man was terrified. I listened to him describe all this, standing there at the wool-smelling bar in the Chemin Vert on a rainy night in Reims, and the look on his face brought to my mind a patient I'd once had who as he drifted off into his narcosis was overwhelmed by an event from earlier in his life (this so frequently happens), a day when he'd thought he'd lost his teenage son to a canoeing mishap on — what river was it? — the Broad. Canoeing on the French Broad River. The man's expression as he relived those minutes, his son missing beneath the Broad's brown current, was as spooked and stunned as Emil's was now.

That was one thing that occurred to me. And the other — oh, Daniel, may I tell you this? — the other thing I realized, as I took in Emil's tale and held his arm and witnessed his living torment and felt I was inside his skin, his mortal, his survivor's skin, was that for the first time since I loved you, I was falling for someone, for someone else. That I might have a chance with Emil. The clamor of the bar had abated entirely, lifted like a ground fog, and the crowd had fled away and the air was silent as a séance and even his voice, Emil's voice, was far, far away, the air full of light. My little swoon caught me so suddenly that I had to struggle back onto the path, had to swim back into the subject and the moment and get the room to resume again.

"I know what you're saying, though, about Willem," Emil was telling me when I'd made my way there. "He's reliable. He'll do what I tell him or tell me why not. He'll do what he's paid for and do what's professional. And do it very well. And if Odile died, he'd review his procedures and make his improvements, and continue on his way a better doctor. He'd be demanding of himself. But he wouldn't die with her. He's too blameless."

"Blameless?" I asked, but I was really just announcing my return and arrival, using my voice to assure myself I had one.

Emil repeated the word. "Look, Willem thinks that pain is an error to be fixed and that evil is an anomaly, a glitch in the great march of progress, and not something alive inside you that you can touch and feel, and fear. That's not something you know unless you're fallen, unless you've touched it."

"And you have," I challenged him, to hear myself.

His rejoinder was sharp in its swiftness. "You have too."

It was exactly then that the wiry imbecile appeared so close in front of me, stepped between me and Emil, his face peering directly into mine with those lidless, urgent, whistler's eyes, and he reached over with a spastic finger and tapped me on the hand.

PART THREE

XV

BLOOD AND SNOW.
Push, pull. Blood and snow.
Push, pull. Again, I'm writing you — or maybe I should say:
Boo, Daniel! A letter, my love, can you believe? — from Portbou, and if
I've been silent these last couple of days, the *incomunicado* is all self-
imposed, for I had written, of a sudden, all that I could bear to write,
and had to stand at the window awhile to collect my wits and catch
my breath.

I'm like the painter of Emil's old painting, or at least I'm the way
Emil described him: he'd get so overwhelmed by the extreme photographic *presentness* of the lions and tigers he was drawing that mid-
composition and midbrushstroke he would flee from the canvas in
terror and throw open the studio windows to gasp and wheeze until the menace had escaped into the atmosphere and his heart could
quiet down. Never mind that to everyone else, his fanged menagerie
was as toothless-pretty as a string of paper dolls, as my words must
seem to you. With every pen stroke in my effort to depict these events
for you and, through their depiction, to prepare to ask my question,
behind each of these words lies a world of detail that I sometimes
fear I've only imagined and whose imagining I fear I cannot begin to
depict.

The more I try to straighten matters out and arrange them plainly
for you to see, the more things tumble together in my mind, and my
conversation with Sahran gets butchered into bits — Emil saying,
"She sounds like a brat," Emil saying, "The only way to make love last
a lifetime is to cut the lifetime short," Emil saying, "*Haraam* also indicates blood" — and then those bits get enmeshed with all this stray

extraneous flotsam, some canoe trip a patient took with his son on the French Broad River, for Pete's sake, and the relative, or was he, who bequeathed you a clarinet. The French Broad, you know, is in North Carolina, but that's what I mean, the walls cave in. *Let us cross over the river and rest under the shade of the trees.* I've never been to North Carolina. My thoughts lie in rubble, and I find I need you more and more. The great orderly comprehension of things I so wish to present to you is something I think I'll gain only on the day you reveal it back to me.

With all the things Emil and I said to each other and all that we did on our trip that day, with all the happiness it gave my heart, why is it that when I think of it now, the phrase that comes quickest to mind is *blood and snow*? Because that's how the evening ended? It was well into tomorrow when our little excursion got back home to Paris. Our return trip was slowed by another turn in the weather, which hit us before we made it out of Reims, hit us, in fact, before we could even get into the car.

It was pouring when we burst from the door of Le Chemin Vert. We huddled resolutely under our umbrella and raced down the street as though evading a fusillade of rifle fire, Emil's urging arm around my shoulder, the rain pounding mercilessly. And then, halfway down the block, silence, complete and instantaneous. The last raindrop thrummed into the pavement with a snare-drum finality as though someone had twisted the tap and throttled the storm.

The air around us stood erect and glistening and mysterious and empty: anticipating. The wet, washed façades of the square's old buildings, the washed giant ribs of the cathedral, the scrubbed glass domes of the streetlamps dripping slowly onto the wet curbs. *Regardez!* they instructed, and when we looked up — Emil had dipped his umbrella in his astonishment and was scowling at it accusingly — we saw it coming, a high, lace counterpane of snowflakes drifting down so, so slowly, billowing so motionlessly it seemed to suspend in the air forever before the first flakes reached our faces and mobbed us at last with their embrace.

I've never known as exact, or as thorough, or as instant a benediction as that snow. A mere degree had shifted, the sky had slipped a fraction of a Celsius degree and thrown the world from yin to yang, and every threat, dread, inclemency, and darkness was dispelled by the gentlest, most cold and weightless white. We headed back to Paris down a country highway brighter by far than the same one we'd traveled at noon.

The next morning, the snow was my evidence that the night before had happened, and I sped to the window of Emil's bedroom and pulled the drape aside as though the miracle in my imagining could be made real only if corroborated by the other on the ground. How relieved I was to see its accumulation! And how frigid it would be an hour and a half later when we stepped out to make our way through it.

I wouldn't have stepped at all, would have remained quite contentedly beside the red embers in Emil's fireplace, if I weren't drawn by a mission, sparked by the thing that Emil had been meaning to tell me. We were almost done with a late-morning breakfast of day-old croissants and marmalade and espresso set out not in the Sahran family dining room by the Sahran family housekeeper, who was off on account of the weather, but prepared by our helpless selves and consumed beside our self-assembled fire. Emil jumped up and ran off somewhere and I thought he was after more tinder. He came back with a large manila envelope that he dropped into my lap. "I keep forgetting to give you this. I ran down a couple things," he said. "About your Saxe and Landers chaps."

I sprang the metal tabs and extracted the contents, which weren't much, some pages from a dot-matrix computer printer — Bureau of Vital Statistics stuff — and photocopies of several newspaper clippings, evidently, from the tatters and the typeface, very old ones. I went for the obvious first, that being the one with a photograph. It was an article from the paper *Ce Soir*. "Gala to Celebrate Election Victories in Spain," the headline stated, and after a dateline in March of 1936, the story commenced about a "dance and dinner reception to be held by the Iberian Daughters of Marianne and Communards d'Espagne" to commemorate Spain's newly elected government "hosted by the distinguished Carlos Perigord Landers, temporary honorary Spanish consul to the Élysée Palace, at Landers's gracious home in the Seventh Arrond." The consul, it was explained, was a dual citizen of France and Spain, son of an Aranese nobleman and a French heiress who had returned to Madrid last month to confer with members of the incoming administration. "Spain is unified in joy behind the prospect of a new era," he told *Ce Soir*, "when workers and peasants will at last lead their beloved country into the front rank of modern democracies."

It went on full of transformative zeals and halcyon expectancies. The halftone photograph above all this was grainy but distinct and exhibited the figures of a man and woman standing amid a crowd at some public ceremony, seemingly (judging from the looks on their faces) unified in joy. Might the woman be his wife? Though I hadn't pictured Alba quite like this, a square figure draped in daunting black. Her contours suggested a cubist rendition of heroic womanhood, while the man beside her seemed an impressionistic tribute to fin-de-siècle aristocracy, dapper in a double-breasted suit and bow tie and fedora, round-rimmed tortoiseshell spectacles perched on an aquiline nose, the two of them laughing fondly together as a clutch of well-wishers gathers around. Then I read the caption and recalled the woman from my history book, a prominent Communist leader of the Republicans. The caption read, "Consul Landers with La Pasionaria in Barcelona Last spring." I stared at them awhile; the photo called up some distant muddling association that I couldn't quite manage to place, and so I quit trying.

That was the longest of the articles. The shortest was from another paper and whatever ballad the gala piece had crooned, this one spat its data in starkest semaphore. It was a single short paragraph long. Its opening sentence, which was not at all a sentence, was all that served for a headline: "Landers, Carlos P., b. Val d'Aran, 1903, philanthropist and statesman, Monday, at his home in Paris." It went on to mention schools, degrees, and titles, while omitting, along with headline and photo and the Daughters of Marianne, any mention of cause of death.

"It's clearer here," Emil said as I set the obituary aside. He pointed to a line in one of the printouts.

"My Lord," I said. "Do you know how?"

"My guess would be violently," he said.

I inquired with an eyebrow.

"He's an old-world aristocrat," Sahran said, "and aristocrats didn't die of poison if they could help it. Or pills. They preferred to duel with death, not cheat him. And consider the times."

I had, indeed, already considered the times. The obit was dated 1942, not quite six years since the *soirée diplomatique* in Landers's home. I kept to myself my mental image of a set of extraordinary seventh-arrondissement rooms as gracious now as they must have been when they hosted an A-list of Parisian high society on a gay night fifty-five years ago, or as they'd been almost forty-nine years ago, when their resident took his life.

My thoughts swirled upsettingly around this enigma — not for the first time I felt the susurration of a malevolent conspiracy of ghosts — and I said to Sahran, as I rifled quickly through the several sheets to be sure, "Is this all? Didn't you say you'd found the other name?"

He shook his head, apologetic. "Mysterious guy," he said. "There was a legal notice regarding an estate, and this." And he pointed to the picture of La Pasionaria and the long-deceased honorary consul in Barcelona. In minuscule Helvetica in the margin beside the halftone was the "taken by" attribution for the photographer: B. M. Saxe.

I left the house on Île Saint-Louis soon after. Not expelled by any discomfort; just wanting to be elsewhere. For reasons I would comprehend only later, I was pulled quite strongly to another and particular spot. I asked Emil to drop me off at Portbou.

He'd kissed me goodbye and fishtailed off homeward before I realized my error, for the café's window was dark and the door was locked. I cursed Passim's fecklessness — such cowards, these Parisians! In the face of such an increment of snow! And then I realized it was Sunday and that he wouldn't have been open were it daffodil time in the tropics. I sloughed off slushward toward my room.

As I made my way, another place where I might find companionship occurred to me, and I headed for rue Nin. The snow was still falling, but hardly; a few drifting crystals, that was all, the last pretty dwindlings of an uncertain storm. The sky remained gray; the air was crisp. I reached the Wisteria and pressed the button, and the very next moment, or so I thought, I went to press it once again and then realized I had no idea how many moments had passed. My thoughts had fallen into a crevasse and had been arduously climbing their way back out, and how long I'd stood there waiting for them to resurface and waiting for an answering buzz, I couldn't say. I pressed the button again.

How suddenly our fortunes change! The whistler, the imbecile soldier at the bar last night . . . or maybe the whistler hadn't been a soldier when his adventure occurred, I couldn't be sure. His friend was — his friend told us later of serving in the Indochine and fighting at Dien Bien Phu — but the whistler's tale had transpired during an earlier generation of conflict, he may not even have been a man in 'forty-whatever, may have been only an adolescent, a civilian prisoner, perhaps. Emil and I fell silent when he interrupted. Then he placed his finger, the same long finger that had tapped against the scar on my hand, to a scar on the side of his neck, and exactly as though he'd pressed a button, his eyes snapped wide and his story commenced.

He mimed the posture of a man aiming a rifle. Then — snap — he showed me his hands, wrists pressed together as though bound, and then put them behind him and started to run in place, running and grunting and running and running, there by the bar with his hands bound behind him and his wide eyes on mine, and he stumbled forward onto the dance floor and let out a whistle from distended lips and pointed to his side with his finger — *See, it hit me here* — and then ran some more, stumbling but not far. This time the bullet that reached him knocked him bolt upright, stiff as a steeple until his knees buckled, and his terrified mute's howl keened like a dog's, and he placed his finger on the scar on his neck again and gave me the dolorous eye.

So that's what had happened, some morning, afternoon, most of a life ago, to the man in Le Chemin Vert, in a field or a forest or on a road maybe not very far from here, and his whole long existence was suspended from that moment like the canvas of a tent from a tent pole, like a tablecloth lifted with a pinch. For better or worse, his moment had come early; soldier or not, he could hardly have been much older than a boy, and the question that it posed he'd had a lifetime to ask, of himself and of everyone he met, reenacting the seconds over and over for any stranger who came through the door on any rainy winter night who might know the answer at last, who might be the one to tell him what it all had meant. His friend studied the boards of the floor throughout this demonstration, absently, patiently, there was love in that, I thought, and no one else along the bar paid any mind whatsoever, theirs was indifference of a different sort, less personal, more communal, but I could see how that was their way of loving him too. With the passion play concluded, the two old buddies went back to their beers amid their oblivious friends.

Twenty minutes later, the eyes snapped wide with horror and surprise, and, as urgently as before, the whistler stepped over and tapped me again on the hand.

Poor whistler; poor Landers. Poor lucky Landers, his moment had waited till the very end; his question was answered before it could even be expressed. The consul's fall seemed nevertheless spectacular. Its suddenness gave me vertigo. Not because of the disparity on display in the newspaper clippings, between party impresario and posthumous pariah — six years is plenty of time to wear out even the noblest welcome. He just didn't bear the mark of such decline. I'd had a healthy glimpse of the injuries besetting him in 1938 and '39 and '40; they were documented in Alba's letters. Yet her every dire letter gave cause for hope. That Carlos had been ground down seemed implausible. That he'd been struck down struck me as much more likely. But what had been the blow? In what precise moment had despair set its lever?

Again I got no answer from the impassive intercom — Mistress Corie must be out sledding — and I trundled my solitude back around the block, musing on the rooms I wouldn't get to visit today. I was more than half glad about that, to tell the truth, and not because I might otherwise transgress my promise to Emil — oh, but my promise hadn't even occurred to me! It was the rooms. I wasn't sure I could confront them. They were where the suddenness of Landers's death showed up. The disparity between his fortunes and his fortune (he was still so damnably well off when despair got its claws into him) was evidence of a calamity as sudden as the whistler's rifle shot.

He was well off even today, albeit quite thoroughly deceased, and what sort of karmic affront was that, to be outlived by one's dwellings? As though his possessions hadn't needed his presence at all. As though moth and rust had forgone his earthly treasures to corrupt his heaven instead. Not to mention that at least one of these rooms that survived him had been spectator to his demise. And exactly which room was it? I wondered, with a shiver of nausea. And what faint signs of his final act had not been cleaned away? For wouldn't you think a trace of such a history would remain? And whose hand had done the actual cleaning? Alba's, possibly? Released with her daughter from a Majorca prison just in time to bury a husband and father, to sponge his gore out of the carpet and his mayhem off the wall? Or could it have been someone else, the same phantom hand that had tidied up after me?

These patient, traitorous, abiding rooms . . . they awaited a restoration I would sincerely have liked to abet, had I known how. As if I could reformulate the man through the lost-wax method, pour molten bronze into the vacancy left by his life — the empty rooms, the half a correspondence — and see what shape resulted when I broke the mold.

Then mostly, of a sudden, I simply wanted to escape, escape my thoughts and the specter of this petty gentry I'd never met and had no reason to care about, and I was incalculably glad to climb the stairs and turn the key and find myself back in my plain and meager digs. I dropped my purse on the divan and gave a quiet inner boo-hoo of gratitude at being alone again, away from all of it, from glamorous Sahran and nettlesome Corie and all thoughts of Landers and his grisly fate, and I was glad I had a closet door (even one held shut with a shoe) between myself and his gilt-trimmed abattoir.

The ultimate test of my alienation from Wisterian mysteries was the envelope awaiting me on the little table. I'd dropped it there the day before yesterday — it held a couple of Corie's translations that we hadn't had time to go through and which I'd planned to read today. Now I shunned it. Whatever its contents, it wouldn't contain the sound of Corie's voice, but that wasn't my only reservation. I'd had my fill of envelopes, is all. I laid myself down to read a book instead, and then didn't even do that.

Dearest Beloved C.

My resolve had persisted, to my extraordinary credit, I think, most of a late afternoon, but then I caved with a vengeance. It occurred to me that right there on my little yellow table by my little pink elbow might reside a crucial clue to Carlos Landers's story, and at some time approaching cocktail hour (sans cocktail, unhappily: I wouldn't be seeing Emil again until his house party, several nights hence) I tore into the envelope like a prosecutor into a material witness.

Oh, what misery my great good fortune's brought! I am reeling, and cannot write you about those things I said I would, I'm shaken. This morning Pilar comes to me on the patio. She brings news. She's been talking with the other women and already knows, after so brief a time here, what I had not figured out. Again the subject concerns my privileges, the comforts allowed me for Alena's sake, for her! Of course for her. I was angry that the others couldn't understand. And now Pilar tells me that the exact thing which I would most fiercely defend and which makes defensible my special status is the very one that other women here have already defended and lost, their children. Last year, before I came, the government ordered all children removed from the prison. A few were claimed by families. The others were taken by the Sisters and sent to the mainland to the Auxilio Social to be adopted and raised correctly (i.e., Catholic) by proper (Fascist) parents. Imagine the monstrosity! Oh, I have cried! Not just for them. I have bruised my hand trying to batter my fear. How many has this happened to? Pilar doesn't know. The children born here, the mothers never see. Others it seems were older when they were stolen, and no wonder I am looked on with hatred. My precious one doesn't justify my privilege — no, she is, of my privileges, the most unjustifiable, the most unfair. How do I shield her? I always knew Alena would strengthen me. With her beside me I could fight them on anything. Now she is made their pawn and hostage. When they come to ask me, how do I resist, knowing what they are capable of? Privilege here is granted only so that it might be taken away. So it is with the mail. So it is with packages. If you don't go to Mass, they tear up your letters right in front of you. How will they use her? What will they do when she's no longer useful, on that day when either I submit to their wish or they give up on their wishing? The life in the balance isn't mine.

The letter ended there, at page bottom and without a farewell, and the next letter was missing its greeting. Some mishap had corrupted its beginning, so that matters resumed in midthought, though Alba's thoughts here were far more contemplative and calm—bemused, even. After the agony I'd just witnessed, I found her sudden complacency disconcerting, until I realized the pages were merely out of order and surmised that the letter I'd just picked up had preceded the one I'd just read.

I must instruct you (dearest, how dearly I miss instructing you!) not to be alarmed by what I'm about to say. I've been saving up paper to say it, so be patient, too, this may take two posts! Nothing has changed here. I'm well in all regards. We go to Mass, we listen to the radio. Alena grows, & so do I. I've put on two kilos, even with my new vice. Though a cig a week does dull one day's hunger. And yesterday, the most exciting thing! My friend Pilar is here! Who was imprisoned with me in Ventas, she was abused there as badly as I was, and was with us in the field when the planes came and when Maria Xavier was shot, & how overjoyed I am to see her, to have someone I can talk with. So do not worry. If anything it's the doing well that's allowed my darkest thoughts. I find myself in a locked room at the end of a terrible road, where luxuries are permitted me that weren't to Maria Xavier & Julio Luiz and how many others whose executions preceded their trials. I have the luxury of contemplation without need & no one could appreciate that more. Why has my fate been forestalled? Why for me such gifts — silence after thunder, solitude after riots, reflection after massacre, kindness after torture, and ample time to ponder? I'm a different person for that time. It's strange. My motivations shift. Always I have been compelled into things. Did I have any choice but to fight? Now at last I am drawn. As I was drawn toward you, but toward a question. Can you imagine how happy I am to have this question? And to have this place to ask

it? Maybe this is what I wish to confess, that I do not want to be anywhere else right now, even with you, & even free. I am ecstatic for my
confinement, & that I am made to be here. What is, is what's right.
I know this. When they killed Maria Xavier, do you know she spun
twice around from the volley before she hit the ground? I adored her
so & they tore her apart, I loved her as I love you, my darling, & the
wood we used to make her a headstone was stolen by dawn for a
cook fire, even with nothing to cook. I think of her life that is over
and was what it was, and I think of mine that continues and is not
yet what it will have been, I look at the burns that cover my chest like
a pox and I'm left with a mystery I'll pose to you. Know in advance
that I am in earnest in asking, and not out to be clever with imponderables and intangibles, there was nothing intangible about what
happened to Maria Xavier. Here is my issue. Which, in your mind,
would give your life greater significance — to be an infinitesimal (to
the point of not existing!) piece of something lasting and continuing,
or to be a quantifiable (notable) part of something over & closed, of
a history that has ceased to exist & about which nothing is remembered? For those aren't imponderables either. You and I, we will suffer one fate or the other. And all our loves & all our battles & ideals
& beliefs and thoughts & passions will suffer the same alongside us.
For we are human, & our race will either continue on indefinitely, in
which case each of us & our earthly span becomes less than even a
negligible piece of the whole, becomes nothing, zero, meaningless.
Or: Our species will die out, as it seems eager to do, and in that case
your life (mine, Alena's) occupies an actual and measurable stretch
of the entirety of things. For if history lasts ten million years, even a
year of life is a ten-millionth part of it and infinitely more than zero.
We will have mattered, but who will know? And so, this faces us. And
thus does life's adorer yearn for death! In the very long run, we will
be measurable in the universe only when the universe itself becomes
finite. By which I mean: over. Our existence is drawn to the end of
things. Do you see where my mind goes? We will exist on the day
the world ends. Or, I must try to put this better, we will be shown
to have existed at all only at the moment when the universe ceases
to exist. And then your love for me will have been a love, and our
fight for the world will have been a fight, and it all will have meant
something, except . . . except there will be no one left to comprehend

its meaning. Oh, I hear you smiling! You think I have been alone too long, or that this is one of your *frivolités philosophiques* to be served overheated late at night with eau de vie, and if that's how you're inclined, then I hate you but you have my blessing, you can make of this a parlor game, if you wish. Take it to the Tuileries and hand out lances and hold yourself a joust, or maces and cudgels on boulevard Raspail and advertise the Battle of Sèvres-Babylone: Come see our gladiators fight for their favorite insignificance! Extinction! Eternity! Death in Life Everlasting or Death in Eventual Death! And then you can tell me how it went.

Good, then, I've amused you. But I want you to tell me, in the meantime, what all that we've been through means. What did it mean that Maria Xavier came to her murder not by accident but with a purpose, and was murdered for the purpose of her coming, what will you tell me of that? That it was all in the service of mankind and progress & fulfilling our moral responsibility & making this a better world? Then I will truly hate you & you do not have my blessing. For that is the coward's way out, & damn the coward who thinks this is about usefulness, for each time as she spun around Maria's eyes met mine. Or about the greater good and our duty to each other. It cannot be just that. I have an answer for this too (I have been using my time here well), though you will not like my conclusion, for it entails a conversion of sorts. And you see that I have run through my paper, & so you get a stay, but I will continue in the next, poor you, you cannot escape, I love you that much. Forgive my ranting, and Alena begs me to convey her incoherencies. (Like mother . . .)   — A.

And so that was her letter, and I confess by the time I finished it I'd developed a brand-new theory about the root cause of Carlos's suicide, for had I been as desperate for news from a loved one as he must surely have been, and had I received, instead, this — Boo! My love, a lecture! — I too might have felt inclined to stick my tongue in a light socket (were that a method sufficiently violent to confirm my aristocracy).

But as I ate a so-called dinner (a crust and cheese) and then drank by lamplight a second glass of white Bordeaux, my dismissive reaction curdled into serious claustrophobia. Not because of my own narrow confines — the snug room was actually a comfort — but because of the threat closing in on the woman in the letters, a juggernaut of harm. She seemed so adroit, this Alba, so full of light and air. Even her densest ruminations were agile, and her darkest ones irrepressible, and that made her situation the more unbearable to me. Her child made a hostage . . . Alba's dawning comprehension that the monster she faced was implacable, that it would consume her no matter which course she took . . . then eat up her girl, for good measure. Once again, how glad I was for my blessed childlessness! Alba's vulnerability was compounded exponentially by her daughter's, and her peril made doubly perilous.

Triply! For I already knew what Alba could not about her future, that beyond her current trials, something more horrible yet awaited her. The morning's news crashed in on me, belatedly. Oh, Daniel, what a disastrous kinship we shared, me and this woman! Not a year hence, she would know what I do, what it means to be bereft in war, to lose your lover to violence. Of course, what happened to you and what Carlos did were different things, Daniel. Still, I felt smothered, as though Alba's fate had reached through the decades to wrap me in a headlock.

Finally, wanting to escape and animated by a persistent anxiety, and deciding of a sudden that my dinner was disappointing and that one cannot live by day-old bread alone, I hopped up and shod myself and headed out to the ToujoursBonne!, the corner market on the boulevard that would still be open on a snowy Sunday night. I took the long way around and walked one more time down rue Nin. No sign of Corie. On the way home, I veered up Nin again, a dread still roiling in my mind.

"*Haraam* also indicates blood," Emil had said that morning as we sat by his fire discussing the catastrophe that had destroyed the life of Carlos Landers, and he'd gone on a bit about suicide being a cardinal Catholic sin but Islam being the world religion that most explicitly forbids such action. "Suicide is prohibited blood. Maybe we should convert your comrades."

"My . . ."

"Anesthesiologists," he said. "Morrison, Massenet ... Didn't you say your mentor —"

"Maasterlich," I said. There were times when Emil knew too much for my own good, and here was an instance, though what he knew I'd told him — that Maasterlich had killed himself.

"Well, then, so it's true. Your specialty has the highest rate of suicide? You're like the Sweden of occupations," Sahran said. I allowed that some people made that claim, but it wasn't a subject I wished to pursue and I wasn't sure it was very fair to Sweden.

"What could explain this?" he said.

"Don't know," I said. "We also like to fly airplanes."

"Pilot them?"

"Yeah. Own them, fly them. Don't ask me why."

"That's interesting," he said. I wasn't sure it was. He said, "Maybe it's just availability."

"Of planes?" I said.

"Of drugs. You work every day with curares and belladonnas and barbitals, whatever, these exquisite poisons. It makes it too convenient, when things are looking grim, don't you think? An easy solution."

I conceded that that might constitute a factor, though more people attributed the danger to the "availability" of a rollicking good time, for anesthesiologists know what a blissful state our poisons can induce. "'The most delightful physical sensation I ever enjoyed.'" I lowered my chin to my chest to achieve a masculine register.

"Who said that?" Emil asked.

"Old Stonewall," I replied. "Jackson. The general. Before he died. Obviously."

"Ah, back on the battlefield," Emil said. "But he didn't die by his own hand, did he?"

"Shot by his own men," I said. "So I heard. Does that count?" I'd learned a good deal about old Stonewall over the years, and not just at your graveside. In any anesthesiology program, he's a darling of the curriculum, having been a prominent early adopter. I told Emil how the surgeon had administered chloroform and the Confederate general had reported back, "Blessing, blessing, blessing." "Maybe we just want to find out what the big deal is," I said.

Though I didn't really believe that then, and I especially don't now, after all that's happened.

"But that's not what you really believe," Sahran said. Knowing too much.

"Well," I said, "no, since you ask. I think actually the connection with the flying is more to the point, if you want to get right down to it. We're like air traffic controllers; we like running the show, but we miss the travel. We spend our lives sending people off on journeys, and they never tell us where they've been, and it's tempting to want to go and find out for ourselves." I asked him if I'd already told him a story.

I said, "Stop me if I have."

He said, "French Broad? I don't think so."

So I gave it to him as the old man had related it to me as I stood beside his supine form and started the IV in his arm, the old man's story of his trip on the river with his son.

The boy was a teenager, the man had told me, and he'd tried to give him some basic knowledge, before they set out in their canoes, how there were two things to watch out for that could kill you on a river: hydraulics and whirlpools. Both were currents that plunged straight down, and both would suck you under. But to survive, you had to know which was which — that was the trick. If it was a hydraulic, you had to fight like hell, because everything it took in, it smashed against the bottom and held there, and sometimes a body wouldn't be released until it was dynamited loose, and occasionally not even then and you had to wait for the season to change and hope for the current to slack. A whirlpool was the opposite. It would release you after it had sucked you to the bottom, but only then. You couldn't possibly fight it, and if you tried to resist, you could drown yourself with exhaustion. The way to survive a whirlpool was to let it take you and hope you came out the other side.

"Are you with me?" I asked Emil. "So this man, he's on the river, it's a mile-wide stretch of river, apparently, and he comes upon a whirlpool, and he skirts away and avoids it, but then he sees his son's canoe has been caught. It's roaring, it's impossible to yell and be heard. He can see his son fighting, and see him losing the battle and getting pulled to the center, and he sees the boy remember his advice and stop paddling. He lets himself go." The boy reaches the eye of the current and the boat flips upright and everything springs out of it, the boy and his gear, and then they're all swallowed down and they disappear.

And the old man starts his vigil.

Had he told his son right? He'd never actually been through a whirlpool himself. A minute passed. A second minute passed. The old man floats on the surface of the water and counts the seconds and waits. Whirlpools are most often in the middle of the river, like here, and hydraulics are behind an obstacle, a dam or a rock shelf, but not always and you can't always tell from the surface which is which. It's beautiful out, a beautiful day. The kingfishers are skimming the calmer currents for minnows. A damselfly, petroleum iridescent, adopts the old man's canoe prow as its private lily pad; it alights, drifts away, alights again to dry its wings. And then, some time before the third minute ends, a paddle shoots out of the current, high into the air, and soon after it comes the boat, breaching up vertical and collapsing on its side with a splash.

And then, at last, the boy. He's nearly sodden dead. But he'd grabbed enough breath and had managed to hold it, and he clutches the side of the waterlogged canoe and gasps and pukes while the old man paddles down to him. "When the man — he was an old river guide and a hard father — reached his son's side, he said to his son, 'You all right, boy?'

"And his son wheezes, 'Yes.'

"And the old man said, 'Well, then, gather up your gear and let's go.'"

That was the story, and I told it to Emil in such detail because I'd rehearsed it to my lonesome self so many, many times over the years, imagining into it damselflies and kingfishers. And especially, I'd rehearsed the way the old man ended it, with his stone-cold stoicism concealing the wreckage inside of him, and all that that stoicness implied — love withheld, restrained, but felt — that he'd then tried to ask me about. The only reaction I'd ever had on finishing telling the tale to myself was silence in my mute-stunned mind, and that's what Emil gave it now, a long, long silence, staring straight at me, and I wondered if he was thinking of young Odile and of standing by her bedside, waiting for her to surface. He said, "That's a mighty elaborate story for someone to tell as he's going under."

"He was fighting it," I said. "And then he quit fighting. Do you know what he said as he let go? He said, 'Now I'll know where my boy went.'"

"Really!"

"Because his son could never tell him, you see. And I think maybe that's what Maasterlich was doing. I don't think he meant to die. I think he meant to come back. It's just that he'd sent all these people away—that's what we do. And he wanted to go where he'd sent them."

Emil nodded and stared at the fire. "Couldn't he just get operated on for something or other? Then he'd know."

"Maybe," I said. "I have, and I know it only makes the mystery worse. You still don't know the answer when you wake up, and it makes you want to go again, and deeper."

"What if," Emil said, and he continued on with his speculations, but my mind had slipped the scene and fastened somewhere else, on another what-if he'd uttered the day before. "What if she thinks she's figured it out, that the only way to make love last a lifetime is to cut the lifetime short?" That's what he'd asked. "The problem's real," he'd said as we sat in the Citroën headed to Reims and imagined Corie's heartbreak, "but the solution's a sin." That's what my fallen Muslim said: suicide was a cardinal Muslim sin.

And maybe that was the thought—the conflation of Corie and suicide—that had me marching nervously past the Wisteria for the third time today, like a sentry on endless duty. Approaching the building on my way back from the market, I was elated at what I saw—a light was burning in the top-floor window. She'd returned! For the nth-plus-one time, I pressed the buzzer.

Exactly as on the nth, I got no answer. Not the one I was listening for, anyway, though I quickly received another kind, inaudible. Above me, the light went dark.

I turned in dismay. A slap! Surely Corie must know who it was calling at this late hour, she could easily see me from the window, did she look, and did she think I wouldn't notice the rebuff? Was she watching now, as I beat a stung retreat? My way back home was a long crooked grumble of chagrin—what had I been thinking, presuming such informality?—and I added to the mystery of the curtness of the darkened window the odd little detail I'd glimpsed through the fence as I slunk from the site. There, in the snow in the blue-white evening, was something so small in its consequence that I was a couple blocks away before I considered what it implied: two sets of boot prints traversing the Wisteria's yard, one set pushing off into its darkest corner, and the other coming back.

The other coming back. "I do wonder," Emil had said as we'd come across town that morning—he'd been pensive and preoccupied since our talk by the fire—"who took the longer journey. That day, I mean. Really, who had more happen to him? The boy struggling all the way to the bottom of the river and back? Or the old man floating above him, the father with nothing to do but drift and wait and hope that his son survived? Did he say more? Afterward?"

"No," I answered, and I would have preferred to let that be all I said. But Emil persisted.

"Didn't you talk to him after?" he asked.

I shook my head and gave him the truth of it. "It was unfortunate," I said, stoic. "It was a risky procedure. He knew that going in."

XVI

T HE USUAL?" PASSIM ASKED when I took my seat the following morning, and he brought me my customary espresso
and customary newspaper, along with something I hadn't expected and didn't want, marked with the customary *confidentiel*. To
my anticipated question, he proffered his customary response to any
catastrophe survivable or dire: he shrugged.

"Saturday," he said.

Inside the package, along with another translation, was a note.
Away, back midweek. XOX, Cor.

Cor? XOX? I felt another light go out. Was I to be punished for one
day of liberty with Sahran? The thought inflicted its own reprisal: no,
I realized, because Corie would not have minded my absence the way
I minded hers. But, anyway, this note was from two days ago. And
then the delayed alarm finally seeped through the cotton of self-pity:
Saturday? Who, then, just last night had turned off the light in the
window?

Jeko arrived with my customary pastry and lingered conspicuously
until I met his eye. "Jersey," he said meaningfully, and cast a conspiratorial nod through the window, as though a snowstorm blanketing
half a continent was just a little secret *entre nous*. I paid him no mind,
as I paid no mind to the war news in the newspaper or the blazing
of wing guns from the far side of the room or the smoke from the Gitanes wafting from the zinc or, frankly, to the taste of famous pastry. I
was at home in Portbou; I no longer noticed it. "He and this room enjoyed quite a history," Passim had said of Saxe the day I first stepped
through the door, and now I marveled how quickly in a place of basic,
daily routines history could establish itself. His favorite table was al-

ready mine, the place where my customary was brought to me, and where any novelty trespassed. Some clever historian applying the lost-wax method might already derive my shape (*quelle horreur*) from the routines I followed here.

That's what set me up to be so startled by Café Portbou on this day. I'd assumed that anyplace where I'd made myself so comfortable must be as thoroughly known to me as I to it, an assumption, it turns out, that was easy to refute. The refutation was hiding in plain sight. It confronted me when I'd finished my espresso and was contemplating ordering a second one to aid my deliberations over whether to read the new letter. To help me deliberate, in turn, over whether to order the espresso, I decided to visit the lavatory.

Sometimes a trip to the restroom advances one's deliberations and sometimes not, but it always nicely postpones the moment of decision, so off I went, and I was returning down the stub of a hallway, shouldering one wall to avoid being strafed from the other, when I saw it. Saw it without seeing it, from the corner of my attention. I'd passed it fully before the snare drew tight, just as I had passed it more than a dozen times on previous deliberative visits without being seized, without noticing anything at all, but this time I stopped. I didn't turn, not right away. Coincidence had ambushed me too often in recent days for me to feel that time and chance were on my side. Whatever was approaching, I wanted a stance to handle it, especially if what I'd just glimpsed turned out to be true. But what sort of stance protects you against a photograph?

I took a step backward and turned to face the image, the image formerly known to me as "Consul Landers with La Pasionaria in Barcelona Last spring," though this print had no caption or credit and was, like all the other photos on the photo wall, in a simple black wooden frame. I stared at it a long while before I sensed Passim's shadow.

"Would you like some light?" he asked.

"That would be nice," I said, and wherever the switch was hidden, the switch was thrown. The effect of Passim's Prometheanism was like drawing aside the drapes and exposing the world, or like turning on the light behind an x-ray panel. There were maybe thirty photographs. Together, they offered a time-lapse vision of an era and place and peoples, those being the peoples of Paris and northern Spain in the era before the big war. The prints bore no insincere autographs, and the faces here weren't those of petty starlets of the sort I had expected — Brigitte Bardot–wannabe types — save for one grand and unmistakable starlet, Ernest Hemingway. He was standing with a clutch of other men, all dressed for the heat in sandals and light shirts, short scarves knotted around their necks and a couple of them carrying guns, at the brink of a bomb crater in the middle of a city street. The party stood in a line facing the camera, somewhat proudly, as though they'd gone out crater hunting and had bagged themselves a big one.

That identification loosed a host of others, as I have since returned to study those photos with a more ambitious eye. Over the weeks, I dislodged photographer after writer after writer after photographer after poet (Tina Modotti, Arthur Koestler, André Gide, and Gerda Taro with her arm around Pablo Neruda), a Who's Who *des artistes du moment,* but on this day and at first glance, I spotted only *vedette* Hemingway and (writer) André Malraux, Malraux conspiring with a group of pals at a table littered with a day's worth of uncleared espresso cups and wineglasses and cigarettes stubbed out in overflowing saucers.

They were nice photos, friendly, well framed, most of them portraits but none of them posed beyond the moment of looking up from whatever battle was being fought or bottle emptied or table pounded in whatever café. I found the camaraderie of the subjects disorienting, as though it leaped from frame to frame, as though the individual photographs were discrete rooms in one great rolling party, as though the comfort of these people with one another extended to encompass me, and wasn't that table where Malraux malingered in some familiar spot? I cast a déjà vu behind me — no, the tables had been changed out, but yes, there was the very window, exactly as it was in its reflection on the wall. Malraux in Portbou! Passim's returning shadow was distinct this time, and doubled, its edges sharp.

"Do you know these people?" I asked him.

"Not really" was the answer. "If my father were here, he could tell you everyone," he said, the father who had owned Portbou before him and who was, of course, dead. "No, no, he's still alive," Passim protested, and explained that he was in retirement back in Algiers.

He offered, with a wandering finger, "Somewhere here, your Papa Ernest."

"And them?" I indicated the "Barcelona Last spring" portrait.

"She's famous too," he said.

And the man? Passim shrugged. "Friend of Byron's." He swept his arm to indicate the entire wall. "All friends of Byron's. I don't know what to do with them. I haven't had the heart to take them down."

So that was it. The chronology I viewed was double-fold: a scattershot history of the people portrayed, and a somewhat more continuous one of the man who'd done the portraying, the faceless face behind the lens, and I was reminded of the invisible omnipresence that photographers share with other gods, the unseen composers of every scene. This particular deity was my humble Portbou predecessor, the man whose café seat I had made my own and whose apartment I now lived in but whose life and art, so visible so close by, I had remained resolutely oblivious to.

His life and art, and "all his friends." Including Landers, whom I spotted in several other photos beyond the first one. Landers giving a raised-fist salute to a squad of marching militiamen; Landers at a diplomatic reception, a sash with medals draped across his tuxedo; Landers with a woman in a starched white smock and cap (La Compasionaria?) beside the hospital cot of a heavily bandaged smiling man, ranks of similarly bandaged, similarly cot-bound men diminishing into the background. And again, with the same woman lithe in a smart sleek dress, you can see she is dark-eyed and willowy, in a smart café by the sleek dark sea, both of them relaxed and elegant and young, and the two of them again at a Paris curbside, Landers toking on an evil-looking cheroot in the front seat of an open cabriolet driven by a man I didn't recognize at first until I discerned his eventual face through the mask of beauty and youth.

"Would you mind?" I asked Passim.

Chrysanthemums had given way to hothouse dahlias in the desk vase, but the familiar dry voices were still heavy at it, consumed in their pleasant, incessant, chiding quarrel, and when Madame Secretary disappeared down the hall, I stepped into the alcove to pay my respects. "I should have listened to you," I whispered, sincere, but the trio burbled on unperturbed by flattery. I understood their urgent advice no better than before. Then we broke off, for Madame was returning. Rouchard dragged along in her wake. He was carrying the photograph.

"I'm complimented," he said.

"I meant to come by earlier," I apologized.

"That you recognized me, I mean." The lawyer was as amiable as his finches were litigious. He invited me into his office down the hall, a burrow at the end of a book-lined tunnel whose conceit of red-leather luxury had been swamped by a mudslide of files and books and papers. Rouchard put down the photograph and hoisted a cardboard box to clear a chair for me — it must have been a while since a client had stuck around long enough to sit — and then resumed talking before he located anywhere to drop it. "Portbou, huh," he said, holding the box. "You've enlisted!"

Back in the day, he explained, the café had been one of several Parisian bistros that served as nocturnal mustering stations for the volunteers arriving from Britain and elsewhere to fight with the International Brigades in the cause of Republican Spain. The young men and women — well, mostly young, and almost all men — had been given their marching orders there, before boarding trains for the south of France and making their night trek over the Pyrenees to get to Albacete. "A highly illegal undertaking," Rouchard offered, over the box.

"They didn't accept me," I joked.

"Good," he said. "It wasn't a trip that everyone returned from."

At that moment, my ankle experienced a startling sensory drenching, as though splashed by a warm, rough wave. "Oh!" I yelled, and kicked the air as involuntarily as though struck by a general practitioner.

"Daisy!" Rouchard scolded, and I looked down at the pink nose of the culprit — Daisy, evidently — the dog beneath my chair.

"Hi, Daisy," I said, and propped both feet out of licking range. "And you?" I said to Rouchard. I was done with the small talk, but I wanted to know.

He'd never once been in Portbou, he said, "because I was never in the Brigades, you see. I wasn't a Communist. I was just a little, lost, dreamy anarcho-syndicalist who found himself in Spain."

"Why didn't you tell me you knew Byron Saxe?" I said.

In honor of the gravity of the question, Rouchard seemed resolved to jettison his cardboard burden. He looked about him and, absent other options, set the box in his own leather chair and came back around to perch on the edge of his desk. "Because I didn't know him well enough to offer you any insight, anything pertinent to his will," he said, picking up the photograph again. "I knew him well enough for him to take my picture, apparently, but that was about it. Saxe was, as you say, a friend of a friend."

"Carlos Landers."

"Ah, you know the name," he said. "Yes, Carlos, to be sure." And so began his account of an association that had started when he and Landers were students together in Sciences Po and that blossomed later as they both became active in politics, unfortunately on what would be the losing side in the coming era, though decidedly "on the right side of history." For a few glittering years, until Generalissimo Francisco Franco kicked off a decade-long European war for Aryan racial supremacy by invading white and Catholic Spain with Moorish legions of his Army of Africa, airlifted out of Spanish Morocco by Adolf Hitler's planes, and before leftist fratricide had turned Barcelona into a Russian nesting doll of civil war within civil war, the politics had remained exciting, fruitful, optimistic, even glamorous in an intellectual sort of way, and the glamorous Parisian apogee had been the group that gathered around the wealthy and revolutionary Landers couple. That was the community and family into which young Byron Saxe had parachuted one day in April of 1933.

"I don't remember him all that well, but even so I can tell you precisely when he arrived," Rouchard said. "Right after the Reichstag fire" in Berlin, when a Jewish merchant from Franconia decided it was time to get his son out of Germany and to safety in Paris and had arranged to purchase a pied-à-terre from Landers.

"Carlos's apartment, you see, it was just around the corner from you, and I must tell you that it was very grand, ostentatious, really, I always thought." It had been built as the Paris home-away-from-home for a Budapest goods trader eager to be taken for an Austro-Hungarian count, but afterward it belonged to the Landers family, and Herr Saxe knew them somehow and he and the family reached an agreement, "and they basically turned one of the maids' quarters into a separate little apartment, do you see? It was rustic, but it was only for the time being."

I saw well enough, because I'd seen more than he knew.

Rouchard remembered Saxe as barely more than a teenager when he arrived, in his midtwenties, maybe, and immediately he became part of the set and was adopted as a brother by Carlos and Alba. "Carlos, in particular. I think they were very close." The two resembled each other: same build, same vitality. Byron was often mistaken for Carlos's younger brother. "And maybe Carlos mistook him for that himself." He bought the boy a camera, "this beautiful art-deco Rolleicord," and wherever Carlos and Alba traveled, Byron traveled with them, the Rollei draped around his neck on a harness-leather strap. "And I think it was one of those things — they were friends from the start and the boy lived in his room and made his photographs," and then the war came, and when they saw it coming ("And of course it was impossible to miss, unless you were running England"),they sealed up Byron's room to serve as a sort of hideaway.

"A sensible caution," Rouchard said. Carlos was prominent, and the apartment's grandeur was renowned. "There was no telling what devil might stop in, and did." The Hôtel Lutetia, only blocks away, which before the war had been a favorite refuge for Jewish visitors, became a headquarters of the Nazi intelligence services, convenient to the prison on rue du Cherche-Midi. "In '42," he said (meaning after Carlos's death — the evasion was obvious), the apartment was requisitioned by the occupiers. "Some high Nazi lived there. I'm sure it was destroyed. I wasn't here, by the way," because Rouchard by then had found himself in Gurs, a detention camp in southern France, and later, along with a lot of other Republican fighters, in Mauthausen, where most of them succumbed to starvation or typhus or exhaustion or lead but where he survived to greet the liberation.

"And do you know where they brought me to be repatriated into my beloved France?" Rouchard asked, and then he answered himself: to the Allies' relocation authority, "in the Hôtel Lutetia!"

It pleased him very much, I could tell, how things changed and changed and changed again, reversing valence at the drop of a hat, since they'd changed at last for the best. "But Saxe," he said, getting back to the subject. "I'd assumed Byron perished. I'm sure all his family were murdered. I did hear he'd taken a journey, that he'd tried to escape and was captured. I thought that was it. Kaput. Then, last month, he summons me to his bedside. I was astonished to see him, I can assure you."

Astonished and moved. Rouchard was still coming to grips with the sorrow of it all, this ghost so firmly lodged in the past that it haunted still the same old unchanged room. "You noticed the peephole, I imagine," he said. There was so much to untangle, and he was making good progress with the estate, still had some of Saxe's instructions to fulfill, leads to run down. Among them the name of a lawyer in Geneva who might have some key to the title search, a tangled affair, as any legal history that coincided with the war years tended to be; incredibly tangled.

A word leaped at me from across the city, off an envelope of blue with a Geneva address. "Barayón?" I said, the name of Alba and Carlos's Swiss intermediary. I was getting a bit too good with the crazy toss.

"Yes! Well!" Rouchard answered. I think it was the first time I'd surprised him. "Well, Corail Barayón's no longer alive, but his firm exists, and it seems they have a file."

"Worth a trip?" I asked, a Socratic nudge.

"Booked!" he said, triumphant at being half a step ahead. "Leave tonight. Back Thursday. We should talk before the weekend, do you agree?"

He studied the photograph again before handing it back to me, stroking its borders, lost in a reverie of touch. "They were lovely people, you see," he said. "The loveliest couple of a lovely moment. Not a long moment, *malheureusement,* and it was a shame it had to end."

He caught my astonishment. "You didn't know?" he said. "Why, yes, that's her. That's me, there, and that's Carlos with his cigar, he was being terribly *méchant,* I remember the day. And there's Alba, dear, intense, brilliant, passionate Alba. How she glowed!

"I thought you knew."

XVII

I WAS DETERMINED TO make the following day a restorative one. I deserved it, was the thing. If for no other reason than because of what I'd exposed myself to on my way to see Rouchard and show him the photograph: I'd had another rendezvous with Willem. Our confrontation unsettled me. From that and much else, I wished the time to rejuvenate. I thought I'd revive the formula I'd envisioned when I'd imagined myself in Paris: one part anesthesiologist to nine parts tourist. The one part was an appointment I'd set up to visit Odile in the *banlieue,* to perform my pre-op courtesy call, check for last-minute problems and anxieties, dispense advice, that sort of thing. Not everyone does it, even in the hospital. It's more to calm my own nerves than those of anyone else and to keep my profession a human, not merely technical, one. Willem had told me to be prepared, that a possible donor was anticipated (I imagined someone on a ventilator awaiting an order to withdraw life support) and that unless things changed (as they frequently do) or fell through (ditto), the operation could very well be next week.

We'd met again in Le Faux Henry, Willem and I. If he'd picked the place to reinstate our vanished camaraderie — hadn't we argued more civilly here than anywhere since? — the ambiance let him down. What a difference the weeks had made! The yard chairs were folded away, and the patio, absent its sun worshippers, had the cracked desolation of an abandoned swimming pool. Willem was waiting for me in the curtained vestibule, his eyes wary and his expression bruised behind the smile. His welcome was efficient, a quick hug before we marched off to our table, a perfunctory patting of shoulders. His cheer blew through me like a desert wind.

"Well, I hear you've been having fun," he said, a tiding so oddly accusatory I felt a "Yes" would be a confession and didn't respond at all. He ordered a bottle of sparkling water and told me to go ahead and get whatever lunch I wished, that he'd had a late breakfast. "Thought we should touch base one last time," he said, "before the surgery." Was there anything I needed to talk over?

"Such as?" I asked.

"You've expressed some concerns," he said, dryly. "At times."

"I think we've got them ironed out," I assured him, adding, dryly, "It helped to find out who the patient was."

"The matter was delicate," Willem stated.

"Meaning you didn't want to tell me I was putting a heart into a blind woman in a wheelchair. I agree. She's not the most obvious candidate, Odile. On paper."

He said, "It was decided it would be better if you met her first in person."

"Precisely what I asked for, as I recall." I felt my exasperation rising, all this insipid thrust and parry, padded and masked with courtesy. "And by chance," I said, "it's precisely what happened."

Willem, vehemently: "Nothing in *his* world happens by chance!" The venom in the words was more than a taint, was enough to choke the speaker. He sputtered before continuing, "Well, Emil's not easy, is the thing, Tilde. That's all."

"He's a perfectly nice man," I said.

"He can be," Willem said. "He can. And he can also be very determined. Overwhelming, in fact, I'd say. And don't think for a moment he'll let what he loves stand in the way of what he wants."

If I sensed a warning, I had no idea what he was warning me of or what he was trying to imply. I knew only that I didn't wish to hear any more about it. I cut him off with a not-so-secret secret smile. "Will," I said. "You've known Emil a long time, but I may know some things you don't."

"I'm quite sure that you do!" he snapped. We were moving to a place beyond the courtesies, at least, and the first thing I saw there astonished me. Despite my lifetime of Willem experience and all my years of Willem analysis, it hadn't occurred to me where Willem's jealousy resided, that he might be desirous not of my esteem and my affection, but of Emil's. Now I saw it clearly for what it was, and saw myself as he perceived me: the home wrecker stealing Emil's (lucrative) attentions, stepping between longtime partners. Little wonder he'd like to pry us apart.

"Just remember who's leading this team," Willem finished, and I saw I'd sideswiped his professional preeminence too. "And remember who we're here for. The patient. That's all. No one else."

The bitterness of the conversation lingered in my mind the following morning as I headed to the *banlieue* to see no one else but Odile.

Drôlet and I had arranged to meet at Portbou. I wanted to stop in and return Passim's photograph. I'd spent much of the night looking at it, looking at Carlos and Alba, imagining their brilliant lives by my dim lamplight, but now I wanted them back among their comrades, in their rightful place on their rightful wall, and so I arrived at the café a few minutes early with my absurdly burdened bag burdened all the more. In with all the usual kit, the passport and ibuprofen and hand cream and wallet and powder and brush, et cetera ad absurdum, was a stethoscope and a blood pressure cuff, an extra pair of light shoes so I could ditch my boots in the car — and a wood-and-glass-framed eight-by-ten photograph still a bit dusty with café dust and aromatic of fry grease and cigarette smoke and smeared with the fingerprints of recent adulation. I didn't think to ask (as if there were time) if that's how the courier identified me, by the morbid obesity of my handbag.

"Madame Anselm?" he asked. He was a young man, and he stepped across the sidewalk to intercept me before I could gain the sanctuary of Portbou's steps. "Are you Madame Anselm?"

"Yes." (Imagination fails me at crucial moments.)

He had a message, he said. Could I come immediately? "You must help her," he blurted, back-dancing in front of me, and he handed me a folded scrap of paper.

Drôlet was already waiting, of course, had stepped out of the Mercedes to receive me and he rushed to the curb to intercede, but the boy took off at a brisk clip. We watched him glance back at the end of the block and resume a casual gait and round the corner. "Do you know where this is?" I asked. The name on the note was not that of a court or jail, but a hospital. Drôlet's eyes were elsewhere, on the other item the boy had handed me, by way of credential, obviously, and I deemed it to be a nice touch, though Drôlet was clearly dubious: the brown bandanna.

And that's how it came to pass that when I arrived at the lycée my opening question for Odile was not about her health, as I'd intended, but the welfare of somebody else. Frankly, I was thankful that Odile couldn't see the stranger I introduced her to, for the girl who arrived on Drôlet's arm was a pitiful, beaten, waifish mess, her tresses straying upward in tense red spirals like the feathers of some exotic sea coral, my overcoat covering her hospital slip, her feet afloat in my gum boots.

"She rescued me," Corie exulted sullenly to Odile, her voice a rasping, drugged whisper, but I wasn't sure, I wasn't sure. The line between savior and impostor, by that time, had grown too impossibly thin.

The hospital was mid-city, a gritty old relic of a charity ward that seemed to me, on entering, closer to my notion of a French colonial prison than to anyone's idea of a modern medical facility. The receptionist at the *guichet* was harried and overwhelmed, the admitting nurse outnumbered. She guarded the cosmic boundary between order and chaos, but before her, chaos was all she surveyed.

"I'm here to see a patient," I said when the approximation of a queue had nudged me to its fore, and she flipped through her ledger to locate the name.

"No visitors," she said with finality, that French finality that is more quintessentially French than anything else could ever be. "Security," she said, and held her finger at the ledger line for me to relish. When she was satisfied she'd rubbed it in sufficiently, she slammed the book closed. I deemed that a nice touch too, and I reminded myself: When there's nothing left to do, there's no risk in a chance.

"I'm not a visitor," I told her, with a little New York persistence. I fished in my purse and found my laminated hospital ID on its neck chain, the one that Mahlev had given me. "I'm a visiting doctor." And to get past the public issue and negotiate with the private one (I couldn't quell the childish thought that Sahran would be proud of me), I held the ID up a little too close to her nose, so that she had to lean back to focus. "Consulting."

"With..."

"Dr. Ulmann," I said. She should never have rubbed my nose in that ledger entry.

I watched her warring impulses: Her imperious desire to inspect my credentials tussled with her proud refusal to be in any way subservient to my imperious demand that she inspect my credentials. She was a pro; she played it down the middle. Maybe she took in *anesthésiste* and the name of the unknown hospital, or maybe just photo and filigree; whatever, I could hear the pace of decision — challenge or not? — and it lasted as long as the silence lasts between snowfall and downpour when you're standing beside a cathedral at night in Reims, and then the verdict arrived and she said, "Orthopedics, third floor," and handed me a visitor's sticker.

So far, so good, I thought as I walked toward the elevators. I didn't usually do things like this, was the truth. If I'd planned it, I could never have pulled it off. The forethought would have registered on my face. Receptionists at public hospitals are the reigning facial code breakers. They have to be. A stranger walks up to say that he's stubbed his tibia or misplaced his sick mother, and the nurse has a third of an eyeblink to diagnose his character and motives and condition: Stroke? Shock? Deranged? Hostile, and if so, to a particular patient or to doctors in general? Munchausen? By proxy? Out-and-out kook? Or just needs a restroom? So I was certain she'd see right through me. And what she had seen was a harried and borderline-irritated physician who'd had other and nicer plans for her day before an unexpected duty call added a troublesome patient to her rounds. What she'd seen was a hundred percent correct, and the correct answer to what she'd seen was "Orthopedics, third floor," and I thought, *So far, so good,* and then, as I got into the elevator, I thought, *Now comes the rest.*

And as I pressed the button: *Pray it's a whirlpool.*

I took the elevator not to the third floor but the seventh, which didn't have an orthopedics office but seemed like it might hold the room whose number had been listed on the ledger page: 7134. The

doors opened onto a corridor, not a ward with a reception desk—
that was handy—and I followed the arrows around a corner to another corner and then caught sight of my goal.

It was the right place, all right. A policeman sat in a chair at the
end of the hall, engrossed in a newspaper, and I didn't turn down the
corridor but kept on going straight. A few corners later I found what
I was looking for, another bank of elevators. I wanted the one that
didn't stop in the lobby, the one marked *Accès Professionnel.* I pulled
off my visitor sticker and hung the ID Mahlev had given me around
my neck and then reached into my bag and pulled out the badge for
my teaching hospital and hung that around my neck also, and to be
sure I was adequately lei'd and garlanded, I threw on my stethoscope
too. In for a dime.

There were several people in the lift, and we ascended *ensemble,*
stopping at floors to take on or disgorge. It was one of those padded
garage-sized elevators with stainless-steel doors back and front, and
when we got to the top I let everyone else get off and stayed on for the
descent. I had to ride up and down twice before I got what I hoped
for. The doors opened and two orderlies steered in a gurney with an
elderly woman on it, her gray head swiveling on the pillow, tubes in
her hand, hooked up for her pre-op.

They pressed a button for a basement floor and when we got there
I held the door ajar while they rolled her out and then I tagged along.
Thank God I'd decided (at the last minute too) on humble attire today, on account of the snow. A dress would stand out in these precincts, these precincts being a surgical ward, what sort of surgery I
didn't know or care. What I did know was that just inside the swinging door would be a canister of soiled, discarded scrubs, and indeed
there was, along with something better. Set on a shelf above the canister were boxes of fresh green scrub hats and facemasks and shoe
covers, and I grabbed what I needed and headed back to the elevator.
By the time I reached floor seven I was in my *doctoresse* camouflage, a
facemask tied loosely around my neck and flopping open against my
chest. It wouldn't fool a doctor—scrubs and a purse?—but it wasn't
a doctor I was out to fool. If a doctor had been guarding the hall, I'd
have gone with a dime-store sheriff's star.

I was as prepped as I could be for my performance when happenstance volunteered a grace note. An orderly was coming down the hallway. "Excuse me," I said and inquired if he'd left the wheelchair I'd ordered in 7134. *Non,* he replied, and I told him, Oh, darn, we need it immediately, could he bring one *tout de suite, merci bien,* and I bustled on before he could claim to be busy. Then I reached the guard.

He was young and bored and professionally suspicious, but being professional, his suspicions were targeted, and I didn't look like anyone he had prepared himself to fear. I knew better than to breeze on by. I asked him how his day was going and if the natives were restless and such — I'm not sure what I came up with — before I asked about Dr. Ulmann. He said Dr. Ulmann wasn't in, and I pursed my lips a bit to express my mild professional disapproval and asked after another couple doctors whose names I just made up, and he hadn't seen them either. I then pulled out Corie's chart — actually, it was Odile's chart on its clipboard — and with a weary sigh and an air of studied distraction, I edged on past. The policeman was monitoring three or four rooms; I saw 7134 and turned into it.

There were two patients inside: a snoring woman in the first bed and Corie, lying by the window, her back to the door. I went around and paused long enough to get a good look before touching her shoulder to wake her. Her appearance shocked me. Her cheek was bruised yellow and violet and she had an abrasion on her forehead. A cut on her temple had bled into her hair, red on red, coagulated into stringy, clotted brown. The blood had not been cleaned away, nor had anything been treated that I could tell. Her lips were chapped from dehydration, and the knuckles on the hand on the hospital blanket looked as though they'd picked a fight with a cheese grater, but I was elated that I didn't see casts or, worse, a traction sling — the invoking of orthopedics had given me a scare. She should have been receiving fluids, but here, too, I was thankful for the neglect. She had no IVs or catheters, wasn't tied down like Gulliver with ropes of polyethylene. I shook her, and before she could even register who this new person was, I demanded, "Where are you hurt?"

She pointed to her ribs, and I winced. *Aïe.* Careful movement. This could require some time.

"You've been x-rayed?" I asked and she knew who I was by now because she looked at me dumb with wonder and shook her head no. Clearly, they had her doped up a bit.

Astonishing, I thought, about the x-rays, but I said, "Good," and told her, "We're doing that now. Do you have any possessions here, or identification? Anything personal?"

"Of course not," she said.

"Clothes?"

"In the cabinet."

"Leave them." I heard a little commotion outside and I went out into the corridor to redeem the orderly with the wheelchair. The guard was getting antsy; the appearance of a conveyance with wheels was enough to start making him nervous, and he'd stood up. He looked down at me from the crumbling cusp of suspicion and opened his mouth to frame what would have become a challenge if I'd allowed him sufficient time.

"Can you give us a hand, Officer?" I asked.

The request had the happy effect of insulting two professional prides with one blow. The cop's irritation that he might actually have to do something distracted him from his suspicions even as the orderly objected, "*Non, non! Docteur,* it's not a problem. Where does she have to go?"

"X-ray," I said. "Be careful with her ribs," and I stayed with the guard to sign Corie out for transit — thank heavens, doctors worldwide are known for illegible signatures — while the orderly went in to collect the goods. By the time the elevator doors opened at the emergency entrance level, the helpful orderly had been dismissed, and my badges and stethoscope were safely stashed in the bowels of my bag, along with my purloined scrubs, and Corie and I hightailed it sedately out to the curb, where I'd instructed Drôlet to wait for us.

Odile had told me to meet her in the lycée's nurse's office, a functional little room outfitted nicely with the rudiments — tongue depressors, cotton balls, half-bath with spritz shower. It was unequipped in one regard, to my relief — there was no school nurse on duty today, thank God. Then I realized who the school's nurse was: Odile. I soon saw why. Despite the fact that she couldn't actually see her visitor's dilapidated condition, Odile didn't hesitate for an instant. She fled to Corie like a magnet to steel and commenced her mending immediately. I'd imagined this hour ahead of time as a ritual establishment of our respective roles: mine as the doctor, Odile's as the patient. Now everything was getting all swiveled up. Odile became the room's attending physician, and among the miracles of the miraculous day was the sure insightfulness of her sightless ministrations. Her hand went straight to the bloodied temple as though drawn by the heat of the wound, and her grunt of dismay when she found that gash wasn't one of surprise but of disgust at suspicions confirmed. This nun, it turned out, wasn't so cloistered from the world's ways.

She appointed me her sous-nurse — Get me hydrogen peroxide; get me the gauze — and cleaned and bound Corie's hurts and searched her over with a blizzard of squeezes and pinches, arms lifted and knees twisted, a tactical reconnaissance for signs of further damage. She pushed her into the half-bath to rinse off, then zipped from the room and returned with a change of clothes: a one-size-fits-the-whole-Arab-world abaya and a brightly colored hijab. She combed out Corie's matted hair and patted the headscarf into place — it nicely hid the bandage she'd wrapped around Corie's skull to keep the gauze tight to her temple — and said to her, "There. Now you're one of mine."

We were all, in truth, indubitably hers, for that afternoon and into the evening (I'd dismissed Drôlet until a late hour). Odile escorted us back to her chamber, the square, dorm-ish, windowless room whose austerity reminded me of Saxe's flat, where she sat in her chair and we lounged on pillows on her carpet and her bed, Corie propped at a comic angle on account of her ribs, which appeared to be only contused, not cracked, Corie and I yakking away quite outside ourselves, as though our outlandish morning had kicked our identities reeling and indeterminate until Odile had come along to gather us into her basket like windfall chestnuts, like foundlings. We were foundlings, chestnuts, newborn chicks; we were giddy with safety and hardly recognizable to ourselves, though I consoled myself that Corie was looking more normal again, if it was yet a somewhat bruised and burnoosed normalcy.

"Weren't you awfully afraid?" Odile asked me, turning the conversation to my daring raid. "You could have been arrested —"

"For what?" Corie interrupted. "Impersonating a doctor?" It wasn't quite a scoff, but she definitely seemed to be feeling more herself.

That brought a laugh from us all, and it also brought a chapter whimpering to a close, and not a long chapter either, *malheureusement*. For a little while there, since the big event, I'd felt an unaccustomed thrill, felt myself visible at long last, the fuddy duckling who molts into cool, not some medical Auntie Mame but a street desperado who could spring a friend from a foreign jail and then (the more astounding) whisk her into an all-girl Muslim safe house, and the whisking, it should be noted — bonus points for élan — effected via chauffeured limousine. The gambit that had begun with no preparation and proceeded move by move on the improvisational fly had turned into a bravura piece of work, if I might say so, and as I say, I hardly recognized myself until Corie exclaimed "For what?" and my newfound identity collided with who I'd always been. Which was a doctor, of course, and I remembered, of a sudden, that I'd put off doing the very thing I'd come to do, and I got out my stethoscope and my blood pressure cuff and went over and pushed up Odile's sleeve.

"So now you must tell us where you've been," I said to Corie over my shoulder as I worked. I hated my voice for its pleadingness. In the car I'd asked what the hell had happened and she'd been too druggy or stubborn to say, but now she recounted the story of her night, the civil disobedience gone haywire, the tear gas and the water cannon and the police truncheon that finally caught up with her, her arrest for resisting arrest. ("Felony tautology!" Odile interjected, miming the fall of a gavel along with her verdict, and I had to say, "Don't move.")

And then, her tongue loosened, Corie filled Odile in on the general construct of her current life — on Alba, and on Saxe's death, and how she and I had first met twice, once in a church and once on a road by accident ("No accident," Odile judged, miming another gavel. "Fate!"), and about the old letters we studied in the vast apartment, and I saw that any wedge that Massue's tirade had driven between Corie and her life on rue Nin had been expelled by her night's heroics: she had nothing to apologize for anymore. The adventures had liberated her from something more onerous than the clutches of the police: the indictments of her thuggish handler. Massue had tried his damnedest to evict her from her garden, but Alba had brought her back home. And I thought, *She's proud.* The lacerations her face bore were hardly hallmarks of bourgeois indifference, and I thought, *They honor the scars on Alba's breast,* and, *What Alba does, she follows without question.* Alba had freed Corie from Massue. As a result, Corie was more than ever Alba's captive and disciple. "Why do you have a mirror?" she asked suddenly.

I looked around at Odile's "window" set in its heavy oak frame. I was aghast (I wish I could say astonished) at Corie's rudeness, but Odile laughed, delighted. "Vanity," she answered as she held up her sleeve for me. Her voice was blithe. She asked if Corie was surprised and noted that she had a lamp too. "Did you notice? No, I can't see them, but I can't see my lipstick either, yet I wear it," she said, and said that if she was going to be vain, "I want a mirror to be vain in." She lowered her voice to a confidential rumble. "Would you put on lipstick without a mirror?" The question was sly; Corie never wore even the simplest makeup, though how could Odile know that?

I reached for my bag to grab Odile's chart and pulled out with it the awkward weight I'd been lugging around through all the day's adventures. I dropped the photograph slowly into Corie's open hands. Even before she looked at it, she received it as something to revere. She scrambled up painfully and carried it to the table and held it in the lamplight and peered through the glass intently.

"Is it her?" she asked.

"Mm-hmm, with Carlos," I said as I put away the cuff.

"Are we done?" Odile said, and then, as though 90 over 50 were something to celebrate (it isn't), she wheeled to her dresser and returned with three small earthenware cups and set them in front of us. She reached into the drawer again and came out with a mischievous half bottle of liqueur.

"Santé," she declared when she'd uncorked the contraband and poured us each a thimble's worth. "To rescue!" We had our sips and she asked, without a sequitur, "Aren't you ever afraid?" She had the Sahran tenacity with a topic, I had to give her that.

"How so?" I said.

"Oh," Odile said, "I'm afraid of so many things. For instance," and she mentioned fear for her brother, whose profession was very dangerous, who went off on missions from which he might not return, who was running off more and more with this war impending, who could be away for months at a time to who knows where, who'd warned her that any time they got together could be the very last, who was not as sturdy as he pretended to be and who'd recently looked (it was her word) unwell, like he was fighting something, "though he'll never admit it. He always has to be the strong one, because" — and she motioned around her as though flouncing a skirt to indicate the circumference of her infirmity. "So he can never be sick, even when he is. He's like all of us, he is who he has to be. And I'm his sister, who's made him be that way. Have you ever had someone disappear from your life?"

I could feel Corie's attention shift, though her eyes stayed glued to the photo. I pulled the cork and poured myself another. "Actually, yes," I said to Odile. "I have." And maybe it was the experience of being there and being as we were, so very dislodged, displaced, each the other and none of us ourselves, maybe it was something I'd wished to tell Corie already, or maybe I just wanted to be seen for myself again, having had a momentary taste of it, but whatever the reason, I talked about you, Daniel, you, whom I've never, ever talked about with anyone, gave them the bones of who you were and what you'd meant to me and what had happened, the base-camp accident with the drunk fools launching the mortar, a party goof gone haywire, how it hit the munitions cache. How the box was too close to your tent. How you'd remained in a coma all that long time after the wounding, long enough for them to airlift you to Saigon to cut out some of the shrapnel and then to fly you to Honolulu for additional treatment, and then on to Philadelphia to get you closer to home, though it wasn't in time for me to see you alive.

Corie's silence, as I talked, was as absorptive as dark is to light, looking at Alba and Carlos and listening to me and thinking I'm not sure what. When I was done, Odile said quietly, almost to herself, "That's exactly what I mean." And then, to Corie, in the bright voice of an older woman who wishes to cordon off and cradle her own grief and fear while bringing a younger one into the conversation, "And you must get afraid, living alone and doing all these things you do."

"No, not really," Corie said absently, but she conceded that she'd been scared for a while in the apartment, because it was haunted. When she wasn't there, she said, someone came through it. "I *sense* it," she said, had sensed it for a long time, and then when nothing bad occurred, she'd realized that maybe she wasn't being threatened at all, but "looked after."

"I'm sure it's Céleste. Doesn't she come in to clean?" I asked.

"Nope, it's not her," Corie said, and then confided, "But I know who it is." Before I could fear I was about to be unveiled, she pointed to the photo. "Who else?" she demanded. She'd seen small footprints — not shoe prints; footprints — in the den carpet once, and then the other day, the clincher, someone had undone the chain lock — "From inside! You know how I always lock up" — and then mysteriously evaporated, leaving not even a trace. "You think I'm crazy!" But she didn't sound crazy. She sounded happy, staring into the photograph and seeing there her guardian made tangible, and when she looked back up at me, she belched a little gray grunt of surprise.

"You okay?" I asked. I had an urge to get the cuff back out and get a quick read on her vitals.

"Look!" she said. She grabbed my arm and pulled me over to stand in front of the mirror, then raised up slowly beside my head the photograph, her hand held over everyone but Alba. We stood that way awhile, three dim female faces, Alba's, mine, and Corie's, lined up in the mirror, and then she said, "Oh." It was a lament, as though she'd lost the thread. "In the dark, for a moment, when you moved —" and didn't finish her thought.

I gave her hijabbed, bandaged head a consoling pat. "Get your stuff," I urged her, but Odile broke in firmly. "She can't go." Then, to Corie, "What if you get home and they're looking for you?"

"I'm in disguise!" Corie said, her enchantment evident, not so much with the costume as with the whole experience of ruse, until Odile tapped herself on the forehead, right where Corie's forehead was scabbed and scarred. "I suspect they may spot you anyway. Give it a night, to be sure."

So I left them there, the two scheming sisters, and headed back into town, without the photo, but with a question. For a moment, in the dark, in the mirror, I thought I'd seen something too.

XVIII

H E WOULDN'T EVER TALK about it," she said. "Not to me, not that I care. Who cared where he'd been?" What mattered was the war, *"La guerre etáit finie,"* and with it over, she'd returned, and found she was still the housekeeper, thanks to the saintlike beneficence of the late Monsieur Landers, "God rest his most generous heart. And your Jew returned too, and crawled right back into his wretched little hole." What he'd been up to in the meantime, "God knows." It was something he never said.

Céleste paused for a while. "Not that I care a whit."

And she paused a while longer, a longer pause this time. "I have some idea, though," she said. "As it turns out."

I had been relieved, as usual, when Drôlet dropped me off and I'd gotten my tired bones back up the stairs to my wretched little hole, but it soon became clear that it would do me no good to be home that night. I had no luck sleeping, none at all, thinking on what I'd seen and done that day and what it might mean for tomorrow. I could see where Odile's prediction might come true, that the police might find a way to track Corie home. Oh, wouldn't that just make Willem blow an aorta, if I turned up in jail! It was almost delicious enough to contemplate actually doing. Less delicious: the thought of what Emil might think when he found I'd broken my solemn promise to keep my distance from Corie.

Or maybe the thing that I really feared had tracked me home already: thoughts of you. The conversation in Odile's room had set them loose to rampage like jinn. Of course, as much as I told the two women, I hadn't told them all, hadn't told them any more than would permit their full-faith sympathy. The rest was left to beset me.

"There was nothing you could have done!" Corie'd consoled me, but Corie had never heard of a marriage deferment and didn't know the full or the half or even the least, least piece of it, that indeed there really had been, there in the snow, in the dark by the steps, something I could have done. You'd given me the chance to save you, and I didn't take it; you'd thrown me the line that I didn't grab. *Come in and let's hear the rest,* you said, and what if I had, for the rest was the rest of everything. But I shook my head and left.

What if.

Though there's also this, and I say this with all understanding, Daniel; I've thought about it, and I understand, so don't take this wrong: It wasn't only me who was silent that night. Do you hear? It can't have been only me.

Lying in the dark, pursued by these thoughts through half-sleep and half-awakeness, chasing an emptiness down doomed paths under blind, forsaken windows, I was jolted by a certainty. I sat up and gave it a body check — yes, it was so, it was clear — and without needing an oil lamp to light the way for my resolve, I slipped into some clothes and put on my coat and went through the closet and the closet door. I walked through Landers's rooms with no more worry or speed or caution or stealth than if they'd been my own and I was headed to the fridge for a midnight snack. I dallied long enough to purloin a flashlight and one of Corie's class books from the study and then went through the flat's front door and exulted in the bang of the latch as it closed behind me. At the bottom of the stairs I exited the door to the street, but this one I didn't let lock. I blocked it open with the *Lexique définitif d'langue Basque.*

My one concern was timing, but as soon as I got outside I saw that my optimism had reason to celebrate. The tracks leading from the gate to the corner of the yard had melted somewhat during the daytime and then glazed into a shining archipelago of rotted dents and craters as the evening air rechilled. The night crust had been broken by a fresh set of footprints, sharp-edged and crumbly new, and I followed where they led me.

The park was landscaped at its inner corners with a dense hell of rhododendron or mountain laurel, and the tracks led me through a gap in this thicket and into a little clearing rimmed half by hedge and half by edifice, a secluded chamber walled around in evergreen and brick. In its center, at the base of the base of the wall, in a circle of swept snow, stood a little cross. It was only a foot or so tall, crude-hewn out of rough stone, its fashion more Druidical (in the beam of my flashlight and to my anthropologically innocent eye) than Catholic. At least, I sensed some pagan power beyond straight Christian symbolism. On its face was the inscription *16 février 1942*. At its foot was a nosegay of small blue flowers, still fresh enough that they hadn't been frozen into black. I pinched off a blossom with my finger-nails, and headed back inside.

The cellar corridors were notably easier to negotiate with a flash-light in hand and no assassin chasing me. I'd hoped for some sign, some crease of lamplight under Céleste's door or the sound of a ra-dio inside, anything to indicate the concierge might be up and awake, but there was no such thing. Still, I didn't pause. I knocked on the door and waited, my fist held up, prepared to knock again, breath-ing the dormant detergent smell from the room just down the hall. I didn't have to wait that long before the voice barked, *"Oui?"*

"C'est moi," I answered. There was a clatter of locks, and the door opened to reveal Céleste in her housecoat, unapoplectic, but ready to be. She looked at me gloweringly, expecting, I could tell, some way-past-bedtime maintenance nightmare whose solution would just have to wait until dawn. Her expectation was as impassable as a granite wall, but she didn't expect what I gave her: I held out the flower.

She took it all in silently: me, the book, the flashlight and the open coat, and the tiny blue blossom between my fingertips, and then she left the door open and walked back inside. She gave me no invitation. I saw a light in a farther room, and I stepped in and closed the door and followed.

She was sitting at a round oak table in the center of a modest din-ing room, in a corona of intensest pink. Her apartment obviously lacked for windows — I saw only a couple of high transoms in the two rooms I traversed. Yet the room was bathed in a cotton-candy radi-ance, and entering, I saw its source. Banks of fluorescent grow lamps shone down on tables that lined three walls, tables crowded with clay pot after clay pot of identical dark, round-leaved plants bearing tiny, pert, violet-blue, yellow-centered flowers. In the middle of this, Céleste sat staring at her hands as though she were entirely alone.

"I suppose . . . Was it this time of night?" I asked.

She stared at her hands as though she had only her two hands for company and nodded, almost imperceptibly. "An hour ago," she said.

"But why do you go there the long way, around the block, through the gate from the street? I don't understand," I said. "Why not just go up the basement stairs, through the lobby, and out the front door?" She cleared her throat before giving me the faltering answer that I'd more than half expected, that she'd walked all night that first night, and preferred to walk each night since, something I heard Druidically, that hers was a pilgrimage that convenience would defile. If his spirit was alive in the night air, she would share the night air with him, were it full of ash or full of sleet or full of nothing at all. I understood. I'm a walker too.

"So," I said—I had to be sure—"he jumped." She nodded again. "From the window?" She wasn't offering, and she wasn't shying away, and I pulled out a chair and sat down, to be closer to her words.

"The roof."

And landed where? I thought, and didn't pursue it, but she heard my thought and nodded: *There.*

"You must have loved him," I asked, and she allowed that she still did, though not in the way I implied.

The young Landers couple had hired her not long before their engagement—and all perhaps she'd ever known of happiness had transpired in the not-quite-a-decade between her arrival in Paris from her ancestral village on the banks of the Loire in the Massif Central, a provincial young woman only yesterday a girl, and the date on the cross in the mountain laurel. She worked for them through the best times, and then worked on as things darkened and turned complicated, a juncture she attributed not obscurely to the arrival, a year after hers, of the Franconian Jew who had taken over a room that had formerly been her supply pantry and who had quickly assumed a prominence in family affairs she could never hope to equal.

It was the beginning of the beginning of the end. God knows what outrage he'd perpetrated against the Franconians before absconding and arriving here, but soon all of Germany was pouring in in pur-

suit. After the *nox horribilis* of February 16, she had continued in the
house and worked for her new overlord — one had no choice in those
days — starching death's-head uniforms and serving wine in Landers's crystal and canapés on Landers's china from Landers's silver
trays to strangers, until she had the chance to plead a family emergency and get herself back to Le Puy, and when the war ended, she
returned to find some things different — the apartment walls had
been stripped of art, for one — but other things very much the same.
And in good time, as matters straightened out, she discovered that
she miraculously had her same old job as a lifetime paid appointment, if she wanted it, and that the little stark room with no electric-
ity where he'd holed up as a fugitive still belonged to that Byron Saxe,
who had stumbled his way back to Paris after her, though God only
knew where he'd spent the meantime.

"But I do have some idea," she said, and after she let me languish
several seconds, she proceeded to tell me what it was. She'd known
when he'd left, more or less, at some point in the early fall of 1942,
months after Landers's suicide and while she was on the other side of
the paneled wall serving French hors d'oeuvres on Spanish silver to
Germans, "and I knew he'd traveled south," trying to make it to Spain.
That was smart, she reasoned, a plausible line of flight. He'd gone
there often with Carlos and Alba; he knew the back ways and spoke
the language fluently and had contacts and places where he might
hide, though most of those had surely been swept away by Franco's
terror. Nevertheless, he didn't last long, and the little she'd gleaned
in the years after their uncomfortable reunion was that he'd been arrested in Bordeaux and sent to a concentration camp and that his
life had been spared only barely and only by a small but vital piece
of miscommunication: like most Spanish Republicans imprisoned in
France, he'd been assigned the blue triangle of a stateless person, not
the yellow star that would more surely have been his death sentence
if he'd been rounded up in Paris. It was capricious fate of the starkest
sort: geometric.

And so, instead of being delivered to an oven in Poland, Saxe was
packed off to serve the Wehrmacht in a slave-labor detachment laying a railroad over sand dunes in the deserts of North Africa. "There
was precious little left of him," Céleste said with what sounded like

disappointment that there wasn't a little less, and she said he lived out the rest of his years hiding from life as fearfully as he'd hidden from the Nazis, holed up in his chamber with the shade half drawn, taking his meals around the corner, walking the streets with his cameras, shooting his photos, a ruined man, how he made ends meet no one knew.

"And then," she told me, "last summer he comes. And he tells me something I cannot stand to think of for the excitement," that a long-lost relative of Carlos and Alba was alive. It seems on his escape attempt south from Paris, all those years ago, Saxe had made contact with some member of the Landers clan, someone he'd then lost touch with, but he now expressed an expectation that this person, or someone associated with her, might materialize, "and he told me I should expect a lady to come and stay in the flat, and that I should admit her and take care of her, but not say a word about the family business because that was her job," to find out whatever she needed to know.

"That's what he said, and it's what I've done," she told me, and crossed herself. I had the feeling Saxe's instructions would have been less compelling if he hadn't died after giving them. She was driven less by regard for the man than by terror of his ghost. "And then, she arrived," Céleste said, and her voice held the wonder of prophecy.

"And you looked after her," I stated.

"I have," she said.

"When do you clean?" I asked, and if she recognized my prosecutorial turn, she mistook it for a slap at her professionalism. Every week was her adamant answer, "Thursdays!," as she'd done for forty-some-odd years, even without anyone around to clean up for and nothing to do but beat the drapes and push the vacuum back and forth as if she were rocking an empty perambulator and run some water through idle pipes to keep the rust at bay, and no one to know if she did it or if she didn't, but she'd never once missed a Thursday, "bright and early!"

"You go in at other times too," I said.

Céleste replied with silence — now she got it — and gave me the side of her head.

"For instance," I said, "you repaired my door, where I damaged it."

She pouted, sourly. "She's a Landers," she explained to me with a telltale hint of haught, and I could see there was more restoration afoot than that of a family heir. "There's no need to expose her to all that other stuff. I did what I could."

"A beautiful job!" I said sweetly, and then, "You were in her office too, one night. Or I suppose maybe . . . many nights?"

"Once!" she corrected fiercely before catching herself, and then stopped to calibrate a bit. "You rang from the street," she confirmed, surrendering, then pushed back with a grievance of her own. "You mustn't make her read those letters!" she blurted, and blurted that, *pardonnez-moi, madame,* they'd lead to trouble. "Haven't they done enough damage?" Hidden safely away for all those years, and now pulled back out to resume their mischief, "what could that Saxe have been thinking of! Every week she reads a bunch more, and it's only because you make her."

"What can you mean?" I asked, and I wasn't prosecuting now; I was genuinely perplexed. "What on earth's in them?"

She admitted she couldn't read them, "mostly," and then caught herself again and insisted she would never be so nosy as to try, "and I couldn't begin to tell you what they say." But there was one she'd read, all right, because she was the one who'd found it, lying on his bed on the night he killed himself, "and I've known where it is ever since, because I put it there myself, at the bottom of the stack, the very bottom, and I know the girl, and if she ever sees it, the blood will be on my hands."

Céleste sat inert for a while, seeming to cogitate — the conclusion was foregone but she wanted to give it its due — and after a few seconds she pushed herself away from the table and stalked out of the room. I counted flowerpots until I heard her stalking back. She flicked on the ceiling light as she came through the door — a brazen noon overpowered rosy *crépuscule* — and flung a folded pink paper onto the table. "So I took it!" she declared, and with her confession complete, she crumpled unrepentant into her chair.

I picked up the letter and unfolded it. It wasn't a letter at all. It was a telegram, in French, and though the light lit the room like a stadium, I stood up to read it as though to bring it closer to the sun.

GENÈVE 15/14 16/02 1200
C. BARAYÓN
NL

C LANDERS RUE GANIVERT 40 APT 50 PARIS 7 FRANCE
WITH DEEPEST REGRET RECEIVE NEWS ALBA DEAD
FALL FROM PRISON WINDOW WEDNESDAY STOP
UNSURE DETAILS ACCIDENT UNLIKELY DEMANDG
OFFCL ACCT GOVS OFFICE STOP NO POSSESSIONS
INTERRED IMMEDLY NO INQUEST STOP WILL SEE WHAT
CAN FIND OUT RELAY SOONEST GREATEST SORROW FOR
YOUR LOSS STOP CARLOS MY GOD WHAT HAVE WE LEFT
STOP

CORAIL

I read it over several times, and when I'd finished reading, I refolded the page along its ancient creases and told Céleste I wished to take it with me. She didn't answer and I'm not sure I expected her to. She really gave no indication at all, of my request or my presence. I flipped off the overhead light as I left the room and then I thought of something I ought to say and stepped back into the glow.

"I agree, it would upset her," I said. "So I won't show it to her." I left the woman in the fluorescent twilight staring at her hands, at the little flower she spun between her fingers like a purple whirligig.

XIX

OREJA DE OSO," Rouchard said. We were in l'Urquidi, ensconced at the corner table that I was coming to think of as mine, having sat there once before. It was Friday night. The particular place was my idea. A restaurant — any restaurant — was his. He wanted to be out of the office, and, it seemed, a retreat of any caliber would suffice, though he hinted that what he had to tell me might go well with a decent wine.

"What's that?" I asked.

"A wildflower," he said. "Like an African violet, but it grows only in the Pyrenees. *Oreja de oso* is to the Pyrenees what edelweiss is to the Alps, if you will. Daisy, calm down." The last was directed at the creature of whom, previously, I'd met only the nose, who turned out to be an enormous red Airedale. She was now curled up under our table, albeit somewhat bumpingly — it wasn't an automatic fit. "I have hiked into valleys when it's blooming and seen cliffs painted like the sky," Rouchard said. The only other place where he'd ever seen them grow was a microclimate in Paris. "Carlos figured out how to cultivate them," he said. "He made a study of it." A talent he must have passed on to Céleste. "He liked to keep a few around for comfort. He and Alba were both from that region, you know."

I hadn't brought the telegram with me to l'Urquidi. I didn't want to be like some road-show vendor, always turning up with an antiquity to appraise. (Last time I'd brought the photo.) There was no news in it that Rouchard didn't already know.

"It devastated us, *bien sûr,*" he said, about the deaths of his friends. "There's no way to indicate how devastating it was." Alba's murder, "or maybe she wasn't pushed, maybe she jumped, but anyway we know it happened on the morning she was to be forcibly given communion and baptized into the faith against her will, so either way, I'll call it murder. A *double* murder," if you threw in Carlos's reaction. The news had chased Rouchard all the way to Mauthausen, "and I can tell you that any event that made a day in Mauthausen worse was a significant event." Until exactly that moment, he said, he, like his friends, had thought there was a chance they would survive to rebuild their world. "Afterward, we knew better," he said. "We might survive," but their world was lost beyond retrieval. "That was the news. That was when we knew.

"It wasn't because of the violence," he said, Carlos's copying Alba's fall. They'd seen too much killing to be impressed by that. It wasn't the violence "but the passion. You must understand that for those in Paris who remember it, the story of Carlos Landers's suicide is a great, tragic love story. He acted as we would not, and we were awed."

Rouchard paused in genuine hesitancy, and then asked, almost shyly, "Would you permit a doddering old Frenchman who walks with a cane to give you his theories on love? I can promise to be every bit as pompous as you might expect." Of course I said yes. It wasn't the sort of offer I would ever turn down.

"You know the old saying," Rouchard said. "When it comes to love, Germans breed, the French flirt, the Americans sell, and the Spanish die. Ah, you cringe; it's offensive, yes, I agree. It's wise enough to omit the Swiss but doesn't include the Italians: *voilà!* I bring it up only to say that there's a geography to love. For instance: We French pride ourselves on being smarter than our emotions. Oh, we pretend to be destroyed by love, but it's only so we can demonstrate how amusingly we outwit it." (He took a diversion here, with apologies fore and aft, to stipulate that American "love" was a mechanical impulse that we still couldn't manage to outsmart, that's how clumsy the Yanks were when it came to matters of the heart, "and when an American dies of love, it's mere incompetence, you will please again forgive me for saying these few truths.")

The Spanish, though, were true romantics, too smart to let themselves be smarter than their feelings, so their brilliance is ever overmatched by their passion. For them, love was no more a plaything than a bull was. You stood before it as you stood before death, and never expected to survive. "If Elsa had leaped from a roof," he said, referring to some others of his war-era friends, passionate lovers and French Resistance comrades, "Louis would have written her a poem. So would we all. Carlos was far too Spanish for that."

This was why, for generations, his country and Spain had danced a dervish waltz, he said, "a tarantella." Between French frivolity and Spanish mortality, French brain and Spanish blood, French abstraction and Spanish belief, a complete cosmology of love and all its meanings had spun on its Pyrenees axis. "It is why we have loved one another as we have. And between these two opposites, and only there, your violet blooms, your *oreja de oso,* you see. But now the center's gone. We won the war, we thought," but only the shooting part. "Today all the world is breeding and selling. We've forgotten how to love and die. The way Carlos and Alba loved, and died. Their deaths destroyed us beyond repair. And now we will order this bottle, and have a good dinner, and I will tell you what I came to say."

What Rouchard then revealed is something I must make you comprehend if you are to understand what I did and said some few hours later, back home, as it were, after the police arrived. The hour was still early when the attorney and I finished up, and the air was balmy — the day had been warm enough to melt all but the most obstinate islets of snow, and the evening kept a pleasant suggestion of its heat — and I walked back home through the Marais, past the Hôtel de Ville, crossing the river on the Pont d'Arcole, dawdling there to observe the lovers and the reflections of lights on the water, musing on what I'd learned, carried away as will-lessly as a bark on the river's tide. As I went, I tried valiantly to keep euphoria from drawing me over a cataract. How greatly I wished I could talk with Emil, whom I missed. But I wouldn't see him for another twenty-four hours, at his dinner party. I might have taken a taxi home from l'Urquidi, or taken the Métro, that is true, so I could quickly hole up alone with my new knowledge, but the thought of haste was as scary as the thought of happiness, and the only way to avoid the terror was to tamp down the euphoria, so I walked the long way, tamping with every step, and dallied on the bridge. I'd dispatched Drôlet that afternoon to fetch Corie home from the girls' school, and when I got to our neighborhood, I went around to welcome her and ask about her stay, which she'd extended from one night to two.

The girl who opened the door seemed transfigured, and not just by the floral hijab, which Odile had made her a present of and which she wore loose over her hair and tucked modishly into the collar of her blouse. The rest of her garb was her own again, and she'd set out my gum boots by the door so I wouldn't forget to carry them home. Attire aside, she seemed to my eyes remade, recast, rejuvenated. She clasped me lightly by the shoulders and gave me kisses when I entered — *trois fois,* cheek, cheek, cheek; I couldn't have been more astonished — and we retired straightaway to the library and she ran to the kitchen, a little bit gimpy on account of her ribs, to set a hospitable kettle on.

It was then that I noticed the photograph, on the mantelpiece where Corie had propped it. It jolted me. Alba and Carlos dominated the room, and more. I realized for the first time how bare were the walls of the otherwise fully furnished house. The portrait, amid this barrenness, seemed to saturate the premises. I went to the icon almost gravely and studied it in its all-new light, and when Corie came in with the teacups and saw me standing there she began asking me all the things she hadn't gotten around to the night before: where I'd got the picture, who was the guy on the left, et cetera, and I told her how I'd filched it from Portbou, with Passim's blessing, and how she really should get over there and have a look at the photo wall before he retired the entire collection to give the cruddy old joint its first fresh coat of paint in umpteen years, as he was threatening to do. He was already picking out the color.

"There are more of Alba?"

"Oh, definitely," I said, and even in the silence I could hear her adulation reverberating, verging on belief, and there was very much more I wanted to tell her about telegrams and newspaper notices and my dinner across town and all the things I'd been finding out, but I dared not, and anyway, though I'd surely broken my vow to Emil, I still had my vow to Céleste to keep, to not reveal the fate of Alba. So for an hour I let Corie yammer, and she pleasantly did, about her stay at l'École Islamique de Jeunes Filles and how generously Odile had hosted her, how she'd joined with the faculty in morning prayers and how Odile had invited her to speak to her students and how she'd answered their questions about activism, about the lesser-known languages of the Iberian Peninsula, about music, about Missouri. She told me how Odile had taken the bandages off and she'd felt so much improved.

Eventually it was clear we were both too tired and cheerful to attempt anything vocational, and I told her, well, I guessed I'd better get my gum boots home, and we said good night — cheek, cheek, cheek — and I headed out and went down the elevator and out the front door to the gate.

Isn't it odd how we get through the world? I think back (so very far back!) on the family of voyagers I observed through the café window as I waited for Corie in Portbou, the man and the girl and the housecat, and I think, now, that my progress is not like any of theirs. I am more like some deep-sea submersible, chugging through the mire with my lamp aimed straight below me, illuminating a circle on the ocean floor — feeling my way with no past and no path, just my little moving patch of visible turf. That's certainly how I was advancing when I left the Wisteria, my eyes on the walk, inattentive to anything outside my immediate radius, as though I were lost in thought and being chauffeured home by Drôlet.

I was several steps along in the balmy air when I looked up and it dawned on me just what I was seeing out beyond the perimeter of my lamp, in the world beyond the fence. A car had pulled to a stop and double-parked in front of the Wisteria's gate, and then another pulled in behind it, and doors were opening and policemen were getting out and shaking out their pants legs, assembling themselves on the sidewalk.

I'll give myself this: As soon as it dawned on me, it dawned full and quick. There could be no doubt what this concerned, and my about-face was as smart as a majorette's. I retraced my several steps triple-time and caught the closing door before it latched and raced up the stairs. The elevator would have been a sorghum torment under the circumstances. I banged breathless on Corie's door. I didn't knock and wait with my fist held up, prepared to knock again, uh-uh. I banged and banged and banged, panting, "Come on, Corie, damn it," until the door jumped open and she stood there gape-mouthed and wide-eyed, asking me what I'd forgotten. She had her coat on; she must have been planning on following me out — what a fine trap that would have been! It was just at that moment the buzzer rang.

"Don't answer that," I commanded, and seeing that she was convinced there was an urgency, if not clear on its source, I said, "Get all your tea crap into the kitchen now."

She raced off to the library and when she came back she said, "Study?"

"They'll look there," I said. I don't know if she attended to my deliberations, for they required only a second, although they were exceedingly and exhaustively thorough, and then it was all decided and I said, "Come on."

I grabbed her hand and we ran as fast as her aches permitted through the living rooms and hunt room and the conservatory, and after we passed the piano, the last object of sufficient bulk that a person might hide behind or in or under it, and headed into the empty oval chamber with the sylvan vistas and the summer sky and the chandelier dangling like the basket of a fabulous balloon, I could feel her leaning back, jamming on the phantom brakes like a passenger in a runaway buggy, for now we were careening across the very last room at velocity toward the wall. I held up just short of a crash and snatched her to me. "There's a shoe," I said, "prop it against the inside and wait for me," and I told her I wouldn't knock but would call her name, "so you'll know it's me. Okay?" And to her astonishment, I pushed open the panel in the wainscoting and more or less tossed her through it. Then I fled back to answer the front door.

It was no small effort to come off arranged and relaxed, and I thought I'd faint for trying not to breathe like a bellows. But I got myself as composed as I could as I waited for the elevator to complete its ascent, and when the grate opened, three of the uniformed men emerged. (Where were the others? Taking up positions?) The trio seemed reluctant to proceed any farther down the hall. The gate shut and the elevator hummed downward and then back up again, disgorging, this time, a single short man in a suit who walked through the others without acknowledgment and led them like goslings to the door.

"Is there some emergency?" I asked when they'd reached me, and the suited man got straight to business, introduced himself as a captain, Cassell was the name, and asked if I was Alba and showed me a badge. "May we enter?"

"May I ask what this is about?"

"Only some questions," he said.

"I see," I said, "of course," and I ushered the little regiment in. I was less spooked by the detective than by the patrolmen, each identical. They reminded me too indistinguishably of the guard guarding Corie's hospital room.

"Do they *all* have questions?" I asked the suit, leaning my stage whisper near to his ear. I thought he smiled, just slightly, at the delicacy of the suggestion, but he got the point, at least, and he motioned with his head for his troops to continue to vigilantly secure the entry hall, and I led him into the apartment.

I was pulling rank, frankly. I'd heard somewhere just recently that uniformed societies harbored a refined connoisseurship of social status, and I thought I'd give the theory a try. Anyway, it couldn't hurt to allow him a gander, let him compare the grandeur of these rooms with whatever he'd imagined his scofflaw's lair to look like.

Even through my nervousness, I confess that I felt a dizzy little thrill; it was my first time entertaining in the consul's "gracious apartments," and I was indulging in a little pride of place. I was glad all the lights were on (and relieved to see only one cup of tea on the table). I was also pleased to be able to receive my guest in a nice dress and hose. At dinner with Rouchard, I'd worried that maybe I'd overdone it a wee bit, finery-wise, but the lawyer hadn't objected, that was for sure, and the lawman didn't either.

"I should assure you, you are not a suspect in any matter," he said as we reached the library and I motioned him to sit. The décor had done its job. He didn't sit.

I let a small and terribly astonished laugh burst out and said, "Well, I'm relieved to hear it," and secretly, I was. I added, sweetly, "But for whom are you searching, if not for me?"

"A young woman," he declared, and then, flustered by his own indiscretion, "student age." American, supposedly, or possibly British, a girl called Alba, "but it's undoubtedly not her name. She's witnessed certain matters and may have information for us." She was involved with others who were wanted for more serious questioning, and he stressed that it was important, "or we wouldn't have inconvenienced you," and that he couldn't tell me any more than that, but in the course of their investigations my address had come up, and he asked me again if I wasn't Alba.

"No," I said. "I'm very sure."

"But this would be the home of an Alba Landers," he asserted, preening until I looked at him funny.

"Name's by the bell," he admitted.

"It would be, Captain, yes," I confirmed, and he twitched to attention as though I'd yanked his tail and said that he wished to speak with Mademoiselle Landers immediately, *s'il vous plaît*, recouping enough gravitas to impress upon me that, delicacy aside, he wasn't the sort to be detained from his target.

"I'm sure mademoiselle would be delighted to speak with you," I said, and I walked to the fireplace and brought back the photograph of a young woman and two young men in a 1930s roadster. "Sadly, she cannot." I handed over the evidence. "Alba died fifty years ago."

The captain frowned at me in a way that tried to split the difference between scolding and surprise and condolence and irritation, and he concluded in surrender. "Perhaps I should back up a bit," he conceded. "Whose home am I in, then? If you would be so kind."

"Hers," I said. "Back then. It's mine now."

"And you are . . ."

"My name is Magdalena Landers," I told him; it was the first time I'd said it to anyone, but then, he was the first to ask. "Alba's daughter. But please just call me Matilde, everyone does."

It was some minutes more before I got the inspector and his drones back out the door. I latched it, as Corie would, with the chain lock and watched through the study window as the cohort squeezed into their cars and drove away, and then I traipsed back through the rooms, kind of giddy, to give the Little One the all-clear.

XX

O F COURSE," ROUCHARD HAD said, "he may have been the only one to see things differently, our young Mr. Saxe. Lovely for everyone else to find his friend's suicide romantic. He thought it a crime, pure and simple. An abandonment. And, what is your phrase — I can see from whence he comes."

Rouchard had used his two days in Geneva well, he told me as we sat in l'Urquidi awaiting our dinner. He'd gone through the document trove in the lawyer's office, dry legal filings, most of which he'd trucked home in his accordion valise, "along with some bric-a-brac," and he placed on the table one of his company envelopes. "To view the rest, you must see me in my office." He now considered the disposition of the estate to be complete: everything reposing in the Swiss attorney's files he was confirming through French property registries . . . cleared up considerable mystery . . . all in order.

The story of the estate was another matter, and pursuing it had taken him into two long bedside chats (the word was his: *des bavardages;* they sounded to me more like *des* bedside *interrogations*) with the Swiss lawyer's infirm last wife, who had met Saxe once, soon after the war (she had been fascinated by his personal saga even as her husband administered his legal one), and whose memory of him hadn't in any way dimmed. She told Rouchard of Saxe's verdict on his friend's romantic Spanish final act: that it was despicable.

"In Saxe's world," Rouchard said, "fathers put their children first. No other grief or love displaced that responsibility. That was the gist of it." It was the very thing that had saved Saxe's own young life, after all. "So, a week after Carlos received the telegram, he kills himself for love of his wife. But where was his love for his child? I will say in defense of my friend, Carlos must have felt he'd lost his child as well. Likely she was dead, and if she wasn't, how would he ever find her? It was impossible." If alive, she would be swept into Franco's giant social-aid baby mill—the Francoists had trafficked in babies, it seems, like the Tontons Macoute in blood. Their state orphanages had bulged with child-of-a-Red infants stolen from Republican mothers in accordance with government decree; the children were renamed, their birth records were destroyed, and they began their lifetimes in "moral reform" limbo. Carlos would have no way of knowing her. "The letter that would tell him otherwise arrived long after the telegram," Rouchard said, and after Carlos had jumped. When it came, via Geneva, it came to Saxe.

"Through the attorney Barayón." Barayón, whom Saxe was now in touch with on account of Carlos's estate. Carlos wished to have the home where he'd lived with Alba preserved as a shrine to their romance. And with no family left, he willed it for safekeeping to the closest friend he and his marriage had had, "along with enough money to maintain the premises in perpetuity. Of course Carlos meant it as a thumb in the eye of his tormentors—making this glamorous property the possession of a Jew. Not that the Nazis would know or care." They assumed he died intestate and would never have seen the will. Anyway, Carlos didn't file it with French courts; "that would have been absurd." But he understood that if the Allies won, Occupation property settlements wouldn't be valid anyway. So he filed it with his friend in Geneva. It was the last act of his life, and it made his young friend Byron Saxe rich.

I broke in to observe the obvious. "But—" I said.

"But Byron kept living in his room, yes, I know. Of course that would be necessary in 1942, wouldn't it, considering his neighbors' temperament. But in 1946? Or '60, or '90?" He shrugged. "Byron could have knocked down the door and lived in luxury any moment he chose. Yet he didn't. And—I'm surmising here—it goes back to how much he detested his friend's decision. He refused to profit from it. Carlos made Byron wealthy, and Byron hated him for it." He'd rather remain in the home of a parent's love than in a headquarters of parental desertion. "By his terms, he picked the grander palace. That's why he did it. At least, that's what I imagine. That and one other thing," Rouchard said. "His guilt."

He paused there. The first of the food had arrived and he could see that until he quit talking to eat, I wouldn't eat for listening. Or maybe he was grappling as hard with his composition as I with my comprehension. Whichever, when he put the tale aside, he put it aside completely, and it wasn't until we had commenced our main course that he segued out of more general talk and picked up where he'd left off. "Guilt," he said.

"But to make that argument requires some evidence, and so I will describe what I found in Geneva." But first he had to tell me that what he'd found had made him "exceedingly sad. Sad that this is an individual I never got to know in life, for now I've come to admire him. He is both outside my history and part of my history, but he is very much what I wish my history had been," what Rouchard wished his home and generation had represented. "He redeems us, at least a little. Even his guilt redeems us."

So it seemed that right after Carlos died, "Saxe lived on here. In the little room, of course. The big place was full of Germans, only centimeters away. He could hear them through the wall. There was a piano in that room, I remember that, a big old Steinway, and apparently that's where they liked to socialize. Imagine. What a hell it must have been! Eventually someone would discover the back stairs, climb them to Saxe's place. Even to use the toilet, he had to cross the hall. A sneeze, a dropped pen, the tiniest noise at the wrong time might give him away. He couldn't warm food, or light his lamps. If he slept, he might snore. He must have been constantly terrified, for he was worse than just a Jew. He was a foreign Jew, and he was a fugitive." In 1940, when the Germans required every Jew to register at the prefecture, Saxe didn't. Two years later, the decree came that every Jew had to wear a star, "but again, he did not. He refused." He took the chance.

"Actually, what he did," Rouchard said, "he took photographs." At some point after Carlos's death, Saxe began slipping out of his hideaway dandied up in his old friend's business suits — he had grabbed some clothes and Carlos's identification papers before the SS squatters arrived. He'd stroll through Paris in his good cloth with his excellent camera, taking snapshots of street happenings. "But not just strolling, not always. And not just snapshots." He documented things he'd heard of through the tympanum of the closet door.

"Was this at the behest of the Resistance, the Maquis?" Rouchard asked. "I don't know. I doubt it. Regardless, it was extremely provocative. I can only surmise that he had become almost obsessed with these others, these soldiers on the far side of the wall, and he would hear all these plots and plans, and he couldn't help himself. He had to see who these people were." Had to see their rumblings play out in the light. "You can't conceive of the risk," Rouchard said. Surely only Saxe's aristocratic attire protected him. "Uniformed societies harbor a refined connoisseurship of social status," Rouchard said. "I can't think of any other reason he would have survived." Carlos's clothes were Byron's suit of mail.

"It's worth savoring, you know. A German hiding from Germans, taking photos with a German camera of *la vie française* under German rule, protected by a Spanish cravat. Well, there's a geography to many things, as it turns out." Saxe stored the exposed rolls in his room, Rouchard said. He could hardly have developed them. The odor of chemicals would have given him away.

And then the event that brought this perilous refuge to an end. One night (so Corail Barayón's widow in Geneva told Rouchard), Saxe heard a rumor through the wall, and the very next morning he packed up his camera and left. "And I can envision even what she didn't say, because I know of the place he went to," Rouchard told me. "Every Parisian knows it and remembers what happened there, though no Parisian wants to." The place was a new Utopian housing development envisioned by its designers as such a peaceful spot that it had been nicknamed the City of the Silent. A mammoth modernist complex with a set of landmark residential towers still under construction when the invasion happened, it wasn't specifically requisitioned by France's new overlords, except briefly as a barracks, but it was turned to their special purpose anyway, under the groveling management of "my countrymen."

It stood on the city outskirts, and when Saxe showed up on this morning, he could hardly have blended in. "In those clothes? Anyway, this wasn't like the crowds in town. He must have just marched right up to it," Rouchard said, "insane as that sounds." Then (Rouchard was told) an extraordinary thing occurred. Two men rushed out at Saxe's approach, but it wasn't to arrest him or turn him away, not at all. "You found us with no trouble?" one of them asked in French, pumping his hand, and Saxe had the presence of mind to answer in German as he was ushered along to begin his scheduled duties as a contract photographer. He spent the morning in Hades, making pictures of what he found there.

"And what he found," Rouchard said, "were children." Thousands of them, hordes of children heaped on one another in squalor, nakedness, and near starvation in the dank shell of a Utopian ruin, the older ones taking care somewhat of the younger, though the youngest were barely weaned and the oldest barely teenagers, "for you see, if they had been even fifteen or sixteen, big enough that the Germans could pretend they were being sent off to work, they would have been deported with their parents to the ovens. But you can't keep up the pretense it's a work camp if you're sending toddlers to it."

The Germans had been afraid of inflaming French sentiment by openly deporting children to the camps. But the French authorities argued that, in the name of humanity—"they damned well knew what it looked like," Rouchard said—the children should go. Outraged at the barbarity of splitting up families, the French insisted that compassion required that children accompany their mothers to their deaths. And in the standoff between these rival decencies, the children piled up, arriving from around the occupied zone and from Vichy; from other camps, established and makeshift (including a bicycle *vélodrome* turned human stockade, a circle of hell in the shadow of the Eiffel Tower); from the massive roundups of foreign-born Jews that were mounted throughout the summer. The parents passed quickly through the transit camp, while the children remained, feral castoffs warehoused for weeks.

Saxe wandered among this rabble, photographing their faces and their world, the wooden, hand-lettered dog tags supplied for each child because so many were too young to know their own names. Then the event he'd gotten wind of commenced, and gendarmes arrived to cull out the selectees who would experience the only thing Saxe could imagine that was more horrific than this captivity—

sealed boxcars packed with children rolling through France and Germany and Poland, the first of the deliveries that would ultimately reunite the orphans with their families through the agency of a crematorium.

All would perish on the transport or in Auschwitz, Rouchard said, and Saxe's photos would survive the war to remain the only visual record of the day. He'd turned in his film as he'd left the compound; the photographs were printed and archived in Berlin, where they are said to represent the very finest photographic work, by leagues more profound than anything else in the oeuvre of the German photographer Saxe was mistaken for — you could see the intensity of the man's roused conscience seeping through his documentarian composure, an artistic awakening made all the more poignant by the fact that it had overtaken this man, the German photographer Saxe was mistaken for, on the very last day of his life. On his way home from the assignment, one of so many he'd fulfilled for the Wehrmacht, he was knocked down by a grocer's van while crossing the street to catch a bus.

"There's a bit of historical confusion on that score," Rouchard said. "The police report of the incident states that he was killed in the morning, though that is obviously an error, because the film he shot clearly chronicles events that can be verified to have occurred between noon and one thirty of the afternoon of that day." The accident report had been cited by one of the photographer's academic biographers, in her volume *The Redeeming Light,* as yet another example of the notorious slipshoddiness of French official record keeping.

As Rouchard gave out his tale, I felt only impassivity, a muffled asbestos stupor immobilizing me against any reaction at all. It was a fearful peace; Rouchard's conclusion bore down on me as inescapably as the truck that had flattened the luckless German photographer. My dinner mate, meanwhile, did not share my calm. His emotions skittered here and there as though he himself had lost control before his careening account. He'd nearly come to tears at one point. Now, concluding his rendition of the caper of the mistaken photographer, he erupted in seeming anger. "Don't you find it preposterous!" he demanded of me, a muted yell. Daisy bumped, alarmed, beneath the table.

"What?" I said.

"The whole thing!" he said. "Understand, I am a lawyer. And at the same time, underneath, I still think of myself as something of an anarchist. And in either of those identities, I am offended by this story. A man steps off a sidewalk and is hit by a truck, okay. But that this accident would then spare the life of another man that morning, one who, as a result, goes on to witness a horror that would have affected the first man not at all but that compels the second to commit a heroic rescue of yet another human being who ultimately would not have been rescued at all if a step had been slower or the delivery wagon's fender just a little to the left or the right or the windscreen not so dirty."

Or look at it another way, he said. "A beautiful woman sits before me in a restaurant in Paris, a woman whose life has been a good one and who has benefited many other lives and who would not be here, at least not with me, and who would not be at all who she is had the man who intervened in her life so improbably, so many years ago, not himself been improbably saved by the precise convergence, according to an exquisite coincidence of direction and velocity and time and inattention, of a delivery truck and a pedestrian going to work. Does this not disturb you? Oh, it does me, madame. For it tells me that life is either a thorough game of chance and the greatest of fates at the mercy of the merest whim, which leaves no room for law, or that the hand of Providence can reach out of the future to shade the wheel a centimeter and give a sufficient tap to the pedal, in which case my liberty is destroyed.

"I leave you the choice," he said, and he bent to comfort Daisy, who was beginning to whimper condolences. I stared at his stooped back — his gray suit coat bulged over the white tablecloth like a stone in a Zen garden — and felt grateful for the idle seconds that let my cognition catch up with the news. When he surfaced, his face was ruddy. "Where was I?" he said.

XXI

YOU WERE ABOUT TO TELL me he didn't go to Spain," I
ventured. A crazy toss.

"Saxe?" Rouchard said. "Oh, but he very much did! But how
did you know of Spain?"

"Céleste," I confessed. "She said he had contacts there but was
caught in Bordeaux en route."

"Yes, well, Marseille," Rouchard said. He seemed unsure which
thread to pick up. "It was much more than contacts," he said. By that
summer, the Maquis, "my countrymen too, I must remember, we
weren't all *collabos*," had established an underground railroad spir-
iting Jews out of the German-occupied zone, funneling them into
Barcelona and the coastal cities of Italian-seized Provence. "Because
Franco was like Mussolini, a dictator who resisted surrendering his
Jews to Hitler. He'd already surrendered his pyrites and wolfram to
the cause of German rearmament. Now the Führer wants his Jews as
well? Ha!" So that's why it made sense that Saxe might look to Spain
for safe haven. "But that's it, you see; that's the problem. They arrested Saxe in Marseille, but Marseille is not on the way to Spain,"
Rouchard said. "Not from Paris. Anyway, he wasn't headed for Spain
when they caught him." He looked at me a long while, as though this
were a call and response and the next line belonged to me. Then he
said, "He was coming back."

Rouchard couldn't tell me exactly what Saxe had done while in
Spain or exactly how he'd done it, only that three weeks after he'd
made his way south along the Côte Basque roads to La Bidassoa,
he'd left Spain by another route, and that once back in France he'd
followed the Mediterranean coast eastward with his companion to

Marseille, "for now he was no longer alone." He arrived in the port with a young child, a girl, whom he left with his Maquis contacts, specifically with the XIV Corps. "Do you . . .? No, of course not." And of course Rouchard told me about the unit of the defeated army of the Spanish Republic that had regrouped in southern France as an anti-Fascist guerrilla force. The corps understood who the girl was; they'd of course have known of her parents. They placed her in the care of two American Quakers in Marseille embarking for Galveston on the freighter *Champlain Ressuscité*, via connection in Rabat.

"And so, you see, I have many details, but no essence, beyond the basics," which Rouchard's French love of delineation divided into two equal parts: his knowledge that Saxe had gone into Spain alone and come out with a child, and his conviction, based on that knowledge, of Saxe's motivation. Saxe had paid off his grief debt to the doomed children of the City of the Silent, Rouchard said, by finding a single Spanish child and saving her.

"What you call his guilt," I said. "Those children."

"Let me tell you something," Rouchard replied. In Geneva, Madame Barayón had spoken of this subject and had recounted what Saxe had told her, that on that day, as he wandered through the prison, he'd endured a sort of regression. Surrounded with urchins, knowing what was about to happen to them, he felt himself a child again as well, one more foreign-Jew orphan no different than the others. Except for the essential distinction that they were being loaded onto transports or returned to their cells while he could turn on his heel and turn in his film and exit through the front door, detained only momentarily by official exclamations of gratitude and promises of prompt payment, "and I think the monstrous inequity of it — the caprice — must have overwhelmed him. Byron became that terrible, inconsolable thing, the child who survives."

Nevertheless, no; this wasn't the guilt to which Rouchard had alluded. That was toward another child (and this part Rouchard had from Byron Saxe himself), the very child Saxe had rescued. Saxe knew there was a more rightful heir to the property he'd inherited, a proper resident for the house he refused to inhabit. But how to make restitution? He'd lost track of the girl, and the comrades who had arranged her passage had perished in the war. "So ultimately he did something inventive." He drafted the legal system into the task — "*Merveilleux!* All of France a bloodhound! And me!" — by appointing the lost girl his heir and willing her both of his independent properties, the smaller one bought for him by his father and the larger one given him by hers, along with the endowment for permanent upkeep and maintenance, to which Saxe had attached a not insignificant obligation, "by the way," that his heir must uphold the continued lifetime salary and support of one Céleste Marie Bowdoin.

"Oh hell!" I exclaimed, and I felt a gush of relief, my consternations and bafflements chased away like humidity by lightning: finally, this saga had burst the bounds of credibility. "But — she loathed Saxe! Céleste. *Loathes* him! Anyway, Landers arranged her support."

"Umnnhhh," Rouchard said, and the single drawn-out syllable presented a thorough legal rebuttal in its intricate and irrefutable entirety. "I recall," he said. "She's quite a dreadful Jew hater, isn't she, our Madame Concierge. But however it may contradict her feelings, or ours, the truth is she owes her great good luck to a Jew. Again, I can only guess how this happened. But that's not so hard, you see."

Just look at it, he said. "Byron's in hiding half a year, more than half, in terror of being discovered and killed. And the whole of that time, who was on the other side of the wall, working among the killers, rubbing shoulders, conversing with them, but someone who knew exactly who he was." And exactly where. "She could have made her life easier by turning him in, believe me, she would have been rewarded. And it could have cost her her life not to, as well." Yet she didn't betray him. "She's an anti-Semite, true, but don't forget" — and here Rouchard appeared to puff up a mite with pure native pride — "she's a *French* anti-Semite."

And of course she didn't tell Saxe that she was protecting him. "She would never! Pheh!" Rouchard expectorated rhetorically floorward. "But he had to have known. Of course. And later he knew to protect her in turn, just as silently. Here," Rouchard said. "Here's to Herr Byron Manifort Saxe."

He reached for the cognac, which at some unnoticed moment had arrived on our table, and raised a snifter. "To my comrade," he said, and we clinked, and he said, "*¡No pasarán!*" and we clinked again. We both downed a slug of the brew. I could tell that for Rouchard, the nightcap was a receding tide, that he was waning now, along with his subject.

"Something I don't understand," I said when we'd set down our glasses. I was desperate to catch him before he faded. "How would he have recognized this child? There was a letter, you said . . ."

" . . . which I haven't seen," Rouchard finished. "But it's a good question and I have pieced together your answer," and he nudged something toward me across the tablecloth. It was the envelope. I picked it up and popped it open — it wasn't sealed — and spilled its contents out onto the table. There were only two items: a small steel key and a barrette. "Alba's," he said, of the latter. "Carlos had given it to her, and she put it in her daughter's hair. If he'd seen it, he would have known. But only if their daughter might still be wearing it, of course." I picked it up. It was lyre-shaped, and a lustrous mottled brown, and just as I seized it Rouchard reached out and captured my hand in his.

"Something else too," he said, "more indelible." He drew my hand to him softly, as though intending to propose. "It seems that their daughter, Alena . . . Magdalena . . . had a scar," he said, "visible on the back of her hand. Now, this I don't know from Madame Barayón. I heard it straight from Byron. He told me how I should identify the person who would come to me. Yes, yes, I'd already noticed. But Madame Barayón explained the rest," that Saxe had applied the same test, all those years ago, in Spain.

"You know," he said; he kept his hand on mine. "This man Saxe. I'm sure he was a terrible and flawed person in this way or that — isn't each one of us? What he survived, one never really recovers from. He seemed to me broken, a shadow inside a shell. Maybe he was petty or mean, maybe he kicked the cat, I wouldn't be surprised. But I will say that I've known some of the best of people in some of the worst of times, and I think this man may have been as moral an individual as anyone I have ever encountered. On top of all else, he has given me, too, a gift. He has dispelled a sorrow that darkened my life since the day I heard the news in Mauthausen. I believe he knew what he was doing. Certainly he could have easily gotten a much better lawyer than I am. But he knew how much I loved them, Carlos and Alba.

I think he understood how much it would mean to me to raise a glass with their daughter."

Maybe it was those words coming after all the others that lofted me so irrepressibly home from the Marais, along the river and over the bridge, amid an astonishment so very great I was sure my joy would wash me right into the maw of reprisal. Standing in the apartment after the police had departed, I realized I no longer felt in jeopardy. Instead, I sensed all of my lifetime curses — *Whatever you love, you will cause to be slaughtered* — departing, deserting me. As though they'd been subdued by the visiting gendarmes and carted off in handcuffs to *le clink*. I watched from the window of the study as the little blue delegation clambered back into its cars, and the impression swept me that it was not the police who were leaving the scene — it was me. I was absconding, released, the long incarceration was over at last. I'd faced my comeuppance and found in it nothing to fear. There was to be no reprisal.

The big cold world had turned out to be not so frigid after all. It wasn't just that I'd found my birth mother — no, it was something greater: that I'd already, remarkably, been so long in her presence. My mind gathered up all the hours that Corie and I had lingered over Alba's letters, letters from a stranger who turned out to be no stranger at all, a woman I'd dismissed at first, and then been drawn to, having no idea how deeply she belonged to me and I to her, that the events she described were as intrinsic to me as I was to those events. What other walls might prove to be permeable? What other untold stories were right now explaining my life? The question itself was another great gift from Alba: What other love was I overlooking, that might be right in front of me? My thoughts flew to Emil.

I sauntered back through the apartment's rooms, taking my leisurely time, testing my liberty with baby steps, getting accustomed to the odd gravity of this new planet, observing my surroundings with all the wonder of my very first visit. What I saw around me now wasn't bizarre opulence but an old, old riddle pieced together and solved. I felt, as Rouchard had said, *"La disposition, c'est complète,"* and my contentment lacked only one concluding element, one last act before I could consider matters satisfied. My amble through Alba and Carlos's rooms was my path to that appointment.

It was a mystical assignation, and all the more vital for that. I felt the need to convene with two central parties to tell them the news, to convey my gratitude for my good fortune and theirs, to cement my new life with my new family, the agents of my delivery. Fortuitously, they both awaited me in the same place: Byron Saxe and Corie Bingham, the one spectral and embodied in the little spot he'd lived and conspired in, and the other very much corporeal, the translator he'd employed to advance this very moment, the young woman awaiting my signal that everything was okay. I'd been allowed a new life, thanks to them, or allowed to possess my old one at last, and there was no one I wished to celebrate with more than the woman who'd brought me so insistently, step by step, through Alba's letters, to the threshold of my miracle.

I reached the last of the grand rooms in a state of rampant anticipation. Untethered from dread, freed from reprisal, I felt excitement romp in my chest until, with my last few steps, I was afraid it might burst me before I could make my rendezvous. I whisked through the oval salon with my leisure cast aside and reached the secret panel with a whistling pulse.

"Corie," I yelled at the blank wall, and yelled again, because I couldn't abide the wait, knocking even though I'd said I wouldn't, "Corie, it's me!" There was no answer, even to my several repeated cries, and premonition encased my heart. The panel hardly budged at first. I'd expected a weight on the other side, but not this resistance, and immediately I wondered if the obstruction weren't greater than a shoe, might be some mortal bulk lying against the sill. I pushed harder, and the door budged inward with a sibilance of cloth on wood, the grudge of garments heaped against the door. The closet's rods had been emptied.

"Corie?" I called, stepping over the pile. No one was in the room. The chair at the table was overturned. Nothing else seemed out of place or ransacked or disturbed, but it was clear that a disturbance had gone on and that the friend I'd wished to commune with had departed. The door to the hall was ajar, and I ran out through it and spewed Corie's name loudly down the staircase, her name spiraling down into darkness like water down a drain.

I didn't notice the other item of disorder until I walked back in and stooped to right the chair. I seized on it merely as something else to tidy up, a small leaf tossed by the whirlwind of Corie's flight. That was before I saw what it was and surmised its role, the pink, fold-creased telegram announcing — and as I spread it open like an origami swan, it divulged its message all over again — the news of Alba's death.

PART FOUR

XXII

DANIEL, I'VE NEVER HAD an instinct for edges. Oh, in my work, of course. There I'm exquisite. I can take a body to the brink and back and never let him step over. I mean in life. Maybe because I lacked one of my own, one edge. Without a birth, a beginning, without a conception, I couldn't conceive of an end, that's true. Happily I dwelt in the middle regions. My story was deathless and my earth was round, you could sail and sail and sail it, and never sail over the edge.

And so I think I just didn't know what he was talking about, there beneath the trees beside the river, the sergeant in his dress greens crisp as matzo even in the rain, he'd come so far. The mortuary's limousine waiting curbside, your coffin in the ground. I suspected he was not still in the service. But he had been, back when he met you, so he claimed. He was there when your transport set down in Tan Son Nhut, your company filing out, piling its gear in the shade of the great wing, while the noncoms who would escort you to your deployments rested on the grass berm and looked you over and placed their bets. Four or five of them, Daniel, relaxing, placing their bets. It's what they'd do, he said, the officers. To while away the time. They had an instinct for the edge. They bet on who among you would make it out alive, and who would not.

This is what he came to tell me, that you were fated, doomed. He had a term of art for it. The word he used was *fey*.

He said that they got very good at it, at guessing, that if you had even a hint of the talent, you could develop it quite quickly in a war zone. They could usually tell, were right more often than not. They weren't concerned with the great mass of boys, your comrades who would survive or not depending on luck and circumstance. Their game was played at the extremes, with the marked ones, those who were impervious and, especially, those who were fated, as he said you were, those who bore the scar, the fatal aura. The players spotted you immediately. You disembarked from the plane, Daniel, and before you'd even mustered out into your unit, before you could get your duffel off the runway, they'd pegged you: fey. Foretold.

That's what he came to tell me. He'd thought I'd want to know. That it had been, as Odile said to Corie, not an accident, but fate. I guess you and I were different that way. You fell so quickly off the end of life, and I crashed through the center of mine. But you don't have to drop off the edge of the earth to drown, Daniel. "Death inhabits you," Maasterlich assured us, and didn't it, Daniel, didn't it, for happily I drowned where happily I dwelt. If you were fated, does that mean I was too?

"It won't be your undoing, though." Maasterlich again. "Life will." And wasn't it. Last lecture, semester's end, the creaking old hall packed to its rafters. Even his detractors had come to gawk. They couldn't pass up a show, and the finale of Introduction to Surgical Practices had earned its reputation for providing one. No one knew what the old man would say except that it would surely be whatever was on his mind. He'd titled his peroration (vapor trail of chalk through the chalk cloud) Systole/Diastole, but I've long ago rechristened it (neuronal trace through clouds of recollection) Silence v. Silence, or Maasterlich's Musical Mystery Tour.

Everyone, he was sure, had warned us, the professor said, smacking his pointer rhythmically against the flank of the lectern, how a doctor must deaden his mind against the constant prospect of death, "the way a soldier does, even though that can be a dying in itself." He was right, for they had. They'd warned us to steel ourselves, warned us how sometimes we'd see death coming but wouldn't be able to stop it, how that particular trauma would take its inevitable toll on our spirits, "or, what will take a worse toll, you'll even cause it someday, and kill the patient you're trying to cure," Maasterlich said, but that was okay, because it was all a part of the fight. We'd elected to earn our daily bread by daily going head-to-head and toe-to-toe with mortality, "and if you do that" — a *whack* with the pointer — "and suit up every day for the battle" — *whack* — "once in a while" — the pointer fell silent — "you're bound to lose. Because your enemy is implacable and huge, is profound beyond all knowing," too dark, too mysterious, too big, too silent for anyone to fight against it and prevail.

"And isn't it all such crap!" he declared and we'd known it was coming, this wasn't September anymore, when we still might be gulled into the misimpression that this man was swayed by his own svelte logic. We knew the drill and its penalties by now, knew that his every stroke was a windup for the whack. So cheerfully we girded ourselves and greeted it when it came. "Crap!" Maasterlich repeated. "Oh, everything they say you'll see, you'll see. But a surgeon afraid of death is an undertaker for the living," embalming his patients prematurely against their certain rot. "That's not medicine." It especially wasn't surgery. "Every good surgeon I know is romancing life, not 'contesting death,'" and the distinction should guide us. "What you're setting out to do, it isn't war," Maasterlich said, though war and its opposite were oft confused. "It's worship."

Worship: "the highest form of fear" by the old man's definition, "and the truest worship is awe to the edge of terror." The thing worth fearing isn't death, because death is not profound, not meaningful, is "not even much of a mystery. It's the only thing we know enough about," Maasterlich said, and then he got to his question.

"I suggest for your consideration two varieties of silence," he said, "and you must tell me which is larger, longer, deeper, more immense, more eternal, more frightening, more *fearsome,* more worth worshipping: The silence that follows the last note of a musical piece and continues on forever, or the silence that precedes it and lasts a single beat?"

Acoustically, they are identical, he said, for as long as they each last. So by all rights, the *silence forever* should be the more profound, "correct? But it is not. The opposite." He found the lowly musical rest, "the *presence* of a silence, not a vacancy of sound," by every measure more sublime. And grander, and longer, long precisely because it fell between two limits, "for without limits there can be no length at all." The meaning of the rest is suggested by two things, he said, "the melody leading up to it, and the anticipation of the note yet to come," and anyone who'd waited for anything dear understood the enor-

mousness of that, how "expectancy makes a second into centuries."
Unbounded time is instantaneous, as death is short, as the shoreless
sea is shallow. But a span — even the briefest span endures, endures
because its moments hold meaning, are *fraught* with meaning. Since
there's no end to the meanings that a moment may contain — "it may
just contain the universe" — any living moment may be endless, and
endless its depths.

Which brought him back to the heart, the magnificent pump
whose wondrous efforts — its systole contractions and diastole relax-
ations — take place in the silences between the audible beats.

"As you watch your patients' vital signs cross the screen," he said,
and resumed whacking the lectern with his pointer, "as you monitor
their pulse and pressure, remember why you are doing this, why you
are undertaking this endeavor at all"; the pointer fell, and fell again.
"It's not out of fear of the silence of the grave. It's wonder, at the silence that falls between heartbeats. A systole inside diastoles has a
beginning" — *whack* — "and an end" — *whack.* "And between those
two beats lies the only eternity on earth."

I understand, Daniel, why my euphoria and my terror were intermingled. More than intermingled: after my conversation with
Rouchard they were identical, one to the other. Over the course of
one short dinner he'd given me back my family and my beginnings.
He'd asserted my existence by restoring its first border (*whack*). With
that came expectancy (no *whack* yet), and I'd never felt so mortal in
my life.

I spent the night on the couch in the library, where I could hear the
front door open. If it would only just please open. Surely she would
return by her usual way up the lift, and not come up the back stairs
through the chamber of betrayal she'd fled from, the offending apartment. Wouldn't she? What a dreadful dolt I'd been, so enthralled
with my savior act I was oblivious to the damage of revealing, unex-
plained, the secret of my residence next door. As the hours crept and
she didn't come home — *seconds into centuries* — my thoughts darkened and my vision swiveled more and more to view things as she'd
viewed them, and the damage swelled in my imagination. Losing
Alba, the protector so alive in the girl's mind that she'd imagined her

footprints in the carpet, must have been horrible. Alba's Scheheraza-
dean chronicle had been Corie's counsel against recklessness and
risk, calling her away from principled self-demolition. *Accident unlikely,* rang the klaxon in my mind. *What Alba does, she follows* came
the echo. Oh, what must she be going through!

And then to suffer, simultaneously, the rape of her sanctuary
and the violation of a trusted friendship. For I'd considered myself
trusted, though now I was exposed as a liar and a sneak and a spy—
Impersonating a doctor? she'd asked, and I could hear Massue swearing, *Flics, fuckin'* merde—and how was she to know that I wasn't,
wasn't with the police?

Though were I only impersonating Tilde, that would seem monstrosity enough. Sneak.

Spy. When would it dawn on her I'd been eavesdropping on her
piano playing too?

I lay awake in a riot of indecision. Lights off? If she saw them from
the street she'd feel cornered. Or lights on, so she wouldn't feel ambushed when she stumbled upon me in the dark? The truth: it hardly
mattered. Toward morning, racked by a vision of Corie grappling
in the shadows with a ghoul, a professorial impostor turned home-
invading, wall-piercing poltergeist—I suppose I must have dozed off
for a bit—I retreated to my own penitential chamber and pestilen-
tial bed, leaving the closet door wide open as an invite, just in case. In
the morning, the bright sun streamed through the window glass into
an empty and unvisited study whose every drifting, sun-struck dust
mote screamed that Corie was nowhere, that Corie was not coming
back.

The day began its spiral. I was afraid that if I left my room I'd miss
her, miss my chance to explain, the only thing that would stop her
from clearing out for good. At the same time I was eager to escape
the unbearable vigil and shatter this spell, to go somewhere, anywhere, so I could return and discover she'd arrived. Twice I stalked
out to Portbou. Only the first time did I ask directly—had she by any
chance come to look at the photo wall?—because only once did I
have to. When I stepped back in for a quick late lunch, Passim shook
his head as soon as I met his eye, and then I wasn't hungry and waved
a thank-you and left.

I considered going out to Odile's, but I knew that that would be nothing more than bustle. The girl would not have absconded from me in the direction of anyone I knew. For a full thrilling minute I was convinced it would be a brilliant move to call up Capitaine Cassell, the police inspector whose business card sat in my pocketbook, and get him on the case. Worst idea yet. I bumped into Céleste in the courtyard and inquired if she'd seen the young lady. My offhandedness fooled her not a bit. The indictment in her gaze was as blank and cold as river ice. *So you've done it after all,* it said. *You've run off the last of the Landerses.* Could I protest? Could she read, in my eyes, my guilt?

Oh yeah! The last of the Landerses! It was afternoon before I gave any thought to that other small matter, Rouchard's recounting of Saxe's old adventures, the cosmic alteration to my history and my identity. My joy in my ascendancy had been eclipsed before it could shine, and even as it emerged again from behind the shadow of worry, it seemed to me wan and immaterial, and its blessing beamed down like a final desecration.

What pulled me through was the prospect of seeing Emil. He'd been off on one of his missions since our jaunt to Reims, and I'd hungered for him. Now he would be home again. His party was scheduled for this evening, the dinner that he'd invited me to so long ago as we stood in the drizzle in the hospital parking lot on that day he'd insisted on addressing me by my title and then called me Matilde instead. A first lapse. A glimmer of intimacy, the source point of that whole wild sweet arc extending from his silly rain hat through his bleeding lip and the blanket on the church lawn and the night of Le Chemin Vert and the miracle snow to some warm intense conspiracy of the stars, the predestiny I sensed we were constructing. What news I had to tell him! I'd have to talk fast — as he'd amply warned me, he would have to be gone again by the time of Odile's surgery, which could be just days away.

I wished it weren't to be such a busy, public evening. Now I had an added reason to wish for Corie's reappearance, and the wish was sharp enough that I fashioned it into a weapon, a way to get angry at the girl I grieved and feared for. How could I be expected to enjoy my gala night out and conjugal morning with Sahran with her Royal Brattiness so inconsiderately lost? Immediately I forged my weapon into revenge. If she could abandon me, why, I could abandon with the best of them, couldn't I? As I'd reminded Willem, I knew how to use my feet. Happiness would be my riposte.

With that resolve to relieve me, I slept, as I had not been able to for two nights running, and awoke in the early evening suffused with a great, grateful, tattered peacefulness, as though I'd overslumbered, like Rip Van Winkle, the advent of the armistice. I bathed, and slipped back into my good dress — the do was to be a formal one (I'd even received, hand-delivered to Portbou, an ornately engraved invitation) — and renovated my lipstick and mascara. (I was getting so good at *maquillage* by candlelight I felt myself downright Josephine.) Drôlet's limousine whispered up curbside, and I jumped in the back with Odile. She was, I'd been forewarned, one of only two among the celebrants whom I was likely to know, the other being, God help me, Willem, but I wasn't concerned about that. With my happiness already steel-plated and bulletproofed against Corie's absence, the presence of Willem presented no problem at all.

The house on Île Saint-Louis was igneous, its windows ablaze as though it were being consumed from within by inferno. The orange heat blushed through the gray stone façade like smolders of magma in a lava field. The eruption came the instant the front door opened. Cacophony burst out, a hive of chatter fervent and indecipherable above the strains of a string quartet. I'd expected formal; I'd had no idea how grand.

Emil stepped outside to preempt Drôlet with the car door, and he kissed me on both cheeks and then full on the mouth, and lingered there an adhesive moment before leaning into the car to lift his sister, an arm under her knees and another around her back, and carry her up the steps like a slumbering child, though she was anything but sleepy. She was as radiant as the house, and I remembered that this had been her childhood home as well as Emil's, and I wondered how often she got back to it, when the last time had been.

Emil introduced me around. He was attentive, and resplendent. A martial stripe of satin ran down each black leg of his trousers; he was shod in patent leather slippers and wore a white bow tie and a white tuxedo jacket with a rosette in his lapel, and did I imagine in his eyes (for his eyes seemed haunted) the same desire I felt, a frustration with the price of his expansive hospitality, a wish like an ivy itch for when we could be alone? In the living room, the discreetly enabling liquor cabinet had been supplanted by a vast open bar staffed with starched shirts and cummerbunds. The buffet in the dining room was still in a primal hors d'oeuvre stage of existence, though that would evolve over the coming hours through an accelerated time-lapse Linnaean order of flora and fish and bird and mammal, culminating after the quail and lamb (and Darwin claimed evolution had no goal!) in chocolate mousse.

Emil introduced me not just as a doctor but almost the hostess of the *fête,* and when he drifted off to apply diplomacy to one or another social tangle, I felt all the more family, because Odile stayed faithfully by my side, holding my hand, introducing me to everyone who engaged her, as many did with cries of astonished fondness. Her homecoming, I could tell, was a restoration before the restoration, poised as it was before her surgery, and she seemed at times almost breathless under her scarf as her chariot did a victory lap through the rooms where her life had gotten its start. She took my hand, not to be guided but to guide, and though I performed such courtesies as regaling her with buffet options and reaching for her water, she was otherwise the leader, steering me deftly around armchairs and coffee tables and standing lamps and potted palms. Here was the oldest tactile map in Odile's mind.

It was a map of a vanished geography. All the furniture she steered me around was gone. Emil's grand divestment was proceeding apace. The house sale had gone from pending to closed, and the furniture had been sold along with the walls, and whatever appointments the acquiring owners didn't want, including everything downstairs except the carpets, Emil had had removed. The resulting cavern must have been desolate by day; tonight it glittered like a discotheque.

Which it became. At some point the old map was altered further by means of rolled rugs to expose an acre of bare parquet, and the quartet returned from a brief intermission transmogrified into a jazz combo, and shoes were shed as though at the door of a mosque, and people danced. I did a couple of turns with Emil, as it seemed the only way for us to be together alone for a blessed moment, and a jig or two with Willem for the opposite reason: it permitted us proximity without our actually having to talk. He didn't seem hostile, but I sensed the risk. In a very few days we would be intensest collaborators; I didn't want to jinx things with a reanimated swelter of grudge and animus, and I could tell he didn't wish that either, though his wish had the oddest quality to it, a lovely warm netsuke of resentment clutched in the fist of aloofness.

I was glad to get away from all that when the time came to wheel Odile out of the havoc and into the sanctuary of a back bedroom. Her party was over and her victory lap done. Now began the launch of her other restoration, gathering peace and strength for her surgery. As I helped her disrobe, her animation dropped away and I saw her weariness. It crept across her face like gratitude. Even her concern was becalmed by the weight of tiredness. "Did you notice?" she asked as I lifted her legs into the four-poster bed and smoothed the sheet down over them.

"Notice what?" I asked.

"My brother," she said. "It's exactly as I told you." And no sooner did she bring it up than I knew what she meant, for I'd already registered what I wouldn't admit about Emil, that something was off. I'd caught him staring at me across the room, as though behind his party cheer, he harbored a dark thought dense in his mind. His expression dissolved instantly into a wink as soon as he noticed I'd seen him, but too late. I'd caught the eviscerated glance. "Who *are* all these people?" he kvetched into my hair as we danced, and I explained away his mood as distraction. "We have so much to talk about!" he said, and promised we'd reclaim the night for ourselves as soon as we could, "though we may have to settle for the dawn." Wouldn't anyone be distracted, I thought, with so much going on? But distraction wasn't his sister's diagnosis.

"I can see he isn't well," she declared as I pulled up the counterpane and tucked it around her shoulders, and that's the phrase I was pondering as I came back through the vestibule and stumbled on the commotion and encountered, as though I'd dropped through a hole in the earth, the disaster that would both end and initiate my evening. Out on the stoop, people were arguing. One of the voices reminded me of a voice I knew, though vaguely. I stepped through the foyer and out the door into the cold night. All I saw at first was the uniformed back of the doorman, his coat's blue bulk obscuring his antagonist, someone below him on the steps whom he refused to let past into the party. The gatecrasher must have attempted a lateral move because the doorman's back jerked adeptly to counter it, and then she emerged from below him in her Cossack boots and tattersall coat. Céleste. No wonder I'd only half recognized her voice—I'd heard her angry, and I'd heard her sorrowful, but I'd never heard her so out of control. Her face blazed with an abject frenzy bludgeoned by desperation; her eyes were those of a madwoman. Then her eyes found me.

I thought she would climb the doorman like a tree. She threw herself through and over and around him, her arms outstretched, barking my name in a hoarse quaver and holding out in one shaking hand the engraved invitation with my name on it. *"S'il vous plaît, madame, s'il vous plaît, s'il vous plaît"*—her dervish whine accompanied by slobberous weeping—and she yelled that the child was about to do something, *"quelque chose terrible!"*

A calm warmth edged up close behind me, and Emil's breath was quiet in my ear. "The Little One?" he asked.

And I answered, "It seems."

XXIII

T HE CAR SLIPPED GENTLY between the cordon poles, and as soon as we were inside, the waters closed behind us and the soldier hooked the chain again. Drôlet angled us into a space that wasn't any designated space but seemed at least sufficiently out of the way, and Emil stepped out and closed the car door behind him and strode toward a knot of men wearing uniforms and loitering in the lot. They spoke. He walked on somewhere I couldn't see. He seemed quietly purposeful, a toreador departing for the chute.

After Céleste's arrival at his house, Emil had ushered her into the kitchen and soothed her with a snifter of Côte de Something and a shawl around her shoulders until she'd settled her nerves enough to deliver a coherent alarm. Her composure collapsed again as her explanation tumbled out. It tumbled out in confessional form, her confession to a petty trespass leading to a petty theft. She'd let herself into Landers's apartment, she said, snooping for signs of Corie. Fear brought her in; she'd known full well what my question about Corie had implied. She found her corroboration crumpled in a corner of the study. The note was doubly terrifying for inducing a fifty-year-old déjà vu. As with the last such message she'd found, the farewell in Aranese from Carlos Landers addressed to his lost Alba, this one was indecipherable except for those few words where its language overlapped with Céleste's: *necessity, sacrifice.* In a panic she ran for a translator — me — the page clutched in her fist.

She found my door ajar and no one home. She went in (clearly not for the first time) and noticed immediately two things amiss: something added, and some other items gone. The added part was the party invitation, which I'd left on the table. The missing items scared her so terribly that she'd caught a taxi straightaway to the address engraved on the card.

As Céleste slurped, and spewed her confession, we ironed out the note with our palms on a kitchen counter and flipped the dial on the tiny kitchen television until we found a relevant news report and then we stood around viewing helicopter footage of a protest gathering near the Bastille and surging down the boulevards a hundred thousand strong. It was heading toward the Élysée Palace and the American embassy, though security forces were positioning to stop it short of that goal. Police and protesters had already suffered injuries, the television claimed, from thrown rocks and the glass of shattered windows. Hospitals were readying for an onslaught. Emil made a phone call, and another, and now here we were, the three of us — Emil, Drôlet, and I — on the margin of the accumulating storm. Absent Céleste, whom we'd left at the house submitting to the forced sedation of a plate of party food, after which she would hurry back to rue Nin on the chance that Corie might reappear there.

Emil was preternaturally calm on our ride, lodged in a distant place. It was a place I couldn't read: Was he resentful? He had reason, certainly, being crowbarred out of his party. At the same time, his mood seemed like some familiar home place, a country in itself that Emil could inhabit comfortably at will. He stared out the window at the passing slate of Paris, his every muscle entirely relaxed, and occasionally asked me a question. What exactly had happened with Corie at the apartment the night she disappeared? I told him about the telegram, the death of Corie's role model. "And this apartment is exactly next to yours, really?" Had she said anything unusual before her departure? The note she'd left, did it sound like her? The note was a hopeful sign, Emil said. Those most intent on suicide often leave nothing, no word at all of their plans. Who else was involved? he asked. No one, I told him, and he absorbed my answer almost osmotically, facing me immobile as though waiting for my voice to diffuse into his skin. Then he turned to stare out the window, placid.

The emergency had swept away his melancholy. "So much to say," he'd told me as we danced, but whatever he'd intended to discuss, he wasn't discussing it now. And he wasn't the only one with news — oh, no! And what I had to relate would thrill him as greatly as it had me.

I'd cheer him up, by God! That, too, would have to wait, though: This wasn't the time. It wasn't the point of our mission. Anyway, I didn't want to squander the wondrous chronicle of my miraculous inheritance by relating it during Corie's wretched crisis. On the far side of mission, our private dawn awaited.

"So what's your choice, ultimately," he asked, focusing on our business, "among the probabilities?" His question swept me back to our night in Reims, and to my broken promise not to get involved with Corie — did his words contain a reproof? Whatever, they also posed a genuine question. He wanted my diplomatic counsel.

"Not school," I answered, and, with reluctance, "and maybe not the war. Love, maybe. Maybe fear."

"Of?"

"Past, future . . ." I said. "I don't know . . . Emil, I'm sorry."

He looked at me directly then. His wan smile held on valiantly.

I said, "What a mess I've caused."

His forehead wilted into my shoulder, and he reached to clasp my hand to stop my explaining further. And then he righted back into his reserve and his vigil. We'd neared the scene of the *manifestation* — you could tell by the angry clots of traffic and the security forces controlling the intersections — and Emil said to Drôlet, "Over there," and I could see the stockade, in a parking lot, under the icicle glare of generator lights, off in the velvet distance. He said to me, "In a way, you've made things easier."

"What do you mean?" I asked him after giving him time to amplify. Then, guessing, "Emil, where did you go these past days?"

He nodded. The question was right. "Not far," he confessed, and not for diplomacy. As it turns out, he said, "Some things are beyond negotiation." He'd needed confirmation of something, though he'd been sure of it already, he said. "Something I've known for a while."

"Confirmation of what," I said, beginning to go numb.

When he answered, it was as though he were changing the subject. "Remember your Stamps and Buses? What did you say you call it when something is both behind you and ahead?"

"Medically?" I said, the numbness cascading. "I said that, as a doctor, I called it remission."

"Drôlet," he commanded, "here we are. Turn through right here."

We slipped through the cordon and Drôlet stopped the car, and as soon as it was parked, Emil emerged from his thought and from the car door in a single and unitary glide of outward motion. The door swung shut and he strode off across the lot.

A few minutes later he was back, tapping on Drôlet's window. "I'm to be let through," he told the chauffeur. "Alone," he said. He might not be returning to this depot after events played out, so we shouldn't wait. Also, as such things went, it might take till morning to resolve matters, statements to be given and so forth; best we head toward home. And then he began to walk off again, just like that, in his patent leather shoes, pulling the lapels of his dinner jacket up around his ears. I yelled after him, "Emil!," and jumped from the car to arrest his flight.

Thankfully, he wheeled around and returned to me and heard my request. "You can't seriously think that's a good idea," he answered, putting a hand on the roof of the idling limousine.

"I do think! I think it's necessary," I told him. I was obstinate about the one thing, Corie, because I was obsessing about the other. Perhaps I thought that if I could contest Emil on something, everything would be contestable. Mostly, I just wanted to go with him. "I'm the person she needs to hear from," I said. "It's me she's upset with."

"Precisely," he said. We were standing in the crotch of the open door. "Do you know how instantaneous this would be?" he said. "A flinch could be fatal. It's no different than a jumper. And if they managed to save her, it might be even worse, believe me."

"You're afraid I'll set her off," I said. "I see. But I won't! Please. I have to help her."

"Anyway," he said, "that's not the problem."

"I know it's not!" I almost shouted. I could feel the sob rising like a bubble inside me. "I know it's not the problem! Emil, you said it was one hundred percent. That you'd dodged the bullet. What are you telling me now? Why did you lie?"

But he wouldn't be pulled off the topic. "The problem," he continued, "is that you'll be arrested before you get ten yards." He motioned with his head across the parking lot. "The boys over there aren't happy about this. Not a bit, and they told me about it. They feel this whole episode could have been avoided if their search for this person had succeeded. And it nearly did. Until their investigator got thrown off the trail by a mysterious, charming, foreign-born aristocrat on rue Nin. Nin, I'm trying to remember, isn't that close to your duplex?"

I searched his face for recrimination, those limpid eyes, and was surprised to find only amusement. He looked proud. "Anyway," he said, "it was just last night, and now it appears she may be an accomplice, this woman. May be the same individual who sprang our would-be martyr from protective custody on a past occasion, which is why this woman is now the subject of a warrant."

"A warrant," I said. "Me?" And he laughed despite himself. "That all depends," he said. "You wouldn't be Madame Magdalena Landers, by any chance?"

"Emil, I can —" I began, and he silenced me with his fingers against my lips. Then he closed his eyes as if hit with an ache, and his hand dropped. "I didn't lie to you," he said. "I answered your question. You asked if my lymphoma was cured, and it is. The lymphoma. It's just" — he paused — "that you didn't ask the doctor's question, where the lymphoma came from, and I was glad you didn't, Doctor. You asked if it was over. You asked the lover's question."

And I wanted to ask him a hundred newer things, lover's questions all, and to tell him we would get through this, that I knew what he was talking about, how cancers sometimes arise from other cancers, and the one they'd fixed was a sign of deeper illness, but I'd help him. We'd turn this around together, whatever it was. But he cut me off.

"Miss Landers," he said, "I have to ask if you've made the acquaintance of a certain Capitaine Cassell."

"Cassell!" I said.

Emil nodded. "Yes, Cassell. Because here comes the good captain now."

I made to turn and he yanked my wrist. "I wouldn't," he said, and he drew a breath. "Listen," he said, and his firmness had a bitter, incontestable finality to it. "I will get your Corie out of this. I promise you. And you must promise me something in return, and promise it solemnly, this time. That you will attend to my sister." And he impressed upon me, urgently, that I must let nothing stop me in that, must not put helping anyone else ahead of helping Odile, and that

I must take care of myself "before the surgery, and afterward," for as long as she needed me, which meant not getting arrested, obviously, and not getting involved in bizarre capers, and also meant "giving me a very visible embrace and getting back into the car now."

His hug was as brief as it was encompassing, and crushingly tight. "Promise," he breathed, as he held me. The voice was as burdened with needing to know as any I'd ever heard.

"I do," I told him. "I promise." He released me, and as he more or less shoved me through the open door and as I more or less crumpled into it, I heard — or imagined I heard, at least — him whisper, "Don't forget." Or was it "I won't forget you," as I came to wonder later? The door slammed, and I slid into the shadows in the center of the seat as footsteps approached and a voice I knew said, "Ready, Mr. Sahran?"

"Never more," Emil answered. His demeanor had made its immediate return trip to jaunty.

"And you're convinced you can help us in this ..."

"This unfortunate situation, yes, Monsieur le Capitaine, I'm sure, but —"

"But you needed to see me alone."

"I do. There's a matter."

"About this girl."

"I've never met the girl," Emil said. "I'll do my best to return her, and you can do with her as you like. Maybe that will help ease some ... embarrassment, if you will, Capitaine. For the department, I mean. If you want to say you called me in, that's fine." The two men were almost leaning against the car; all I could see were torsos and elbows, a cigarette in a rising hand. "No, I must request your consideration with someone else," Emil said. "It's this Landers person."

"Oh, I see," the captain said.

"Let me strike a deal with you," Emil said, and the two began moving across the parking lot, Emil's hand on the captain's shoulder, a cigarette arcing redly into a puddle. I peered back as the car moved forward, hoping for a stray glance as we exited the stockade, but there was none. He didn't look around.

Our exit was via a different gate than the one through which we'd entered, and when we'd left the depot behind us by only a few dozen meters, Drôlet braked to a halt in the middle of the street and put the car in park. He leaned his arm along the back of the seat and craned his neck around to face me directly. His question was his ancient and only and eternal question, except that this time it was all in his eyes, and, as I'd never known him to ask it so oddly and silently, I was shaken for a moment. Then it came to me that his effrontery was actually an invitation, and that *silent* was as brash as he could get.

"*Toward* home?" he asked finally, echoing his boss's orders, but his emphasis was front-loaded, and he left conspicuous air between the words, and as soon as I recognized the nature of the offer, I took him up on it, gladly.

"Yes, Drôlet, thank you," I said. "'Toward' would be perfect."

The streets were spookily calm — the police had cordoned off the neighborhood. The only movements were the shifting of drivers in the dark cabs of the paddy wagons lined up in convoy along the far curb. Drôlet let the car drift forward at an idling speed with his window rolled down, gazing up through the windshield as if navigating by the stars. Which he was, in a way, or at least by *son et lumière,* sound and light, though his only quicksilver constellation was a helicopter whose gyrations brought it whipping suddenly over the housetops for a few loud seconds of grinding glare before it disappeared again. When its searchlight crossed our path, the world was turned a blinding antiseptic blue. Then it clattered off and left us with another sound, a low throbbing murmur like a pulse beneath the pavement, punctuated at intervals by squalls of whistling whose shrillness pierced the dark like the helicopter's glare, bleaching it the same cold ozone blue. At some point, his inner sextant satisfied him, and Drôlet parked and locked the Mercedes and we walked in the direction of the throb.

We came upon it full blast, suddenly, as we turned around the angle of a last narrow side street into the rumble of a human avalanche. The street before us was a thoroughfare, judging from its width — it must have had multiple lanes and generous, tree-lined sidewalks, all now buried from battlement to battlement beneath the throng of protesters, their multitude flowing over everything indiscriminately. Stoop, stair, truck, curb, car — all was stood upon, the streetscape elevated two meters up into a rolling topography of human heads. Our tributary conjoined the avenue down a small flight of steps, which allowed us a momentary vista over this vast molten flow that extended to our left back through pools of lamplight and under the inane stop-and-go of intersection signals, block after block, as far as we could see. To our right, several score yards away — Drôlet had placed us deftly — the sea met its seawall. We descended down into the mass; it was in that direction that we tried to move.

It was effectively impossible, the pressing so great that at times I was lifted off my feet and rocked back and forth in the stagnant tide. I was afraid to exhale, afraid I wouldn't be able to re-inflate my lungs. The tide had nowhere to go. It washed in place for long minutes and the pressure built and then some shift would occur and the whole mass would adjust an increment in one direction or another and the whistles would blow and we would accommodate to the new equilibrium. Whenever there opened any piece of leeway or when we were set down firmly enough for Drôlet to get traction, he would push us mercilessly ahead through the mass, and eventually in this gradual way we came to the foot of a tall crowd-shape enshrouding, as in amber, a delivery truck.

Drôlet yelled through the roar — I could read the *Madame* on his moving lips better than I could hear it — and he pointed to a person above us who was reaching down a hand. Drôlet gave me a sufficient moment to decline the informality, then he grabbed my waist and lofted me up to meet it. With some scrambling and yanking (you try spelunking in your best silk sheath), I got myself to the top of the palisade and found a place to perch on the edge of those heights and survey the source of our impoundment.

The impediment was only some thirty or forty yards ahead, at a point where the number of people didn't diminish but their mass changed color and character. The road was bisected by a Plexiglas barricade, shields behind which an army of helmeted riot police pushed toward us. Their front ranks wore gas masks; the vanguard of protesters drummed a tattoo on the impassive shields and screamed with an added fury, the two sides facing each other intransigent, warring continents contesting a fault. Like a fault, it would slip once in a while, abruptly one way or the other, and the mass would slide an increment more and the great terrifying whistle would rise into the night.

In the center of the straining line was the most bizarre sight: an embolism, a vacant space half as large as a tennis lawn and placid as a drawing room, delineated only by the solid wall of bodies that respectfully surrounded it, an incredible bubble of peace. The eight or ten people inside the bubble seemed neither pressured nor concerned nor even noticeably interested in the rage without. A column of light from the gyring plane burrowed down constantly onto it, and the little group glistened sharply in the ray like diamonds in a display case. Some of the men (and the one woman I could see) were in uniform, the others in suits. Whatever game was under way evidently required on their part a display of bored equanimity equal to the fervor of the troops. It occurred to me that this was some ghastly mockery of the party I'd just left, the celebrants pacing their parlor absorbed in concentration or in conversation, lost in the mood of the moment, until regularly they coalesced again into a central huddle — all they lacked was stemware.

By these odd rules of engagement, some vital brinkmanship was being advanced. I sensed beneath the bonhomie a massive mutual ongoing accounting of force and resource and nerve, for when one of the suited generalissimos looked out of the circle at the crowd, the crowd responded with a plebiscite of whistles and amplified roar. I recognized Massue's ponytailed head.

Then the row of shields parted, and through the opening, two new parties were admitted into the light. The first was Cassell, who stooped as though crawling from a culvert, and right behind him Emil. The newcomers shook hands around the group, and the huddle reconvened. There was evidently some contention or excitement, and people stepped away from and back into the conversation, and after five minutes or so it seemed a resolution had been hammered out, for there was more shaking of hands and a delegation struck off out of the bubble, tunneling through the crowd. The crowd that had seemed so impermeable found a way to let the delegation through. We (for Drôlet had spelunked up beside me) could follow their progress by the disruption roiling the pond. As they neared the far curb, a new beam, cast down from the whirlybird, landed ahead of them on the building façade. It illuminated, with a supernatural clarity, their destination, a second kingdom of utter calm even larger and even calmer than the one in the middle of the street, guarded by an outward-facing picket of rifle-bearing police. At its center, all alone, was Corie.

XXIV

S HE SEEMED, AT FIRST sight, more eerily oblivious even than the generals, more oddly insulated from the tumult. She was at the top of some sweeping steps, the building at her back, sitting in a lotus position, forearms on knees, an icon of contemplative serenity. Her gaze was concentrated on the ground just before her; the police guards at the foot of the stairs held the crowd at bay as though the girl were a bomb that might detonate. I discerned the source of their caution. In one outstretched hand was a large open bottle, and in her other an object that glinted like a heliograph in the searchlight and glowed like a candle whenever the beam skipped away. It was Saxe's hurricane lamp, its wick aflame, missing its crystal chimney. The pavement around her glistened with spilled oil, and her jeans and coat were dark with it.

The ripple through the crowd arrived at the steps and eddied there a minute, and then I could see the pickets relent to admit someone out of the swirl and through the cordon. Emil emerged onto the steps. He climbed them without haste or hesitation, neither slow nor especially fast. His walk was without worry, it had purpose without guile, and a destination without any urgency. It was a walk without qualities. His hands were in the pockets of his jacket, and his head was down, and I imagine the effect, as he approached her, must have been like one of those cobras I've read about that hypnotize their prey with a lullaby of swaying. If Corie felt threatened or had moved to ignite herself, I couldn't discern it from where I was, but no flames rose and there was no conflagration. Emil strode to her without rush or pause, and with an almost blasé unconcern he sat himself down beside her, right in the puddle of fuel.

Somewhere inside of me it occurred to my conscience that a man I'd accused of being so self-serving he would pilfer a stranger's heart was engaged here selflessly in rescue, so selflessly he'd sat down in kerosene beside a stranger wielding an open flame, a stranger whose Armageddon he'd volunteered to share. Traitorous first impressions! Emil's tuxedo jacket shone like the brightest snow, and they began their conversation.

Impressions. Daniel, you must forgive me, I cannot seem to keep the whole thing straight. It all conflates from midnight on, Emil and Corie sitting at the top of the steps so side by side, so grave and close and calm in the jitter of the hovering beam—they derange in my mind with the other quiet huddle under the other and closer lamp, the lab coat Willem always liked to wear, like a lucky garment beneath his scrubs, as white as Emil's tuxedo. The street crowd had fallen in two as Emil ascended and sat, and its sound was cleaved in two, for everyone on the boulevard who was close enough to see fell silent, and the silence echoed off the wall of chant persisting from far corners. The silence spread by word of mouth, grew deeper. Wall to wall, the block became a chapel, you could hear the masses breathe into the apse of the sky as the whistling stopped and the drumming against the shields stopped and the only sound was the sound of waiting and the dry pulse of the helicopter rotors in the high distance, and Willem announced, "Begin quiet," and the Bach invention that had accompanied our preparations was killed with a punch to a button on the CD player, and our work began in earnest.

I had arrived at the hospital on the morning after the night that followed the night of the demonstration, knowing with relief that Corie was alive and Sahran somewhere, but not knowing where they might be. In jail, I assumed, in Corie's case, and in Emil's? Had he headed out so soon? Without so much as a word?

I used irritation to keep my anxiety at bay during the empty intervening day between those nights, but it hardly worked. My Sunday was spent in a torpor of agitation. The trauma of the standoff on the steps, of Corie's flirtation with death and Emil's hinting about it, induced a sort of narcolepsy in me whenever I thought about it. Every excitement incited deeper somnolence, and I lay physically exhausted to the precise degree that I was racked by worry inside. I was thankful when the next day dawned and my morning call to Mahlev brought a summons to the hospital. Drôlet drove me over, and I distracted myself with routines, chatting with Odile about this and that as she settled her system and we awaited word of when an organ might arrive.

The moment word came, our surgery would commence. Once a heart is cut from the donor's chest by a harvest team, it has only four or five vital hours before a metabolic despair sets in and it begins to die, a loneliness of tissue. That single imperative sets the pace for everything else that happens: transport alone can eat up an hour — or longer, certainly, depending on where the donor is. The first thing required is readiness. This was the event I'd come for. I slept the last night in the hospital, in an empty patient's room.

Willem was nowhere to be seen during that day of hospital waiting. Then, in the evening, I heard his voice in Mahlev's office. There was some eleventh-hour fracas over the arrangements, and in the lounge down the hall where a couple of us had gathered, we could hear the tenor, though not the details, of the discussion. It wasn't hard to guess the situation — these things are common at the last minute. Was there a holdup? A likely donor discovered to be inappropriate? But at five the next morning I was awakened by Mahlev, who let me know with a knock and a whisper that we were on. I washed and got into my scrubs and hustled to the theater. When the transport arrives with the donor heart, the recipient should be open.

"Still There Drips In Sleep Against the Heart," I murmured to myself, running through my equipment and my drugs. I stroked Odile's hand. The hypnotic had been added to the IV, and she was succumbing; her talk had faltered into senselessness and soon it would stop. "Grief of memory." Memory: my meter — the pulse oximeter — was attached to her fingertip; her vitals were scrolling across the display. Her voice was supplanted by a different and deeper reporting.

Her repose at this moment was the profile I consider the most unfathomable and most disquieting point in surgery (it's the aspect some observers find the most unbearable, aside from the smell), the hardest thing to acclimate one's mind to, for surgery's most remarkable aspect isn't its violence; "That's just what's bound to happen when those most weak are prostrate before those most ambitious," as Maasterlich liked to say. It was the weakness itself, the breathtaking vulnerability of the anesthetized patient. The patient, as Odile now, lay exposed before God, a sacrifice, utterly naked and unconscious and defenseless, supine on the tabernacle, inert as a roll of veal, a billowy bag of acids.

No one but God noticed, generally. The crew was now quite busy. Odile was officially a thing. She'd been unrobed and slathered orange-yellow with antiseptic, her gentle belly jiggly as tired aspic as they swabbed her, the swabbing as unceremonious as painting an apartment wall or basting a fowl, her legs spread wide. The circulator nurse was bent between her legs, parting away from the brown folds of her labia the stray thin wisps of her pubic beard as he fed a catheter into her urethra.

The bustle in the room, the general obliviousness to the profundity of this human frailness, exacerbated the impression I always had, whenever I thought to notice it, that the patient was an invisible angel. She might have descended out of her celestial plane just as unnoticed to levitate anywhere — over a city sidewalk or midfield in a playground — but she had chosen to descend to the center of OR 5. The impression was exact. We in our scrubs were proudly at our knitting, busy people busy with our worldliest routines, while Odile, divested of all will (and all clothes) and tossed so thoroughly out of conceivable existence, reposed in a submission so complete it was tantamount to grace. I gathered two short pieces of transparent tape and moved to seal her eyelids to her cheeks, to keep her eyes protectively closed, as is customary, and then I paused — and then put the tape on anyway.

Willem had come in and was leaning against the tile wall completing his paperwork. The scrub nurse was counting her array of calibrated gold and silver clamps, and the perfusionist had pulled up a stool behind the heart-lung bypass machine, a contraption the size of an upright piano made of stainless steel, a carillon of big and little bottles and long and longer tubes. When Odile drifted off, I took her to the final level, administered the paralytic, and prepared to put the line in.

I swabbed her neck, and inserted the hypodermic. I could feel it enter the vessel right away, and I pulled back on the syringe and checked the color of the blood. It was dark, not arterial crimson, thankfully — there was always a tiny ping of relief; you didn't want to get that one wrong — and I said to myself, "Jugular," and fed in the guide wire. I made a nick in the skin around the wire to accommodate the large hollow dilator sheath. I floated the catheter over the guide wire, slowly, pushing an increment with each throb of her pulse, down the living tube. The vein coursed beneath the skin of her neck before submarining into her chest. I advanced the catheter to the vena cava, just above the heart, removed the guide wire, verified the blood flow, and then sutured the catheter in place. "Line's in," I announced when I'd gotten it arranged the way I wanted it.

I inspected Odile's pharynx with a laryngoscope, and edged a breathing tube down her throat and between her vocal cords, lungward. She accepted it easily, the dear. Some throats are so resistant (some in fact almost impossible). I attached the bag and squeezed the pleated fabric and released, and squeezed it again, and watched the rise and collapse of her shiny chest.

"We're breathing," I told the room.

The yellow corpus was gone now. The circulator nurse had packed Odile carefully in prodigious layers of Sanidrape, so that only a rectangle of her chest was visible through the sky of blue shrouds, and her face and neck, and I stretched the ether shield across her neck, the blood-brain barrier between Willem's world and mine: his rectangle of thorax, my cradled head. Soon Odile would be an inert mound of cornflower blue trailing gussets of reddest red through seven-foot-long tubes into a contraption by her feet.

Willem said loudly, "Hard stop."

Activity ceased, even the flurry of fingers, even the shuffling of clogs, and there was only the slow electronic *beep, beep* of heartbeat on the monitor. The circulator nurse reached for his checklist.

"Patient name?" Willem said.

"Sahran, Odile," the nurse said.

"Procedure?"

"Transplant, simple."

"Organ?"

"Heart."

"Surgical site?"

The assisting surgeon said, "Not marked."

"Allergies?"

"None," I said.

"Any clinical or nonroutine issues?" It wasn't for me to answer, but no one else spoke.

"Cerebral palsy," I said. "From birth. Lower-limb paralysis, blindness. Past surgeries for associated complications, abdominal and orthopedic."

"Have you given any pre-op antibiotics?" he asked me.

"No."

He looked up and around the huddle.

"Does anyone have anything to disclose?"

A brief silence, then six consecutive individual noes, followed by another, final.

"No," Willem declared.

The circulator nurse tied the strings of Willem's mask behind his head, and as I watched him nudge his goggles back onto his nose my affection overwhelmed me. It had been a long time since we'd worked together, and I was reminded why I liked to, because he was so very thorough. Not every attending surgeon does a hard-stop time-out, but Willem always did, assuring we had set out to commit the right acts on the right patient. Everything up to now was reversible. What was to come was not. With a scalpel, he sliced a shallow, straight incision from clavicle to diaphragm down the center of Odile's chest, parting her skin to expose the fascia beneath.

"Bovie," Willem said, and the scrub nurse handed him the hot-tipped wand of the cauterizing knife. Out in the night air — the air of a couple nights past — the conversation had lasted nearly half an hour, and the impatient crowd had set up its clamor again. For a while, the pair on the steps had occupied the center of an excruciating concentrated quiet. I was glad when the resuming roar gave them back their privacy. I stood immobile in the crush and tumble, feeling, except for Drôlet's protective, restraining arm around my waist, untouched and alone.

Across the avenue the two of them sat, tiny adjacent figures in their bubble of back-and-forth. I could see the talk ebb at times to nothing, to sulk, and then come animating all the way back to argument. I tried to conjure the words at play, the moments of risk and reassurance, whether the end would spell life or disaster for both. And ahead of the crowd's noticing, I noticed. And my heart whistled long, so long, before the crowd's great deafening whistle marked the moment when she moved her arm and reached out to hand Emil the lamp, and before he reached to set it aside on the stair and rolled back to hug her with her head in his hand and pulled her temple against his chest, and before the centurions turned from guards to jailers and rushed to bury them in a mountainous tackle, I saw him draw down the wicked wick and, between tongue-moistened fingers, pinch the heat out of the flame, and the little puff of ash-smoke ascended like an offering on the air. Willem lay the hot point of the Bovie knife to the top of the incision in Odile's chest, and drew down the first long line. The yellow flesh cringed from the livid scorch to reveal an arroyo of magenta and honey, and the white puff rose, and with it the atrocious aroma of Odile burnt to bacon.

XXV

B Y THE TIME I SENSED trouble, she was split full open, her rib cage pulled akimbo by the windlass clamped into her sternum, her pericardium unzipped and her heart exposed. For a girl who'd been on the dance floor several nights ago, she sure did need a new heart. Oh, it beat like a bean, dancing away merrily in there, bumping with insurrection like it would leap out onto the table, but you could see right away what the trouble was. It was big. It was congested and far too large and its bump was gimp. It didn't have the nice rolling ventricular gallop that marks the contractions of a healthy beating heart. Some of the muscle of the wall or septum had probably died to deadweight. It would pull the rest down eventually. Willem snipped into the aorta above this antic creature and sewed in the cannula for the bypass machine, banging on the tube to get the air out, and after I'd got the anticoagulant started and had announced, "Heparin is in," the plastic hoses flushed table-length with that indescribable, electric bruise-bright crimson of heart blood, and the perfusionist said to the room, "We're on the pump."

The room temperature was plummeting by then, toward the high 50s Fahrenheit that would slow Odile's metabolism and keep the iced replacement heart from warming up and beginning its rot before we could get it into her. The climate would convince the rest of us we were descending into the crypt, and soon I would reach for a blanket to shawl my shoulders, in ecstasy. I could feel myself back in the current of surgery's lovely, seductive sway, reentering the altered state it had always allowed me.

Patients after an operation notice the constrained, private look on the surgeon's face and assume he's being stoic about all the gore and corruption he's been made to witness, and they feel a bit chagrined about putting him through such horror. They want to say that they're better than this, that their best side's more human than their insides, but they're wrong. What the surgeon can't confess is that he's already witnessed them at their most magnificent, seen a side of them they'll never have the privilege of knowing, so brilliant and extraordinary, so exceptional to their dreary daily exterior that to admit the preference in its full blunt force would trouble people, would seem to revel in a ghoulish perversion of blood-love. For blood-love it is, an awe for the whole wet, mad, divine, ingenious jalopy, and even its genius afflictions, because the tumor and the lesion also attest to miracle, are full of the mystery of striving.

And the colors! To delve beneath the skin is to part the lapping flannel of the grim Atlantic and dive into a South Sea paradise, its coral reefs and tropical grottoes inhabited by every outrageous iridescence. Organs are as day-shy as deep-sea creatures; they oxidize to dun in the open air. The heart that appears a rump-roast russet when hauled out of the chest is a carny of neon inside of it. Its atria are aubergine and violet, and the red-veined fat swaddling its ventricles a synthetic, delicate, cautionary orange, the whole of it moody and mercurial, spangled as a butterfly and glistening like a poisonous frog.

Willem and his assistant stood face to face over their exquisite excavation, cutting and cauterizing and tying off. I was surprised at the rapidity of their work. Usually, a surgeon as cautious as Willem will want to have the replacement heart in hand before cutting the old one out, on the odd chance the courier has a flat on the freeway or the chartered jet hits a fog bank. But here they were, already lifting out of Odile's chest her crippled, poisonous, butterfly heart and setting it aside. The core of her gaped like a shoebox.

Odile, who had relinquished control of her lungs, now emerged into the abeyance, a category of existence unknown and unknowable; she was living but unequipped for life, her circulation waveless, her respiration breathless, her diaphragm stilled, her heart discarded, her systems supplanted by motors and regulated by chemicals, she was demi-organic and fully unviable, as incapable as a carcass. She was a thing of the future, alive without a pulse. She was a cadaver with a brain, her brain sustained by pumps and pistons over which her brain had no control, for we did. Wherever was the panel for the hospital's circuit breakers, there was a switch inside it bearing her life's label; throw it and she'd wink out like a light bulb, and what must her brain think of that? (In case of power outage, the heart-lung machine had a backup, a hand crank like a hurdy-gurdy, which fact had never offered me much comfort. It was my job to turn it.) The nurse opened the insulated cooler (a courier had just stepped in to drop it off, like clockwork) and Willem plucked the replacement organ from its bath of freezing saline.

For a while, I was swept along in the sway of all this wonder, drawn down the irresistible conveyor through the melodrama of Odile's inner workings, and I was happy with that, indescribably. As Willem kneaded the replacement heart to force the air and saline out, and then set it not delicately into its new apartment, and flopped it over face-up and edged it into position, I was sincerely glad to be working with him again. I relished him as a surgery partner for reasons that went beyond his rigor, I admit. Whatever our recent disagreements, we were still the oldest of teammates, he and I, our routines and movements shaped to each other's according to the decades and thanks to the experience of acquiring our hand trades side by side, all those many years ago. If he'd called for a Chrysler, I (alone here today) would understand what he meant — the clamp that old daft Dr. Barber had forgotten the name of that time, lamenting to the nurse absurdly that he wouldn't know it from the Chrysler Building. And if Willem demanded, "Madison," I'd sluice the unattached organ with a dose of cold-preservation fluid (one variety of fluid is named University of Wisconsin solution). A dozen like that, a score, a gross and bushel of such. Every stable operating team coins its own language, and he and I had ours, and our own routines too, and so I knew what Willem meant when he said (to the assistant's visible surprise), "Miss Anselm, if you please?" and I slipped around the ether shield, and the circulator nurse got me elaborately antiseptic and scrubbed me in with new gloves and I joined the scrum tableside, standing next to the surprised assistant, ready for my cameo.

The particular occasion was the suturing in of the third of the four great vessels (in the order in which Willem liked to work), the

inferior vena cava. It's a tricky one to stitch. Well, they're all tricky
—the rubbery aorta; the flimsy, floppy pulmonary—but this one's
location makes it harder to reach, and its inconsistent size makes it
easy to pull or pucker. Willem had developed his own best method
for reaching it, which worked reliably to relieve all strain on the su-
ture site but benefited from an extra set of hands to prop the heart in
position, and over the years and especially in private hospitals where
our teams weren't augmented by fellows, those hands had often been
mine. "Miss Anselm, if you please?" he said (and this its own bit of
homebrew, from the first time I, a resident then myself, had been invited to dig into cardiac doings, by starchy old Dr. Oldenmeyer), and I
glowed in the acknowledgment of our long association, and stepped
around and got scrubbed in and as soon as Willem keyed me with a
nod, I reached through the clamp into Odile's chest and cradled her
luscious new bauble in my fingers, lifting it exactly the degree and
angle that I knew Willem wished (he must be glad to be working with
me again too!) so he and his assistant could perform their magic with
arc needle and ligature.

It had been years since I cupped a heart in my hands. It was like
holding a newborn, a tiny miracle ready to kick like hell. Odile had inherited a lovely, bright, eager little heart, I could feel how game it was,
and ready to go, as though it were imbued with mission and warmed
by its own anticipation.

And I thought: *Warm.*

At first what I felt through the latex was what I anticipated, the
warehouse chill of a well-packed icebox heart. Oddly, the cold ran
only surface deep, like the skin-chill of a child who's been playing too
long in the snow, and within a dozen seconds it had burned off like
hoarfrost, or as though my touch (though my touch was statue still)
had chafed the rose back into a chill-bit cheek, and then the infernal thing kept warming and warming, was warmer than the room,
was warmer than Odile, and I had a moment's irrational alarm that it
might keep on heating up and heating up, might combust inside her
like a coal in a brazier. I looked up in panic. I expected the astonishment of a gallery of wide-eyed onlookers, but my comrades were all
busy at their tasks, oblivious to the alchemy playing out right in front
of them.

"Solution!" I demanded, and someone gave her a dose of cold Wisconsin, but the little furnace still felt like it was coming alive in my grasp. And as it did, as it divulged its secret heart to hand and I absorbed through my fingers what it had to say, I sped through confusion, through disbelief and terror and revulsion, and felt the tears start sharp behind my eyes, and immediately I had to stanch them, for to weep into this open chest would be as deadly to Odile's prognosis as would any shift of stance or posture before they wrapped up the sewing-in. With a strain of effort I immobilized my panic to immobilize myself, and I braced my knees against the side of the table to keep them from buckling under me and braced my mind against hatred.

Oh, Daniel, the news, once it came, came from everywhere. It poured out of every vacancy, from every lack I'd willingly overlooked, the absence of his usual restraint as Willem cut out Odile's heart so quick, the absence of relief when the new one arrived like clockwork. Clockwork, Daniel: the absence of allowance for the sloppiness of scheduling of a transport between two hospitals down French backcountry lanes, and what other hospital could it possibly have come from? The absence of any hospital near enough to this one, that a heart from there would still be so warm on arrival.

Willem and me, our collaboration was like this: a room where every time you've entered it for twenty or thirty or fifty years, a lamp has stood on its place on the shelf, but this time when you enter it's not there, and you derive from its absence the whole slow enormous fact of things, the future foretold in the missing crystal ball. The new heart had arrived and Willem had lifted it out of its cooler and plunked it into her chest with less than his usual sizing-up and turning-over, as though he already knew what he had to work with. He'd made his first three running sutures and tugged them to snug the newcomer into place and set about his tailoring immediately, the slicing and snipping, the edgework of artery and atrium that would permit the two parts of this hybrid to precisely coincide without any pursing or bunching or stretching out of shape at the stitches, and that's how it worked, one soft tissue adjusted to fit another. But with all the leeway the softnesses allowed, there were still so many reasons why one heart might be restless in another heart's nest; even the best of hearts

was sometimes unsuitable, for reasons you couldn't anticipate—
Hatfield and McCoy stuff, stuff like that, incompatible families.

That too: the absence of incompatible families. I expected Willem
to do as he always did, to tumble this newcomer over in his hand, interrogate its heft and take its measure, apprise the cut before he paid
the butcher, but he hadn't, or hadn't sufficiently, not quite as much as
he used to do. The curiosity and the superstitious fidgeting, checking
for injury or imperfection, for the congenital puncture between the
two atria that is so common and so easy to repair (at this point) with
a single stitch, settling the interloper this way and that to see how it
fit the pit, almost the way a gardener plants a tree, musing how the
roots should go this way and the branches that—all that procedure
was absent, absent.

The way Willem had always been, he wasn't, quite, and the ab-
sences gathered to accumulate to a certainty. I couldn't admit it then,
couldn't have accepted what I already knew without bringing on general catastrophe, so I did what I had to with my every nerve immobilized, and my only advantage was a great one, that what I was at-
tempting not to think was wholly and entirely unthinkable. As soon
as I had been freed from my rigid duty—"That will suffice, Miss Anselm," Willem said, quoting again, jocular; he had no idea I'd caught
on, no inkling of the emergency storming my brain—I checked
Odile's vitals on my display and gave the nurse a nod and excused
myself from the room. It was a traditional time for the anesthesiologist to leave things with an understudy and grab a swift break, if
needed. Soon they would take Odile off the bypass machine and it
would be time for redoubled vigilance as they reventilated the lungs
and extracted themselves, retracing their steps, drawing her breastbone closed with heavy lengths of stainless alloy wire like closing a
boot with a lace, then hammering the twisted steel pigtails flat to the
bone with the side of the pliers and basting her fascia shut over them,
and then her skin, and there she would be again, orange and unremarkable, restored.

I excused myself calmly and pushed out through the swinging
doors into the recovery area, the central reservoir into which all the
ORs emptied. No one was about; no other procedure was scheduled
for the day, another incriminating absence. I looked around at the

several sets of doors, their portholes darkened, indecisive. Then it occurred to me: of course. It occurred to me in Mahlev's remembered voice. *I directed you to the wrong room:* Mahlev that day in his dither. With a somnambulist's sureness, I stepped to the middle door and entered.

OR 3 wasn't completely dark; someone had left the light on in the light box for viewing x-rays. I stood just inside the door awhile, letting my eyes adjust to the dim glow and preparing my mind for what it was about to confront. How thoroughly that confrontation has haunted me since! — hounded my thoughts and bludgeoned all my dreaming into a single, inescapable dream.

In the dream, I walk not slow, not fast to the table in the center of the shadow of the room. They haven't removed him yet. They are waiting for everyone to vacate the ward. I imagine the harvest team is already on a plane. He is covered with a sheet. He is nothing now but a shape in a shroud. I go up and stand beside the shape, blue cloth bluer in the gray light from the light box. I lay my hand on his chest, on the cloth where the rise of his chest is, and let it rest for a minute there, consoling him or me. Then, with a surge of strength or will — it's the last bit of usable anger in me — I punch him hard in the sternum with my fingers, and the drape plunges into the open slit, and as the hollow sucks my hand into its absence, the hem of the cloth retreats to reveal dark hair and a forehead, then a noble nose, and his busted lip, and then I awake, my bedclothes twisted around me like a truss. In my dream, whoever put him under taped his eyes.

And maybe it would have been better if that's how it had been. Maybe it would have settled me to see Emil, to have found some certainty to accompany what I knew. Horror can be a useful paralytic, administered in sufficient dosage. The hysteria in my skull would still wail for a lifetime. Just maybe it might not be so shrill, so unabating, if I'd found him before they could whisk away the evidence. If I could have been granted that confirmation.

Instead, I flipped the wall switch and the light erupted onto emptiness. The table smiled back without subtlety or shadow and was hard and chilly when I laid my hand against it. The room was absent not only Emil, but everything, every sign of any past at all: *not even a ghost.* The tile walls gleamed innocently, and the floors; the light box held no films. The normalcy of everything ridiculed my suspicions.

Maybe it would have been better for me if I'd found him, but I was so, so relieved not to, so very relieved to be wrong, to be spared the worst, if only for a while, so willfully glad for the precious gift of just enough illusion to last me through the day.

In gratitude, I returned the room a favor. Before leaving, I stepped over and darkened the x-ray panel. I'd flipped the light-box switch and turned back to head for the door before I saw it. I noticed it just as I turned to exit, the little flat coin flat on the floor, lurking there directly in my path. I stopped and stared at it in utter perplexity, this little daub, this crimson dime on the spotless tile floor. My perplexity was that I knew right away what it was and what it meant, recognized immediately what a grievous debt this dime would cost me, even before I knelt to inspect it more closely and extended my arm slowly and tentatively to tap it with the tip of a finger. Yes, it was wet, still as wet as it was red. A single fresh drop of blood.

XXVI

G RIEF IS A SOLIDER THING than suspicion, Daniel, solider than fear. Grief is work, and all I could do . . . all I could do was begin it. Kneeling there by the blood spot in the blameless, spotless room, that's just what I did. I ordered my tasks and began.

And that's what got me through the next two hours, barely, some oil-and-water admixture of grief and disbelief. The serious and immediate and main thing was Odile, and I stepped back into OR 5 and took up where I'd left off behind my ether screen, a presentable zombie, putting Odile through her remaining paces, alert for the last-minute danger, any reflux requiring suction, any reluctance to breathe again. How fatally reluctant she would be, did she know! And did she ever find out, she would rip her chest open with her own two hands, of that I was sure. *Before the surgery, and afterward,* I heard, and heard myself say, *I promise.*

And so I became a conspirator.

Willem alone had noted the minutes, known to make anything of them beyond a regulation break, and I could feel his quizzing eyes on me when I took up my task. I didn't say anything, wouldn't even look at him until later, when he accosted me in the stairwell after we'd gotten Odile to intensive care, when he'd try to begin to explain it all, and I would give him my verdict, straight and unadorned, that he and I would never speak again.

I fed Odile the palliative and watched on the monitor to see it counteract the anesthesia. On those rare occasions when someone doesn't make the climb, it's generally on the first step that they stumble. They refuse to do the about-face. Was that where Odile had dallied at the end of her childhood operation? What had tempted her to stay that time? I could feel myself pushing her with every wish I had. When I saw on the display that she'd turned and stepped, I thought, *Good: come. You're beyond the abeyance, the room is warming, wherever you've gone to, come.* Her pulse beeped steady on the oximeter, and it occurred to me, *Emil,* as though I recognized its voice.

I saw her through the finalities. She came to in the ICU and I stayed with her long enough to kiss her forehead and assure her everything had gone beautifully, to welcome her back before she drifted off again, holding her hand as though pulling her up the last yard to the surface, and when she let go, I sank.

For that's what I did, Daniel. Whatever the spirit was that had buoyed me most of a lifetime gave up and gave out and lost its spell and let me all the way, all the way down. The sensation wasn't, as I'd always imagined it, of slipping smoothly through a satin vortex, but of banging down stairs the rough way into oblivion, down a rotted ladder rung by rung by rung. Each rung had a name on it. I couldn't see through the dark where the ladder led; I wasn't drawn by destination. It's just that each rung had a name on it and the name was a question, and the answer to each question was the question written on the rung below, so I took the first step and asked, *What have I done?*, and embarked on my descent. *Done, with* all my smug prattle about the morality of things.

[Step]

Who cares? He didn't, to leave you in such a way.

[Step]

But he did care. I do. He had no choice.

[Step]

He made a choice.

To save his sister.

To not be with you.

He couldn't have, not for long.

Not saying how very sick he was.

[Step]

Willem did. Willem said "pancreas."

Afterward.

Yes, afterward. In the stairwell. Said, "Emil knew he had pancreatic cancer, knew he was dying and that death would be soon, and ugly, and pointless." And that I was being . . .

[Step]

. . . illogical.

Willem said that?

Said, "Look at it rationally. We've put a cancer patient's heart that no one would have accepted into a cripple whom no one would have saved. We've spared a man who was going to die anyway a few months of agony and made his end a happier one and converted a sure and purposeless death into the wondrous gift of life." He demanded I tell him why I wouldn't call this . . .

Call it what?

My "finest hour as a doctor."

[Step]

That's hard.

Not hard. Wrong.

You call it wrong.

Oh yes!

And when Emil sat in kerosene beneath a wobbling candle and risked his life to save the life of a stranger, your friend, at your behest, was he wrong then too?

[Step]

Oh, but . . .

[Step]

Why not? Explain. Is it because his death then was merely possible, not certain?

That's a fine distinction.

Though the good was merely probable too — with your Corie, it was never more than a maybe, at the best. But in Odile's case, the good was as guaranteed as all his sacrifice and all your skill could make it. Doesn't certainty of good justify certainty of sacrifice?

And so?

So your grand morality is really a matter of bettor's odds, is that what you're saying?

I don't think . . .

And your absolutes a matter of degree . . .

Because I . . .

—and this distinction you draw between murderer and saint comes down to some secret gambler's balance of sacrifice and risk.

No.

And if you had the chance to take the risk . . .

[Step]

. . . to save someone . . .

[Step]

Would you?

I might have.

[Step] Silence.

And did you?

[No step]

[No step]

No.

[Step]

No?

No.

I see.

I didn't take the chance.

I see.

And with the concluding of the questions, I gave up the struggle and let the current have me. I'm not sure how I'd even gotten home from the hospital, got myself to Saxe's place and up the stairs to shut myself in and set out the pills in their cheerful array on the table and draw the glass of water from the tap. I don't know how I got there and don't know why, considering what I had planned, I waited for the water to run so cold from the faucet before I filled my glass and pulled down the blackout curtain against any intrusion of light.

But then the twilight was breaking through everywhere around me, a Perseid of quick white sparks, spinning past like fireflies as I tumbled. I tumbled for days, pursuing him. Was I? I could taste him sometimes, ahead of me, a soft linger in the charred air, and my hurtle fled downward at terrific speed through a darkened plain, through an upended farm of shadows whose nearnesses eluded me, though distance still stood patient on the brink, a far gradual picket of tall trees. We were in the rolling cabin again, the snowflakes curled against the speeding glass, and you'd bent your legs up beside you on the seat to recline across my lap. I watched the snow through the window as you slept, thinking so slowly in the warm crust of your slumber of how everything were, and of how it was going to be. And it would have been, maybe, if the night had turned out differently, but now the train was another one, hauling along the wet plateau and the trees that stalked the horizon were a march of linked children, standing to stare as the lights flashed by on tall poles in black fields of blacker violets, and after some immediate curt great span we burst at last through a blinding jamb of doorway, and I hit landing. My hand that could still feel against itself your warmth was grasped in another's hand.

"Are we here?" I asked in the quiet, breathless.

"Do you promise?" came the voice. We stepped out from a room down steps, across a yard into a wood. Oblivion claimed the twilight and all shone clear and sharp along the length of a path where we wandered for hours dayless without rest, or needing such, with the shade drawn down against any chance of dawn, and I inquired, "Is he ahead?" And at one point: "Close?" And at another, "Is here where it happened?" And I was answered, again, "Do you promise?" And the word I heard was *patience.* The woods ended. The flash and shadow of the woods subsided and the clouds were behind us like a storm shore. We stepped out from the edge of the trees. We were in a garden lit by a clear dark stark as moonlight, the path flowing through it a twist of palest sand. I felt in his hand my wounded hand. We curved as the path did, a long swept beach through a ledger of midnight pansies, aligned in an order of orderly contemplation, and no sooner did we arrive there at the edge of those thoughts than I met the only thing in all our journey that cast its own shadow and moved of its own will.

It moved like an abstraction. The geometry extended itself as inexorably as a dream and so absent hurry or halt or acceleration that I couldn't tell really if it moved at all. It extended relentlessly across the path without ever extending all the way, or getting any farther, as though the source receded equal to the brilliant point's progressing, like a river contained in a pure and widthless line that never got longer or the least depleted as the river rolled past unpassing. Its brilliant point was a ball of tannish yarn, unspooling without diminishment. The hand that guided me stopped us there. I saw beside the path and beside the little blossomy hedge the mottled cat's face grin up at me, deranged, and the paw push out across the trail the resolute, tempting, and fascinating line.

The tail twitched. The voice said, "I only go this far."

I stepped to the string and made to leap over it but couldn't. The voice had released me, but the hand had not.

I was surprised at this restraint, and irritated, and wished wonderfully to go, and made to step again, and again felt the grip. Angrily, I shook it off. I looked ahead, past the hedge of thoughts at the country beyond the string, and saw where the path led, over a high suspension bridge through a bower of gold vines to an island in an alabaster room, and I knew that here every splendid friend awaited me, that here you awaited me also, Daniel, you among the others. Then, out of this most cool radiance, a couple materialized, and a man and a woman ambled down the path to greet me. They liked each other, you could tell that they would. Tell better than they could what future lay before them. It was me they'd come to visit! They loved me, and their eyes met mine in welcome, the gentleman in his buttoned brown suit, the woman in not the very nicest pants, and he turned to say to her, "Then you'll never be alone."

My foot lifted toward them into its step, and just as it did a thought swept my mind, came to mind in the very most visceral way, or, that is, maybe it came to my touch, for the vision was entirely in my hands. I didn't quite recognize it right away, it felt so distinctly like music. As though I could hear from another place the last notes of the Brahms again, the chord and then the silence, and as I awaited the arrival of the ultimate note, my step suspended, it was then I felt the spasm. I'd only just set my burden back into its chamber. The command hadn't come to release the cross clamp and let the flow engorge the atrium and summon this stranger's muscle back to life, but somehow the heart must have gotten a foretaste, some rumor of blood must have dripped its way in and sent out its funny current, for just as I laid it to rest in its den, the muscle grabbed and spasmed, and I waited, suspended, and another, stronger spasm came, and came again, and Emil's heart — hers — Odile's heart beating of her own twin's life-will took up its cadence in my hand.

All this swept through me with an onrush of greater grief and horror. And with something else that was greater by far than sorrow, and I set my foot back softly in the sand of the path. I reached behind me for my companion's hand. "I do," I assented, more silence than whisper. "Take me back now, Byron. Please."

I came around vomiting in a bucket.

"Enfin!" Céleste exclaimed. She was holding me propped off the edge of the bed, one hand garroting my wrist, her strong grasp circling my shoulder. "That's right! *Et voilà!* Now she comes nicely!"

The world blazed. The shade had been lifted all the way up and the morning light pierced mercilessly in. I must have been out overnight, for the hour was earlier than when I'd made it home; it was the early hour when the sun probes all the way to the back of the room, but things were much brighter than they should have been even then. Brighter than that.

I heard another voice, mumbled by distance, and someone entered through the closet door, set something glinty by the sink. "This'll work," she said, and ran some water, stooped to plug the object in — I recognized the drumming sound as the tap water filled the teakettle, the electric kettle from Landers's study. The girl came over and knelt down beside me, put her face in mine. I looked up and reclined back into my pillow, relieved to see her but my mouth aghast, embarrassed, my face an ache, my heart a scream. "Sorry you're sick," Corie said. I covered my mouth as Céleste handed me a washcloth, saying, "There you are," her triumph audible.

"Thank you," I mumbled through the cloth.

"Your lamp's out of oil," Corie explained, apologetic, but only for dispelling the pre-electric mood of the place. I saw they'd dragged in extension cords from Landers's rooms. That explained the brilliance. Two tall torchères glared into the ceiling.

"You came last night?" I asked feebly, and Corie said no, she'd just come in, but Céleste had been here. "You know how to scare an old woman," Céleste said. "Too sick to move, you were!"

"We thought we might have to call a doctor," Corie affirmed.

"Ach," Céleste scoffed at her. "None of that!" and said that doctors brought only trouble, that she knew what to do.

And knew how to do it quietly, sweeping the evidence off the table before anyone, including me, could see it, a mess of pills no different than dust and splinters. Her wall of denial was so immaculate I could never broach it, even to ask her how many pills had remained.

And so commenced my welcome home, Céleste brewing teacup bouillon to spoon into me while Corie ran out for ginger ale, which for some reason was all I craved and which I downed in excess with my soup while she slipped next door to play something else on the Bösendorfer. The closet door stayed open, accommodating the music, though I think it was intended to accommodate only the extension cord. It was a unification, generally comprehended.

Thank God for their busyness. Whatever had roused me — and I'm sure I did owe some large grain of gratitude to Céleste's home-remedy purgatives — I wouldn't have wanted to come around all alone with just my thoughts, and the bouillon tasted good.

She was sure, Céleste said the next morning, that my recuperation and Corie's safety had finally broken the fifty-year spell that "that Saxe" had placed on this household. In commemoration, she and Corie drew open all the heavy drapes in all the rooms and let sunlight sweep the ghostly chill from the mausoleum. The rooms seemed resurrected. Then, immediately, day-shy and ambushed by splendor, they just seemed faded and worn. I asked Céleste if she wouldn't bring some flowers up, and she loaded the elevator thrice with violets and set them in every window.

"Were you not safe?" I asked Corie.

"Oh, it was nothing, I'll tell you about it," she answered, but she didn't tell me while Céleste was there. Céleste, I took notice, didn't let on that I was playing dumb, and I let it all rest until later.

All, everything, later. For days I lay about recuperating from my "illness," wrapped in a blanket on a couch in Alba's living room, listening to Corie practice, and piecing my mind back together. I felt well physically quickly enough. Within my darkened mind, the drapes stayed drawn. I had survived my attempt to escape. There was left to me now no recourse from what I understood, no safety. I was afraid to move before I could handle it. Afraid to attempt the empty world.

I sent Corie out to Portbou to phone Rouchard, to relay my apologies for missing our office appointment. The following morning he made a house call, ringing the buzzer from the street for the first time in decades and peeking through the premises timidly with a face of anguished astonishment. At the door of each room, he'd poke his head in and peer about with his clear gray eyes before his body would allow itself to follow. I could tell he verged on tears. "They stole the art!" he muttered, but it wasn't the missing paintings that moved him. Feeling with his cane through his friends' home, he seemed halfway summoned by his own old youth, tempted by an already trampled optimism. Promise blossomed directly into wilt. When he left, he looked older than I'd ever seen him.

His visit altered things, of course, altered everything. It announced my ascension. Céleste encountered the news most directly when she came around a corner and met the gentleman face to face, and she stood trembling in place until his greeting made him real, then collapsed into him sobbing when he leaned to give her a kiss.

Her demeanor toward me never recovered. I had to instruct her firmly (firm instruction was all she now desired from me) that the arrival of a long-lost Landers did not quite constitute a second coming and that I would not tolerate adulation and obsequy, an order she complied with obsequiously, and I realized too late my mistake, for now independence and subservience were rendered inextricable, and even her returning to her harridan self (a person I missed remarkably) would bear the taint of compliance. I was forced to concede that a wall of good feeling had sundered our relationship beyond repair.

Corie, for her part, seemed benignly and bizarrely pleased with everything, me included. Had her evening on the steps really settled her soul, removed some long-dangling sword of threat? The police had treated her gently on the condition that they never see her again, but that alone didn't explain her gaze, which was bright as a crayon and impenetrably, synthetically happy.

It fell to me to broach the issue of her unsafety and on several occasions I tried, dashing myself against the coasts of cheer, swimming against the tide of disengagement. I couldn't admit my motive, that I just needed to talk about him, talk about him any way I could. "Why do you assume he wasn't a cop?" I asked, and she said, typically, "Who?"

"Who do you think?" I said.

"He just didn't look like one, I guess," she answered. "More like a waiter. With shiny shoes."

I managed to get some tidbits out of her, odd fragments that dropped out willy-nilly like puzzle pieces spilled across a table. That's how I judged them, by color and shape, and tried to fit the jigsaw back together. Without much success. I pressed her only as hard as I could without confessing my cause. "When?" she said, when I asked what they'd talked about.

"On the steps. What was the first thing he said to you?"

"Nothing!" she said. "Not at first." And so it went. She maintained resolutely that the whole big event had been a mere caper, a bagatelle, a stupid prank with no lethal intent, and when I noted that the cops didn't seem to see it like that, she responded, "What do they know?"

"Well, they want you out of the country," I said. "That sounds serious." That was the other condition of Corie's parole, that she get herself out of France.

"Oh yeah, and gave me two weeks to do it," she said. We were standing in Carlos's library, whose collection I'd set us to cataloging, because I desperately needed some utilitarian preoccupation. And, too, because Corie was leaving and I couldn't get it done without her help. Only half the volumes were in French. "I'm not, like, public enemy number one or anything," she said.

The cataloging consumed a shocking stretch of hours (blessedly —we'd wrapped up the last of the letters. I no longer had Alba to distract me). The index cards stretched across the polished parquet, and the stacks of volumes, yanked from their shelves, ascended like the columns of a temple ruin. Céleste's compulsive cleaning (it now never ceased, and only of necessity paused) was avaricious of the dust we raised, but in the name of order I forbade her to enter the library.

I still lodged in Saxe's room. I couldn't muster the gall to move into Alba's bed. Anyway, secretly (secret from Céleste, that is), I preferred Saxe's humble, day-cot perspective. It fit my prison. It was easier, lying there, to turn my face to the wall. I preferred awake to the echoing caverns of sleep, and preferred the tangible, touchable wall to invisible doors that refused to budge or that slammed shut to seal off my every advance. All around me, that's what I sensed. Guilt slammed the door on grief, and anger slammed the door on guilt. Then I caught sight of my own two hands and horror shot the bolt.

Once or twice, I headed out to Portbou. Intentionally, I didn't get there. I couldn't bear the welcome, the prospect of a casual conversation. I diverted for the boulevard, on the pretext of stopping in at the ToujoursBonne! to pick up some supplies, then didn't go there either. The haste of the sidewalk, the glare of the street, made those places as dangerous as the silence of my dreams. Every passerby was an assassin, and every truck and every taxi a missile intent on leaping the curb and lunging directly at me, and every thought of Emil, especially, and of Willem and Saxe and Carlos and Alba and Corie — of all of them, and of you — a stone to trip my steps.

So instead I gave both sleep and glare the slip and made my rounds at night. My odd reaction to Corie's equanimity was to develop a resistance to her music. I couldn't help it; it deepened like a rash. I hardly noticed it during the day, but as the clock came round to evening and the hour of her practice, my unease became unbearable. To escape it I'd slip out onto the street. Once through the *cour* and beyond the gray doors, I'd stomp off purposefully for a block or so, a point of no return. I needed momentum to carry me that far, before I confessed I had nowhere to go. Then I'd begin to go there.

Some nights I headed east, some nights west. Toward the milling crowds of Saint-Germain-des-Prés, or away from them into the emptiest streets I could find. No flowing river appeared overhead to guide me. I never went to Île Saint-Louis, or to anywhere I'd visited with Emil. I wished to avoid encounters. Encounters with Corie's music, with the past, with anyone I knew, anyone at all, and most of all with him. Or, not really "him." But to encounter Emil in any spot where we had gone together would be to encounter "us," and "us" was far more than I could handle. The merest thought of a museum or restaurant or any place he'd brought me to or anything we'd experienced — a churchyard picnic, a soldier on a rainy night on a street behind a cathedral, a whistler rehearsing his life's central moment for friends and strangers in a bar named Le Chemin Vert — any such pierced me with pain. My walks were epic. Whatever hour I got home, the lights in the grand rooms were always dark and the music already over, and Corie, I supposed, back out with her protests, though I never asked. She never said.

Several nights into this habit, I was aware of being followed. My initial alarm dulled quickly past worry, into acquiescence. I could spot no one around me who seemed to show an interest. I'd round the corner and hear my pursuer, or catch a glimpse at the edge of my vision, and turn to find only the echo of my steps, my own face in a shop vitrine. Still, it was there, a spectral watching. I remembered Corie's conviction that a benevolent Alba haunted her. I recalled how I'd scoffed at the notion. Now I wondered if the same woman's tragic ghost had shifted its attentions to guard her daughter instead. The company enabled my solitude, allowed my longest and darkest routes. I'd loop around the Panthéon toward the Jardin des Plantes or up toward the Observatoire to cross behind the Cemetery Montparnasse, the hour quieting into ever greater stillness, my overseer nearing until I could sense its presence behind my ear, ready to perch on my shoulder, and was afraid to look around.

Then I realized who it must be, that this must be Emil. The spirit was his, equal parts elusive and insistent. My nightly mission shifted from push to pull, avoidance to assignation. I went into the street not to seek, really—more to be sought, attended. And to ask. All those questions I'd had for Corie that were thwarted by her silence were satisfied by his. His calm confirmed me. Especially in the bleaker streets, where only he and I were about, I took my every agonized question and asked it of him outright, and let it sit as still in my mind as though I'd laid it on the sidewalk for him to gather up later as he passed. One by one, I set them down and left them there behind me.

On the ninth or tenth night of this, I wandered down by the Esplanade and across the river to stalk the grounds of the Grand Palais, then angled up toward the Madeleine. The night was a drippy one. The rain was more of a mist, though. I didn't deploy my umbrella until I'd gratefully begun to tire and had turned back along a wide street through a placid, pretty neighborhood that felt close and intimate though its avenue was broad, the sidewalks lined with plane trees. I could smell the bark in the moist air. A slight breeze crossed the avenue and shook the raindrops from the branches above me, and I raised my umbrella against them, and maybe that's why I didn't see where I was at first, as I walked along, because the umbrella cut out the sky. The last time I'd been here, the sky was all there was of nature, though pierced by the beam and racketed by rotor blades. The ground had been buried beneath the crowd. My whereabouts didn't dawn on me until I was at the steps.

It was so very quiet, where I stopped. The night was so quiet, the raindrops and the wind's whisper were all I heard, as though my attention to these smallest sounds had drowned out the roar and the whistling. A marble plaque on the building entrance declared an institute, evidently eminent, apparently defunct. The glass doors had been painted black from inside, their iron grates chained and padlocked. The ceremonial steps ascending from the street were sodden with stray leaves. I set my foot on the bottom step and climbed.

When I reached the top, the portico was empty, except for a few empty wine bottles and the leaves. Whatever gas phantom had been chalked on its floor had been washed away by the rain. I turned and scanned the street as though I might find the multitude, but instead saw only the wide blank pavements, a picket of dark trees — or as though I might even discover myself amid the crowd, constrained by Drôlet's arm, on top of a truck mired in the chaos like a mastodon in pitch. Instead there was only the vast prospect and the solitary silhouette, waiting at the bottom of the stair.

It faced me like a penitent, forlorn, ancient, resolute, the coat hood raised around a faceless shadow. The hood was the vacant hood of the cloak of the messenger who is himself the message. It stood so motionless, this figure, I was teased by the thought it might be my own reflection, cast from an upright mirage. At the same time, I knew in an instant who it was. I walked down the steps. When I reached her I held the umbrella over both of us, and with my right hand pulled her hood back, off her auburn hair. Her gold eyes stared into mine, taking me in, expressionless. We stood that way, silent. It wasn't clear who wasn't speaking, me or Corie.

"You were here," she said, finally.

"I was here," I admitted.

"You saw it?" she asked.

"I did." The news rippled across her brow, and her eyes glanced away. Once again, I hadn't told her something. Before I could finish with the "I'm so sorry," she cut me off.

"It's okay," she said. "I understand it."

There was another awkwardness.

"I'm surprised you come back," I offered, and she shook her head vehemently.

"I hate this place," she said. "I followed you."

"Really," I said.

"Why do you go out at night?" she demanded. "It isn't safe, where you go."

I told her I had some things I needed to think through.

She absorbed that, and guessed. "About him," she said, and I nodded.

"You knew him," she said.

I nodded again, and she considered, and then the wave washed through and her eyes seethed with that same sudden panic I'd seen in them before: panic for me.

"You know that he's dying," she said, urgently. "Do you know that? That's what he said, that how was it I could want to die when he wanted so badly not to."

She was tense with the necessity of having to ask if I knew. "He told me I mustn't tell anyone," she said, "that I was not to tell what we talked about." I answered her question — "I know" — to ease her, but she wasn't eased, just rigid as she let it all occur to her. It seemed to occur in stages. I watched her march through the logic step by step. As much as she couldn't comprehend me, this child, she knew more about me than I'd ever know of her, already knew about Alba, and knew what happened to you, Daniel, and what that would mean to me now, under the circumstances, and knew that I'd been sick, suddenly, then suddenly well, and what that might mean too. It took her a minute, but she put it all together. When her eyes found mine again, they were filled with moisture and intense with anger, and she seemed about to speak. Then she seemed not to, and instead, almost as though to catch her balance, she reached up her hand and clasped it over mine, my hand on the hasp of the umbrella.

I smiled at her. "What do you say we get in out of this rain?" I said. She nodded, grateful. She recognized the offer — to set us both down gently. She accepted it, and we turned. A little ways down toward the end of the block, I said, "You really shouldn't follow people around like that, you know."

She glanced to see if I was really okay. I was. "You always worry me," she said. "Ever since we met."

"Why on earth?" I asked. She dismissed me instantly with an "I don't know!" but then gave the question its thought. "Because you kept the bandanna?" she offered, sure but not quite, and then, more surely, "Because you didn't even know what hurt you." I thought to myself to ask her, Was she so confident she'd always know what hurt her? But I kept it for a future conversation.

I awoke the next morning to see that the rain had ended, and the lovely sky was a wash of lightest Dutchman's blue. A fleet of gray clouds was scudding through, on its way to some other overcast. I was halfway to the kitchen when a thought stopped my steps, and I turned and went back for my purse. In the galley, Corie was already up and making tea. She asked did I want breakfast and plopped a second egg into the pot to boil beside her own. "I brought you something," I told her. I fished Rouchard's envelope out of my purse, the one he'd given me in l'Urquidi, and spilled its inventory onto the countertop. Big inventory: two items. I pulled Corie's hair back and clipped in the little lyre barrette.

"Oh!" she said, appraising it with her fingertips, and then she walked out of the kitchen to the dining room, to the gilded convex mirror that hung on the dining-room wall. "It's beautiful!" she yelled back. I watched the vapor rise from the copper pot, listened to the clacking of the eggs jostling each other contentedly. "Is it . . . ?"

"Tortoiseshell," I yelled, and yelled, "It's old!," thinking, *Old as me*. Then I realized that Corie had already returned to the kitchen, and I lowered my voice. "It's one of those materials you don't get anymore." The barrette, in her hair, did in fact look beautiful.

"So what's that?" Corie asked, nodding toward the counter. Beside the envelope lay the rest of Rouchard's bric-a-brac.

"Mystery key," I told her. "Mystery keys to forgotten doors. Life's full of them."

The eight minutes were up and the timer went off and I ran some cold water and cracked the eggs against the side of the sink and rolled the shells between my palms and peeled them. Corie stirred some pepper and salt together in a plate, and we carried our feast to the dining room and consumed it at the corner of the Biedermeier, dipping our eggs in the communal spice plate, sure the candelabra disapproved. We ate without talking much, lost to morning thoughts. I'd just stood up to gather the plates and bring some more tea when it struck me. It struck me like someone had cuffed my ears. I looked at Corie and saw from her gaze that the thing that had struck me had struck her too. Our thoughts had run convergent. "You don't think . . ." I said, and her head bobbed.

I palmed the key. We left the china unwashed in the sink and went off through the rooms to Saxe's closet. Corie went ahead to fetch a light, and I kicked some shoes aside. She was back right away, with the torchère already turned to its highest wattage, grasping it in both hands like a vaulting pole, tossing wild shadows around the ceiling. The closet squinted in the unaccustomed glare. Splinters still lay in the corners from my brief day job in demolition; plaster dust frosted the top of the little safe. The steel slid into the key slot with a stutter of tumblers, and with the first turn of my wrist, the heavy square door sprang eagerly off its moorings.

We sat there in front of it, Corie and I, blinking at each other. As though we weren't quite sure what safecrackers did once they got the safe cracked. I reached and swung the door full wide. The crypt contained one item, a large wood letterbox. I dragged it out but didn't open it right away, not squatting there on my haunches in the dust. If, as I supposed, its contents had not seen the light of day in years, they deserved the best daylight they could get. Corie moved the table to the window as I lugged the box into Saxe's room, and I set it in the sun and pried open the lid.

The thing that came to view I took to be a miniature Chinese birdhouse, a square-cornered cube with two round holes in its façade and a little squat cupola on top. Then I saw that the holes were lenses, covered with a pince-nez of painted tin, and that the box was an ancient camera, differentiated from any of its type that I'd ever seen by its ornate cloisonné skin, for it was clad entirely, top and sides, in a herringbone of nickel and black enamel. I pictured it immediately on its sly tours of occupied Paris, dangling on a harness-leather strap from the shoulder of a fine Spanish suit. Beneath it was a stack of envelopes, and inside the envelopes were sheaf after sheaf of square photographic negatives encased in numbered plastic sleeves.

"Oops," I said to Corie as I opened the first. She was busy pulling envelopes out of the box and froze midmotion, and I told her to be careful. "Just don't lose their order," I said, and (to placate me) she continued doing exactly what she had been only slower.

I held a couple of the plastic sleeves up to the window light, careful to obey my own instruction. I opened another envelope and looked through its array, and then another, witnessing through the acetate the lost world of a Franconia-born Jew during the era when he, Byron Manifort Saxe, was traveling around the south of Europe with his friends Carlos Perigord and Alba Solano Landers, and then the era to follow, without the friends, as his world spun from happiness to tragedy. The photographs were hard to make out in any detail, being in negative and given the cloud-spersed light, but I could see that some were cityscapes, and others portraits, and I kept up a stream of exclamations to Corie as I spotted anything interesting and she gratified me with a grunt or an "Oh, amazing," once in a while, and once or twice stepped over to squint through the film. And then I came on a heavier envelope that disgorged a sheaf of not film but paper, a thick ream held together by a spring clip. The jaw of the clip had rusted into the top of the first page, branding a brown signature across the title, התשובה שלי. "What in the world," I exclaimed, and instructed, "Look," and asked, "How's your Hebrew?" but I was talking only to myself.

I had been for a while, I realized, for Corie had disappeared. Except that she was still right there, actually, standing in the window with her face buried in a leaf of blue paper. "What have —" I started to ask her, *What have* you *found?*, but she waved me to silence with a slow open hand and edged herself blindly onto the bed. The paper was obviously a letter, on aerogram onionskin, and she clearly was determined to read it through before saying a word about it. "From . . ." I started as she finished the first page and shuffled it behind a second, but I didn't bother to conclude the sentence.

So I plunked down beside her, and watched her face, and waited.

At one point she glanced over at me, as hard as though I were a stranger, then went back to reading. When she got to the end she didn't move, and I had to speak to free her.

"It's from Alba," I said, and she nodded and shuffled the pages again and began with the salutation. "'My dearest C.,'" she read.

How afraid I am for you. Things are becoming worse here & I'm sure there is worse to follow, but I'm not afraid for myself but for you, when you know what I must tell you, & terribly for our Alena. Wednesday I am to be baptized into the church. Voluntarily, they say, or, in the event I compel them to compel me, voluntarily by force. For them, this has become imperative. They'd hoped I would serve as a role model. Now that's what they fear. I have become for them a living repudiation, and they are done putting up with it. This I sense. I cannot know exactly their plans, but I fear my immunity — my prominence — now only adds to my indictment, and will harshen my sentence, for they will devise a penalty to match their shame. I no longer think my conversion will spare me. My Eucharist may be meant as my last rites, a last humiliation to repay me for humiliating them. I have made my preparations & you must attend to this carefully. First of all, C., if anything does befall me you must find your way to your daughter. Not here, though. Get to Madrid. She will be on the mainland within a week. It's how the system works. The mothers here have pieced together much of it, by now, & I have set down what I know on this separate sheet for you, which ferries are usually used & their arrival ports, & the orphanages where she is likely to be sent. They'll keep her for a while, because there is such a glut of children and of course the customers prefer the newborns. But do not wait long. She is lovely & someone will want her. And my poor C., you do not even have a photo, but she will have my barrette & I have also to tell you that she bears a mark, a wound on her hand that is fresh and should be visible, it is as large as I was able to make it, may God and our daughter forgive me. That is what I have to tell you, to look at these details & make yourself a plan, my desperate hope is that you can find a way. Also, I must tell you, because you know everything about me & do not know this, that I do not ask God's forgiveness mockingly, but in the most fervent way. They will not succeed this Wednesday in converting me to their faith but they do not know why. Because Maria Xavier won't let me, true. I cannot betray her by accepting the thing they killed her for refusing. That's one reason, but there's another, simpler. I cannot convert because I've already converted. I have accepted their God, & it wasn't they who led me to him; it was Maria Xavier herself, she is my saint as you are my confessor. For I saw what they did to her, & it was an evil of great consequence. I insist, with every ounce of hatred I can muster for what they've done, that their sin will not be meaningless. But this is where logic has led me, that whether the human race lives on infinitely or dies out entirely, & one or the other must occur, there is no alternative, in either case she will not mean anything, her life, her death, mine, Alena's beauty, the things we fought for — our lives' significance means nothing without a presence outside our puny human sphere, a mind outside of time. I see this now. Our only worth, the meaning of any moral or immoral act, cannot exist solely within us. To exist at all we must be witnessed from beyond us. They tell me prisoners who have experienced torture learn to doubt God, and perhaps they do. For me it has meant the opposite. What I saw, God witnessed, that's the only truth. Otherwise the importance of all I've seen was a passing joke, & all that I have done. And, oh, my C., the thing that I have done. I planned for it & saved up my cigarettes & didn't give them away & when Sister Serafina offered me a light last week I came upstairs and used the first to light the others. I know the ceremony. In this I have experience. How not to douse them & what the burning smells like, & what sort of sore it will leave. When I had three going I clasped her to me with my gentlest arm around her neck and committed on my perfect girl the thing they'd done to me, & made it as bad as I possibly could and could stand to with her screaming. Was that all for a joke, my C., what this mother has done to her child? Something time will forget or diminish, so who cares? I say not. I choose the alternative; I demand to accept my consequence. And into my hell I will drag all these righteous. Only their God can avenge us on the proselytizers. Only a living & attentive God can attest to the weight of my hatred.

PART FIVE

XXVII

ANIEL, NOW YOU HAVE all that I'm able to tell you, though I can't tell you at all what it means, or even exactly what's happened, what I've been through, for I've been to a place that I'm helpless to describe. At the moment, I'm seated in my study at the partners' desk. I've just come from Portbou. Passim says the forecast is for snow tonight, and I am glad, as though somehow that might make it easier, though it won't. It will cover the grave, there's my solace, but where the grave is I can't know, and who will I share my solace with? Corie left this morning and I am afraid of not having her around to protect me against my mind, which dwells on Emil and cannot leave him alone, and I cannot decide what part is enormous sadness and what even larger part rage. She was so excited to go, my Little One. I saw her off at Charles de Gaulle with the flowered hijab draped around her neck and her russet hair held back by the tortoiseshell barrette that was the one thing Alba ever gave me. I consider it a fair trade: Corie gave me Alba. Anyway, I've kept the brown bandanna. Drôlet drove me home; he assures me I'm still on the tab. I wonder what he knows, but he knows enough not to tell me.

So at last I'm alone in the great house, alone with Saxe and Alba and Carlos, without the garlic of Corie's presence to protect against the ghosts, and now the din of the echoes grows too loud. The wind blows through, and it's no use pretending I can flee again into Saxe's hideaway, whose air would be empty of music. I thought of returning to the Clairière, or finding some nearer hotel. Instead, I think I will open up my parents' bedroom and pull out the linen from the closet and make my home there in whatever way a home can be made, for the little time it's bound to last. Tomorrow the man from Century 21 arrives to give the joint an estimate. Céleste will hate me, but it is for the best.

And then I can begin my preparations for my return to New York. I'm postponing a while longer, to see Odile through her convalescence, and so she can see me through mine. She does not know my injury, but she does know me, whoever I may be, me, unchanged at last into the woman I always was. For I am Magdalena, born and marked and abducted and rescued, and I am her twin, Matilde, who had no idea what past lay in her future, who was raised by friends and summoned by a stranger, to whom it was restored what she had lost, and who lost what she was given, *for whatever I love I will cause to be slaughtered,* as I did you, Daniel, you remember. I've instructed Odile to move in here with me for several weeks, until she's stronger. She can care for me better that way.

And I think to myself, Isn't it funny how we get through the world? At some point in our wanderings, we stumble on a home. And then, in our wanderings, we are never again to leave it. And somehow what has happened here has brought me back to an older place, though not to the place you'd suspect. I see now the chamber I've occupied all this time, the scant few moments that expanded to envelop my life, from which I'll never depart, for all of my departing. For I have burst out of my smallness and entered the whole grand immensity of it.

This you will remember: that afternoon. We'd gone up to New Haven for the day; I had an appointment and we'd thought we'd stay for a meal and race home in time for you to get to work, but then the snow started. It drifted down so light at first, white out of the white-gray, then heavier, and we recognized its determination, knew this was a gathering siege, and we thought of phoning your students and canceling their lessons and getting a room for the night but decided instead to catch the early train back into the city, while we could.

What with the blizzard, the day got dark so early, and Connecticut through the train window was a pen-and-ink Connecticut, a charcoal wash through a gauze of falling snow, the land stunned senseless by multitude, and every sign of life, the headlights at the grade crossings, the smoke trails lashing from chimney pipes, bundled against the mobbing. The forest flew by fast in its nearness, I couldn't begin to grasp it, and the fields ran blue with twilight. You slept. I caressed your head and watched the still world pass.

Then it seemed that we were the ones who were stationary, and the world was the thing in motion, whirring past my watchfulness. I felt your love around me like a kingdom. All was peaceful, not a peace of quietness, but of perfect equilibrium, and my peace took everything into account, understood how it — it itself — would come to an end and dissolve again into the ordinary mess and noise of life, but that's just the thing: its comprehension of its own destruction only compounded my peace. I thought how I loved you, and how someday I would lose you, and I kept you close and perfect inside me through Darien and Stamford and Greenwich and down into the Bronx, the night solidifying outside, and then kept it with me as you roused and gathered and we walked through the clamor of Penn Station — such ominous thunder; above us, the wrecking ball was demolishing the old terminal — and took the local downtown and got off earlier than we had to because, after all, we had the time, and the city was ours entirely, and the snow was falling that would powder every step with confectioner's dust. Every step of every adventure, even a crazy couple assaulting each other in a rocking automobile, even a sonata through a recital-hall window — absurd, sublime — and in between them that other time, incalculable.

We cut through the park after our little curbside intervention, laughing at the joke of it, laughing in relief that it hadn't been what we took it for. Nervous. Laughing in sheer silly nervousness over all that was impending, of just what happiness could be. And then you stopped laughing. We were nearly out of the park. You stopped beneath the giant elm there at the corner of Waverly Place, the enormous branches umbrella'd high above us, and you gathered me to you. I was shocked that your face seemed so serious and sad, as though shaded by that bare-limbed elm. You set your violin down right in the snow and asked me if I would marry you.

Of course I would, Daniel. Of course I would marry you. If I hadn't just wished to dwell a while longer in anticipation of the thing I most wished for, if the suspension wasn't such a bliss that I wanted just to relish it for a day or two, a week or month, before I said, "I will, I do."

And if only you hadn't been so pure about it all. You could have — no, I have waited all the years to make you hear this, so you must hear it — you *should* have told me what was going on; keeping such a secret from me all the way until your induction wasn't the least bit right, now you know, don't you? Of course you do, you found out worse than I did, though quicker, at least, so who's to say what worst is. You said (later, in your uniform, and damn you for being so proud of it) that you didn't want to contaminate my decision by telling me what depended on it, a deferment, your future, your life, as it turns out. That you would want me to marry you only for love and not to save you from something as drab as the draft, but only out of love, and for that, my love, I have hated you all these years. Hated the memory of every step we took that dear night, you with your secret, me with my hesitation, how it could all have been different, and the cramped room that I have lived in could have been our palace all this time. But I didn't hear your need. I stroked your face and said you were lovely and that you must ask me some other time, soon, since for some things I wasn't ready. Wasn't ready.

We walked on through the Village, as beside each other as we'd been before, but pulled away now an increment too, and I wanted us back in the space of the peace that had held us, on the train and along our walk. I was crying out against this wedge of air that had let your thoughts and mine run off apart. And there before the conservatory, listening to the piece that spilled through the window: What possibilities perched on that last bridge of silence? How much of *almost* fell into the time between those notes? I wanted so much to say, *Put down your fiddle. Hold me again.* If you ask, I'll tell you that I love you as I'll never love another, that I was yours and that we were young, so, yes, let's begin. But there was the increment to cross, and the moment passed and the chord landed, and you said, again — it was your second invitation of the night — *Come in, and we'll hear the rest.* But I didn't.

And you went through the doors and I went off, and those several weeks later you showed up in your uniform and your hilarious scary haircut, and we made some talk about what would happen when your tour was up; you seemed content to be going, and resolute, and it all seemed so strange and public, this was a war, there was a war to be fought, for you to fight, and who could get their lives straight with the world demanding so violently into every soft thought? I got your letters, and the announcement of your furlough, coming up soon, and then the call from your mother when the visitors came with the news, and we prepared to see you bedside except that you just didn't give us time, Daniel. And where you went as you lay in that bed, and why you didn't come back, back to me, has been my prison for all these years, until now.

For now I know something I didn't know a month ago. That across the path at the bottom of the well lies a string. And at the location of the string lies decision. And maybe you couldn't have, maybe you knew the damage done and preferred it to be like it is, but I've touched where you were, and I know the step you took. And what I have to tell you, Daniel, is that I have hated myself for a lifetime for your death, and found myself past forgiving. But now I have found forgiveness, at last: I forgive you.

At last I can live in that moment without remorse. For that was my time, Daniel. On the night the stranger steps into my Chemin Vert, that is the moment I'll relate to him, along with the question of what it all meant, how one person's heart can beat for so long in the center of the story of another.

And with that little bit to console me, I will close up this house as soon as I can, and will have the carpenters and the painters come and seal up the wall in the oval room for good, for I think I will have Saxe's apartment spruced up a bit, and the peephole plastered over and the shade taken down and some curtains put up, and maybe have it wired with an outlet or two in case I'd like to plug in a radio. In a certain way, my life has existed longer, more continuously, in that small room than in any other place on earth, and though I'll never meet the man responsible for that, I'd like to keep his room in the family, since family he is, as a pied-à-terre for the occasional trip back to Paris, or in case Corie might find the French at some point hospitable to her return. And I will take some of the money from Saxe's will, a little of what's left over from supporting Céleste, and make a donation to l'École Islamique de Jeunes Filles. This is what I will relish telling Odile tomorrow, when she arrives to take up her recuperation: that I intend to buy the painting from Madame Ralanou, the portrait of the woman on the garden path. I will pay an exorbitant price for it. It will fill the wall over the day bed.

Odile and I have planned a few things to do as she gets stronger. I told her I'd like to go shopping on rue de Rivoli to buy a good pair of traveling shoes. And then we'll go to visit Buttes-Chaumont, to stroll through the park along the paths around the lake. She will wonder where her brother is, what mission has pulled him away for so many weeks this time, and I will tell her to think about happier things and not to strain her precious new heart, and we will visit the belvedere temple on the island on the far side of the bridge that spans the chasm, and there I will leave a coin for the sibyl, and a little blue flower too, in honor of being older, and to tell you that I forgive you. For I know why we must try so hard to live. And why we must not live too long, for we mustn't tire love. For love will outlast us, however long it takes, Daniel.

Daniel, however long it takes.